EHUD A
GREAT V
JERICHO

Bogo de Chair

www.amazonprohub.com
First Published 2023
Amazon Pro Hub
® 515 Flower's Street
 Los Angeles
California
United States
90071

Table of Contents

To Jeremy Clarkson,
Scrapper, straight speaker and superhero.
Just like Ehud

I would like to acknowledge the cheerful help and efficiency of the staff at the National Library of Scotland on George IV Bridge in Edinburgh. They managed to maintain some kind of service during most of the Covid pandemic and provided me with the books to research life and times in the biblical world of 1600 BC, everything from A for Arrowheads to Z for the tribe of Zebulun.

I would also like to pay tribute and thanks to my wife for the patient correcting and constructive editing of the various drafts which preceded publication, a grim and lengthy task.

Bogo de Chair was born in Washington DC but has spent most of his life in his native Scotland. His career, in the military, financial services and television production, has brought him into some of the wilder parts of the world from the jungles of Mexico to the sand dunes of Southern Oman, and he has published several articles and produced documentaries from his travels. He lives in Edinburgh and is a member of the Speculative Society. This is his first novel. It is based in the Middle East and in Old Testament times and was written during the Covid 'Lockdowns' of 2020 and 2021.

The Ehud Papers Foreword

One day in the autumn of 2010 I was sitting at a desk in the Vatican Library researching life in second-century Rome. The librarian had pointed me in the direction of various archives which included a box containing the accounts, inventory et cetera of a well-to-do Roman, Lucius Albinus, a cousin of the general who lived in the Villa Giulia on the Caelian Hill. A bit on the dry side for some, perhaps, this was truly the stuff for academics, and it was exciting to think that, perhaps, I was the first person to review this box. It was all higgledy- piggledy; some scrolls, a few scraps of papyrus, but mostly codices, those early books made out of skin. They all had faint markings on the outside. All in Latin, of course, like 'Furniture Inventory – Villa Giulia' or 'Silverplate – Villa Giulia' and then I came on a whole pile of codices simply 'Ehud'. There were ten of them. Eventually, in my meticulous way, I got around to opening 'Ehud 1' and found myself transported back from comfortable second-century Rome to the Old Testament and the Siege of Jericho.

A lot of 'killing' happens in the Old Testament. Probably the best-known story is how David slew Goliath. Then there's Judith cutting off the head of an Assyrian general, and many, many others. Most of these can be gorily observed as great paintings in art galleries. But Ehud? Who is Ehud? Well, the Bible tells us that he was sent to assassinate the King of the Moabites, Eglon the Corpulent, and he was chosen for the job because he was left-handed. It was going to be difficult to get a dagger past the guards but, when they searched him, they only looked in the places where a right-handed man would hang a weapon, so Ehud got through with his dagger. Demanding absolute privacy to impart his message the guards departed. Ehud leant down to whisper his message and, instead, plunged his dagger into the belly of the King where it got stuck in his fat. Ehud abandoned his dagger and escaped by a window. Just another assassination story, and there is no mention of Ehud ever again in the Bible.

Now we can date Eglon the Corpulent, and therefore Ehud, to about 1150 BC; but there in the codices is Ehud at the Battle of Jericho, about 1600 BC, Ehud with Sampson about 1000BC, Ehud and the conquest of Jerusalem around 600 BC. So – there we have an Ehud who lived about a thousand years playing a part in all the great events of the history of the Israelites.

My explanation is that Ehud was the eternal boy, a bit of a 'likely lad' and storytellers would use him to enrich the history of Israel to their audiences. These stories got passed down, mainly verbally, perhaps sometimes written down, until they came into the possession of a second-century Jew, a slave or servant in the house of a rich Roman. He was probably the archivist, in charge of records, and had time enough to collect the EHUD stories which he translated into Latin. What was his name? We do not know; so, let's call him Pakeed, the Hebrew for writer.

So, 1800 years later we are lucky enough to see the

history of Israel, from the fall of Jericho in 1600 BC to the fall of Jerusalem through the adventures of Ehud. You have to like him, and you can see why boys through the ages identified with him. He's brave enough, when he has to be, pretty cynical about authority, always on the lookout for the main chance, sharp witted in a crisis and, above all, a survivor. And he never ages; for the best part of a thousand years he remains a young man in his prime, probably around 25 or into his early 30s. Just what we would all like.

Bogo de Chair.

Chapter 1

I prodded the rock with my stick. It rolled over and there was a big black scorpion. Ugh! I hate scorpions. I have been terrified of them ever since my sister put one in my bed and I got badly stung. In fact, I nearly died. I rolled my tongue slowly around my mouth collecting saliva, then spat it hard at the insect. The shining spittle landed a few inches behind and the scorpion scuttled away. Phew, not towards me or I would have bolted, hardly a dignified action for a chap in charge of his father's flocks for the last time.

Of course, I had no idea that I would never again be sitting in the middle of the wilderness with five hundred goats grazing, copulating or simply standing still with that fixed look of theirs. Actually, I quite enjoyed being a goatherd. There is a pecking order which proclaims shepherds are better than goatherds, or rather gives them a God-given right to look down on us. But it is pure snobbery. Of course, sheep get all the good publicity with that wool for fine garments and nice soft leather, but for life in the desert give me goat any time. There is goatskin for lining our tents, the milk is better, they can eat anything, and they can look after themselves. In other words, a lot less trouble than sheep which are always breaking their legs or toppling over, helpless on their backs with their feet waving in the air, needing to be rescued.

But back to the day. It was a day like any other day. The hot sun was the same in the high hot blue sky, all around was the hot sand and the hot rocky hills of the Jordan Valleys, and scratching a living out of this hot arid landscape were the pale green grasses and the acacia bushes which the goats fed on and had learned to like well enough.

But then things started to change. From down in the valley, a few miles away, came the faint sound of a trumpet.

I don't know how knowledgeable you are about the time when we were a bunch of nomads who had escaped from Egypt and all that pyramid building under the leadership of a pretty remarkable guy called Moses. I mean he was not a dashing leader or anything like that but he just set out a vision and told us we were a people chosen by God and he was taking us to a land of Milk and Honey. Great talk but we found ourselves bumming around the Sinai Desert for forty years; and that the 'Promised Land', or anything with half reasonable grass, was occupied by people who did not like us at all. Canaanites! As far as they were concerned, we could stick right there in the desert and if we all died so much the better. And in the occasional clash of arms the point was quickly made. The Canaanites, they had weapons of iron, or bronze at least, and each soldier had a spear, a sword, a breastplate and a helmet. And they had chariots to run us down and archers to shoot us up. More than a match for 'savages with sticks' as they called us which was true enough. Our main weapons were spears with charred points or flint heads and a few captured swords and bits of armour.

And these guys were more numerous, had better commanders and unfortunately Moses was not a man of war. But before he died, he appointed firebrand Joshua as his successor to lead us into the 'Promised Land'.

'Hurrah, hurrah, forward and conquer; Milk and Honey and all that'. Those were Joshua's war cries and we all cheered that to the stars. Well, we younger ones, did but the older generation was a bit more sceptical. My dad especially scoffed at Joshua and regarded him as a big talking buffoon.

"Look at us," he said, "we're just a bunch of nomads and he's thinking of taking on kingdoms with cities with walls and well-armed troops." You can imagine Dad was not the only doubter.

But then nothing happened. Nothing! Joshua was all a big bluff! And we got back to scratching a living in the desert. Or, like my family, became one of the many small nomadic groups who 'strayed' out of the Sinai desert into the lusher

– yes, I mean that, this place was the Garden of Eden compared with the Sinai – territories of Canaan with the talk of faraway cities built with stone, running water and Kings dressed in scarlet.

The trumpet sounded again. I kind of scratched my head. The trumpet – and, thank you very much, it was due to me that they had got the trumpet. I had had the wit to swap it for some turquoise with some Amorite herdsman we were quite pally with. I remember when I saw that trumpet, beautiful, long and shiny. I knew I just had to have it even though I could not get it to make a sound myself, just a kind of spluttering noise, which made the Amorite boys roll with laughter. Of course, back home it did not go down too well initially when I told them I had swapped some of Mum's turquoise for this bronze thing. But then Dad made the best of it and declared that it would be used to announce important occasions. Actually, he loved it. He could blow long blasts and even fanfares, which you could not do with the horns of animals.

But today the blasts were short, not just tootles as if some child had picked up the trumpet and was having a go, and they spelt urgency. Then the blasts stopped, just like that and I was not sure what to do. One option was to stay put and wait until one of my brothers brought up the food in the evening when all would be revealed and I would feel a bit stupid for getting into a flap. The other option was to leave the flock and belt down to the camp and see what was going on. But that would probably take me a couple of hours and I could just see them, my parents and the other people at the camp bemused, at the appearance of a flustered me, Ehud, simply because of a few blasts on the trumpet. Bemused is not quite the word. Angry, furious angry more like and, with many furious angry words from my father, being rifted back onto the hill pretty smartish before the flock dispersed. And, of course, by then the goats would be all over the place and my reputation as a reliable goatherd in ribbons. Everyone would then have to come up and spend the next week grumpily rounding them up and I bet we would be down a few goats as well. Another thing I

4

would not be allowed to forget quickly.

Actually, I did not have to ponder the mystery blasts that long. Looking up the valley I could see two war chariots with half a dozen men trotting alongside. Yes, war chariots in the middle of nowhere – and Amorite war chariots at that because we did not have any chariots. You can bet the next moment I was scarpering up the steep sides of the valley to find a safe vantage point. No difficulty in making that snap decision I can tell you because I knew this was trouble. Yes, we were nomads and by tradition we would wander from pasture to pasture with our flocks and there was plenty of room and people generally did not get too fussed about it. Certainly, that was the way in the Sinai desert where we had been for the last 40 years but Moses had promised better things and taken us north and the reception here was more mixed.

Yes, we had 'strayed' into Canaan and had been for some months, in the territory of the Amorites, the ones who probably despised us most. On the third day after setting up camp, a contingent of these Amorites arrived, not in war chariots, but with the leader on a white mule. They just advanced into the middle of our camp and stood there waiting. The chap on a mule in his white tunic and red skull cap looking haughty while his guards with their fine bronze helmets and big, long spears grumbled and joked amongst themselves. Thank you very much, point made, just a bunch of savages! Eventually, my father came out and, law of the desert and all that, ordered the women to give Haughty some goat's milk and the men some water.

That done Haughty, still on his mule, addressed my father in Amorite, which we barely understood, but the clear gist was 'Pay up or get out' adding 'pay in goats, if you like'. This he said looking around at our tents and showing that he was well aware we had nothing else of interest for him. Dad paid up, paid up regular and that seemed that.

"Uds," a voice cried from below in the valley where the two chariots had stopped, and one of the men had come forward and was standing below me. It was Rim, one of the Amorite herdsmen, and my best pal.

It was funny, the Amorites could not pronounce H which gave them complications with my name. Only my parents and their generation called me Ehud; to my brothers and sisters I was known as Hoods or even Hoody but the Amorites could only manage 'Uds'. We used to tease them about this and call them Hamorites, which rather annoyed them, but this was all just good joshing because after our initial meeting we were on good terms.

It had not started like that. I remember the first time I met Rim it was a stand- off, a deadly stand-off, Amorite bows versus Hebrew slings.

Rim always swore since that it was all a joke, just having a bit of fun to scare the shit out of a couple of Hebrew boys out with their herds. But it did not feel like that at the beginning when a couple of arrows, in quick succession, whistled over our heads and we looked up from our herd and saw two Amorite boys, our kind of age, loading up for second shots. It was just me and my elder brother, Chilion – well, half-brother if you like or even, if you want to be pedantic, no relation at all. Anyway, I had been adopted by his family. So there we were, out in the middle of nowhere, with one of Dad's herds – and we certainly were not expecting trouble, especially not from two boys with curved composite bows taking pot shots at us from thirty yards away. All we had were our slings, little strips of leather with a pouch which we would load with a stone, swing and fire off at any predator that came near the herd. A direct hit wherever always dictated a change of mind and the animal would turn tail, possibly limping, in search of easier prey.

So the skilfully crafted and glued composite bow with its feathered arrows versus simple leather sling and piece of rock is not the unequal struggle you might think, and we were not going to abandon Dad's flock and flee off into the hills without a fight. First Chilion and I rapidly split up so we would not have the problem of trying to avoid two arrows at once. My bowman fired again – it was Rim actually – and the arrow was going straight for me but at that range it was easy enough to duck. He was still fitting his next arrow when I managed to get a quick stone at him. It did not hit him but it was a big enough shock for him to drop his arrow, which gave me time to load again, this time with a handful of fragments. I waited and watched, the loaded sling hanging from my left hand, and he fired again. Once again, easy enough to duck but this time I was able to give the sling a good whirl and released half a dozen sharp rocks in his direction, a couple at least guaranteed to find a target. They might not have the stopping power of a larger rock but they hurt all the same. He leaned back sharply and I saw blood appear on his forehead. I quickly loaded my sling with a nice round rock, the size of a small pomegranate, a real stopper if I could land one on him, and let fly. Now it was his turn to do the ducking and my killer stone whistled past his ear. I heard a sharp cry from his mate over on the right. *So Chilion has landed one too*, I thought with relief.

Every so often, I have found, there comes a moment in a contest – it can even happen on a busy battlefield when you are engaged with your enemy and both giving it all and suddenly you each get the same idea and lower your weapon. You look at each other, even smile. "Well," you both are thinking, "We've had a good little fight, haven't we? And we are pretty equal, aren't we, and frankly I think it's time for us both to go off to other bits of the battlefield rather than continue bashing away at each other." You do not actually say 'And let's meet up for a drink afterwards' but it's almost like that.

Actually, I probably had the upper hand on Rim because at that range I could duck his arrows and, if I went back to loading with fragments rather than a single stopper, I could hurt every time and a lucky pebble could disable him. But then, thinking ahead, it was not going to do any good for business if I killed or wounded an Amorite; so it was with a certain relief that I suddenly saw Rim raise his bow in the air and laugh out loud.

That was two years ago and we had been friends

with Rim and the local Amorites ever since. Whatever the huffing and puffing by Moses and Joshua about smiting the Canaanites and taking over their land, the reality was, out in the wilderness, everyone got on, because we had to. What with sandstorms, wolves, eagles, snakes and scorpions and the constant need to find water, there were enough problems without getting in a battle with the other herdsman because they were not, like us, the chosen people. They had their sheep and we had our goats but we found we could share the waterholes and the vast scrubland waste without quarrelling. Better than that we drank together, traded together, had girls together. Of course, Rim and his mates gave themselves jokey airs and looked down on us.

"Chosen people!" Rim guffawed when we told him about Moses. "You are just a bunch of runaway slaves. Whoever gave you the idea that you were something special? I mean, look at you!"

Well, of course, it was not hard to see his point. My dad might be rich in Hebrew terms with flocks and concubines but home was still a collection of goatskin tents and our women stank. Rim could talk about houses made of brick and stone, white bread, furniture of ivory and girls, what girls! Actually, we challenged him on that, teased him, called him a liar and even promised some goats. And all credit to him, Rim was as good as his word. The next time we met up he had smuggled up two little Amorite tarts with their own slave who scraped and oiled them before being introduced to the boys. I mean, I do not want to be unfair to our girls, they were good enough in their way, but the daily grind in a nomad settlement does not do much for looks and temperament, and frankly the men coming in from the fields or down from the hill could not care less if their woman stank of garlic and had hands like cheese graters. Tizzy and Topsy, we called them and I can tell you they were worth every silky black hair of the two best goats in the flock which Rim was allowed to choose. Actually, it became a bit of a regular thing especially after Amorite festivities when the whore business became a bit slack. I had a bit of a job explaining to Dad about the losses in goats, and always the best ones. He certainly suspected something but he could not work out what. "Oh, dear me," he once said shaking his head sorrowfully, "that's another two of the best billies taken away by that lion, or was it a wolf this time?" And I would mutter something, shake my head and know I looked as guilty as hell with my brothers sniggering in the background. It was not really fair; they had their share of Tizzy and Topsy but it was always left up to me as the 'half-brother' to give the excuses to Dad.

We even got into God-talk. We had the best stories and would brag about the escape from Egypt across the Red Sea and the manna falling from heaven but Rim and his mates just tended to shrug their shoulders.

"Were you there?" Rim would ask disbelievingly, and just smile. It was infuriating.

In retaliation, we had a go at his Baal and human sacrifice, throwing live people into furnaces and all that.

"Not very nice really. Why, it could be your turn next?" said I, thinking I had him there, but he was good at turning round the argument and counter-attacked on our rules and rituals.

"Not much fun being a member of your sect" – I know he used the word 'sect' deliberately because it used to annoy – "You've got all these silly rules, haven't you? Can't eat pig, can't eat camel and then you all have to have your knobs cut! Where did that come from? To please the girls?"

Of course, he said that to get a laugh from Tizzy and Topsy who did actually titter marvellously. It was worth a joke against us to hear them. Of course, by now, Rim was enjoying himself again.

"Or is it to avoid passing on a nasty infection from your female friends here?" He guffawed nodding at the herd of goats, and his mates, of course, just burst out laughing. This was a sore spot; we really didn't like to talk about what happened on the hill. It was another of those things which Moses condemned outright and declared it a death-by-stoning offence.

I touched my brow and Rim had laughed. This was my sure-fire way of ending a conversation when we were on the losing end. That shard of stone had scarred his forehead. All I had to do was touch my forehead to remind him who had drawn first blood.

But Rim did get us once and good. They were close by when there was some kind of Baal feast and Rim's dad had told them they could kill a couple of grass- fed Canaan sheep and have a bit of a binge. No mention of us of course but Rim invited us over.

"Don't worry, there will be no human sacrifice and you won't have to dance around in the nude cutting your arms," said he mockingly. "And we have got some proper booze with us, wine with a bit of a kick."

Well, of course, we accepted and tried to look a bit blasé about the whole thing. I mean we did not want them to know we had never eaten Canaan sheep – of course, we had our own sheep but the desert diet did not make for particularly tasty lamb – and we had never had wine.

So along we went, me and three of my brothers and it was a boys evening with no girls that night. The wine flowed, there was plenty of lamb and it was delicious. It was all good fun when suddenly, even in my slightly fuddled state, I was aware that the Amorite boys were grinning silently at us. Rim leaned forward;

"Ah, my dear friend," he announced in that smooth way of his which was never a good sign. "What a pleasure it is that you enjoy our fare. Please, take this last morsel." He picked up a bit of crackling and held it out to me. "To my victor!" he concluded and touched the scar on his brow. Mug that I was, I felt flattered, took the piece and crunched it up.

"Thanks," I said, slightly embarrassed and feeling rather uncouth. The Amorite boys simply collapsed in laughter nudging themselves and pointing their fingers at me and my brothers in derision.

"You've done it." Rim laughed uncontrollably while rolling about. "Naughty boys, naughty little Hebrews," he jeered.

I was getting a bit fed up with this and touched my

brow. They all stopped laughing and Rim leaned forward again;

"That wasn't lamb we've being eating," stated he, matter-of-fact. "It was pig!" And he and the Amorite boys once again fell around laughing.

Well, as you probably know, eating pig is probably the worst thing that you can do as a Jew. I mean if Dad found out, I do not know what he would do. The official punishment was stoning et cetera but Ma would not have allowed that so we would probably have been disowned and slung out into the wilderness. Or was Yahweh going to strike us down and turn us into pillars of salt or something? "Oh, don't worry, we won't tell," said Rim consolingly, seeing the absolute genuine horror on our faces. "Come on, there's some wine left. Fill up your goblets."

In the morning, back with our herds and feeling a bit fuzzy we were shamefaced.

"Agreed, we don't tell Dad or anyone about last night," said Chilion, and we all nodded.

There were lots of other happy memories! But now there he was, Rim, standing on the valley bottom shouting up at me with two bloody war chariots champing behind him.

"It's bad news!" he shouted up. "Very bad news. And don't come down." I said nothing, I just raised my hands as if to say 'What the hell is all this?' Rim cupped his hand over his mouth.

"Your guy, Joshua, has just invaded Og and Sihon up north and the orders are to slaughter everyone. Men, women and children, the whole lot. So we're taking revenge down here." He paused then shouted up, "I'm sorry!"

He pointed in the direction of our camp. I looked. In the distance, I could see black smoke rising.

"Run for it, Uds, and good luck," he said, and turned away.

I have been at the scene of a few massacres in my life, played my part in some of them I have to admit, and they always finish the same way. There is the smoke of the scattered campfires, the litter of upturned cooking vessels, pieces of discarded clothes, corpses lying distorted and bloody, and the awful stink of the burning goat hair. And there is an eerie silence but that silence is always broken by something. Once it was a baby which the mother had hidden. Another time I remember it was a goat bleating, scrabbling in the dirt with a broken back. It is always the same, an uncomprehending cry for help. This time – yes, my first massacre scene – it was that little dog of my mother's, yap yap yap. I could hear it a mile away. Persistent, frantic; it just got louder as I got nearer.

The little dog was barking over the dead body of my mother speared at the threshold of the tent, presumably, come out just to see what all the fuss was about. In the daze, I walked through the settlement strewn with the bodies of my family and tribe. Inside our family tent it was the same. Death! Chilion just lay there on his rush mat, eyes open in horror, his chest a mass of spear thrusts. Outside the tent I shouted out. Perhaps someone had got away into the hills and, frankly, I did not care if the Amorites came back and killed me. But nothing, my voice just echoed and echoed. I remember going and sitting on the big stone by the fire when Dad used to sit and tell stories. Yap, yap, yap, that little dog continued to bark, then started to howl but I just sat there and wept.

I suppose I was really feeling sorry for myself. Gone, all gone!

I would like to say that I could remember the day my real mother and I struggled into their camp all those years ago. But I cannot because I was unconscious with hunger and thirst. Not surprisingly my mother died shortly after but I do remember standing there and these two grown-ups looking down at me.

"Look at his crinkly hair and that funny stub of a nose." They laughed but it was kind. Then the woman took my hands. "Entwined snakes," she commented looking at the purple tattoo on the inside of my left wrist. Then she looked up at her husband.

"We must take him in. He must become one of our family." And she knelt down in front of me;

"We'll call you Ehud. That means Glory. Will you like that?" I nodded. So they became Mum and Dad and I got a whole lot of brothers and sisters who called me Ehud and its variations, or Snakes, after the tattoo, depending on whether they felt like being nice to me or not.

So, sitting on that stone with everyone dead all around me, you can understand my weeping a bit. But, of course, you cannot weep all day, eventually your survival instinct kicks in. "Ehud, my lad," a voice – your voice – is saying, "it's all very awful and very sad but tears are not going to bring them back and there's no point hanging about here. Leave it for the vultures, they'll be here soon enough." Looking up, the first ones were already there, their wings languidly beating the air, watching, listening, waiting for the moment to flop down and start the feast.

I really did not want to be around for that. I stood up; the sun was high in the sky. Yes, I could follow the sun, go south back into the Sinai and become once again a nomad in the wilderness. But I didn't. I turned round, my back to the sun and headed north. To find Joshua.

Chapter 2

"Name!" barked the grizzled commander, an old soldier if ever there was one, sitting behind the desk. He looked at me with a mixture of scorn and total lack of interest. To him I was just another ragged boy 'going for a soldier' in Joshua's army. He was stocky, round-faced with a ragged beard and on his head was a strange helmet of black leather and shiny bronze studs. Obviously, something which had belonged to an Amorite once, and probably recently to judge from the crudely sewn jagged slash across the top.

It had taken me about seven days travelling north to find Joshua's army at Abila. Just living off the land is surprisingly easy when you have not got a whole herd to look after. Any small spring will do for water, and finding them is just one of the skills you acquire as a goatherd. And where you find water, you find animals. I was admittedly lucky; on my first day I was able to trap a small gazelle coming for a drink and that, along with my bag of barley, kept me going. I preferred to travel at night when the moon was up with the North Star to keep me right. Then I would lie up in a cave when the moon went down or the sky clouded over and everything became pitch, pitch black. Whenever I met someone, and the only people I met were Hebrews fleeing east with their herds, the news was always the same. The Ammonites are on the rampage, massacre, with no quarter! And our folk were escaping back into the hills to the east of Jordan for a harder but safer life.

It was all bustle when I arrived at Joshua's camp up at Og. I quickly found myself in the queue of other boys, some as ragged as me possibly with a similar story, who had come to join Joshua's army. But there was no talking in the queue. "Name!" he repeated at me when at last it was my turn. "Tribe and occupation!"

"Ehud," I said, "Benjamin. Goatherd." The scribe sitting beside him wrote this down.

The commander sniffed. "Another bloody goatherd, another Benjamite." He glared at me. "You think you know it all. Well, sonny, we'll see about that!"

It took me a bit aback. I am not saying I had been expecting a hero's welcome or anything like that, but it is true that I probably did have quite a high opinion of myself. My dad, poor man, had been a respected figure, and I had escaped the massacre and found my way all on my own to Joshua's army. Others, in my situation would have curled up and died, and some had.

So I suppose it did hurt, this leathery old bastard's total lack of interest in my history and his contemptuous dismissal of me as a mere goatherd who thinks he knows it all. Of course, I realise now, that is just the army for you. The recruits arrive all cocky and derring-do but basic training does not care a hoot about that! All it wants is to turn you into another tiny cog in an enormous wheel. And that it will do by Hook or by Crook, or rather Carrot and Stick but mainly Stick until you become that cog. And Stick, whether it's being forced to stand in the sun for an hour or a good beating, gets everyone down eventually, and then you are a soldier.

And actually, standing in the queue for an hour and half in the sun with the other recruits, I did not fancy the job ahead of turning this lot into soldiers. Okay the easy ones were the bums, pimps or pickpockets, or on the run for some petty crime; a few good beatings and they would knuckle under soon enough. But looking at them, most looked like village boys who had simply joined up to get away from the daily grind, and for a bit of a colour and glory. I mean, it is fun to play the hero and announce to your family that you are off to take part in this Yahweh-ordered great landgrab – not those words, of course. Anything to get away from flaying your fingers sewing tent flaps, humping buckets of sewage out each day to empty on the crops, cutting down trees and bringing the wood in to feed the inexhaustible requirements of the women for hot water and that kind of thing. Dull hard work and little respite. And don't make me laugh saying that was the work the women did. All that talk about women being 'the hewers of wood and carriers of water!' Ha, anything heavier than a twig or a cup, there were always those pathetic little screams of 'Ehud, can you help?' and 'Chilion, this is too heavy!' and some boy would have to take over. I tell you, they, the women that is, ruled the roost, and being a goatherd may have been tough and sometimes dangerous but it was a hundred times better than sitting in camp or village at the beck and call of every woman with a sore back or varicose veins.

Now, I reckoned, those village boys must be beginning to wonder what they had let themselves in for standing in the baking queue behind me.

Of course, old Barker had not finished with me.

"And you don't look like a bloody Benjie, more like a bloody Amorite," he snarled, now looking at me closely. "Where's your bloody hooter, for one thing? And that snub thing of yours and that crinkly hair. Are you a spy, boy?"

Inwardly my anger gave way to a sigh, or rather a cold feeling in my stomach. Of course, I had long been used to being teased about my nose and my hair. My brothers, or so I called them, and Dad had big noses and long straight hair whereas my nose was, well, stubby and my hair crinkly.

But these questions, were they just the patter of a bored commander, the kind of stuff any rookie has to endure, or was he on to something more serious? With all my family and their friends' dead there was no one to vouch for me. I could be a spy just turning up like that out of the desert with a cock and bull story about a massacre and then travelling a week on my own to get here. Oh yes, it was not hard to see his point of view.

I raised my left hand. "I'm left-handed," I said back to him. "Doesn't that prove anything?"

He grunted and shrugged his shoulders. Being left-handed was a rarity but it was something more usual with Benjamites. I must have inherited it from my mother. Of course, some of the other tribes looked on it as an infirmity, called it an infliction by Yahweh for

20

the sins of our fathers and all that. So we called them the whore's children in return. I mean, we may have been the twelve tribes of Israel with Moses leading us out of Egypt, and wandering around the desert for forty years and all that, but that did not make us the greatest of friends. Or friends at all! We just quarrelled with some tribes more than others. It all stems back to our common ancestor, old Jacob. We are one of the four tribes descended from his wife, Rachel, so we do more or less stick together. But Jacob took a new piece called Leah and the other tribes are descended from her and her crony, and they, of course, hate us. Sensibly, Moses tried to keep us apart most of the time, but now Joshua had his orders from Moses on his deathbed – obviously straight from Yahweh himself – and here he was trying to collect an army from all the tribes for the invasion.

Nogram – I discovered that was the grizzly old soldier's name later, or Noggy as he was known by us soldiers – looked back at me and snorted. There were a lot of men behind me, waiting in the queue, and he knew he ought to get on. If I were a spy, and frankly I did not look like one or sound like one, I could see him thinking, that was going to be someone else's problem.

"You'll be joining the other Benjamites, of course. Go and see your tribal commander and he'll tell you where to go. Get on," he finished shortly gesticulating with his hand. "Someone will take you to his tent."

"Name, tribe, occupation." I heard him bark out again to the next in line, as I set off around his table towards the beckoning arm of another soldier.

21

"Dreadful, dreadful, absolutely dreadful," muttered Micah, leader of the tribe of Benjamin, when he heard my story. "Your father, your poor father" – he paused – "You know we go back a long way?"

I kept silent, shifting awkwardly from foot to foot in front of this comfortable-looking kindly-looking man. I reckoned he was having a conversation with himself and there was not much I could say or add. Or rather I could, but it would not do, now or ever, for me to inform him, my tribal leader in charge of my destiny for the immediate future, that Dad had thought he was amiable enough but a useless old fool.

"Hm," he went on. "Your father was a rich man. Had the finest flocks of black goats in the tribe. All gone, I suppose?"

He paused long enough for me to start to open my mouth, but he went on. "They will have taken everything, they always do," he finished with a little chuckle. Then he seemed to suddenly remember that for some present – which of course was only ME – it was no laughing matter. He became more sympathetic and business-like.

"Poor lad, poor lad, so you've got nothing. But you will do well here. Your skills as a goatherd will adapt easily to soldiering. In fact, unlike a lot of the lads I've seen this morning who will have to go through basic training, I'm going to put you straight into an operational unit." He beamed at me and I tried to look back gratefully.

He called out and a boy of about my age appeared. "Take Ehud to Seth's tent." And turning to me he said, "Seth is one of my best junior commanders. He needs chaps like you. Yes, you will do well there. And, my boy, I will keep an eye on you. Good luck!"

*****

"That's Seth." The boy nodded at the tall sour-faced man in a white tunic with a black leather belt standing outside a big open tent before slipping away without another word back to Micah through this brand-new maze of Joshua's army.

Seth stood there silently, eyeing me. I reckoned that it must be pretty obvious to him that the boy standing in front of him, very ragged and very dirty, had been sent to him by Micah. A sardonic smile, not welcoming, slightly distorted his face but he didn't say anything, he just waited.

"I'm Ehud," I said. "I've been posted to you." He motioned me forward with his head. I stood uneasily in front of him. "Keep still," he hissed, then barked, "Where's your kit?"

I shook my head. He frowned, then eyed my spear. Well, I called it a spear, it was actually just a stick with one end sharpened to a point and hardened with fire. I reached down with my left hand and touched the sling.

Seth brightened ever so slightly. "Use that, can you?" he asked. I nodded unsmilingly. All this parade stuff and putting down was getting to me. All the same,

I felt I was getting back into my territory and touching the sling gave me my confidence back. I was itching to say, "You want to see what I can do, commander or whatever you call yourself? Choose your weapon and let's face each other at thirty paces and, I tell you, this ragged boy here with his sling will make you dance."

I think Seth saw my anger and reckoned the conversation was over for the time being.

"Your scratcher's over there. Big Abs will sort you out," he said tersely, pointing with his hand towards the interior of the tent where rush mats, laid out in lines a yard apart, filled the tent. There were quite a few soldiers, all in simple coarse white tunics, in the tent; some were sleeping on their mats, and others were just sitting around. I followed Seth's arm towards a bare mat over in a dark corner of the tent.

I suppose it is one of the things you do lots of when you are younger, arriving somewhere for the first time, and not knowing what to expect. You can't shout for attention, call out 'It's me! Here I am!' to a lot of total strangers, and beat your chest for good measure. I mean, I think you would get dumbfounded silence at best and otherwise a hail of old sandals or anything else every man in the tent could lay hands on. So I think most of us go to the other extreme, which is certainly what I did that day, pretending to be invisible and threading my way carefully through the throng towards my mat. *Then, should I lie down, or would that show disrespect to my new mates*, I was thinking. Would that provoke a hail of sandals or whatever? My compromise was to sit down on the mat and, head down, pretend to examine my sling. *Your move, my new mates,* I thought*, and the sooner the better.* I suddenly realised that I was very, very tired.

I heard someone sit down on the mat beside me. Was this the Big Abs who was going to 'sort me out'?

"What's your name?" a voice said, brusque but not unkindly, and I looked up and there was a big chap observing me while behind him the others were all glancing in our direction. I told him, and he nodded.

"I'm Abner, well, Abs," he said. "You don't look as if you've come from Boot Camp." He looked at me puzzled. "How come you've been posted to us without basic training?"

I shrugged my shoulders and mumbled something about being a goatherd.

Big Abs laughed.

"Right on," he laughed. "So that qualifies you to tramp all night, bake all day and then kill with a smile on your face? Does it?" He paused then added, "Oh yes, and drink your own piss on your third day without water! Well, I guess that's all the basic training you need in this man's army," he paused again, "or this tent anyway, because congratulations, Ehud." And here he leaned forward and patted me on the shoulder. "You have been posted to one of the elite," and here his voice took on an exaggerated tone, "yes, one of the elite long-range units," he continued, "and 'That' – tramping, baking and killing is what we do. In fact," – and here he leaned back and put his hands behind his head – "looking at you, ragged, gaunt, burnt and completely bloody knackered, you could have just come back from one of our patrols." He finished with a laugh, and the other men in the tent joined in. All I could do was smirk back feeling foolish.

Abs bent forward and put a hand on my shoulder. He smiled. "I guess you need sleep. Better get it in. We'll sort you out tomorrow."

Frankly I have known many worse first-day experiences.

*****

"Start panicking, details later!" Seth's bellow had me sitting bolt upright and awake. Around me the other soldiers laughed.

"That got you up all right," said the man on my left, leaning over on his elbow. "We thought you were never going to wake up. Come on. It is lunchtime. I'll take you over to the cookhouse."

Seth's 'Start panicking. Details later' – the nearest he ever got to humour incidentally – was his way of announcing that he had orders for us. That could be anything from a medical inspection – he had a particular thing about lice although I never remember finding them a particular problem – to a seven-day raid into Canaan. We always just had to wait and see. That day, I suppose my second in Joshua's army, it was orders for a raid.

"This is Ehud." Seth nodded over at me when he started addressing us, standing, while we all sat on the mats in front of him. He then proceeded with his orders. Nothing more than that, nothing about where I had come from, nothing – I was relieved – about Micah keeping an eye on me. No, it was just 'This is Ehud'. That was all, nothing more, and typical Seth.

He then went on to give short orders for a two-day operation in Canaan. "I'll be wanting ten men," he finished, and read out a list. There was a groan from each soldier as his name was mentioned. This was routine and a tent tradition which Seth ignored.

"The tenth man will be Ehud," he finished, looking at me. "This op is only two days so it's a good one for you to start on. We'll see what you are made of." Of course, the other men laughed.

There are two big differences between being a goatherd and being a soldier out in the desert. As a goatherd your only kit is a stick, and a knife; your only food, some barley cakes, and for water, a small goatskin. Your job is to make sure the goats do not go thirsty so you are never far from water and, frankly, for food you can more or less live off the land, snaring rabbits and eating the odd goat that is stupid enough to break a leg. In other words, you can travel light, very light. Not so the soldier. First, he needs a spear with a good bronze point to it. Then he needs a sword to strap around his waist. Weighty objects! Then he cannot rely on finding water so that is one big goatskin filled with the stuff slung around his neck; and he cannot live off the land scavenging for food, so he is carrying a few days rations as well. So, I would say the bits and pieces add about a tenth to your body weight. Okay, that may not sound too much but it certainly takes the skip out of a man.

Which brings me onto Difference Number two. Being a goatherd is leisurely, your speed over the ground is dictated by the speed of your flock. Those goats are never in a hurry and they feed as they go. In front, there is scrub, behind them bare desert. They pick clean so progress is slow. Being a soldier in enemy territory you move fast, the faster the better, and that is when you really feel the extra load and all the kit you are carrying. Oh yes, and one other thing. The Good Book says that goatherds watch their flocks at night but actually there is nothing to do so they wrap themselves up in a big comfy cloak and go to sleep. Not so the raiding soldier. He cannot move by day in case he is seen by the enemy, so he has to sleep by day and march by night, lucky if there is a bit of a moon but often stumbling and cursing in the pitch black and with the occasional rainstorm to make the rocks slippery and dangerous.

Most of the other soldiers in Seth's tent were fully equipped – if you can call it that – with sword, spear and water skin. These had been picked up on operations although the rules were that all loot had to be handed in. As I learnt, this was a typical Joshua order. He would make these grand pronouncements, declare the official policy if you like, and not interest himself too much in the various interpretations down the line, well, as long as no one boasted about it. Even sticklers like Seth did their own little bit of interpretation. He had built up a small stock of weapons and certainly was not going to hand them over for distribution to the rest of the army. Well, he did hand in some weapons just to show willing but you can bet they were bent or broken.

It is no wonder the Canaanites, those inhabiting the West of the Jordan with their lush pastures, orchards of fruit trees, terraces and vineyards, sneered at us. We had nothing or rather started off with virtually nothing. No wonder they dismissed us as mere 'Savages armed with sticks'. We did not have chariots; we did not have foundries to make metal weapons or armour; all we had was manpower and our flocks. You have to give Joshua credit for the big bold decision to invade Canaan. Sorry, 'Take possession of Canaan' because that is the language he used. We were 'The Chosen People' and Canaan was our 'Promised Land'; a promise by God; and 'THAT', with our sharp sticks, would send us victorious.

So the reality was that every bit of fighting kit that was any good came from loot, came from the enemy. Most of it came from the sacking of Og where Joshua's instructions had been pretty much carried out to the letter and every man, woman and child had been killed. With that came a good chunk of weapons and armour; swords and spears, helmets and breastplates, even some chariots and a good few bows.

There were a couple of other soldiers new to Seth's tent with clean white tunics and cropped heads, clearly straight from Boot Camp. The three of us followed Seth to a corner of the tent where a couple of soldiers were unwrapping his cache of arms, a mixed bag of swords and spears.

"You wait, Ehud," Seth said roughly to me as I

leant down to pick up a nice- looking sword with a good blade. Seth picked it up and a spear with a shiny iron tip and gave them to the first soldier. He did the same with the other one and dismissed them with an 'Off you go, lads'.

"Take your pick, Ehud," Seth now addressed me waving towards the diminished stack. The two soldiers who had done the unwrapping onto the floor of the tent now knelt there grinning. There was not much left and a lot of it looked broken and rusty as I sifted through.

"Now that's a nice sword," Seth said encouragingly and, of course, I fell for it. It was a fine sword with a big thick blade and an ornate bronze handle. I picked it up. It weighed a ton. The soldier squatting on the floor laughed.

"That's Mighty," he chortled. "I had to carry that monster on my first operation before I picked up this boy." He tapped the much lighter sword at his side with a simple handle. "But Mighty will go through anything you touch. We think it was a sword used for executions, don't we, sir?" Seth just nodded. "You need a spear too. Go ahead."

There was not much choice. The other two soldiers had been given five-foot spears, javelins really, wooden hafts with a short bronze point, nice and light, but the remaining spears were either broken, or solid bronze and very weighty.

"Yes," said the soldier – obviously Seth did not mind this running commentary at my expense – "These belonged to the Guards of Baal. Big guys! All they had to do was stand there with this thing in their right hand

and look impressive." He paused. "Easy meat, weren't they, sir?" Seth just grunted.

"Thanks," said I as I turned away and walked back to my bedspace wondering how I was going to cope on patrol. *Nice little test,* I thought, *Seth*. Nice little test for the goatherd, is it not? Thinks he deserves special treatment because his dad was someone and his dad knew Micah? We'll see! Give him a big bloody sword and a big bloody spear! Let's see how he gets on these next few nights. And do not think of losing them out there accidental-like, by the way, because that is a very serious offence; which probably means being tied to a pillar and stoned to death. Quite frankly, at that moment I do not think I could care less.

When I had calmed down a bit, I took myself in hand. "You've survived bullying on the hill, you'll survive the bullying in the tent. Just work it out!" said I to myself. The tent was now fairly quiet, just a few soldiers present sorting out their kit. Big Abner was one of them.

"You're not going out tonight, are you?" I asked. Abner nodded. "Can I borrow your sword and spear?" Abner rocked back cross-legged thinking.

"I'll tell you what," he said ruminatively, "we'll do a deal. I've a couple your kind of size. They are yours for the op for your daily pay. That's two Tent Shekels a day every day you are away."

"That's a bit steep," I said. "In other words, you get all my pay while I am away on operations."

"That's about it," said Abner. "But remember, you'll be travelling light like the rest of them. And remember, from my point of view, I don't get paid and I lose my valuable weapons if you don't come back" – he paused – "not everyone does, you know," he added and languidly pointed out the empty mats. "But let's think this through," he said quietly leaning forward.

We were due to set off after dark. Seth did not like anyone seeing us leave the camp so he held his inspections and rehearsals at four. The ten of us duly turned up. There was some smirking around me as I stood there with the big bronze spear in my hand and the heavy sword hanging from my belt, almost touching the ground. Seth, of course, as he inspected me, was imperturbable and we were all dismissed when he was satisfied.

Then I did the swap. A couple of hours later in the sudden blackness of the early evening when we all became shadows, I doubted that Seth would notice. Or frankly bother at this stage. And yes, it was a quick look to see that we were all there and off we went.

Chapter 3

They were always the same, these terror raids into Canaan; a scramble down the hills into the Jordan valley, cross the Jordan – that could be quite hairy sometimes

– then out the other side and a hard tab along the beds of valleys, through scrubland, over plateaus, with dogs barking ferociously whenever we were near an encampment. Seth did not believe in short rests so we just kept going for eight hours and then stopped a couple of hours before dawn. Of course, by then, we were well into Canaan and everyone was an enemy. Our job was to take out an encampment. Two or three families was about the right size. We certainly did not want to go to all this trouble to butcher a lonely nomad; on the other hand, we did not want to find ourselves with a major fight on our hands. So any encampment with a single dog barking was too small, and any with a great many dogs was too big. Three or four dogs was ideal and Seth rarely got this wrong. The business done it was back across into our territory at the speed of light.

Stragglers did not last, Oh no. They were picked up pretty smartish by the chariot patrols which buzzed around from dawn till dusk. Then it was a slow death, normally just staked out under a burning sun but otherwise it was anything which took their fancy, impalement or burning your feet off at the ankles with a charcoal fire. With the same ending of course, a treat

33

for the vultures. Lessons learnt! You could not really blame the Amorites. What else could you expect from an enemy whose families you had slaughtered in their beds the night before?

I will never forget my first terror raid, although actually they were all much the same. That night Seth identified his three-dog encampment and went forward on a recce. He took me as the new boy, and one other. Of course, the dogs went increasingly mad as we got nearer; people came out of their tents, looked around a bit, then cursed the dogs and went back inside their tents to sleep. We could hear the women still complaining. Then we returned to our cave that night and the dogs eventually shut up. We lay trying to sleep in that bug-infested cave all day, then up again at nightfall. Soon we were crouched in the circle of rocks on the side of the valley, the three tents stretched in the moonlight on the flat floor of the valley. The dogs, of course, started to yowl again, out came a couple of blokes for a look around, a bit of shouting and then back into their tents. We gave it a couple of hours and then went in.

Seth, that man of few words normally and none on this occasion, had simply pointed. We had already been split into three groups and I was with Seth and a couple of other men. He silently indicated our targets, one tent for each group, then looked round at us raising his hand. Then he pointed and we rushed forward. It was all quite simple; if it moved you stabbed, if it squealed you stabbed. I kept stabbing until there was silence. It was the same everywhere else, grunts, screams, a bit of babbling, then silence. Apart from some retching from nearby;

I remember thinking that someone is not enjoying this, probably one of the new boys straight from Boot Camp.

"Grab any weapons, lads." I heard Seth cry. I looked round quickly by the dim light of the swinging lantern trying not to look at the bloody blankets and contorted limbs. There was a simple knife lying on the floor which I grabbed. As I emerged from the tent a dog came for me. I gave it a short stab in the mouth and it went away whimpering. Elsewhere more dog killing was taking place.

"Everyone here? Everyone all right?" Seth did a silent count back in the rock circle. All present. "Let's get out then," he said. A solitary dog continued to bark; otherwise, silence.

Jeez but we did hammer back! Once we hit Jordan again, we knew we were safe and we splashed around for a few minutes washing off the caked blood. Then up those hills again and we were soon back in sight of our camp as the red fingers of the rising sun spread across the dark desert. It was good to be home! We stood in front of our tent and threw down the weapons we had taken, a spear and a couple of swords, nice ones too, and a few daggers. Seth looked almost happy.

"Help yourself, Ehud," he said curtly, and I leant forward and picked up a spear. Mine now, well, for terror patrols anyway. Then it was the turn of the other boy, the one who I think had been retching. This was Seth's way of saying, 'Welcome to the team'.

No one ever talked about the killing, but there was a routine after each patrol. In the evening, Seth would arrive with a bucket of date wine, rough stuff but it certainly did the trick, and ten tent shekels each as a bonus. He would dish these out with a knowing wink, one of Seth's ghastly and thankfully infrequent attempts at being laddish. Of course, ten shekels was the price of a quickie in the Boxes where the camp tarts did the business. So, after our skinful of date wine, we would set off roaring to the Boxes, and then brought up sharp by the Madam and told to wait quietly in the queue.

I will give Seth his due; for all his petty faults he was a good commander. He took care and could think fast. I am not saying he had much imagination but he always seemed to know what to do when something happened.

Of course, what worried us all was breaking a leg or getting wounded or even lost in deep Canaan. It happened to us a couple of times and each time Seth came up trumps. One guy twisted his ankle and each of us took it in turns carrying him home piggyback fashion. It was slow work and we had to lie up an extra day in a cave, which was pretty hairy with the chariot patrols looking for us. But we got back okay. Another time a guy got a spear in the guts. He was a newbie and I suspect he hesitated in the dark tent for the first time. There, what business must be done must be done quickly. When we got back to the cave, he just lay there groaning with Seth kneeling behind him.

"Get ready to go, lads," ordered Seth and in the

darkness of the cave we slung our half empty water skins and put on our cloaks. Over in the corner we could hear Seth talking to the man. "Drink this, lad," we heard him say. Then we heard a gurgling noise, some coughing, and silence. Seth loomed above us.

"Let's go," he announced laconically, and that was that. Again, no one talked about it but I did ask Big Abs afterwards out of earshot of the others. "Apple of Sodom," he said. "The seeds. A few will give you the shits but it's a quick death if you get the dose wrong; or right in that case." Of course, Seth was not going to admit anything, but it actually was rather reassuring.

I always went out with Seth or rather, after our first patrol, I became a fixture. It's not that he liked me or anything; it is just that after all that time as a goatherd I could see, smell and hear better than those camp-based boys. So I always travelled just behind him. We would stop and get down and listen. Then Seth would turn round to me and I would either shake my head in the darkness or point where I could hear or see something going on.

One day a patrol led by Seth's deputy simply did not come back. No one said anything. After a couple of days, another ten men arrived from the Boot Camp to take their places.

Overall, barring mishap or accident, which I was lucky enough to avoid, it was not too bad being a member of a long-range patrol group or terror squad or whatever you liked to call it. There was a certain glamour to it. After all, we were soldiers doing soldiering, whereas other soldiers were day in, day out doing all the tedious things which soldiers have to do, like building fortifications and digging trenches, doing endless carrying duties and all those things which commanders dream up because they think soldiers need to be kept busy. We guys had it fairly easy when we were not on patrol.

In the tent, we were all from the tribe of Benjamin. We joined as Benjamites, we lived as Benjamites, and we fought as Benjamites, and Joshua liked it that way. It was funny; we were all Israelites; we all had a common history in escaping from Egypt and all those years in the wilderness but we weren't exactly a band of brothers. In some cases, it was healthy competition between the tribes, more often it was pure hatred harking back generations. Joshua was from the tribe of Ephraim which, like us, was descended from Team Rachel; that is from Rachel, Jacob's second wife and her maid, Biha; and by tradition our tribes got on well with each other. Which meant we were disliked by the other tribes or Team Leah, which were descended from Leah, Jacob's first wife and Zilpah, her maid.

Joshua tried to be a uniting figure, rising above tribal rivalries and, on the whole, he succeeded but he still made it his policy to keep the tribes separate and not mix them up. We all had our separate tent areas and any necessary meetings between different tribes, planning and operational something like that, always took place in a central neutral area. Of course, there is a certain amount of nicking between the tribes. The Reubenites, or Reubs as we called them for short, always seemed to manage to get the best share of the spoils so we would mount scavenging expeditions against them when we knew they were out on overnight operations. Obviously, they would leave sentries in the tent but the game was to distract them and then slip someone into the tent with a bag. It wasn't big time, just nicking bits of kit or clothing but it really annoyed the Reubs and they used to complain to Joshua. He made a big noise and declared it a serious offence punishable by whipping. But on the whole, we reckoned he didn't really seem to care. We were much more concerned about being caught in the tent by the Reubs themselves because that would have meant a severe beating up.

*****

Of course, we did begin to wonder where all this was getting us. I mean six months of raiding into the Promised Land and we were still stuck on the wrong side of the Jordan and living on a diet of roasted barley and bad beer. Not a pomegranate, fig or wheat cake in sight!

We were quite some army by now what with all those boys coming in from the villages looking for glory and the boot camps churning them out into half-decent soldiers who could walk all day and survive on mush. There must have been ten thousand of us by now. Surely, so the big talk ran in the tents, we were big enough to invade Canaan? And not just a big hit-and-run but a proper take possession job, camp followers and all; that's another 30,000 from priests to prostitutes. But then someone would spoil the fun with.

"What about Jericho?"

And a kind of silence would then prevail because there, across the Jordan and about fifty miles south of us, dominating a flat landscape was a huge, fortified Amorite city called Jericho. Rumoured to be impregnable with miles of thick high walls and towers, and cisterns brimming with water and granaries stuffed with wheat and barley. Strong enough and with plenty enough to last a long siege. Yes, and just forget the military challenge for a moment, the real problem of taking on Jericho would be straight-forward, simply to survive. It was late in the season so all the fields and orchards were stripped bare, too late for this year's 'Milk and Honey', for us anyway. So that kind of living off the land was not an obvious option and an army cannot survive on berries. Water too. The Amorites would be quick to drop dead animals down the local wells so there was every prospect of Joshua joining that long line of generals who lost a campaign with an army dying of thirst or their soldiers reduced to squatting in the sand all day shitting themselves to death.

And what actually was our knowledge of Canaan beyond a few miles west of Jordan? Precious little! In terror raids we always moved at night so saw nothing. We carried our own supplies so needed nothing, and we were always moving at top speed or hiding in caves. Whatever else these raids achieved, they were light on information gathering.

It was not altogether surprising when one day Seth marches into the tent all smiles and fake honesty.

"I'm looking for volunteers," he calls out. "Good rates. Double pay while you're away."

One of the first things I learnt on joining Joshua's army was to go cold when I heard a call for volunteers. Or be very wary anyway. Any 'call' was always dressed up with a 'bit of excitement' and promises of time-off or extra pay – which normally meant you could afford a better tart some evening – and all the various tricks which men like Seth use to lure a bored soldier from his rush mat. So, my Rule Number One when I hear a call for volunteers is to keep quiet and sit on my hands.

Anyway, Seth went on to explain that there was a requirement for 'experienced lads' – another giveaway, that was Seth being flattering, and not the real Seth – to slip over the Jordan and move about Canaan at night and then lie up and watch by day. The idea was to report back on where there were food stocks and, perhaps most important, good sources of water.

"About a week, that's all," said Seth. A few hands went up, one from Gam but the rest from new boys.

"You'll do," said Seth marking out four soldiers and ignoring Gam. That was another giveaway. Seth knew this job was dangerous, whoever was going out to do this spying was unlikely to come back, so Seth chose the disposable.

"What got into you?" we asked Gam afterwards. He shrugged his shoulders. "Bored! Just teasing Seth!"

But Joshua also wanted spies who could infiltrate, listen to the gossip, find out the weak points and that meant people who could pass themselves off amid the local population. That suggested travelling merchants and there were any number of these in the camp who would keep us supplied, or rather those who could afford it, with goodies from the land of Canaan. All strictly forbidden but of course it went on, so Joshua, or rather his henchmen, arm-twisted a few of these and packed them off to Canaan.

Of course, it was a complete disaster. None of those 'Sit and Watch' guys, including our four, came back. No surprises there! It is one thing on a terror raid to sit at the back of a dark cave during daylight, and quite another to perch on the top of a hill for a good look around. There are eyes everywhere; you will be seen and they were. Nor did the merchants with their bags of gold do any better. Even worse the rumour went around that they simply changed sides, and had a good old laugh with our enemies about those 'Savages with sticks' stuck in the foothills to the east of Jordan; and the very idea that we could ever be a conquering army! Yes, a good laugh they had, and all with Joshua's gold.

Which all really displeased Joshua. But what made him hopping mad was the two spies who were sent into Jericho. I mean, Jericho was the key; Jericho had to fall, in other words, we had to take Jericho somehow. So, the spies were there to report on the walls, sentry rosters, alarm signals and all that.

It appears they got into Jericho all right with their bag of gold and slipped into an inn just inside the city, set into the main wall, to start their 'infiltration'. Well, the inn was actually a brothel and, surprise, surprise, they did a deal with the Madam, called Rahab, to hide them. They said there were search parties out in the city but, whatever the actual truth of that, they decided to hole up in the brothel for the week. All very comfortable, no doubt! And, to give the story a bit of zing, they said they escaped from Jericho on a rope from a window in the main wall on a dark night. Them with their soft merchants' hands? More likely let out by the main gate for their last piece of gold. And the information, the intelligence gathered? Zilch! Thank you for telling us that the walls of Jericho are eight feet thick and guarded day and night. As if we didn't know that already! No wonder Joshua was hopping mad. No wonder, as we dreaded, his next cry was 'Forward, with Yahweh we shall conquer!'

One day Joshua simply called us all together and walked among us. Just like that. One moment we were sitting there in the sand and next moment he was among us, small, clean-shaven and with greying black curly hair, but impressive with black piercing eyes. He spoke quite a while in that low slow voice of his. There was quite a lot about us being the Chosen People and how 'He' – Yahweh in other words had promised us all the land to the west of the Jordan, how it flowed with 'Milk and Honey' and all that stuff. All deadly serious and the only funny bit – awkward actually – was when one of the guys shouted, "And what about the women?"

We all burst out laughing but Joshua turned on him and grimly spelt out the words, "Spare no one. They must all die." That sent a big chill around; there was no more laughter after that.

Then it came; he went on a bit about how we had proved ourselves as warriors but now we had to tackle something big. He paused there for effect and we all looked at each other. Then he said it.

"Jericho! Yes, we must take Jericho."

Of course, we all cheered and clapped ourselves on the back but I was thinking, *Taking on bloody Jericho, how lunatic is that?* But that was Joshua all over; typical bloody Ephraimite, full of vision and bold ideas and expecting everyone to jump about and do what he said and not tell him he was bonkers.

*****

"Here we go again. What's up this time?" growled Big Abner as we were stirred to Seth's favourite shout 'Start panicking, details later!' You never really knew with Seth what it was going to be. It could be the patrol orders for next week, a pep talk on camp hygiene, or it might be to collect some money to give the priests to sacrifice some chicken or something. Seth was rather hot on this but we just paid up and shrugged our shoulders.

"There's one thing, lads…" he started and, well, that one thing certainly brought us up short. Yes, WE were in Yahweh's good books and Yes, HE promised us victory over the Amorites and the others living in Canaan, but No, oh dear me, no, some of us were not ready; or, as Seth put it;

"There's no crossing the Jordan until you've had your knob cut."

Big silence in the tent at that, and probably all over Abila as the About-to- enter-the-Promised-Land army heard the message. Some tittering in the ladies' quarters, I'll bet!

You see some of us had become a bit lax. When we were back in Egypt, and utterly under the thumb of old Moses, we did everything by the book. Sacrifices, ritual cleanliness and, of course, circumcision, they were just part of life; but out in the desert for forty years these things just slipped. I was lucky, I suppose. When my real mum died and I was adopted, the first thing they did was to give me the cut. The man I called Dad did not really care about these things but my new mum was a stickler and all her boys had been circumcised; so this was me joining the family. I must have been five at the time and there was this old man with a bit of flint. It was pretty quick but I cried a lot; not so much at the pain, I remember, but the humiliation; and I could not help feeling the horrible old man was enjoying it.

But I laughed now, looking around at the glum faces of the other chaps sitting on their rush mats, and put up my hand.

"That means everyone," Seth continued apparently ignoring me. "They'll decide up there who's had it done and who hasn't."

I looked a bit morose at the prospect of more fingering. Big Abner nudged me in the ribs.

"They can't do it again," he laughed. Gam, on the

other side, murmured, "They might try!" Which, of course, Big Abner and the others found extremely funny.

I can tell you there was some grumbling. Of all the rules we had to obey this seemed the silliest. Yes, there was a case against pigs because they do not thrive in the desert, do not like being milked and anyway have sixteen teats which makes milking a nightmare but circumcision? No one else worried, not the Egyptians, not the Canaanites, no, just us!

"Sign me up for Baal," murmured one guy and we all laughed but warily in case Seth heard. Another thing which rattled was this operation traditionally took place within a week of birth. It was one thing to be an infant under attack with a bit of flint but quite another if you were a big strapping soldier boy.

"There will be light duties for a few days after," cheerily announced Seth to more groans.

Actually, it was all pretty straightforward. Seth marched us up to the Temple and we stood in a row with our tunics up and a very bored priest scrutinised each one of us in turn.

Good old Mum, I thought when the priest nodded to me to fall out, one of the five in our tent found to be 'pure' enough to enter the 'Promised Land'. We went back to our tent rejoicing and how. And guess what, another bonus! Of course, this was having a big impact on business at the boxes, the camp brothel, so the girls were put on half price while the rest of the army was 'sore' and went around with their tunics held out in front of them.

Chapter 4

It took us about a week to get from Abila down to Shittim where we sat on the hillside waiting for orders to cross the river.

"I'd like to see those priests crossing the Jordan, what with the Ark of Covenant and all that, sir." Abs voiced what many of us were thinking to Seth as he fussed around on one of his inspections.

Of course, we all laughed. You never quite knew what to expect from Old River Jordan. Sometimes it was a trickle, hardly any water but dangerous, and on our patrols, we would cross warily from one slippery rock to another. At other times, it was pretty much a roaring torrent; pretty frightening if you are charging back from a terror raid and find yourself stuck on the wrong side and in Amorite territory when the sun comes up. It happened once but Seth was up to it. We filled our waterskins with air and floated off. It was still pretty hairy. I must have been carried about a mile down river paddling furiously for the other side. Eventually I caught a branch and someone pulled me in and I lay on the ground spewing water.

"Yes," continued Gam, chuckling, "I would like to see the priests floating on them skins." Seth cut into our mirth.

"Joshua's got Jordan in hand," he stated matter-of-fact. "Joshua has said that the riverbed will be dry when we cross," he continued curtly hoping to finish this line of questioning. We just looked at each other.

"Is this going to be a 'Yahweh moment' then?" drawled Abs continuing with his favourite trick of Seth-baiting. I mean we had all heard about those Yahweh moments when the Red Sea parted or when Moses struck a rock and water spewed out; but that was all part of our story, and well, most of us thought it was just a story. There had been no 'Yahweh moments' in our lives; things went well or things went badly and that was it. I'm not saying we did not believe in Yahweh, just that surely he was too busy to interfere in our day-to-day lives.

Seth was not to be drawn. He ignored Abs with a sniff and turned away.

Now I know the Good Book says it was a 'Yahweh moment'; the Jordan miraculously ran dry and we all crossed one night without getting our feet wet. And, yes, it is true, one moment we were all on the east bank of the Jordan and the next moment we were across the river and ten miles into the Promised Land. But actually, it took about a week and dozens of men were drowned, mainly from the tribe of Simeon. Which gave us a bit of a laugh, they being one of the tribes which disliked us.

"Start panicking. Details later," sang out Seth one afternoon as we sat there high up on the east bank with old Jordan gushing below; and we guessed this might be the big move.

That evening, immediately after it grew dark, we set off, that is the fighting men of the four tribes descended from Rachel, which included us of course. And so, about an hour later, there were several

48

thousand of us sitting on the east bank of the Jordan with the water flooding past.

"We are going to look a bit stupid if we can't cross tonight," muttered Gam, out of earshot of Seth of course. Around seven was normally quite a good crossing time with the river low but not tonight; Jordan was in roaring form.

Then, at about ten, the river started to drop.

"Fill your skins. Who knows when you next will get a chance?" ordered Seth and we dipped our water skins in the swirling muddy water and drank as much as we could as well. As the river continued to fall, I used the opportunity to pick up a dozen nice small, rounded stones perfect for my sling for general use. With them, I could kill a man at fifty paces with a headshot and sting him up badly elsewhere. I did consider a few fist-sized stones, great stoppers and useful in a close fray but then, I thought to myself, *better ten small stones than one big one.* "Orders are that we cross now," Seth announced suddenly out of the night;

"Link arms and we should be okay."

We started; the river was now wading level but, in the middle, it came up to the chest. So, it was quite a struggle but eventually we got over and flopped down on the other side. Then the river rose again and the crossings stopped.

"So now we're stupid and outnumbered on the other side," said Gam, expressing what we all really feared. There we were, a couple of thousand, easy meat for the Amorites that night. Or would they wait until daylight. What with their chariots, their archers, and a swirling river at our back not a man of us would get away. Yes, Joshua and his generals would enjoy a grandstand view of the massacre.

But the Amorites did not attack. Of course, we laughed about it afterwards. They were just so cocky, those Amorites, why descend to night fighting when they could pick us off in the daylight in their own time? Or so they thought! We jeered, and more fool them, we laughed. Yes, that was the big noise, the bragging, loud but not loud enough: because there was still this voice, yes, it was small but it was persistent, which we all heard. Hey chaps, it said, hold on, you've just had your 'Yahweh moment', your miracle; but it wasn't the miracle of the Jordan drying up and crossing in a night. No! Yahweh saved you from being chopped to pieces on the other side on Day One of the big invasion!

Did Joshua hear that voice? I wonder, but anyway, he kept to the priests' version which everyone knows. And it certainly makes for a better story.

Even so we did not hang around. Once the crossings stopped half our tribe, about five hundred of us, got orders to move. Our target was Gilgal, a village, proper buildings and all that, about six miles west of the Jordan which had plenty of water. We had left it alone until now; it was too big for a terror raid. Now it was to be Joshua's headquarters and our new base. Our job was to take it at first light.

I can tell you it is not much fun moving in a big body of men in the pitch dark. In terror raids, we were small groups moving fast – you see and choose your next footstep. Not so in a big group! There you are clumping along falling over rocks and bumping into the man in front, and all the time worrying about getting a spear up your arse from the blunderer behind you. So we trudged on, the skins lacerating our shoulders, heads down, just following the man in front, hour after hour, and no stops, not for resting that is. Yes, there were stops enough, sudden, for no obvious reason and you were told to lie down; then the madcap panting rush to catch up when the guys move again and start to vanish into the darkness.

It started with a lone dog, starting to bark, just as we started up from the riverbank, and increasingly the other dogs joined in as we got closer. No problems over navigation with fifty dogs barking their hearts out. I must say I wondered if we would find the village empty, that the folk had cleared out in the night alarmed by the dogs. Just wishful thinking, of course. After all, where would they go, hide with their families and children in some nearby caves?

We stopped in a flat wide part of the valley and the tent commanders fussed around as the barking of the dogs rose to a frenzy. We lay there silently as Seth went off to report.

In the end, it was just a mad rush, a charge in the light of dawn screaming our heads off, louder than the dogs. There were those same old figures emerging from their tents or buildings to see what the fuss was about, or sitting up on their sleeping mats, wide-eyed and shrieking. Except this time, they were not figures in the dark, shadows, these were terrified faces illuminated by the grey light. Of course, as usual I did my bit. Then we just flopped down but the whisper went round with fingers pointing to the still dark south:

"Jericho is just over there."

*****

"What a dump!" Big Abner spat out. We were sitting on a hill overlooking Gilgal, a series of strong pickets surrounding the town in case of Amorite attack.

"One hell of a first taste of the Promised Land," grumbled Gam.

It was true. I am not sure what we were expecting but certainly something a bit better than a clump of single-storey buildings spread over a few acres mainly along the valley floor, probably a hundred families or so.

There was no sign of the enemy so we simply had a grandstand view of our army, tribe after tribe, snaking its way across the desert to Gilgal. About midday along came Joshua and his senior commanders in chariots, either ones with iron wheels which we had captured or rubbishy things which someone had managed to put together. After Joshua came the priests, in their long robes and high hats, with the Ark of the Covenant, a great big gleaming box with two gold cherubs sitting on the lid, containing various holy things, including the Tablets of Stone. Pretty heavy it looked; it was borne on the shoulders of some really big guys. Then came the escort to the Ark of the Covenant, from the tribe of Levi, heavy bearded and well-armed, each with a proper spear, shield, helmet and breastplate, proper battlefield kit! Finally, there came the camp followers, a huge loose collection of men and women whose job it was to look after us, soldiers, cooks, doctors, labourers, clerks, prostitutes and, of course, what we called the 'Wealth of Israel', our vast herds of goats and sheep.

It was pretty easy those first few days as the army streamed in sitting up on the hill half the day and lying around in our big tent the other half. Until Seth turned up suddenly and not with the usual 'Start panicking. Details later!' cry, which was ominous.

"There's some clearing up to do, lads," he said just standing there. "You'll need your spears."

I suppose it had all been in the back of our minds about the prisoners. I mean when we swept through Gilgal, we killed everyone who got in our way but then herded the rest of them, old men, women and children into a big walled space in the centre of the town. But when Joshua found out he went completely berserk foaming at the mouth shouting, "Kill, kill them! All must be killed!"

I suppose we were not really surprised. He had never given a hint that he was letting up on his massacre approach.

There they were. There must have been about a hundred of them or so, old folk and women clutching their children, crouching in the sand of the enclosure. The women were cluck clucking their wailing young telling them that everything was going to be all right. The old people just sitting there silent and rocking gently; they knew what was coming. For us, the trouble was that in the bright sunlight, ragged and poor, they looked just like our families.

Noggi was there, roughly separating them into four different groups.

"Here you are, Seth, these are yours," he rasped out. Seth nodded grimly, and turned to us.

We escorted our group out along the valley and then Seth turned up into one of the defiles. I had not heard Amorite for six months but I could still roughly understand what they were saying, the mothers reassuring their children that they were safe and were going on to Jericho. Nothing to be frightened of, they repeated, but that did not stop the screaming.

We eventually stopped. On the right side and a bit up the hill were some caves. We ushered our group into the shade of some acacia trees. The rest of us stood around in the sunlight.

I think we must all have been thinking the same thing at the same time but it was Gam who broke the silence:

"Go on, Abs, talk to him." Big Abs nodded and went forward to Seth, speaking quietly. *This was not going to go down well,* we all thought.

Seth turned on us. "Well, lads," starts Seth, not quite angry, certainly not placating but just matter of fact and brutal. "You know the score," he spelt out slowly. "Our job here…" he shrugged his shoulders. "And we just put the bodies in a cave. End of story." Then he added. "No different from terror raiding."

We were silent. Of course, he was right. These

were the same people we had killed in those raids except then we were stabbing in the dark. Seth looked back at us stonily.

"Let this lot go and Joshua finds out, there will be hell to pay," said he stating the obvious. Yes, Joshua would make an example of us. We could all see it, tied to pillars and stoned to death.

I suddenly found myself talking. "But, Seth, they could hide in those caves until nightfall and then set off for Jericho. They should be there in a couple of hours and Joshua would be none the wiser."

Seth turned on me. "And who's going to tell them that? Leave 'em here in the caves and they swan off as soon as we are out of sight. Then they'll get picked up, and that will be that as far as we are concerned."

"Well," I said, "let me speak to them. You know I talk Amorite." A bit of a boast maybe but I hoped I could string a few words together.

Seth paused, then nodded sharply to me. I went over to the big Acacia tree. One of the older men hushed the soft wailing when I approached and stood up.

"Caves," I said in Amorite pointing, hoping that my sparse vocabulary and a bit of sign language would see me through. He looked over, and nodded.

"Nightfall," I continued, pointing and making a sleeping gesture. Again, the old man nodded.

"Then you walk to Jericho," I finished with a walking motion of my fingers. The old man was looking at me keenly. I needed to make a point. I put my fingers to my lips and then make a cutting motion across my throat, pointed to myself first and then the others behind me.

He came forward and knelt in front of me, grasped my free right hand, raised it up to his mouth and kissed it. It was embarrassing, but I guessed he had got the message. And Seth saw it too.

"Go quickly," I said.

Get up into those caves, you fools, I thought, *before Seth changes his mind.* But the old man was no fool. He rapped out commands and the group scuttled up the hills, this time mothers smacking their children into silence. They disappeared into the caves and all was quiet.

"Fall in," was all Seth said. Turning away, we started back up the valley to Gilgal. Then he stopped suddenly and turned round. I think we all thought, *Oh ho, what's coming now?* But, good old Seth, what he said made sense:

"We can't go back like this, clean clothes and weapons," he stated simply. "Someone's got to go back to the village and get some stuff."

"I can go to my butcher friends in the Temple," volunteered Big Abs, and Seth nodded.

We waited about an hour in the large loose rocks before Abs returned with a bag of offal and discarded joints glistening with blood. A few minutes later our clothes and weapons had that caked blood look of a returning terror patrol.

"You took your time," growled Noggi, standing at the entrance of the town. Seth said something about finding suitable caves far enough away from the camp.

Noggi just grunted.

For the next few days, we sat around picketing the surrounding hills and watching the army stream in. The good thing about finishing Bout One of 'The Cleansing' was that Joshua decided that we all needed a bit of a treat. But it was not the usual skin of date wine to share and ten shekels to spend on the boxes that we were hoping for. Instead, he declared that that we celebrate the Feast of Passover, so it was all rather religious but it did mean a bit of meat for once, a welcome change from the constant diet of parched grain and gruel.

We were all kind of wondering what next, was it going to be more terror raids or what when we heard Seth's singsong voice, "Panic now, lads. Details later."

"There's urgent work to be done, lads," he started. "Building, fortification of the camp, well-digging." He paused. "Or sentry duty. It's a choice between hard work and dangerous work." He looked around. "So, who's volunteering for sentry duty?" he asked with that cold smile of his.

I was quick to put up my hand; I did not want to be lifting boulders and shifting dirt all day. Anything rather than that, and I could not see what was dangerous about being a sentry frankly.

"Good," said Seth, with a bit of a laugh or was it a sneer? "Our brave Ehud for the first stag then. Go over and report to the captain and you will get your orders. We'll send a replacement in four hours' time."

The captain proved to be my old friend, Noggi, the grim old soldier who had welcomed me on my first day in Joshua's army all those months ago. We used to laugh, that his name meant 'Brightness', yet he was all dour and discipline. I joined a group of about ten 'volunteer' sentries. He did not remember me, of course, and looked at us without enthusiasm, then roared out;

"You lot are going on public display." He paused and eyed us slowly. "Your job, believe it or not, is to scare the shit out of the enemy. So, you are not going out like the rabble you are!" We all bridled. Agreed, we had all started our fighting days dressed in rags, barefoot, and armed only with a stick and a bit of bone at one end for a spear or a club for a sword. Agreed, we had no armour or helmets; but we all had something. I mean, I had my sling and a light spear, and I also had a dagger, which I had managed to pick up on a raid, and a tunic too. So I was a far cry from the 'savage with a stick'. And that went for the rest of us sitting around, but of course no one objected.

Noggi went on to explain how we were to picket Jericho, keep a watch, and guard against a sudden attack. Then he went on about a big new look for us because Joshua did not want the guys on the walls to see just how short of weapons we were.

"So you lot," he went on, "are to get kitted out to look like well-equipped infantry soldiers. D'you hear?" he rasped and led us away.

"Help yourself, lads, and parade in five minutes." He showed us a pile of ropey old spears, armour, shields and helmets, all captured stuff from the Amorites or other poor sods who had got in our way. So, we set to and grabbed what we could. I managed to get a black leather breastplate with a gash in the front. There were holes for my arms but the straps at the back were gone, so I had to hold it on with one hand. It was quite ornate, with elaborate stitching enclosing brass studs set at intervals. It must have belonged to someone important. *No longer,* I thought grimly.

The helmet was quite fancy too, thick hard black leather with a wide bronze brim and ridge across the top. It too had seen service, been hacked about a bit, but otherwise it seemed solid enough except it was too big for me. The previous owner, owners more likely, must have had large completely round heads. I did get a proper spear though, nearly twice my height but with a good iron point. Fortunately, there were not enough shields to go around as the last thing I wanted was the extra weight. Fast legs, after all, are the best friend of a soldier; well, for the kind of soldiering I was used to.

When we lined up for inspection, even Noggi allowed a smile to cross his face.

"Well," he said, shaking his head. "You'll just have to do, you'll just have to do," he repeated. "Now," he said, getting stern again, "out there on sentry duty your job is to look impressive to those guys on the walls of Jericho. You!" he shouted at me, first in line, "Go on. Look fierce. Frighten me!"

Yeah, yeah, I thought resentment boiling a bit, what have you done all these months except shout at raw recruits? But of course, I said nothing and just gave it my best. I waved my spear at him, hammered with my feet on the ground, and roared an angry cry. *Good stuff,* I thought but just as I finished my helmet tipped forward and almost broke my nose. Everyone laughed but Noggi did not.

"Right, the rest of you," he said shortly. "You do better!" And, serve them right, he just kept them there shouting and waving their spears while I looked on. I was careful not to smirk. Then he cut them short with a wave of his hand.

"Dressing up's the easy bit. Now, your real job is to protect the camp from those buggers in Jericho. Any sign of activity, horses neighing, dogs barking, a gate opening, someone coming out on the plain and you give the alarm. Immediately!"

We were each of us given a black ram's horn. "You blow on this," he said and put the horn to his lips. It made the sound of a sheep bleating but loud and harsh. "Now you all try," he ordered. My heart dropped. I remembered my failure to get anything resembling a blast out of the family trumpet. A ram's horn was likely to be no different. And so it proved. Gradually the others picked it up and achieved a proper blast but not me. All I could get out of it was a low farting noise. There was some giggling at my efforts, but Noggi just frowned, thought I was playing for a laugh, and gave me a sharp cuff.

"Laugh if you like," he remarked with disdain. "Don't get me wrong. This is serious. Your job is to protect the camp. And, if you want it, personal-like, that horn could be the only thing between you and a very horrible death! Our friends have a nice way of grabbing sentries."

Everyone shut up after that. We knew that was true. Sentries had simply disappeared, even from our old camp. With that we were each given a piece of hard cake and a skin of water and led out of Gilgal and into a broad valley of light scrub and started marching south.

We must have been marching for a couple of hours when we came upon an encampment of about fifty men, all from the tribe of Reuben.

"This is the reserve," said Noggi. "Any breakout will be dealt with by them." And he led us up the side of the valley.

Breasting the ridge there suddenly stretched a huge city. We just stopped and goggled. I had lived in tents all my life, and the only other Amorite habitations I had come across so far had been some pretty grotty villages, just a few single- story buildings made of bricks of mud.

So, this was the famous Jericho. Perched on a low-lying plateau there were these great high walls lined with battlements, about four storeys high, and towers with another three storeys. The frontage must have been over 300 paces and everything was shining white and shimmering in the sun. And invincible!

But we were not allowed to dawdle. Noggi moved quickly, endlessly repeating, "Keep that armour on, keep your helmet on and stick your spear on the ground. And face the bloody front, so they can see you!" Noggi had further barked. "Or woe betide you…!" His voice had trailed off but that was no empty threat from him. We were soon spread out, about two hundred paces apart, in a crescent covering the three main gates of the city.

Chapter 5

"That's your spot and you stick to it, my lad," were Noggi's final words to me. Thanks, Noggi, 'that spot' was prime position, slap bang in front of Jericho, with just five hundred paces of sand and scrub between me and the main gates.

The first thing which dawned on me was my job was pure suicide. The 'big and brave soldier' stuff from old Noggi had never really convinced me; I just felt clumsy with my borrowed bronze-tipped spear, my borrowed – overlarge – ox leather helmet with its fancy bronze crest, and my borrowed leather breastplate, which stank. And that stupid bloody horn.

Now you all know the official story of how we captured Jericho. How Joshua was ordered by HIM to march around the city blowing horns. All that's true, we did. And then so the story goes, on the seventh day we all gave a big cheer and the walls fell down. Well, it certainly was not seven days! More like seventy that we were parked outside that bloody city, roasting by day and freezing by night, and most of the time hungry as well. But it is true, the walls did just fall and that really did amaze us.

But back to me on sentry duty and that great fortified city. It just looked so impregnable to a simple country boy like me. Okay, we had managed to beat up a few villages, and perhaps the word had got around that we were both numerous and formidable, but this was something different, one of the main cities of the

Amorites, well-armed, well organised and well fed. As if to make the point all along the battlements there was the constant glinting of the sun on the metal points and armour of their men at arms as they manned the towers and battlements and changed sentries.

Were we besieging them, or were they simply staying put while we starved to death? I wondered.

There was nothing between me and the city except some scrub and a rocky hard plain. All the sheep and goats and other stock had been rounded up and taken into the city and the crops had been harvested a month earlier. I tried to make myself comfortable, leaning against a rock with my spear stuck in the ground.

But it was hot, and boring. I had to remind myself, *Think of those poor buggers back at camp digging wells and breaking rock,* which made me feel better.

By now, the sun was really high and the whiteness of the city walls was almost blinding as it shimmered in the heat. I then started to hear noise. From the city, came the furious barking of dogs. I shaded my eyes. Yes, there was some movement at the huge great wooden gates between the two main towers opposite, when suddenly they were flung open and I saw a chariot clatter down the cobbled causeway. And heading straight for me!

"So, this is what you are here for." I remember saying to myself with remarkable nonchalance. *Now don't panic, Ehud, my son, just blow the bloody horn!*

I grabbed the horn and put it to my lips. *Help me, HIM, help me*! and puffed. But HIM did not oblige; the result was worse than my earlier attempts, just a watering wheezy sound. Of course, that is what panic does when confronted with a war machine, black horses neighing, iron wheels grinding the rock and with a three-man team armed to the teeth.

Thinking back now I must have been mentally better prepared for a confrontation like this than I had thought. In the first panic of the chariot appearing, I cannot remember consciously thinking what I would do. All I know is that, horn blasting apart, I was pretty cool, aware that time was short but I knew what to do. Which was off with that breastplate, off with that helmet and I was free. Free, I hear you say, free to do what? Pray?

The chariot is a pretty formidable weapon, do not get me wrong. A mass charge can flatten a massed enemy or harass them when they turn and run. But against a single man? There is the driver but he has his hands full controlling the horses. Then there is the commander, probably armed with a sword and spear, who does the fighting but then he is on a moving platform, not so good for throwing an accurate spear. Then there is the third member of the team whose main job, when the charity is moving, is grip the sides, act as a kind of rear gate and prevent anyone falling out. With the Amorites, this third member usually was an archer, so dangerous as well. So, this thumping great war machine coming towards me had a number of options; the charioteer could run me down, the commander could spear me, or the archer could put an arrow through me. In other words, three simple ways of killing me.

Well, we'll see! I remember thinking. I picked the sling from my belt and reached into the bag with the stones I had collected from the Jordan. I picked one about the size of my nose; just about right for general scrimmage like this was going to be. Into the pouch it went and I started the swing, around and around...

Now you may be thinking that a lad with a three-foot strip of leather and a stone is pretty feeble stuff against a three-man, state-of-the-art, iron-wheeled chariot but here's the thing. At fifty paces, a sling shot can do some proper damage. Hit the horse and it may buck and all three of the team end up in the dirt, an easy target for the next shot. Hit the driver – well, he is the most likely one being in front – then he will probably lose control. Hit him on the head – unlikely but always a chance – and he's dead, big bonus there. Hit the commander or the third man, well, that would give them something to think about. Or you might miss, in which case you have already got another shot on the way, and another one, and another.

And one other thing you ought to know, and I'm not bragging; I'm pretty hot with the sling. Remember how I saw off Rim all those months ago. There's not much doing when you are out with the flocks as a boy, and the sling is your weapon against lion, wolf, or thief. On my fifth birthday, Dad gave me my first sling. It was just a narrow strip of hide about two foot long with a pouch in the middle for the stone and a loop at one end. He taught me how to set the stone in the pouch, put my thumb through the loop and grip the other end of the cord between thumb and forefinger. Start to swing in an arc, watch your target, and open your thumb and forefinger. Of course, the stones went all over the place to begin with.

"We'll start at five paces," said Dad, and put up a sheep skull on a stick as a target. 'Three hits out of two, and we add an extra pace' was his cry over the years. "It's an extension of your arm," he explained to me. "Think of your slingshot like a club, and you are right close to your enemy except he can't touch you!" By the time I was sixteen I was getting three hits out of two at fifty paces, which Dad said was 'Good enough!' At forty paces I had killed an old wolf.

Fifty paces then! I suppose I had mentally identified a small bush at that distance in front of me. It looked horribly close. The chariot was closing quickly.

"Wait, wait, wait." I kept repeating out loud as my sling made long, slow rotations. I was searching for the best target. My father's words came back to me, *At distance always go for the centre!* And that was the prow, armoured and glinting, of the shaft between the two horses steaming towards me. A final fast rotation of the sling and I let fly.

I did not bother to watch; I put another stone in the sling, and started to swing. But the chariot had stopped and turned sideways on. Then I saw the charioteer was bent over the side.

Must've got him, I let out a breath of relief. *That's 2 to 1 now.*

The commander dismounted. He must have been in his early 40s, a powerfully built man with a black beard wearing breastplate and helmet, bronze with a red coxcomb, sword at his side and a red cloak. Clearly a senior commander.

"I come in peace," he shouted, a bit haltingly but at least speaking my language. The sling continued to rotate; I was taking no chances. I could deal with the Amorite commander but there was still that archer. He was now standing beside the chariot holding a short bow in his hand and quiver on his back. Duck behind the chariot and pick me off, I worried; bad odds, an archer behind cover against a boy in the open. He started to move. I loosed off another shot. Quick reload, and my sling was swinging again, but he had dropped his bow and was holding his chest.

"Tell him to sit on the ground away from his bow," I called to the Amorite commander. He chuckled, turned around and gave a quick order in his language to the archer who promptly sat down.

"And you, stop where you are!"

The Amorite halted, grinned and raised his hands in mock surrender. I dropped my sling with its stone to my side. I could kill him at this range, a man's head in a helmet is about the same size as a sheep's head.

"Good shooting, boy," he announced. I kept silent; I really didn't know what to do, but I didn't like being called 'boy'. So I just glowered at him.

"I am Zemri. What's your name?" Horns were blowing to my left and my right, so the other sentries were giving the alarm. Good, help would be here soon, but he did not appear concerned, just kept on with the small talk.

"And you are young too!" he continued. I said nothing; I mean I do look young for my age, but I am nineteen, not that I was going to tell him.

"Well, I'll just have to call you Babyface!" he exclaimed happily. "Well, Babyface, I've got a message for your great God-botherer-and-Goat-buggerer- in-chief."

Well, that certainly surprised me. I mean, we all around the campfire had the odd crack about our General Joshua, about how he is always saying *Yahweh is on our side, Yahweh will help us win* and not to upset HIM and all that, but I was not expecting that from an Amorite commander. Nor was the crack about being a goat buggerer something we would ever have dared suggest. I mean, okay, we joke about things with sheep and goats around the campfire, laddish talk if you like, but that's it.

He detected my discomfort, and chuckled.

"Tell him that we propose a release of prisoners. If he is here with his army in front of our walls at midday on the Sabbath, your day of rest," he emphasized and laughed, "your men will be released."

I nodded. I could hear troops coming up behind me. He looked over my shoulder.

"Well, it's been nice meeting you, Babyface. You're lucky. I had plans to either take you alive or give you the message. You fought well, so you got…the message!" He laughed again and turned on his heel and walked back to the chariot where the driver was once again in control and holding the reins. The archer got up and glanced angrily at me but he saw my sling already loaded and swinging. Zemri turned round before mounting.

"Ready as ever, Babyface! Well done! Here, I like a brave, alert boy!" And he tossed a coin at me. "Left-handed too, I see." He nodded. "Quite an advantage in a fray! Perhaps we'll meet again!"

He shook his head and mounted, and quickly the chariot galloped back towards Jericho.

I stepped forward and picked up the coin. It glittered, I reckoned it was gold.

I had never seen a gold coin before.

"What the devil was that all about, Ehud, and why the devil have you taken your armour off?" Noggi puffed angrily at me as he and a dozen men, fully armed and out of breath, arrived in response to the alarm being raised. "And why the devil didn't you blow your own bloody horn?"

Well, I thought, to myself, *I will show you.*

"I have a message from an important Amorite commander for General Joshua," I replied exhibiting coolness, almost haughty. *Look, you cannot blame me, why should I not feel fairly pleased with myself? I had seen off a war chariot, got an important message for the boss, and even made a bit of gold on the side. Indeed, ripe for a bit of name recognition, Ehud,* I thought. *Time to gracefully accept promotion out of the world of terror raids and sitting about in dusty tents!*

"I will take you along to General Joshua now," Noggi grudgingly agreed. "It had better be good," he continued still focusing on that bloody horn, "or you are in for a sound whipping. Get dressed and follow me."

I put my armour and helmet back on and tramped along behind him.

*****

I suppose I had only been away from Gilgal half a day but already the area had been transformed. It was now a sea of tents amid the buildings, grouped together by tribe. There were the black tents of the tribe of Judah, the red of the tribe of Reuben and ours, the tribe of Benjamin, with our distinctive hotchpotch coloured goatskin. Some men were busy lifting jagged rocks into low rough walls around the tents. Others were sealing off the lines of approach through the shallow valleys where the ground was hard and flat, ideal for a surprise attack by massed chariots from Jericho. On a small hill, near the centre, was a very large tent. Fluttering from the flagpole by the entrance was a blue flag, the sign of the general, and on guard were two soldiers, just in simple tunics, barefoot and with a sharpened stick for a spear.

"No frills here," I murmured to myself and followed Noggi in through the entrance thronging with soldiers coming and going. Inside we were stopped by two of Joshua's bodyguard, both in embroidered white tunics and daggers in their belts. We were told to wait there while one of the bodyguards went off, returning a few minutes later with a curt order "Follow me".

We set off, the bodyguard pushing his way through the others until we came to a roped-off enclosure. This was empty except for a dais in the middle spread with a coloured rug on which sat Joshua and several others.

I had never seen Joshua close up before, only from a distance from which you could only make out a black beard and a bronze skull fitting helmet with a spike on the top. Exciting stuff, here I was meeting the great man himself, especially chosen by good old Moses to lead us into the Promised Land! Ordained by HIM! I mean most of us do not claim to be anything special but those guys did, they talked it and they walked it.

Among the commanders on the dais was a stern-looking man with a scar on his cheek and a ragged beard. He was addressing another soldier standing in front of him. I guessed this must be Amram, a commander with a pretty fearsome reputation as a disciplinarian and administrator. Very much Joshua's right-hand man. Joshua might order something – and these somethings could be a bit airy- fairy at times, most times in fact – and Amram had to put the nuts and bolts together and create a reality. He was good at that; and no one, but no one, got in his way. What he said went! Of course, no one liked him, not even Joshua, we suspected.

There were five others on the dais. Four were commander types bearded and wearing breastplates; they taken off their swords and their helmets which were lying on the rug. But there was another guy up there, who was very different. Nothing warlike about him, he was wearing white tunic with a thick heavy embroidered collar and clean-shaven face topped with short fair hair. And soft brown eyes. Very unusual! I wondered if he was Obed, Joshua's Egyptian guru, one of the 'special advisers' who hung around Joshua which the other commanders rather resented. There was a story that when one of the old blood- and-guts brigade was advocating a particularly violent course of action Obed had simply interrupted with 'Warfare needn't necessarily be that simple', then came up with a much cleverer plan. Consternation of warrior types and 'One up' to special advisers! Good on Joshua, was the word in the tents, for always having a few smart guys around to come up with alternative solutions to frontal bloody assaults.

Amram finished speaking and nodded; the soldier saluted and left.

A courtier came forward. Our escort whispered in his ear. He nodded and approached the dais.

"General and Commanders, this is the sentry who failed to give the alarm," he announced with what I detected to be a touch of scorn in his voice. *Steady on*, I thought, *I have an important message, that's the story today, surely?* And, oh yes, he did not leave it out.

"He says he has a message from the Amorites." Just scorn, more scorn. *Not on my side, this boy,* I thought grimly. Bet he had never skinned a sheep let alone faced a hungry lion with a sharp stick.

On the dais, they all turned towards me, one in

73

particular. I found myself looking straight into the eyes of the great Joshua.

"What's your name?" he asked abruptly but with a certain gentleness. "And your tribe?" I told him. "Hm, tough fighters you Benjamites," he mused, and stopped.

There was a short pause, then Amram leant forward. "Come, come closer," he waved his arm impatiently motioning me to the front of the dais.

I started to obey and walk the short distance when disaster struck. I do not know whether it was because Noggi gave me a push, or I just stumbled, but over I went sprawling in the sand. Off shot my helmet in one direction, my wretched breastplate in another. I sprang up quickly enough from the sand, stepped forward and looked up at the four men but I felt very foolish in my ragged tunic still holding the borrowed spear. Noggi was mouthing things behind me furiously, and I could hear sniggering around the tent which stopped immediately when Amram rapped the hilt of his dagger on the wooden boards of the platform. Amram just looked at me and I dropped my head. He seemed unfazed by my transformation from well-armed sentry to 'Savage with a stick'. There was some whispering on the dais and then Amram spoke.

"You have been reported for failing to give the alarm." He nodded at that wretched ram's horn which Noggi was holding. "That was your first duty as a sentry. The whole army has been endangered by your failure. The penalty for this offence is death."

It is one of those things in life. Just when you think

you have done rather well and are hoping for a big pat on the back someone comes up with a different angle and it all starts to look rather black. Noggi had been mumbling about my getting a whipping but I had reckoned that seeing off an enemy chariot and getting an important message was reward time. This guy, Amram, was clearly picking up on Noggi's angle but not talking about a mere whipping.

I found myself stammering as Noggi handed me the horn, "I tried to blow it…but I couldn't get a sound out of it."

"Show me," ordered Amram shortly. I put the horn to my lips. The same watery sound emerged. No one laughed, no one smiled. Amram was about to continue when the softly spoken Joshua intervened.

"Give it here," he called gently and Noggi, all action and prompt obedience, snatched the horn from my hand and passed it up to Joshua. He raised it to his lips and blew. Another watery sound. Again, complete silence in the tent.

"I can't either," he said, giving it back to Noggi, and sitting back.

"But you could have raised the alarm in other ways," Amram resumed. "You could have shouted, you could have beaten on your shield, you could have even run back to the reserve. You failed to do any of these things." He paused. "You endangered the entire army."

I got to thinking he reckoned this was a straightforward case with a straightforward solution, thank you very much, and not something to waste time over.

"What have you got to say before we pronounce sentence?"

He didn't even look at me, he was looking at other papers in his hand.

I started to speak. I told them about the chariot galloping straight towards me, how I had quickly discarded my armour and brought the chariot to a halt at about forty paces with a couple of slingshots. I stopped there, sensing that I had lost my audience. The courtier who had led in me was smirking at another courtier across the room and the men on the dais were looking at me, a kind of bored curiosity in their eyes which said, *Go on, what are you going to say next?*

Amram, all speed and let's get this over and done with, looked up from his papers. "Continue," said he.

I found myself stammering. The unfairness of it, I was telling the truth yet I knew I was sounding like a burbling liar. How could they believe my story? Anyway, I persevered. I told how the Amorite had approached me and described him. When I got to the bronze helmet with the red coxcomb, there was some muttering between those on the stage. *Gosh, are they beginning to believe me?* I thought.

"That could be Zemri," Joshua said to the others.

I dared butt in. "Yes, yes, he said his name was Zemri." Amram just nodded. "Now what did he say?"

I hesitated. This was clearly no time when on trial for my life to inform Joshua and his commanders that he was known as the old God-botherer-and- Goat-buggerer-in-chief. So I pronounced clearly, "The message was for Joshua that if the army stand before Jericho on this Sabbath at midday, he will release the prisoners."

I had not really thought about the message until now. But that was what Zemri had said and I was duly passing it on. I had not even considered whether the message was credible or not. But now I could see the impact of my halting words on an utterly unbelieving audience. Of course it was nonsense! Everyone knew that Joshua gave no quarter. HIM had commanded it. Prisoners were killed and that was all there was to it. So it was ludicrous to expect quarter from the Amorites. The offer did not make sense.

When I had finished speaking, I just stood there. I could sense what they were thinking; here is a man in a hole and he just can't stop digging; and there was murmuring behind me.

Of course it was Amram, who had been shaking his head impatiently throughout, who now spoke, clearly fed up with this absurd interruption to a busy day.

"First, the prisoner" – I was a prisoner now, was I? And it was said with such contempt in his voice – "fails in his duty as sentry. That alone is punishable by death. Secondly, to compensate for his negligence, the prisoner invents a story of stopping an Amorite war chariot, and thirdly, further to aggrandise his position, the prisoner brings us an impossible message for us to believe."

On the dais, there was a nodding of heads. Except for Joshua who was looking at me intently. I somehow felt that he believed me. The fair-haired guy was leaning forward and whispering in Joshua's ear. He gave a small shrug of his shoulders.

"Well?" Joshua asked, addressing me without emotion. "Your story does not convince my military commanders."

He was giving me a chance, I thought, *otherwise I am a dead duck.* I have had quite a few moments like this in my life when I've been in big trouble; sometimes I've been in the right, more often in the wrong. Well, you can't just stand there whimpering, or babbling some further explanation, or just hoping silently for mercy, you have got to go on the attack. *Here goes,* I thought.

I straightened up, head back. *Do your defiant best, Ehud,* I thought! "General Amram mocks my claim to have stopped a chariot at forty paces as a fantasy. Let him therefore stand at fifty paces fully armoured, and I will prove the truth of my account."

Well, that caused quite a sensation. This was a bit out of the way of everyday business. No one had ever spoken to Amram like that. Everyone in the room was listening now. There were even signs of mirth on the dais, plus a deep chuckle from Brown Eyes, the Egyptian guy. Amram looked extremely angry, and held a whispered conversation with Joshua who nodded.

Amram now spoke, "General Joshua has consented to put your story to the test. You will be confronted, not by General Amram," – pause here – "but by another fully armoured man whom you must bring down at forty paces."

There was a bit of commotion behind me, and I looked over my shoulder. A muscular soldier had pushed his way to the ropes in front of the dais.

"I will be that armoured man. Let the prisoner drop me, and live!" he announced proudly, finishing with a loud laugh.

I knew him immediately. This was Zophar, a kind of army favourite and typical of the tribe of Reuben but more so. Handsome and strong, he was the big brave soldier we were all meant to be. Zophar did that, Zophar did this! Or Zops rather, as he was called by his numerous toadies. Feats of arms, shows of strength, his were the stories round the camp fires of the new recruits. Okay, perhaps I am being unfair; so I will give him this much. He was a good fighter, and brave too, but do you know what? He was also just plain thick. No imagination! He just went where he was told, did what he was told, and had, so far, been lucky. The commanders just loved him; he was their pet. I suppose they reckoned that he had his uses, unquestioning loyalty and all that. No backchat from him, just 'Yes, sir, no, sir, quick as I can, sir'. They gave him the best of the captured armour and weapons and he just loved strutting around the camp bragging to anyone who would listen, mainly the younger soldiers who were just in awe. The rest of us found him a complete pain in the arse. But it was still sensible to keep out of his way; he could be mighty spiteful and punishments descended from nowhere on those who mocked him.

Joshua and the other two commanders were looking at Amram's grim face and smiling.

"Well," said Joshua. "That's a challenge, Amram. What do you say to that?" He snorted, and muttered something.

"That is agreed then," said Joshua. "In the afternoon at four, let this test be made."

Then he addressed Noggi. "Bring the soldier here with his sling and shots at the time."

With that Noggi saluted and escorted me out of the command tent. He did not put his arm around my shoulder but I knew I had his sympathy.

"You've done it now, lad," he said. "That big mouth of yours!" He was not a bad type, Noggi, I reflected, he just wanted me to get a good whipping. But execution was another thing.

Chapter 6

Waiting is always the thing. Back in the tent it was empty. I sat down on my mat. *Not much I can do to prepare for this,* I thought. I took my sling off my belt and checked it. Same old sling! I went to my bag of pebbles and carefully went through them selecting six of the smoothest. I heard Big Abs crouch down beside me. He was a good shot with a sling too.

"I would lend you some lead shot if I had any."

Lead was the best shot for slings; it was denser than stone which made for a smaller missile; and it could be cast into a uniform flattish shape so was more accurate.

"Why not go and see old Pecah?" Abs continued. Pecah was the blacksmith of our tribe and looked after our metal weapons, for those lucky enough to have them – even, for reward, sharpening them on his grindstone.

We found him in a corner of the camp with his clay oven and anvil. He was examining a spear with a bent bronze tip. He looked up at us; the news had travelled.

"You've got yourself into a bit of trouble, young man," he stated. "Some people would say you had it coming." *Thanks,* I thought grimly, *and a good start!*

He pushed the spear tip into the oven and looked back, wiping his hands on the big leather apron.

"Can you make some lead slingshots for me?" I said shortly, and he laughed. "So that's your game is it! Well, you're lucky. If it's a contest between you and that loudmouth, Zophar, I'm on your side."

He turned round and inspected a table covered with metal tools. He picked up what looked like a pair of tongs except at the end on each rod there was an open small almond-shaped mould.

"Here's the one, the right size I reckon. Good enough for you?"

I nodded. Pecah went over to another table and picked out a small crucible and put it on top of his stove.

"Lead, lead where's my lead?" he muttered to himself as he shifted his hand through a box of bits and pieces of metal. He pulled out a few black nuggets and put them into the crucible. Minutes later they were bubbling and silver. Bringing his tongs together the two moulds united to form a single almond shape the size of a large grape. He gripped the moulds together hard and held his tongs over the anvil; then, after carefully dipping a long spoon into the molten lead, he poured the liquid carefully through a small hole in the top of one of the mounds until it overflowed. He put the tongs on one side and went back to his bronze spear.

"Just let it cool a bit," he said. We waited. Shortly after, he went over to the tongs, snapped them open, and out fell a smooth almond-shaped piece of lead.

"Perfect," I said.

"How many more do you want?" "Can you manage twelve?"

"Huh, it'll cost you." And, with that, he returned to his crucible of bubbling lead.

Half an hour later he gave me a bag with twelve

shining shots. Then he held out his hand. In ordinary times, I would have given him some cloth, something my mother or sisters would have woven, or some goat leather, or just asked him what he wanted or needed at that time. But out here on campaign we did not have access to those things so it was just a case of trading with whatever we picked up, mostly stuff we had acquired in raids – cooking things, agricultural implements or weapons. But Joshua was pretty sticky on this and everything had to be given in and redistributed. Then I remembered the gold piece that Zemri had given me. All gold and silver were for the priests and I certainly was not going to do that. I had thought I would just hide it until all this campaigning was over.

I made a fast calculation. If I failed this afternoon, I was a dead man, so would not need the gold piece. If I triumphed – and I hadn't really worked out what 'triumph' meant – I might be rewarded, possibly promoted, and in line for greater enrichment. Or so I fantasised! In which case, I would not need the gold piece. Of course, given my luck so far that day 'Triumph' would simply mean survival and no gold to show for it. I looked at Pecah and thought, *it is good to have friends in useful places. So, goodbye, gold piece!*

I placed it on the anvil. Pecah gave a low whistle, quickly looked around to see if there was anyone watching, then snatched it up and put it in the pocket of his great black apron. He nodded at us, and returned to his bronze spear. Abs went back to his wall building and I strolled back to the empty tent.

It was hot outside in the midday sun and I flopped down on my tawny rush matting. Too hot to be outside, too hot inside to sleep with the flies buzzing around in their thousands. *Resting but not restful, as usual,* I thought ruefully. I suddenly felt dog-tired; I had been at it since dawn, and it had been quite a day so far. I put my sling and pouch of lead shot in a bag and clutched it to my stomach. I didn't want to risk any thieving fingers and you could never quite trust your mates.

It was irritating all those flies buzzing about my face so I put a scarf over my head. The noise of flies stopped but I could feel them landing and walking over the cloth. I faintly heard soldiers coming in for the afternoon rest.

Then I must have fallen asleep.

*****

"Get up, get up!" It seemed only seconds later and there was Noggi towering above me, shouting and kicking me in the ribs. I sat up groggily.

"All right, all right, commander." I stood up and donned again my belt and bag.

"I'm ready," I said, and Noggi led the way out of the tent. There were cries behind me of 'Good luck, Ehud!' and 'Stick it to him, Snakes!'. It was kind of encouraging that they were rooting for me, but I knew that they would be out to watch the fun in a moment.

A tent had been erected for Joshua and his commanders, perched on a low- lying hill. It overlooked a wide expanse of valley and it was on this flat area that the challenge was to take place.

As Noggi and I approached the area we could hear a thumping noise. Noggi looked at me with a sidelong look as if to say, I *suppose you know what that is?* I soon saw; it was a couple of men driving a wooden stake into the ground in a gully leading off into the hills opposite. I knew immediately what it was, it was the stoning stake. Already a few vultures, those clever birds, were circling this activity which from past experience always preceded a feed. But it did not make me frightened, it just made me angry. I did not know what I was going to do, but I would get the bastard!

Already men were coming out of their tents and lining the plain as Noggi and I stood with some other eager spectators by a green flag flopping in the light wind. Then Joshua and his entourage arrived at the special tent and were shown to benches covered in rugs. They sat down, frowning except for Brown Eyes who just sat there looking around smiling, observing the scene as one might at a feast and waiting for the dancing girls.

Over on the right the roar of applause started. Soon, lo and behold, there clumped the mighty Zophar. Of course, he was fully dressed for battle; a bronze helmet covered his head and his cheeks and a short chainmail bib protected his throat and overlapped a bronze breastplate. On the front of his legs and thighs were strapped bronze greaves. So much I had expected, but it was a shield which caught me badly by surprise.

"Look at that bloody shield!" I exclaimed in shock,

not to anyone in particular.

Let me explain. When you go into battle, fully armoured like Zophar, you have your spear or sword in one hand and a battle shield in the other. It is a lightish thing of leather on a metal frame with a boss in the middle. It's really an extension of your other arm, you can fight with it using it like a club or you can defend yourself. That is what I had been expecting; that would have been fair play; the same kind of shield every Amorite had. But Zophar was carrying a great big round bronze thing presumably backed by a thick layer of wood, the type of shield which men-at-arms lug about on battlements, great for defence but not much use for anything else. A good slingshot – my speciality – on a normal battle shield would numb the arm, even break it, but this thing could take any amount of punishment.

Zophar bowed to Joshua and started to descend the hill, preceded by Tamesh, Joshua's bodyguard commander, head-to-toe in armour of pleated bronze plates and carrying three short poles, each with a coloured flag. They stopped a dozen paces from me; Zophar disdained to look at me. Of course! Tamesh, clearly brimful with self-importance, continued down to where Noggi and I were standing by the green flag. Already many of those in the camp had gathered and standing around on the grounds overlooking the plain.

Well, this is some send-off, I thought to myself. The stoners were still thumping away at the stake, others were now busy gathering stones. *Very cheerful!* I thought.

Tamesh barked at a nearby soldier, one of the casual spectators. "Measure out forty paces, then fifty, then sixty." He pointed, "In that direction."

He handed over the three flags and the soldier set off at a walking pace counting each step.

"Stop," shouted bloody Tamesh. "Come back and do proper paces!"

Bastard! I thought. The soldier returned and set off with exaggerated paces, counting out loud, "One, two…" he counted to forty and stopped.

"Put the blue flag in there," ordered Tamesh, "Now another ten paces."

The soldier marched on, stopped and stabbed his second red flag into the desert floor. Tamesh nodded to him. He marched on a further ten paces and drove the last yellow flag in at the 60 paces point.

Zophar, without looking to left or right, turned his back and tramped down the valley towards the flags, a rhythmic squeal and rattle at every pace. He stopped by the 60-pace flag and turned round to face us. Tamesh looked towards Joshua and his fellow commanders on the hill.

I was looking straight ahead at Zophar, shimmering but deadly in the near distance. I heard Joshua pronounce;

"Let the challenge commence."

Tamesh, puffing himself up, addressed his massed audience.

"Ehud, soldier of the Tribe of Benjamin, failed in his duty as a sentry to sound the alarm" – he paused – "thus endangering our army!" He shouted this with emphasis and waited until there was an audible ripple of disapproval from the watchers.

"The penalty for this is death by stoning," he continued to a low murmur. "This soldier," he continued weightily, "then claimed that with his sling…" he paused; it was obvious this court soldier was relishing his time in the limelight. He then roared out, "…then claimed he had halted an Amorite war chariot!"

Well, what a laugh that was! This time he got it, the masses erupted into laughter and Tamesh smiled. *Talk about having the audience on your side,* I thought to myself.

"And that he received an important message from an Amorite commander," he continued.

No applause this time from the audience. Come on, we want action, it said. Tamesh sensed the impatience and went on more quickly. Clearing his throat, he continued.

"General Amram accuses this soldier of lying and has volunteered proof with a simple demonstration. This soldier claims to have stopped the chariot at fifty paces. When the command is given, Zophar will advance from the sixty-pace mark. If he crosses the forty-pace mark, the soldier, Ehud, will be deemed a liar, and thus guilty," he finished ponderously to a silent audience.

Tamesh looked up again towards Joshua, who nodded back. "Get ready," he ordered me curtly.

I only half-heard all this. My thoughts had been in another world until then, a world of whirling sounds and images. There was the noise of the stake being thumped in, the jostling and joking of the crowd, the pageantry of the top commanders of the hill, and the sheer dominating presence of the armour-plated Zophar in the near distance. These had completely swamped my mind but now, with that sharp 'Get ready' a kind of focused deliberation came over me.

I blanked out the sounds around me, blanked out the grinning faces lining the plain, blanked out the flapping of the vultures above the stoning stake, blanked out Noggi just standing there. Nothing but focus on the task ahead. I looked up and across the plain. There was this armoured figure, quite small at sixty paces but formidable, peaks of sharp sunlight glinting from his helmet and the great polished bronze circle in the middle of his giant shield.

Everything started to move in slow time. I unhooked the sling from my belt. It snagged briefly, a quick tug and it was in my hand. I put my right hand to the bag on my belt, heavy with the twelve lead shots, and loosened the string which secured the opening. I put my hand in and took out the first slug, smooth and sharp and deadly, then cursed myself for not practising beforehand. Faster slugs mean a lower trajectory especially at fifty paces or so. I will have to drop the height of my aiming point with these little devils, I considered. I placed the slug in the pouch and slowly let my sling rotate orienting it towards the seemingly indestructible figure in the distance.

"Okay, you bastard, I'm ready. Let's go," I murmured to myself, and I prayed. Yes, I prayed!

I know that back around the campfire we all joke about Joshua and his commanders and their 'In the name of HIM we will triumph' and how all the best goats and sheep go to the priests and their 'sacrifices' which means they get meat daily while we are left with parched grain and all that rubbishy stuff. But I still prayed.

"Well, Yahweh, do your stuff for Ehud and help me beat that pompous arse!" I found myself saying.

There was complete silence except for the slight whistling noise made by the slug as it whirled around in the leather sling. Then I heard a voice call, "Ready." Followed by a pause, then, "Begin!"

In the distance, I could see some movement, not much, just the sun glinting back on different parts of his armour; but I knew that Zophar was advancing. I rotated my arm until the sling was whirling fast, a tiny continuous hissing noise, and lifted my forefinger to release the slug. And watched.

The slug was small compared with river stones, but it was fast. Smack on for direction but too high, I knew at once. It went a couple of foot above Zophar's head and I think I saw him duck. I doubt he even saw it, I guessed, but he will know what to be looking for next time, I reckoned.

Aiming lower I let off another slug. There was a sharp crack as it hit the big shield, and the audience cheered. But Zophar did not even stop, he can hardly have felt a thing behind that great wooden shield of his. My only chance was to get him on the head. I altered my aim and got off two slugs in rapid succession. Two more cracks as Zophar raised his shield and caught the slugs racing at his head.

The crowd groaned. They were beginning to see the unfairness of this contest. It was not a trial of skill; my shooting was spot on, but nothing could get past that great bloody shield. I fired more slugs off. Crack, crack, crack on the big shield. And still Zophar advanced. More murmurs from the crowd and I could feel myself panicking.

I have always thought I am quite good at reacting to a situation and seizing an opportunity. It has got me out of many tricky situations. I am proud of this talent and I have kind of laughed at people who do not have it. They get stuck in a rut, try immensely hard and do everything right except think round the problem. Losing, losing, losing! But that was me now, firing slug after slug at Zophar's head and all he had to do was raise his great shield and my slugs, misshapen by the velocity of the impact on the shield, would drop uselessly into the dust. Losing, losing, losing? Something for others? Well, it was cocky me this time, And panicking. And, believe it or not, praying. Yes, praying again.

I remember thinking, I may have even said out loud, "Bloody hell, Yahweh, lend a hand won't you!" And then suddenly I heard the deep voice of God,

"Hit him in the balls!"

Of course, it was not Yahweh but it was Noggi, good bloody-minded old Noggi with his old soldier sense, and skill at spotting a weakness.

It was so obvious now. Zophar had my measure.

He knew I always aimed for his head, He knew I was dead accurate, and all he had to do was watch my throw and rely on his shield. He did not even have to follow the slug. When I fired, up went the shield and 'crack', another well-aimed useless shot. And another pace forward.

A few paces more and that execution squad would be making an example of that cheeky, lying Benjamite who fancies his skill with a sling.

I loaded my sling with two slugs, double shotting it's called, and gave an extra swirl before releasing. No crack this time, just a dull thud and the figure appeared to rock. Zophar had stopped and suddenly the spectators erupted in cheers as his shield crashed to the ground. He slowly bent over clutching his groin and rolled over.

It is silly but my first thought was that there will be no more 'issue' from that branch of the tribe of the Ephraim!

I could hear the roaring of the crowd and Noggi with his deep Yahweh-style voice saying, "Well done, lad!" I just stood there. Soldiers went over and laid Zophar on a stretcher. One slug must have hit an artery because he was spurting blood which a medic was trying to staunch. But I did not care.

I did not know quite what to do. Then I looked at Tamesh. He had kind of lost his supercilious look and now looked simply angry.

"Bring him up to see the general," he ordered Noggi and turned away. There was little love lost between the bodyguard types and old soldiers. I wondered if he had heard Noggi's intervention. Probably!

Noggi just sniffed and started to push his way through the crowd after Tamesh with me following. There were lots of cries of 'Well done', 'Good shooting' and the like and pats on the shoulder.

It is funny this. Just when I needed support the most, at the beginning of this conflict, they were not there, the audience. Okay, most of them were not of my tribe but we were all common soldiers together, all campaigning for the last few months. You would have thought they would be rooting for me instead of coming along to enjoy the spectacle of man of bronze versus boy in dirty tunic followed by aforesaid boy being stoned to death. Of course, no point in being part of the losing crowd, and that bullying shit, Zophar, was 100% on to win. But once Zophar was down the roaring started, the pent-up hatred flooded out, or was it guilt? Sorry, am I getting serious? I think I would have probably done the same if I had been watching instead of being the Number One Participant. And I would have been first in the rush to go over to the fallen man and kick him in the groin, or what was left of it after the havoc of my two slugs.

*****

I think that many courtiers have missed their vocation and they should really be actors or actor directors. They like to be in the centre of things, and in particular they like to be the focus of attention. Now, if you do not have an important part or have the best lines you just have to do the best you can. Most of the time the courtiers around Joshua simply had to carry messages and stand around looking pompous. Okay, the consolation was that they fed well and did not have to go out and fight or do the ordinary everyday tedious jobs of a soldier in the field. But it was pretty boring all the same so they make the most of it when the moment – any moment – comes.

So it was not altogether surprising that Tamesh, a soldier courtier if ever there was one, should want to make a bit of an appearance. There was a lot of self-important 'Make way' and waving of his staff as we progressed, his armour clinking, slowly up the hill to the tent. Then a portentous 'Stay here' while he went in and announced us to Joshua, "Ehud, the Benjamite, is outside, Oh Joshua." Yes, he really said that, "Oh Joshua!" I fought a smirk and took a sidelong look at Noggi, but he knew the game all right, not a crack in that stern face of his.

"Let him enter." We heard the low quiet voice of Joshua.

Out came Tamesh with his solemn face. I think he was searching for a grand statement because he hesitated a moment before rather weakly saying,

"Enter," for good measure, he added, "Benjamite."

So we followed. That is Tamesh first, then Noggi, and last of all me.

I could not help thinking that all this limelight was getting to Noggi and he was feeling a bit out of his depth. I mean Noggi was in his element strutting around camp supervising work parties, posting sentries and inspecting things. All armies need their Noggis and they know their place, they are at a level where they are competent. And, like all old soldiers, they have got the comfort thing sorted out – good tents, plenty of food and even the best beer in the army, you can count on that. But he was uncomfortable with all this court stuff, poor fellow. Anyway, he just tried to look stiff and stern. Of course, he had a bit of a conscience too. After all, he gave me the winning advice and he could not be sure that Tamesh was not going to split on him.

So there I was once again that day with Noggi grimly beside me in front of the great man himself. Joshua was talking with the other commanders, and smiling – that was good – he was not a man best known for smiles. On the other hand, old Amram, from whom a smiling face was completely unknown, was looking like thunder. *Not a man to disguise his feelings,* I thought. *Ever!* But at least you knew where you were with Amram, some people used to say, which was not much consolation to me at that moment. Yes, I had ringing in my head a chirpy little voice. 'I've won, I've won, I've won'. But simultaneously there was another voice, grim and commanding. "Beware the Bad loser," it said.

I just stood there. There was some urgent consultation on the bench, then Amram rose.

"Under the terms of the challenge, you, Benjamite, are the victor." He ground these words out slowly. Benjamite, ha! Bringing my tribe into it as well. Oh yes, I could see what he was thinking, *You little bastard, you got lucky this time. But I know your type, there will be another day when you won't be so lucky!*

Problem solved, I was thinking back, *tomorrow is another day!* Did I allow a smirk? Possibly!

Anyway, I was just about to bow or salute or something and turn round to go when Joshua ordered, "Wait." He then continued in his slow voice.

"Furthermore, we have had another message from the Amorites in Jericho concerning the release of prisoners."

So there you are, that proves I was right all along, I thought. Not an apology, of course, not in front of bloody Amram but that admission by Joshua was the next best thing. There was another awkward pause. Amram returned to the bench, thunder-face again. He had said all he was going to say. For the time being.

Joshua turned his head towards the Egyptian. Brown Eyes had been watching the proceedings with a certain slightly bored detachment but now took his cue from Joshua. He sat back and addressed me. His voice was soft, lisping slightly, "We saw you stop a fully armed man with a simple sling at fifty paces." He paused. "An impressive feat," he continued. "Just a lucky shot, wasn't it?"

Well, what was he wanting? Perhaps it was luck, but perhaps it was not. If Zophar had not had that big clumping shield, I could have dropped him with a head shot, I am pretty sure. But it had not worked like that and I certainly was not going to tell him that it was all thanks to Noggi and his old soldier's advice of a groin shot.

I should, of course, have bowed my head, been meek and said nothing. But no, a disembodied voice took over, and I heard myself say in an amazingly steady voice, "I prayed to the Lord, and the Lord guided my hand!"

Crass, absolutely crass, what was I doing? I mean it was okay for Joshua, he could say that kind of thing, the Lord guiding his hand, the Lord smiting the enemy and all that, but that was commander talk, not the kind of stuff which goatherds-turned-soldiers do. Try that kind of talk on the other blokes in the tent and guarantee a resounding raspberry!

At my answer, Brown Eyes leant back, silent, and surveyed me with amused eyes. He gave a sidelong glance at Joshua as if waiting for him to comment, *That is your department,* he was implying. Joshua, however, said nothing, and into the silence once again plunged Amram, but not with all the usual fury or a man utterly out of control and exasperated by my cheeky answer.

"Now," he almost drawled, in a way I did not like. To me it very much sounded like 'Gotcha!'

"Invoking the name of the Lord," he continued in a matter-of-fact voice, a voice which said I am going to finish this whole thing off, this farce, this affront, this waste of time, this brat. Now! He paused and looked around at the other commanders and shrugged his shoulders. They knew the seriousness of this accusation.

"Yes," he went on. "Invoking the name of the Lord." Another pause. Silence.

They knew what was coming.

"That is blasphemy!" he pronounced with finality.

And then it happened. Suddenly the ground began to shake and there was a terrible grinding noise. My feet shot out in front of me as if someone had pulled the carpet I was standing on. I tried to get up and fell over right on top of Noggi who was cursing in his confusion. I managed to get up on my hands and knees and, as I looked towards the benches, which were now a chaotic jumble, I found myself focusing on the tall thin tent pole rising to the goatshair roof. It suddenly leant over towards me. There was a crack and down came the roof bringing darkness. Something hard hit me on the head. There was a terrific flash and I just remember being hurled to the floor.

I do not know how long I was unconscious for, probably no more than a few moments. When I came to, I was in dusty darkness and all around a pandemonium of screams. I found I couldn't breathe and my eyes were filling with sand. Groggily I rolled over and put my head to the ground with my hand over my mouth and nose, and started to breathe again. I was conscious of a terrific pain in my head and I put my hand up. I brushed another head lying very still. It must be Noggi, either dead or just unconscious.

My brain was working very fast – that's me in survival mode! – and I reckoned there wasn't going to be any help for a while, not soon enough to prevent being smothered under this heavy hair roof. I had to get out, and the only way out was a straight line to the edge of the tent. But could I leave Noggi behind?

Obviously! Then I found myself reaching out across his back, hooking my arm under his armpit and slowly starting to crawl away. I still had to keep my hand over my mouth to breath, and with incredible slowness and pushing the heavy hair roof up with my head I slowly wriggled away yanking Noggi with me. Noggi was still unconscious and the ground was still shaking. Hazily I could still hear screams but now there was shouting. I crawled on; I was getting very tired now. I think I was slipping in and out of consciousness when suddenly I felt the smothering heavy blanket of the tent roof lifted and I was once again in dazzling sunlight. There were voices and I was lifted up to my feet when I promptly collapsed. I recollect being picked up by the legs and shoulders. Then I passed out.

Chapter 7

When I came to, I was lying on my thin mat back in the tent. Oh, my head hurt! I touched it; it had been shaved and there was a thick bandage across the top and under my chin. I stiffly shook my shoulders and limbs. *Arms working, legs working, not too bad,* I thought.

"He's awake," shouted Big Ab, and he came over and sat by my bed. He gave me some water. I hadn't realised how thirsty I was. He had to hold the cup. My lips weren't really working so quite a lot of water was spilt, but he kept topping it up.

"Drink away," he said. "You got a bit of a knock on the head but you seem okay now. You've been out for quite a while."

I nodded, I gestured to him to remove the cup.

"Oh yes," he said. "We've even had Spices over. He dressed your wound!"

And he laughed. Spices – real name Mordecai – was the slightly cruel name that we gave our official physician, a self-proclaimed expert on the healing properties of herbs and all things medical. We didn't really have much time for these guys. When it comes to sickness, give me someone who had been a mother every time, and there were lots of those among the camp followers. Anyone who's been through childbirth and brought up a dozen kids can do anything from patching a grazed knee to setting a broken leg.

"Yes," said Abs. "You got us special bandage with

honey on it. Only the best for you. But he was a bit sniffy about it all, clearly not too pleased about visiting our tents."

I guessed as much. Before all this crossing, the Jordan stuff and taking us to the Promised Land, Mordecai was doing very well hanging around the rich, especially rich old women, and appearing to take their ailments seriously. He wasn't for the likes of us, and didn't mind us knowing it.

Abs continued, "And he said he would come back when you are awake. I'd better let him know." He rose and spoke to one of the new arrivals who scuttled away.

I lay back.

"What happened then?" I asked. Abs shrugged his shoulders.

"I dunno, I was asleep at the time and suddenly the ground seemed to shake and swing. We were lucky, our tent stayed up but there was devastation outside. Most of the tents came down and quite a few people were hurt."

"What about Noggi?" I asked, but he didn't know.

Then Mordecai arrived, and, greatly to my surprise, Brown Eyes as well. He had a scratch on his face and was limping. Seth was all over them of course. Eventually they got to my mat.

I have to give him his due, Mordecai had a certain presence. He was tall and stern of feature, with a forked beard. He always wore a smartly trimmed brown tunic and yellow scarf and could occasionally be seen walking around the camp dishing out instructions to his staff running along behind him.

Mordecai looked down at me with a certain irritated detachment. Here I am, the great ME, I knew he was thinking, called on to treat a mere soldier boy. Was this on the orders of Brown Eyes? I wondered.

Anyway, he leant down and ran his smooth hands over my bandage, pressing until I yelped. That seemed to satisfy him. He nodded.

"Look up and follow my hand," he ordered, and waved his hand from side to side with my eyes following. He stood again and looked at Brown Eyes. He wasn't deigning to address me.

"Yes, just a knock on the head, that's all!" he announced pompously. "He needs to keep quiet for a day. Plenty of water and sleep, and he'll be fit for duties. All duties," he finished sternly. *That's not how you butter up your old ladies, I'll bet,* I thought.

"You will come around tomorrow and check the bandage, won't you?" said Brown Eyes. The physician sniffed his assent and left.

Actually, he wasn't such a bad chap, old Spices. I think his brief from Joshua was simply to discourage sickness; we were always having to dig proper latrines and keep food covered up. There was also an official dispensary run by his minions. Anyone ordinary going along there feeling a bit ill was discouraged by doses of oil, and told to come back in a few days if that didn't work, and he would get something stronger. Very few went back, so that was Mission Accomplished as far as Spices was concerned. That's not to say he didn't know his business, understand his herbs, set a broken limb, or bleed someone, but that wasn't for the likes of us if he could help it.

"Now," said Brown Eyes, settling down cross-legged in front of me. "Where were we?"

I just looked back at him.

"Let us cast our minds back, shall we, or has that knock on the head affected your memory? Do you remember me asking you how you stopped Zophar with your sling? And what your answer was?"

I nodded back warily. *Where was this going?* I thought.

"And Amram was scornful, accusing you of blasphemy? Yes?" he went on.

Again, I nodded.

"And then what happened?" He put his clean-shaven chin in his hand and looked at me, amused curiosity in his eyes.

"Well, something happened, didn't it?" he continued. "The ground started to shake and the tent fell down. All over the camp it seems."

I said nothing. Brown Eyes put his hands together.

"And what caused that, d'you think? Was it HIM, a sign from heaven?" He raised his eyebrows. "Was it because of your blasphemy, or was it HIS anger at Amram's contempt for the idea of divine intervention on your behalf?"

He laughed shortly.

"It may interest you to know that Amram has a broken arm, so the priests are saying that Yahweh's fury was directed at him, not you! Not saying outright perhaps but that's the murmur. Which is fortunate for you, isn't it? Another lucky escape in a busy day!" And he again laughed that deep laugh of his.

"So?" I asked warily. At least, I felt that I was out of blaspheming territory with this man. He looked back at me.

"That was an earthquake."

A bald announcement. I looked back at him dumbly. I really didn't know what he was talking about. He continued, "Why does it rain? Why does it get dark? Why is it windy? Why do plants grow? You don't understand why. Why not?"

I shrugged my shoulders. I wasn't getting it. "I suppose I just take these things as normal."

"And you are quite right, Normal!" he announced, then continued. "And an earthquake is normal. It is quite simply the rearranging of the ground beneath our feet, but it only happens at certain times and in certain places. Today and here was the time and place for a rearrangement."

"So it's nothing to do with, er, HIM?" I queried, and he laughed again. "Everything is to do with HIM. There is nothing without HIM." Lots of emphasis on HIM, I noticed.

"Whoever HIM is," he added casually. "But the idea that HE interferes with the natural processes of HIS creation…" he paused, then continued, "especially in some squabble in a tent in the middle of nowhere…" He just shrugged his shoulders again.

"So all this Joshua talk…" I stopped as soon as I started. *Fool*, I thought, *don't even go there!* But he had already raised his finger to stop me.

"Enough," he said quickly. Then he added more softly, "We can talk again perhaps. My interest in you is military. But you are tired and have been told to rest. Come to my tent after the physician sees you tomorrow."

He rose. Seth rushed over to lift the flap of the tent.

"By the way," he said, before ducking through the entrance. "My name is Obed."

I was right. So he was Obed, Joshua's genius, the man who knew everything.

*****

Not surprisingly Spices didn't turn up the next day but sent a minion, who, while not an iota less in self-importance, entirely lacked his boss's stature. Small and rather fat he waddled over and stood in the entrance of the tent and surveyed us with distaste. Clearly, he thought the best way of 'Getting on' was to copy the boss because he had the same brown tunic and yellow scarf, albeit faded and of rougher material. He also had a little beard which showed signs of attempts at shaping, which wasn't the same as having the daily attention from a trained servant.

Well, everyone ignored him so he eventually announced, "Is this the tent of Ehud? If so, show him to me. I am here on the instructions of chief physician, Mordecai."

"I'm over here!" I shouted, raising myself on my elbow.

He sniffed acknowledgement and padded over to

my bed and knelt down. He didn't talk to me; he just flipped his hand at me for silence and set about his work. This meant unrolling the bandage as one might open a bundle of dirty clothes, ignoring my wincing where the blood had dried the linen to the scalp. He then examined the stitches; he did not talk, just sniffed occasionally. He paused and I put my hand up and gingerly felt for the wound. It ran crossways over the top of my head and was about the length of my hand; I realised it must have been caused by one of the roofing supports. He resumed, mopped the top of my head, then dipped the end of the bandage in some water and dabbed away at the dried blood on my skull. Another sniff, then he looked at the long brown stain on the bandage.

"No sign of pus there," said Seth matter-of-fact who had just come up and was standing over us.

Spices Junior ignored him. He certainly wasn't going to acknowledge an observation from a humble Benjamite, tent commander or not. But when Seth picked up the bandage for a closer examination, he snatched it out of his hand with an angry glance. His anger said it all – bandages were valuable. Why a fine bandage had been used on this humble soldier he had no idea, but it was going back to the dispensary to be washed and made ready for some more senior wound. Or there would be questions asked by his esteemed Mordecai.

"Water," he cried out to no one in particular.

There was a pause and Seth went off. I just think Spices Junior liked seeing people double around on his behalf. When the pot came, he allowed Seth to hold it while he dipped and fussily rubbed together his fingers. They didn't actually look dirty to me; I think it was more a gesture towards our lowly circumstances, compared with his. He gave a final sniff, rose and left. Seth smiled after him, and looked back and down at me and yes, even winked.

I lay back, I was still groggy and very tired. The flies had already started to buzz around the dried wound and I suddenly felt terribly homesick. I remembered my mother treating my arm when it got bitten by a goat. She had gone out and picked some figs and made a special cooling compress for my wound, then sat by waving away the flies and singing gently to me until the pain got better, just willing me to be happy again. All night she sat there. Out here, in the desert with these guys I was just a bit of meat.

Then I simply dropped off and slept, and the next thing was Seth shouting out, "Start panicking. Details later."

Then, rather quick off the mark for him, "Get up, get up, we're going to Jericho, Sabbath and all!" said he in that hectoring voice of his. He was fully dressed and repeated the message. Around me the other men sat up from sleep and started to put on their kit. I lay doggo, I reckoned I deserved my rest. I was thinking he can't have forgotten that I am a casualty with orders to sleep. But I should have known better.

"That includes you, Snakes. Yesterday's little hero!" Seth gave my mattress a kick and moved on. Others were feigning sleep.

"Everyone on parade. No excuses," he sang along. "All up for the big parade." This was invariably followed by the sound of a kick, followed by a groan from a semi-sleeping figure.

Then I remembered. Of course, this was the big parade in front of Jericho when the prisoners would be released. Word got around that Joshua had ordered everyone on parade. We were all a bit puzzled by this offer of prisoners. Who were they? I mean we had been campaigning for several months and men went 'missing' every day, some picked up on patrol, or snatched from forward sentry posts. We had lost a dozen only last week – never came back from patrol, they had simply disappeared. Of course, we didn't like to think about what happened to those who fell into the hands of the Amorites. Lock them up or put them to work? Death by torture more likely. And why not? They knew we killed everyone, Joshua's orders! Or had they deserted, gone back east? There were plenty of moans about living in the field after the initial excitement had worn off. I must confess I was very, very curious about this release of prisoners. If that second message had not come in confirming what I had heard from Zemri, I would be having second thoughts.

I rolled off my mat. Seth was in his usual no-nonsense mood. Everyone was to be on parade. That was it. It didn't matter if they were half dead, as long as they could stand more or less upright with a sharp stick or spear that was good enough for him. That is one of the things you learned on campaign. Yes, when there was fighting to be done you needed to be fit, able-bodied. But often, we soldiers were just there for the show, to impress someone. Parading before Jericho was clearly one of these occasions.

We all jumbled out of the tent and Seth roughly paraded us into ranks. There were thirty of us, standing there uniformly barefoot, in rough kilt, and headband with spear and dagger. I, of course, had my sling dangling down from my belt on my left side and the dagger which I had got as part of my share of the loot a couple of weeks before. And, of course, a bag of ordinary stones on my right side, not the little lead killers, they were for special occasions. And that spear Seth had given me after my first patrol. I had hung onto that. Okay, it was just a stick with a long metal point but it was good for throwing as well as lunging. An adversary with a bronze spear might sneer, call it a 'Throwing Stick' and all that, until he got my point in the guts from five paces.

Seth walked up our ranks with his usual jibes. He didn't miss much. He made one or two spot checks of the satchels we wore across our necks. We all had much the same, a small skin filled with water and some parched corn, enough for a day. He finished his inspection. "Now, from now on, you are all to wear the same headbands," says he with finality, and he took out of his satchel a bundle of multicoloured cords. They were passed round, one to each man.

"The boss wants each tribe to have a distinctive cord and here is ours."

Each cord comprised a few strands of red, blue and green. That's the colour scheme for our tribe and every tribe had its own colour. I suppose there are physical differences between the various tribes. A typical Benjamite is small and wiry with long dark hair and a prominent nose. And often left-handed which is my only Benjamite characteristic. Those of the tribe of Reuben tended to be taller with long straight brown hair but, frankly, if we were all in a crowd, we all looked much the same. So it wasn't surprising that Joshua wanted to put us all into some kind of uniform even if it was only a distinctive headband. It meant he and the other commanders could be sure to recognise the tribe each soldier belonged to. "And you, Baldy," Seth, handing me a cord, was addressing me, "can wear it around your neck until your hair has grown."

The other soldiers tittered. Hero worship doesn't last long in the tent. That stunt with Zophar was good but it's in the past, they were all thinking. Next trick please!

We then joined the rest of our tribe and lined up on the east of the wide watercourse with the hills and narrow valleys rising sharply on the other side. There must have been about a thousand of us, Benjamites, all divided into Tent sections, standing three sections deep with the multi-coloured cord round our heads, except me, of course. Each section had its own tent commander, like Seth. Then there were three sections to a command and each command had a commander. Ours was Chiai who was quite small and his bumptious fussy manner irritated some of the more senior commanders. He had fair hair which probably meant some Phoenician blood. Anyway, he didn't look pure

Israelite, and some commanders – sucking up to Joshua or so they thought – tried to get him sacked, even getting some priests on their side. So off they went muttering away to Joshua about the pretty certain dodginess of Chagai's blood with all that fair hair, and Joshua listened quietly, then abruptly dismissed the accusers and their accusations. It was reported that he said, "I decide who is an Israelite and who isn't." But I doubt he did, he would probably have been more tactful. But we all pretty much knew the reality. What Joshua says, goes! For all his starry- eyedness Joshua could be very pragmatic. Anyway, he knew at bottom Chagai was fairly competent and dead trustworthy. He also knew he was popular and he didn't want to upset us Benjamites.

Chagai, or Chaggy as we called him in the tents, was fussing his way up the ranks in his usual manner, stopping occasionally to talk to a man or ask a question. We Benjies had a reputation for being a bit individualistic. I mean, in the Reubs, they all had to wear their hair like this and carry their spears like that. Everything had to be uniform but we weren't like that, and we rather prided ourselves on being different. So in our section there were 30 different ways of fastening the headband. This individualism rather annoyed Chagai because he would get teased by the other commanders, saying we were scruffy or sloppy and all that, but there was nothing really he could do about it. But he would still make a bit of a show and here he was doing his fussing bit during the inspection. Today he was fussing about spears and checking on the sharpness of each man's spear, in many cases just a six-foot stick sharpened to a point and fire hardened. Chagai was very keen on fire hardening.

"Everyone sharpened and hardened the points, Seth?" he asked as he eventually came to our tent section. "Hm, hm?"

Seth came to attention, his best parade manner. He knew how to please Chagai.

"Yessir, yessir, all points sharpened and hardened, sir."

This was a bit of a bellyache among us, this fire hardening of our spear points. The theory was that charring removed the moisture and made the point harder, and Chagai firmly believed in this. I supposed the sharp black point did add a somewhat deadly aspect to a stick, more threatening, but Seth back in the tent was sceptical about its value. Before parades, Seth always told those with sticks to make sure points were blackened but he never bothered to check if they were properly charred. All he was interested in was that each spear had a sharp point and looked okay. Anyway, all this charring didn't matter to me because I now had a stick with a nice bronze on it which could go through anything.

I was wondering what Chagai was going to say when he came to me. He had been away on patrol when I was in trouble but he had obviously heard all about it.

"How's the head, Ehud?" he asked when he eventually got to me, and then frowned. "You can't stand there with the sun on your bare head, man, you'll

112

get sunstroke. Cover your head, you fool. With your scarf!"

Seth took my spear while I removed the scarf from my shoulder and wrapped it around the top of my head, like a turban. I could feel the men on either side of me smirking. I now looked silly but probably no sillier than with a head reddening in the sun.

"And that dagger? When did you get that?" Chagai had noticed my dagger. *Silly me,* I thought, *I should have left it at home.* I took the spear back from Seth and held it smartly by my side, the way Chagai liked it. "A present, sir, I was given it yesterday. After the fight!" I announced proudly.

Well, I wasn't going to tell him that I'd nicked it from Noggi's stocks and anyway here was a chance to brag a bit. And I've learnt that if you're going to tell a barefaced lie it's best to do it with confidence. No umming or ahing and you will probably get away with it especially when dealing with those who think they can spot a lie from ten paces. I think I learnt the trick from Seth. He was a past master at buttering up senior officers. Any question he answered promptly and with confidence.

I think I saw Seth smiling at my explanation. He knew Chagai knew that I'd been in high places, had somehow done quite well and so it wasn't altogether surprising if I had been given a 'present'. And he certainly was not going to give the impression he didn't know what was going on. Might he check later? Almost certainly not!

Chagai finished his inspection.

"Carry on," he said, nodding to Seth who gave out a quiet order to stand easy. More waiting. That's the first thing you learn about armies. You are always waiting for someone, and the most junior person has to wait the longest. So first we had to wait for Seth to inspect us. Then it was Chagai's turn, and now we had to wait for dear old Micah, the commander of us Benjamites. A short while later, up he turned in a rather racy yellow chariot with bright red wheels drawn by a couple of black horses.

"Good old Micah, always gets the best of everything," muttered Big Abs on my left.

Certainly, Micah had a certain parade-ground style. His armour fitted, he had a magnificent bronze helmet with a very large coxcomb and he never seemed perturbed or in a hurry. His driver put the chariot into a walk and Micah slowly passed in front of our tribe. He nodded to each commander, then wheeled round and faced away from us. I will give him that, he was not one for pep talks, the bane of the soldiers who are standing for hours in the hot sun.

First came the Reubenites, probably of all the tribes we Benjamites disliked them the most. The leading Reub, all decked out in bronze breastplate and tall bronze helmet with polished iron bands, was holding aloft the tribal banner of waves on a red background. Red was the senior colour representing mankind and it, of course, had gone to the Reubs. I am not sure why they had water on the banner too, probably something to do with being a vital resource. The other symbol was the mandrake plant. The Reubs have kind of claimed

114

top dog among the tribes and, just to rub it in to us as Rachel's descendants, they put the mandrake on their banner.

They were quite a horde, the Reubenites, and they had clearly been given first grabs at all the kit we had captured. Pretty much every man had a helmet, a shield, and a bronze-tipped spear. A big contrast to our tribe still in our clothes as nomads with the odd bit of military cutlery that we'd managed to nab.

They marched slowly and stiffly and proud with their heads in the air. *Yeah, just like their fallen hero, Zophar,* I thought.

"Let's give 'em the dog," whispered Abner, and I laughed.

One of the rudest things you can say to another Israelite is 'Go piss against the wall'. It sounds harmless enough but actually what you are doing is comparing the bloke to a low male creature which sits around whimpering, feeds off scraps and, of course, every so often, pisses against the wall. And so it started; first with Abner and then it spread along the back ranks and forward until there was this loud hissing noise running the full extent of the tribe of Benjamin. The commanders obviously felt they had a responsibility to stop the noise but no one had their mouth open so it was impossible to identify the guilty hissers. Quickly the sound reached the Reubenites.

"Keep looking to your front," ordered their commanders, but most of them could not resist a venomous look in our direction.

Obviously, Micah couldn't let this go on. He was

115

never against a bit of tribal rivalry, and disliked the Reubenites as much as we did, but he would surely get a rocket from Joshua for not stopping it. He slowly turned his chariot round and faced us.

"This noise stops now," he said with finality. All the commanders promptly shouted the message along the ranks, and we stopped.

The Reubenites continued to tramp past us, heads high, line after line. Well, we'd had our fun! Well, not quite, it was not over yet. As the line came level someone, once again from the back rank, cried out, "Where's old Zophar?" And of course, we all burst out laughing, which got another terrific frown growl from Micah. It was true, Zophar was nowhere to be seen.

Chapter 8

All at once that terrible sound pierced the air, the cacophony of a hundred rams' horns, a mixture of a sobs, wails and grunts. We all looked over to the right and, being in the back rank and on the side of the hill, we had a good view. There they were, the priests, in their long white tunics and white pointy hats, marching along blowing on their horns. The horns were all sizes, none of them smaller than the horns that Noggi had given me. Some were black, some white and there were one or two really big horns which must have come from some other animal. It wasn't clear if anyone was orchestrating the blowers; occasionally you did catch some kind of rhythm, but I rather suspect their job was just to make an awful noise, which they did. They passed in front of us, and we muttered amongst ourselves which drew an angry 'Quiet there!' from Seth.

Then came the escort to the Ark of Covenant. They were all soldiers from the tribe of Levi, the top tribe if you like because they had been loyal to Moses at a tricky time, so he gave them the smarmy job of looking after the Ark. Any good kit came their way so they were pretty well dressed. Then came the Ark of Covenant itself covered with a blue cloth and on a platform supported by two poles with bearers.

"They're hamming it up a bit today, aren't they?" I whispered to Abner, and he nodded. It was true, the four bearers were really making heavy going of their task, puffing and stumbling. I reckoned it was all a bit of an act. They looked strong enough but then this was not what they had joined for.

Frankly, being a bearer of the Ark was one of the cushiest jobs in Joshua's army. There was to be no sitting about camp gassing about the good old days and phoney feats of arms. Oh no, not in Joshua's army! All had to be useful, and of all the ways to be useful in Joshua's army a bearer was probably the best number. The perks were good too, from left-over food from sacrifices, a rake-off from the donations, to the ear of the priests. All told it was a darn sight better than sewing hides and shaping tent pegs, let alone going out on patrol.

We had a joke, 'Pure as the blood of Levi'. Officially bearers had to be from the tribe of Levi but because they had to be big strong guys there was some unofficial recruiting from the other tribes. Of course, there was never any shortage of volunteers but don't even think about it if you are from the tribe of Benjamin, or descended from Rachel or Biha.

There is a bit of a story here. Jacob, the father figure of all of the twelve tribes, married Rachel but she was infertile so he bred off her sister, Leah. Reuben, her firstborn, took pity on Rachel and gave her mandragora which cured her fertility and she gave birth to Joseph and Benjamin, the father of our tribe. So while we, the descendants of Joseph and Benjamin, are the children of Wife Number One, the others, Reuben and the rest of them were born before us. Who has pride of place is a tricky point among us Chosen People? Joshua had tried to play fair with the tribes but it had never worked out like that. Only those descended from Leah or Zilpah ever became a bearer, so most of them were Reubs, Sims, or Zebs as we called those of the tribe of Simeon and Zebulun. It was funny, Joshua had tried to break this monopoly, not just because he was an Ephraimite and closer to our lot, but in the interests of fair play. But he didn't succeed and he wasn't going to risk his authority having a run in with the Ark bearers. They, of course, were in cahoots with the priests and the priests didn't want to have a strike on their hands.

Micah called us up to attention and they tramped past us. It was probably the first time most of us had ever been that close to the Ark. It was a bit of a moment. There before us was this box with all those rules written on tablets of stone and given by HIM to Moses.

After the Ark, came Joshua and his commanders, also on captured chariots. We let the other tribes pass us without any further mockery. Then it was our turn to join in, bringing up the rear. Micah led off in his chariot, at marching pace, with a really big Benjamite carrying our banner, multicoloured with the image of a wolf. We liked our wolf image. Although the wolf was the herdsman's biggest enemy, it was also our protector because most of us out on the hill eventually got a wolf skin to keep out the cold of the night.

And so we followed the big procession, on this fine hot day under a blazing sun, along a wide winding watercourse and towards Jericho. Of course, overhead we had an escort, vultures. They always knew when there was business to be had and accompanied us, languidly flying overhead or dropping down and perching among some bushes while we passed. From there would come a sinister cacophony of sound. We knew them all.

"Ah," said Abner. "There's 'The Old Man Dying'." It was true, there was a chorus her-her-her of noises like a man wheezing from his deathbed. And over this sound, there was the occasional plucking noise, like someone playing staccato on the mandolin. 'Baby Laughing' was another favourite, a long he-he-he, high but harsh. Then there was the 'Clearing the Throat' – a series of deep gruffs, and 'Spear in the Tummy' like a gasp of pain and many others. But the sound we hated most, which seemed to rise above all the others, was the Screamer – a long shrill wailing, rising and falling, that gave us all the shivers.

I'm pretty tough. I can keep going in hot and cold, wind and rain. I've been thirsty. I've been hungry. I've been lost. That's just everyday life and experience as a herdsman. And I'm not frightened of walking long distances on rough ground under a hot sun. But today was different, and those vultures weren't helping. Old Mordecai was right when he told me to rest for a few days, and putting that thing on my head to protect it from the sun wasn't helping at all.

"Hey there, Ehud," cautioned Abner as I lurched sideways into him. "Sorry," I said suddenly waking up and focusing once again on following the man in front. Then my knees went and I flopped down. The next thing I realised was that I was being supported on my left and my right.

"What's the matter with you, lad?" Seth's face was close-up and looking hard at me. I tried to focus and incoherent words tumbled out.

"Just keep going," said he crisply. "You two keep him upright and we'll sort something out," he ordered Abner and Gam on my left.

At least, they aren't going to leave me for the vultures or an Amorite patrol, I remember thinking as my feet started to drag and I passed out.

The next thing I knew I was seated on the edge of a chariot and someone was pouring water down my throat and splashing my face at the same time. Micah and Chaggy were looking down at me.

"He had that crack on the head in the tent," Chaggy was saying. "Mordecai saw him. I don't know why he is with us but we can't send him back now."

"Poor boy, poor boy," Micah grunted. "Yes, I knew his father, a fine man." He then looked sharply across at his chariot boy, tall with short fair hair, watching, bored and uninterested.

"Yes, Ehud can take your place. He can sit in the chariot."

The chariot boy looked startled, puzzled, then alarmed, and looked at me with scorn in his eyes.

"Yes, you can take his place in Seth's command,

Barak," Micah continued. "Do your good," he added.

Scornful-face looked daggers, first at Micah then at me, but Micah simply picked his spear from the wicker panier of the chariot and gave it to him. The sun glinted on the four-edged bronze point of the spear with its long smooth dark shaft. *This boy knows how to look after himself,* I thought.

Micah climbed up past me onto his chariot to stand behind his charioteer. "Not sure my nephew is very pleased," murmured Micah out loud to himself.

"Now," he said, looking back and down at me, "make sure you hold on!"

And with that the driver shook the reins and the chariot started to move. I quickly grasped the wicker handles on either side and sat back as far as I could from the edge with my feet dangling a few inches from the rough ground below. I had never been in a chariot before and it was curious looking back at the landscape as it rolled away at the smart trotting speed of the horses. Of course, I could see why commanders like chariots; being the height of wheels they have a better view of what's going on and, depending on the ground, the chariot can move as fast as a horse can gallop. But comfort? No! At trotting speed, the chariot bounced from side to side as the big wheels struck and bounced over the rocks. Micah was standing, his knees slightly bent, and holding on to handles on top of the chariot sides, and he too lurched backwards and forwards, striking me occasionally with the back of his legs. The driver was holding onto a handle at the front and held the reins in his other hand. Okay, it wasn't comfortable but I was feeling better now. That water had helped, and my head had stopped throbbing.

"Well, Ehud?" shouted back Micah eventually when we slowed to a walk. "Glad to see Jericho again?"

I stood up, holding the sides of the chariot, and indeed there it was, those great walls broken by towers all glistening white against the dun-coloured landscape and great belt of blue sky. Around were the fertile but empty fields which a month ago had been waving with barley, orchards of fig trees, and long lines of vines. It was all such a contrast to our land east of Jordan, hilly, dry and hard to grow on.

And there we were bringing up the rear of a snake extending into the distance. I could just see the Ark of Covenant but the horns were not blowing now.

A man was running down along the snake, stopping every so often to speak, and eventually came to us. He was dressed in the white tunic and red and white scarf of a runner, one of the innovations that Joshua had brought to the army to speed up communication.

He puffed to a halt by our chariot.

"Commander's respects, and would you join him at the front?" Micah nodded back and his chariot wheeled round and trotted back along our line to where Chagai was standing.

"I'm going forward to Joshua," said Micah. "So you are in charge."

Chagai nodded. Micah's chariot quickly turned round and trotted past the columns of men until we joined the other commanders just behind the Ark of Covenant.

I'm not saying that this was all fun, but things were definitely looking up. One moment I was trudging along on the sand and rock with the sun beating down, passing in and out of consciousness and supported on either side, and next moment sitting, bumping and crunching along with my legs dangling over the edge of a senior commander's battle chariot. Admittedly this meant hanging on for dear life with my arms being wrenched with every jolt, but I wasn't going to create a fuss about that. Not that Micah would have bothered. I was just the newly promoted temporary chariot boy having an easy time.

Everyone wanted to be a chariot boy. It helped if, like me, you were small and light because there wasn't much room in the chariot and they weren't that strong. And with a bad bump a heavily laden chariot would go over. The main job for the chariot boy was to prevent the commander falling out of the back; so you would stand at the back with your arms outstretched holding the hoops like a kind of gate. Otherwise, your job was to run errands and look after him in the field.

We drew level with the other commanders, mainly the leaders of the other tribes, each differentiated with a scarf of the tribal colour. I glimpsed Amram, wearing the green scarf of a Simeonite. I ducked my head; this was no time to attract his attention.

"Let's halt here," ordered Joshua, and a shout went forward to the priests and the Ark of Covenant.

"So," continued Joshua, in his wry way and waving

an arm towards the city. "Here we are, in front of Jericho."

He looked up at the walls in the distance where the sun struck on the helmets of the sentries who sparsely manned the wall. There was no sign of alarm in the city. No sudden surge onto the walls, no trumpets or drums beating as we appeared. It was eerily quiet. Joshua waved his hand towards the city looking from side to side and back at his entourage of commanders.

"We're a bit early, of course. Your thoughts, gentlemen?"

So here was I sitting in on a council of war but I reckoned it wasn't my place to be seen to be listening. I remained with my back to the speakers.

It was Amram, with his arm in a sling I was pleased to notice, who first spoke. "It's a trap, General, definitely!"

As he spoke there was that heavy flapping noise and a dozen vultures descended onto a small raised rocky area nearby with some scrub and began one of their conversations, a mixture of 'Baby Laughing' and 'Spear in the Tummy' as they pecked around and observed us.

The other commanders laughed quietly.

"Thank you, Amram," Joshua agreed politely. Amram was known for his strong but not always very helpful views. His strength was in doing, not thinking. "But what form is this trap, as you call it, to take?" continues Joshua. "They would be mad to come out from behind their walls and face our army. Or is there a relief force hiding in those hills?"

"Whatever we do, we must protect the Ark," growled Amram, and there were murmurings of agreement. It seemed pretty obvious; there the Ark was, a thousand paces from the main gate, an obvious target although it was difficult to see how the Amorites could get to the Ark before we could redeploy. Anyway, I could feel that Joshua wasn't going to take that risk. He turned round and addressed the commander of the Reubenites.

"Deploy your men round the Ark and the priests. That will protect the Ark from a sudden attack. And you, Blam," he addressed the commander of the Zebulun force, "I want you to picket the hills and report any sign of enemy activity. Once you are in place, we will march round the city with horns blowing and trumpets blasting. And let's see what happens."

So off went Blam and the Zebs into the hills nearby. The Reubenites surrounded the Ark and when Joshua was happy, he gave the order. Off we set from our position in front of the main gates, a thousand paces off, in a clockwise direction. First the priests started to puff away at the rams' horns, then the trumpets started, and the army started to move forward. The Reubenites, out in front, had the toughest going, breaking ground through the vineyards and across the walls which marked the freshly harvested fields. They just kicked over or cut down anything which got in their way creating a broad path strewn with overturned walls and broken vines for us to pass over.

Micah dropped back to keep level with the leading files of the Benjamites, keeping himself on the side facing the city, and his chariot dropped to a walking speed. I resumed my position sitting on the edge looking back but I could tell Micah was apprehensive. Amram had put his finger on it; Zemri was up to something but still the city walls looked barely populated and there was complete quiet within.

Jericho was, of course, huge. Wherever you looked, there were these same crenellated and daunting walls, the same occasional sentries just visible, the same dominating towers at the same intervals. It was only by observing the sun that you realised we were completing a circle of the city. It was eerie, touring round this great shimmering dead quiet white city which we knew was full of determined and well-armed Amorites who knew we were bent on their destruction.

"Not even the dogs are barking," muttered Micah, and he was right; there would normally be some market noise and the dogs barking at about this time. Jericho should be all a bustle, but instead it was silence.

Having completed the long circle of the city we stopped for the second time in front of the two massive towers on either side of the main gates. As Benjamites bringing up the rear we were on the extreme right flank facing the city. It was quite impressive standing behind Micah looking along the straight line of our army standing six deep.

The sun was now high overhead. "Should be about time now," said Micah. He was given to making these pronouncements without expecting any reply. He raised his arm and beckoned Chagai over.

"I'm going to HQ to see what's going on. You're

in charge. Keep a sharp lookout all around."

Chagai nodded agreement, and called the other commanders together for a briefing, while Micah's chariot moved to the centre.

A short while later we had joined the other commanders facing the main gates. They dismounted from the chariots to create a loose huddle around Joshua. Dogs started to bark inside the city and there were signs of movement behind the white battlements between the two main towers. The red coxcombs on the helmets of Amorite commanders could be seen joining the simple bronze of the ordinary sentries. We could just see the tops of their helmets until they passed in front of an embrasure when they could be seen from the waist up.

Then one of the red cockscombs, an especially big one, stepped forward and filled an embrasure, facing us, and put his hands forward on the edge. I felt sure it must be Zemri. Even from that distance I recognised his silky movement. Then he took off his helmet and put it on the flat stone surface in front of him.

"Welcome," he called out, in Amorite of course, and, yes, it was Zemri. "Welcome to our city," he drawled again. "You are welcome to the prisoners."

He seemed to laugh, but nothing happened. I think all our expectations varied between extreme optimism and pessimism. Hoping against hope was the expectation that the gates would open and out would pour our soldiers, probably in pretty poor condition, the best that we could hope for. Our worst fears were that they would be mutilated, blinded, with their tongues torn out.

Still the gates stood firmly shut while Zemri remained leaning forward as if expecting something to happen. Even from the distance I could see he was smiling.

There was a noise and we could see something being pushed up onto the battlements to the right of the main tower. Up and up it went until it sat, a great big wooden box on top of the battlements, long and flattish about five paces wide and perhaps three high.

There was a scraping noise and a crash as the box was pushed over the battlements for it to fall and stop with a jerk about half way down the wall as the retaining ropes tightened. It seemed to bounce, then bump against the city wall and become stationary. It was easier to see the box now against the white background. But it wasn't a plain box with solid sides. It had the crossed struts of a cage. And now it was no longer stationary. It seemed to be moving, lurching jerkily from side to side.

There was a dead silence as we strained our eyes in the blinding sunlight. Even the caw cawing of the vultures stopped. Then there was a collective gasp from our army as we spotted movement within the cage. Another look and we could see they were human beings, and then we realised the ghastly possibility. I'm not sure what came over us. Was it our curiosity, our impatience, or simply our desire to confirm the worst? Without any commands to go forward, all those opposite the gates rushed towards the city to get a better look. I had already dismounted but the chariot with Micah shouting and horses rearing was simply swept along in the mass of soldiers. I desperately held onto the handle at the back to avoid getting separated.

Eventually the commanders were able to assert themselves with threats and shouts and the mass of soldiery came to a halt. The flanks had held, they hadn't been close enough to see what we had seen.

"Get back into line," shouted the commanders and soon some kind of order was re-established.

By now, we were about three hundred paces from the city walls and the cage and its contents, our men, naked, legs and arms sticking out of that overcrowded box, were clearly visible. They were waving to us and crying for help. Help or otherwise a slow death, hanging on the city walls, without food or water, roasting in the heat of the day, freezing in the night until weak enough for the vultures to finish them off.

Up on the battlements Zemri raised his arms. "Behold your soldiers. Come and get them." He laughed.

"Steady there, steady, lads," the commanders growled along the ranks. We stood still. Not so the vultures which had already taken off and flapped over to a new base nearer the city. The cawing started again. Their numbers seem to be growing. They always seemed to arrive from nowhere, and their instincts were rarely wrong.

Looking back now it was pretty predictable. I can remember it all in slow motion. First, we heard a loud order, a bark of sound, from within the walls of Jericho. Then a kind of loud humming twang, and a thin black curtain rose against the blue sky above the battlements. They were arrows, hundreds of them, and up and up they went. Our necks craned upwards as we followed their slow trail high above and towards us. Then suddenly they were coming down, fast. Around me, the better armed and more experienced crouched down with shield above the head. I, without thinking, hugged the side of the chariot. Some were simply transfixed by panic and gazed open-mouthed at the descending. Others, with a very good sense of self-preservation, simply turned tail and began to run. As the arrows fell amongst us the screaming and chaos of a battlefield began.

Almost within touching distance I saw an arrow bury itself in the backside of Micah's horse. It reared up overturning the chariot and tilting Micah and the charioteer on top of me. Then both horses set off and I felt a sudden weight lifted as the chariot with Micah's charioteer screaming was dragged away, the reins still fastened to his wrist.

Micah pushed me to one side and started to stand up. He was cursing. There was another whoosh of arrows. I instinctively looked up and there they were, that sinister black shower. Another moment and they were falling again all around me biting flesh, bouncing off armour, penetrating leather, some spitting up sand and pieces of rock as they plugged uselessly into the dirt. I heard Micah cry. We were both on our knees and he was clutching his left shoulder. An arrow had penetrated through the leather of his armour and was deeply embedded. He was now swearing.

Chapter 9

I suppose I've seen more than my fair share of fighting and this includes being pitched into a fighting situation unexpectedly. I reckon there are several possible reactions. All involve panic. The first is to panic and do nothing; for most people that just means standing there, mind and limbs frozen, and if they stick in that position long enough, they'll get a spear through their guts. Or rather an arrow in today's fight. Another is panic and bolt, get out of the danger zone as quickly as possible. Obviously sensible but it is also called running away and can get you into a lot of trouble later on, stoning to death for cowardice and all that. A third is to panic and drop to the ground, make yourself as small as possible preferably under some kind of cover. That's me, at that moment anyway. Okay, there is another reaction, the aggressive one, which is to give a wild whoop and charge. That works too but not when your enemy is shooting arrows at you from the other side of a big white wall.

So there I was crouched in a mass of shouting men, screaming horses with the military head of my tribe sitting on the ground cursing and holding his shoulder with a black feathered arrow sticking out of it. I might be okay but another whoosh of arrows might end that run of luck.

Which brings me back to reactions. I know, time after time, that after the initial panic I'm quite good at working out the options, even with all that noise going on around me. I suppose that's why I'm still here. So increasingly attractive was the option of joining the others who had simply turned tail and run away from those terrible walls and the deadly arrows as quickly as possible. Strength in numbers, I was reckoning. You can't stone to death half an army. *Hmm,* I thought, *even better, grab a shield and run with that covering my back.* "But, Ehud," and I could hear me saying this to myself, "and this is a big 'But', do that and you will be abandoning Micah and that could be trouble." Okay, I coldly considered, if he dies my survival will not really stick out after the chaos of the afternoon, and I can probably bluff my way out of any awkward questions. But I thought looking over at poor old Micah, he's only wounded, he may survive and there will be hard questions. Ouch! Why had the chariot boy deserted him? Why indeed? The most likely outcome a most unpleasant one for me, and a feast for the vultures.

And then it all fell into place. Yes, I wanted to scarper back as soon as possible. Yes, I didn't want to be struck down by an arrow as I scarpered. No, I didn't want to be accused of abandoning Micah but yes, I did want to be the guy who saved Micah's life. God knows, I didn't want to spend the next few years of my life as a common soldier on parched grains and being bossed around by Seth and the like, so this was my chance, was it not?

I 've given you my thought processes rather like a

lecture in the classroom but it wasn't like that. In the sand and the dust and the noise, the mind can work mighty fast, mine does anyway.

The next moment I was by Micah's side, the arrow still sticking out of his shoulder. He looked at me, and I remember looking back at him almost impertinent-like, with my head cocked on one side.

"With your permission, sir," I said rather inanely, then simply grabbed the arrow and gave it a pull. Micah screamed and went rigid but the arrow remained fixed in his flesh. Obviously, an arrow with a barb, a vicious triangle, impossible to remove without a doctor and a lot of pain.

"Sorry, sir," murmured I in response, then grasped the shaft where it had entered the shoulder as gently as I could. With a rapid twist of the wrist, I snapped the arrow, so there were just a few inches left. Micah groaned again and went silent.

Moving to his unwounded side I yanked Micah up, ducked under him, and raised him on my shoulders. I think he was almost unconscious with that last attention of mine. I took one last look at the great white walls. They were no longer firing in volleys, the archers were simply firing as fast as they could and the arrows were falling all around finding soft flesh, metal or wood, rock or sand. "Let's go, sir," I shouted back, I'm not sure why except to encourage myself.

He was unconscious now because I was able to hitch him up on the top of my back without any complaint.

And so I left the killing zone, as fast as my legs

could carry me with my boss on my back as a shield against more arrows; and thinking of the great future ahead of me!

And did I run! Of course, I was only one of many, but what a mess of writhing screaming bodies. Worst of all, the horses which had been wounded and were still stuck in the traces of their chariots were charging around all over the place. I tripped and fell to the ground, staggered up and continued. The whoosh of arrows. There was a twang in my ear and an arrow fell to the ground. It must have hit Micah on a bit of armour; my human shield tactic had worked. That arrow would otherwise be in my back and I lying with the rest of them gasping in the dust and trampled by the flying horde.

Then, all of a sudden, I was aware of no whooshing, the arrows had stopped. I reckoned I must be out of range so I halted for breath and looked back at those great white walls. *Good running,* I thought, *Ehud, perhaps you are safely out of shot here.* True, the arrows had stopped but 'Crash' went the great gates as they were flung open suddenly and, three abreast, out came flooding Amorite war chariots.

Well, it was pretty obvious. We had walked into the trap. The arrows had done their bit, and now they were to finish us off. It is an old, old tactic of which we were the past masters. Challenge a bigger army which is all smug and self- confident, create a tiny upset, and the next moment they are on the run and easy pickings for the chase. Slaughter ensues. Always! Of course, it happens easier with untrained troops. We were untrained, just a bunch of boys who had turned our sticks into spears and done a bit of successful raiding. We had always been on the front foot, in small groups and never experienced massed panic before. Of course, that's what Joshua had realised, sensible old bugger that he was, it's much easier to do hit-and-run than be defensive. Now he had made a mistake, and he was paying. You can't let green soldiers like us use their imagination or, when shit hits, they'll run quicker than you can say 'parched grain'.

I could feel Micah stirring on my back.

"The Ark, the Ark, they're the going for the Ark," he called weakly. Of course, he was right. Capture the Ark, kill Joshua and we were busted. I quaked as I thought what next? Don't tell me the old fool's going to play firebrand and, with his wounded arm and a very reluctant chariot boy, make a heroic stand against the charging horde. Yes, and become mincemeat quick time under those galloping hooves and ironclad wheels. But no, what a relief – Dad was right all along – Micah was no firebrand.

"Get to one side, boy, lie down, let 'em pass," he rasped out. "And keep still!"

Good appreciation, I thought. The Ark was well back and the Amorites chariots were heading straight for it grinding those caught in the way but unconcerned about the disorganised fleeing rabble on either side. I bolted to one side and slumped down behind a small frankincense tree, then squirmed from under Micah. Heads down, lying doggo, both of us still pretended to be just another couple of corpses. And prayed, or I did.

Yes, prayed, "Please, Yahweh, don't let those bastards spot us." Okay, you don't brag about it in the tent afterwards but frankly we all do it at times.

The Amorites were screaming past, loaded about five or six to the chariot, armed with spears and bows and arrows. Micah was right. They paid no attention to us.

But we didn't run, or rather the rest of our army didn't, and soon the Amorites were caught in their own trap. Our flanks had closed in and now a strong group had come across and cut off the Amorite retreat back through the main gates of Jericho. The fray around the Ark seemed to be diminishing. The Amorites were turning back, their chariots battered and their passengers bloodied. It had clearly been a desperate fight around the Ark.

Soon the chariots were returning, ragged this time with their drivers screaming at the horses.

Micah and I were now sitting up. The danger seemed past, but that was a mistake. There was one last chariot, well in the rear of the fleeing Amorites, trotting, not like the others in a frenzy to get back to Jericho. With red wheels. Red wheels! Where had I seen those before? I swore under my breath as the chariot started to turn towards us. They must have seen me move or caught a glimpse of Micah's grand helmet. There we were one last kill before they escaped back into Jericho.

Red wheels, red wheels, of course it was Zemri again! No time for a second look. By the time the chariot was coming towards us, I had my sling out, stone in the pouch, and rotating, picking my target. I had one shot, that's all, and then it would be over. From where I was, with the chariot galloping towards me, one horse's head was more or less aligned with the head of the charioteer behind, so at that double target I let fly. I followed the grey stone as the chariot grew bigger and bigger before me. It glanced off the brass band around the horse's head and ricocheted further to strike the charioteer on the curb chain of his helmet. He buckled over and the chariot came to an immediate halt. It can't have been more than six paces away and I already had another slug whirling when I heard the mocking voice.

"Well," it drawled, "it's our baby-faced slinger again. You do get around."

Unhurriedly he wrestled the unconscious charioteer back into the chariot and took the reins. I knew I should have put my stone into that lean laughing face. At this range, I wouldn't miss but I couldn't. Something held me back. It's like this often in combat, you are in a fight to the death with someone; there is a lull and you just look at each other, and the killing goes out of you. Okay, I found myself weakly apologising to myself, my sling whirling, at least I was ready to kill him if I had to.

That face of his, still laughing, he knew what I was thinking, and turned the chariot away.

"Enough for the day!" he shouted gaily at me over his shoulder, cracked the reins and, urging his horses, galloped off to catch up with his fleeing command. "Coolly done," remarked Micah grimly as, clutching his left arm, he rose on one knee. "But why didn't you kill him?" I mumbled my excuses about how my job was to protect you, Micah et cetera et cetera and if I'd missed Zemri he would have cut us to bits. Micah sniffed, a bit unconvinced. I carefully put my hand under his right shoulder and lifted him up. We looked after Zemri and his chariot force. The main gates were shut but they had broken out through our cordon and we could see them trotting round the walls of Jericho to another entrance.

In front of the gates where we had been standing, the ground was strewn with our dead and wounded, struck down by the showers of arrows. Now the walls of Jericho were lined with archers. They were laughing and jeering while they picked off the wounded down below and anyone who tried to help them.

"Poor devils," Micah commented turning away from the continuing carnage. "There's no helping them. We must leave them for target practice for now. We'll come back at nightfall."

It didn't surprise me that the great man, Mordecai himself, tended to Micah's arm. I suppose it was a bit of a credit to him that, when the fighting started, he hung around and didn't find some excuse, like many others, to belt back to Gilgal. He arrived on a white donkey followed by a minion walking with a small leather trunk on his back.

"You are lucky," he said to Micah after he had gently removed his breastplate and, with a small sharp knife, cut off the leather jerkin at the neck exposing the broken shaft of the arrow. The point was deep in the flesh of his shoulder.

"The arrow has missed the bone," he continued. Micah mumbled something. It obviously still hurt like hell and he looked away from the wound. Mordecai pushed him onto his back and told him to look over his unwounded right shoulder.

"You there, put your arm up in the sky," Mordecai ordered me standing on Micah's right. I raised my arm.

"Now look at his hand, Micah, crane your neck!" Obediently, Micah did so, not of course knowing why. Down on his left Mordecai swiftly placed a stone under the left shoulder. The minion, who had eased the medicine trunk off his shoulder and opened it up, handed him a small hammer with a stumpy circular flat head.

Micah gave a piercing scream and leapt to his feet clutching his shoulder. Mordecai kneeling, leant back, hammer in one hand and the arrow dripping with blood in the other. He was smiling. Micah became silent, then started to complain, but Mordecai cut him short.

"See this barb, Micah," the doctor held the wide sharp barb to his face. He was almost gleeful, gloating, "Can you imagine the pain digging it out with a knife? You were lucky to get me and my hammer." He flicked the broken arrow onto the ground and wiped his hands on a small towel.

"Now I will dress the wound," he announced cheerfully. The minion obediently handed Mordecai ointments in sequence. With each, Mordecai poured a little onto a fresh section of lint and applied it, murmuring as much to himself as to Micah an

140

explanation of what was going on.

"First, we wash the wound." Mordecai cleaned away the blood with the lint which the minion had first dipped in water.

"Now we disinfect it, in case the barb was poisoned." Another dab, a different ointment. Micah looked grey and grim faced.

"And now something for the pain." He poured out some purple ointment. "This will sting," he added, as Micah winced and gave an involuntary groan. Mordecai smiled.

"But now you feel nothing, eh?" Micah just looked ahead. "And finally, we start the process of healing."

I recognised the jar containing the fig ointment. He poured it onto the wound, added some lint and carefully wrapped the bandage.

Then he rose and seemed to hesitate. No, he couldn't, he couldn't just depart like that. He had to remind Micah that he, Mordecai, was after all the chief medical officer of the army and how lucky Micah was to be treated by him.

"Tomorrow, I will come myself," he announced with ceremony, "to see you." And with that he mounted his donkey, waited haughtily for the orderly to pack and shoulder his trunk, and then set off at a smart trot.

A strong detachment, out of arrow shot, remained in front of Jericho in case the defenders made another sally. Elsewhere on the plain and in the broken fields before Jericho, our standards, the flags of the tribes, were being raised and bugles sounded. Men, who had been washed away from their units by the tide of battle, now returned. Then there was the shouting of roll calls, orders to form back into units, and arrangements made to carry back the dead and the wounded, the grim aftermath of any battle.

I spotted the Benjamite standard and pointed it out to Micah who nodded. He was limping. I put an arm under his right shoulder.

Chaggy, always ready for a fight and ever at the front, had been wounded in the leg and was lying on a stretcher. He had done well. Hero of the day, good old Chaggy! When Zemri and his chariots had burst out, Chaggy had rushed two commands over not only to stem the flow but also to prevent the Amorites returning. They, in the city, had panicked and, thinking Chaggy was going to storm the city, closed the gates. But it had really been a bit of a suicide mission for Chaggy's men as the Amorites on the battlements shot arrows directly at close range into their packed ranks.

"We couldn't rescue the wounded," Chaggy dolefully admitted to Micah, who looked over at the carnage in front of the gates. The archers on the wall were still picking off the wounded and shouting with glee as an arrow found its mark. The cries of triumph continued as one by one our wounded soldiers were picked off and lay still, while we looked grimly on.

"And they are ours in the cage. That lost patrol," Chaggy continued. "Hmm," Micah acknowledged and sat down by the stretcher. They talked in low voices.

The war artist would have had a field day. The wind had risen and, sitting there with his easel, he would have painted us with our scarves wrapped around our faces as protection against the sharp dust as we lifted the wounded onto stretchers. In the painting, every man would look dead tired, collapsed by the horror of battle, and absorbed in thoughts of regret for the loss of brothers, cousins or comrades-in-arms. Our brave boys, tired but triumphant and all that; a doleful picture if you like but that is what the public want. But what a load of rot! 'True', everyone was tired. 'True', no one was talking, and for many this had been a first blooding and a bit of a shock. And 'True' again, there may be a bit of sorrow for the loss of Ham, Lam, Sam or whoever, but what we were all really thinking was, "Yippee, I've survived. Yippee, I'm okay. And, yippee, I did all right." Furthermore, there was the feeling of *Yes, of course I'm bloody knackered but, hey, who knows, by the time I get back to camp, I bet I'll be raring for a woman and a skinful of date wine!* Then a long sleep in and the expectation of a lifetime ahead of recounting 'What I did that day'– with, of course, the necessary embellishment – to eager audiences, from rapt young soldiers to eager grandchildren. Obviously with not a mention of when you were shitting yourself in the sand and praying desperately for Yahweh's help.

It was time to go. Micah turned to have one last look back at Jericho. Back at the litter of dead and wounded men, the broken armour and discarded weapons of the killing area where the arrows had first fallen, back at the tall white walls where the archers were still taking pot shots at the wounded, and back at that terrible cage which was beginning to sway and bounce against the walls in the wind. Behind the crossed wooden bars, you could see movement but the men inside were silent, hopes dashed of rescue, and only the prospect of a slow death by thirst, cold or heat exhaustion ahead of them. And they were members of our tribe too.

There, first in the rain-of-arrows killing area and now in front of the gates, the vultures were busy congregating, pecking around for the dead. Once found it was quick work, slicing open the skin with sharp beaks, and tearing out the flesh in long ragged pieces. The birds seemed undeterred by the archers on the battlements who got quickly bored of vulture targets. Perhaps they too were tired of the killing. The thrill was over.

More vultures were flopping and descending into the area. We marched away to the horrible frenetic caw-cawing of the excited birds in our ears.

We brought up the rear of the Benjamites, alongside Chagai on his stretcher. I was carrying Micah's breastplate and helmet and he leaned on my shoulder, quite weak from loss of blood. There was no sign of his chariot or his driver; he had probably been killed in the Amorite sally or, dragged by the maddened horses, cut into a thousand pieces by the sharp rocks of the rough plain.

"Poor fellow," Micah mused kindly, and frowned with genuine sorrow.

Well, that was alright for Micah but my immediate thoughts were how I was going to make the most of all this. Here I was lugging along the senior commander of my tribe, and, arguably, I'd saved his life not once but twice today. First, I had humped him away from that killing area; maybe a calculated act of self-preservation but it still looked good, indeed, another perfect pic for the war artist! And then, my Micah lifesaving act number two, I'd seen off the Amorite general just when he seemed particularly keen to pigstick a senior Israelite before leaving the field. All good stuff but what next? Oh yes, I could just see what would happen; we'd arrive back in camp and he would be surrounded by flunkeys and I would be shooed off, like some inconvenient insect, back to Seth and tent life.

I was still chewing all this over when, about halfway back to Gilgal, a chariot, scattering dust, galloped up and halted in front of Micah and me. The driver raised his hand to his brow, saluting.

"Orders from Joshua, sir. You are to report forthwith." And he wheeled the chariot round.

Well, I could just as well have helped Micah over to the chariot, helped him up onto the platform, helped him grab a handle with his right arm, and that could have been that. Off they would go and I would have been left to join the marching column. But no, that's not what happened, and it all went seamlessly. I helped Micah over to the chariot and then I jumped up on board! I then helped pull him up – mouthing expressions of concern – took his right hand to grip the wicker handle of the chariot, and swung my body round like a gate at the back of the chariot. Yes, the place of a good chariot boy!

"All ready, sir!" I cried rather officiously. I heard the charioteer complain, "I need to pick up another commander," but Micah ignored him with a pleasant enough, "Drive on, please!" The chariot started forward again and Micah looked over his shoulder at me with a smile. As much as to say, "Smartly done, lad." Or was the smile a touch sardonic, a touch wary, and saying, "More cool work, Ehud, eh?" I wasn't sure. *Perhaps he is getting the measure of me,* I thought, *and perhaps that is still, okay?* Anyway, I looked past him stony-faced. You don't wink back at senior commanders.

Half an hour later we were outside Joshua's great tent. I helped Micah down from the chariot and, supporting him, he limped into the assembly. I took the precaution to wrap part of my scarf around my face; I didn't want someone pointing the finger at me and saying, "What, you again?"

Chapter 10

Most of the generals were there in the middle milling around or seated. They clearly had had mixed experiences. Some were pristine in their armour, others showed all the signs of having been in the heat of combat. Amram clearly had. He was covered in dust and, while there was no sign of a wound, he had blood on his face and his breastplate had a huge dent. And, of course, his arm was in a sling. Joshua sat in the middle, cool and detached as ever. He had just finished washing his hands and a boy was handing him a towel. He looked over and welcomed Micah, raising his arm in salutation.

"Great deeds by your tribe today," he started. "But how is Chagai? I hear he's wounded. And you too?"

But he did not wait for a reply. "Pray, be seated," he finished. That was Joshua all over, a bit of conventional small talk and then smartly to business. I lurched over with Micah to a long sofa, and lowered him.

This was, I suppose, the moment for me to bow and scrape and exit left but that voice again rang in my ears, "Stick around, boy, stick around!" I obediently dropped back behind the sofa and sat cross-legged in the dust. Not, of course, on the rug! Play the humble and which commander will stoop to draw attention to a mere foot soldier humbly sitting by his master? Well, Amram for one but I was careful to keep out of his line of sight, and fix my scarf more firmly around my face.

I'm not sure what I was expecting. Somehow I thought that each commander would be asked to speak and we would be regaled with the great and noble deeds of his tribe that day. But no, Joshua nodded at Amram, Amram who could always be relied on to tell things as they are. Which he did, standing up so he could look over at all possible culprits. He started by laying into our gullibility over the release of prisoners, our folly at following the Amorite instructions, while Joshua, clearly the target of these accusations, just nodded. Then he got going on the other commanders. He laid into the failure to control the troops when the cage dropped over the wall, and he laid into the chaos which ensued, the headlong flight by some, the frozen inaction of others. No one escaped, not even the Benjamites, and that grudgingly.

"It could have been a complete disaster for the army had it not been for Chagai" – he paused – "Dear old Chaggy…" he continued slowly and with a certain irony, then paused while the other commanders allowed themselves to join in the joke of hearing his pet name. Dear old Chaggy, indeed. Everyone knew Chaggy. Amram continued, "…with his brave band of Benjamites. Rushing to stop the Amorite charge."

We were all expecting more but he sat down He had finished, but all the commanders knew that his post mortem had only begun. He had a list as long as his arm, and there would be roastings, demotions, and whippings galore before he would consider today's work finished. But perhaps promotions for some, I smiled to myself.

"Thank you, Amram." Joshua nodded his approval almost as if he had just been given a nice cup of tea rather than a pretty damning critique of his own leadership and the conduct of his army. "Now we have two urgent items on our agenda. The first is the recovery of our dead and wounded in front of Jericho and that, of course, must be done tonight, and the second is the rescue of the prisoners in the cage."

Micah stirred uncomfortably. "I propose we, that is my tribe, rescue our wounded and recover our dead in front of Jericho. Arrangements are already in place," he said flatly. That broke my little reverie. *The old fool can't be wanting to go out again,* I thought. *That'll mean me as well! And fat chance of anyone still being alive. This is just a 'straw bag and recovery' job.* Micah went on, "And we will also try and communicate with the men in the cage. See if we can come up with a rescue plan. They are from our lost patrol, let the other tribes recover those others in the killing ground," he added.

Joshua nodded. "And you will go yourself?" he asked, clearly a touch surprised at this offer from his battered and bloodied commander.

"I have been treated by your physician, sir, and my arm is in no danger. My leg is merely a bit sore. We leave in two hours."

Damn, damn, damn! I suppose he fixed all this up with Chaggy. There wasn't much more chat. Soon I was helping Micah to his feet and, with him leaning on me, I led him from the tent.

Outside there was a brown donkey held by – no

149

surprise here – my old friend, Scornful-face, but this time all smiles and welcoming back the master. He then stepped forward and nodded at me dismissively.

"Get out of my way," he seemed to be saying. "Back to your tent, creep.

Micah is mine!"

But I didn't budge. Why should I having come this far? I clung to Micah's arm. Yes, I reckoned, being a chariot boy was just the step up the ladder I was looking for. Okay, this little extra outing tonight was a bore but Micah, whatever Dad thought of him, seemed a genial enough chap and, as part of his household, I was in for better food, better accommodation and better care if I got sick. And, it was always said, there were other perks. No, I was not letting go.

Micah had obviously been expecting all this.

"Thanks, Barak, but Ehud has saved my life twice today. So he's replacing you and I'm posting you back for general service. You can take Ehud's place back in a tent," said Micah without any signs of distress in his voice. "You can pick up your things now."

Barak was about to speak, but Micah just looked at him and he stopped, looking furious. *Not a good loser, our friend,* I thought. *Just the time to rub his nose in it!*

"Hold the donkey still, please," I commanded him blithely – fury and astonishment on his face in equal measure – "while I help the general mount."

We weaved slowly up the hill, Barak leading the donkey bearing Micah with me walking alongside. Already the better housing had been taken over by the senior commanders and extended with tentage.

Micah's new house was a mixture of old adobe walls with straw roofs and tented walls and roofs.

I helped Micah off the donkey and Barak, exuding sulkiness, stalked forward and raised flap of the tent. I helped Micah through the entrance and glanced at him.

"Shithead, I'll get you yet," he snarled in my ear.

"Welcome, master." A tall very dark man with a heavy nose and moustaches bowed to Micah within. He wore a long white tunic and a heavy gold chain around his neck. Behind him was a servant in a white tunic with a belt of multicoloured cotton. He beckoned him forward.

"We will take over now," he announced, quite gently, taking me by the arm while the other man took my place. He led Micah over to the cushions against the wall and slowly eased him down. Micah gave out a sigh. More servants appeared bringing bowls of water and refreshment, lots of fussing over the return of the master. A woman, dressed in a tightfitting red and yellow shiny material– okay, but I had never seen silk before – watched on from the side. It was difficult to tell the expression on her face. At first, it looked immobile and unsmiling, but then I could see that she was heavily made-up, and kohl, smeared darkly around her eyes, made her face into a kind of mask with expressionless olive-shaped eye holes.

I stepped back to where Barak was standing in the entrance and stood there uncomfortably. *The woman looked over at us, or rather not at me but at Barak*, I thought. I got the feeling that there was a brief communication between them. I looked round at his face but there was nothing except his usual impassive sneer. *Ho, ho*, I thought to myself, *I wonder if there is a story here,* as I began to take in my new surroundings.

I have lived in tents all my life. They have always been the same with the same old walls and roofing of goatskin, and the same old tent poles, rough sticks of acacia or anything else strong enough, supporting the heavy goatskin. Yes goatskin, black goatskin, great for keeping an interior dry, and cool in summer and warm in winter. Sheepskin just does not do, nor camel, it has to be goat. Then inside, one big room with rough matting on the floor for sitting about and sleeping on and, through a flap into another room, a kitchen area where food was stored and prepared for the cooking outside. All simple, dead simple.

But this, Micah's house was something different. There was a woven coloured rug on the sandy floor and the walls, instead of being bare goatskin, were draped in different coloured material. Then the tent posts were actually thick, smooth and fluted, painted in gold and red. Around the floor were cushions of many colours, with golden tassels.

I mean, in my time and later on in my long life, I have been in Assyrian palaces, villas on the Euphrates and whatever, all a hundred times grander than this, but nothing has ever made the same big initial impact as Micah's house in Gilgal.

Barak interrupted my thoughts with a curt 'Follow me' and led off out of the big room with the golden pillars into a warren of passages thronging with servants. Eventually he stopped and raised a flap of goatskin. I followed him in. "Here," he said with mock graciousness. "This is yours. All to yourself. Quite a boudoir!" And he laughed. But he was right. Okay, it was a small room, but huge compared with the bedspace in my tent, with a broad straw palliase lying on a thick coloured floor covering of rough wool.

Well, I was just standing there looking around, not really wondering what next, when His Nibs suddenly steps forward and slowly lowers himself onto that palliase, rolls over on his back, folds his hands behind his head and closes his eyes. Just like that.

Now, I'm not cool but at least I know I'm not cool. Okay, sometimes I can act cool but most of the time I am pretty frantic, my mind working 100% and chasing all over the place. I get by in my way, but that does not mean to say I do not admire other people being cool. Yes, I do, but not when it's at my expense, no way! Then I hate it, and it just makes me see red.

I remember grinding my teeth and thinking to myself, or did I say it out loud? "Well done, Barak, you've done it now."

I was blind furious, I don't even know I knew what I was going to do! But I found myself striding over to a pile of weapons, clothing, and bits of armour in the corner. Then I saw it, that smart deadly spear of his. I grabbed it and moved to the end of the palliase, and looked down on Barak still with that sneer, pretending or actually asleep, the cool bastard. His long body stretched out on the broad straw with his legs slightly open, an uneven bulge prominent under his neat white tunic. I raised the spear up above my head, and hesitated. Not the flicker of an eyelid from the figure before me. Gritting my teeth I brought the spear down with all my force.

The spear must have missed his groin by a couple of inches, as of course I intended, but, oh joy, did it give Mr Cool a shock. He sat bolt upright with a gasp, and I saw a flash of fear in his astonished eyes. I gave the spear a wrench and out it came, pieces of straw and cloth snagged on its shiny barbs. He gasped again and looked down at a spreading stain of blood around the jagged tear in his tunic. I just stood with the spear over my shoulder, breathing heavily.

Barak looked down at the bloody tear and pulled up the tunic. High up on the inside of his thigh the flesh was broken and bloodstained. It had probably been done by a barb as I pulled the spear out. He lowered his tunic and looked up at me, still shaking with fury and now glowering.

To give him his due Barak recovered quickly. Once again, he lay back on the palliase but this time resting on his elbows and looking up at me – still with that hateful smile. Then he raised his hand towards me. I couldn't think what to do. Did he want me to help him up, the bastard? I boiled again. I just wanted to bring the spearhead crashing down but into his face this time. He must have read my mind, perhaps he was a bit frightened as well, but he just shook his hand again towards me, and I understood. I found myself putting my hand forward and taking his. He clenched it slightly, then let go, and rolled off the palliase. He stood up, pointed at the bloodstain on his front and opened his palms towards me.

"No harm done, just a cut on my leg and a torn tunic," he announced without rancour. "And good shooting, I'll say!" He chuckled. "Luckily for me!" Then he paused and looked at me quizzically. "I'll say Micah has certainly got one here," he said slowly. "Quite a one for surprises!"

I lowered the spear. I knew I was still quivering. I knew my face was still contorted with fury. Not cool at all but I could not help it. But 'Cool' wasn't the winner this merry time!

Barak knelt down by the pile of things in the corner where I had grabbed the spear, and picked up an empty leather bag. He started to go through his possessions putting some in the bag and discarding others. They were mostly bits of clothing and armour but there were also daggers, belts, sandals, some embossed with jewels.

"A bit surprised, are you?" he said lightly. "A chariot boy with all this kit? Oh, there's plenty of it around here for grabs before it gets down to the chaps in the tents. When the loot comes in, just make sure you get in first and fast," he said, shaking the bag.

He picked up a brooch the size of a hand, set with jewels.

"Not all loot," he said tilting the brooch so jewels glinted and sparkled. "Sometimes presents..." He stopped with a snort, looked quickly at me, tossed the brooch briefly in his hand and thrust it into the bag. *Something to tell but not telling, eh, Barak my new friend,* I thought.

He now picked up a short dagger. The hilt was ebony embossed with silver and it had a smooth silver scabbard attached to a small linen belt. He drew the dagger. It had a short blade. He felt the tip and then put it back in the scabbard.

"Here, have this! A peace offering!" He proffered the dagger. "The prize, if you like." And he laughed.

I took it. I had never seen a weapon for killing so elaborate or even beautiful. Back in the tents weapons were crude, heavy for smashing, pointed for piercing, sharp for slashing and all requiring a lot of brute strength. This little dagger looked an easy little killer, and killer it certainly was, with a blade sharp on each side and a needlepoint tip.

"You see there's a belt there, so you can wrap it around your leg." And he pointed to his thigh.

"Oh," he then said raising his eyebrows. "Of course, you are left-handed. Better still, you will be wearing it around your left leg. Less likely for anyone to look if it comes to searching."

He stood up and took the spear from my hand.

"I guess I'll need this again if I'm back in the tents for a bit," he said, as he picked the strands of straw and linen from the barb, and polished it on the edge of his tunic.

"We'll do a swap of bedding," he continued, looking down at his finely woven multi-coloured woollen blanket and slinging his bag over his shoulder. "Let's go." I had been wondering about that blanket, and how it would have gone down in the tent. The swap suited me. I didn't want Micah's servants laughing at my coarse and threadbare stuff.

"First, some business," said he gaily, as we headed, not towards the lines where I lived, but into the administrative area, the tail of the army which followed us about wherever we went. Accumulating daily the longer we stayed – shops, eateries, laundries, tailors, brothels – they were all there and that was where we spent our pay when we had the chance.

We pushed our way through the crowds, mainly soldiers like myself getting away from the monotony of life in the tents.

"What are we looking for?" I asked.

"My banker," he replied shortly, and then looked at me. I was bemused, I didn't know what a banker was.

"Come on, what do you do with your pay?" He went on. "Don't tell me, you just spend it here as quickly as it comes in? Fine, it doesn't go far, does it? But what would you do if some real loot came your way? Swap it at one of the shops, for a tunic, for a woman? You'd be diddled all the way."

I had sometimes thought about that. Of course, like all the others I dreamt of searching a corpse and finding a bag of gold or some precious jewels and what I would do. And then hard reality would kick in.

"The rules are pretty clear," I replied lamely. "Anything valuable has to be handed in to the priests

157

under pain of death."

Barak scoffed. "Good old Joshua. He is a great one for these pronouncements but who obeys them? You've seen Micah's tent. That's mostly booty and no one is chasing him. Okay, for appearances he gives something to the priests, enough to keep them happy or rather their mouths shut, but the rest he keeps. Everyone in that position does the same."

He kicked the sand, and continued. "Because when they get into the Promised Land, when they get given vineyards and fields, the bosses will be those with silver and gold, not with iron and bronze," said he with finality.

"Well," I said, a bit shocked by what he had said and unready to yet accept that reality. "They did stone that guy the other day. What had he kept, a measly silver bowl?"

"Of course, and that was Amram's work. He has to make an example now and then to keep Joshua happy. But come on, what would you do if a bag of silver came your way? Keep it with your kit and 30 pairs of eyes watching your every move?" He laughed derisively. "Bury it under a tree out in the desert?" He waved his hand at the surrounding low rocky foothills. "Hope to come back here in a year and find it?" He laughed and shook his head as we stopped by a tent behind a low wall. The entrance was blocked by two big black Nubians with huge swords.

Barak spoke sharply. His voice was surprisingly loud. "I've come see Rameses. My name is Barak."

The Nubians looked back and down at him without

expression. Seconds passed, then a voice from within, refined and lazy, called, "Ah, indeed, indeed! Let him in, let him in." The Nubian raised the flap of the tent for Barak and me to enter.

From the scorching whiteness of the outside, the interior of the tent appeared at first pitch black except for a single bronze lamp. The dark figure of a man stood in front and, in a heavily accented voice, ordered;

"Take off your belts and raise your arms."

"Just do as he says," muttered Barak. I saw the dark hands run down his body from shoulder to knee. I took off my belt and dagger and then it was my turn. The hands slowly descended from my shoulder, and then ran slowly down my thighs before reversing and rising up into my crotch. *No shortcuts with this gent,* I thought, *he would have found any knife strapped to my thigh.*

The bodyguard called through in a strange language, then lifted another flap and lead us into a large chamber lit by lanterns. I found I was treading on a richly coloured carpet and the walls were covered with cloth panels illustrated with flowers. By the steady light, I could just discern three or four figures sitting on the carpet facing a very fat man, cross-legged on cushions. He waved his hand as we entered, and said something softly but commanding, not in a language I knew. The figures on the ground scuttled off like rats disturbed at the feast, and disappeared behind him.

"Sit down, sit down." The fat man beckoned us in front of him. The bodyguard sat down, facing us, in the front and a bit to one side. Now we could see our host properly. He was a huge man, naked and glistening to the waist and wearing an Egyptian-style white pleated skirt with thick golden bands. He put our belts in a heap in front of him and then drew a short heavy double-bladed dagger and held it in his hand across his legs. *Takes no risks, our Fatty,* I was thinking.

He clapped his hands. A boy, also dressed in the same Egyptian skirt appeared. He didn't look more than sixteen. Rameses spoke to him quickly and, as the boy bowed and turned away, explained;

"You are indeed fortunate. My friends have just bought me very fine wine and cake." He finished with a little laugh.

I looked at him carefully. He was certainly very fat and had a great wide head with eyes, small black and twinkling set deep behind a heavy nose and flat forehead. His hands were almost white, and in contrast to his overall appearance, the fingers were long and sinewy and with plain gold and silver rings. He smiled and laughed as he talked, his head and shoulders rolling from side to side. *All that ha, ha, ha stuff, jollity with a menace,* I thought.

And now he turned towards me. "They call me Rameses. That is a name for the rulers of Egypt. As I am Egyptian it is their little joke." He sniggered and I kind of managed to smile back. "But now," he continued, "Barak, who is your new friend?"

He continued to look at me, still smiling, still with twinkling eyes but I felt I was being subjected to a very cool appraisal. He saw the soldier's rough and ragged tunic, the bare feet, and his glance lingered on the dark scar on my nearly bald head.

The boy appeared from behind and put down a large bronze tray in front of us. On it, all matching and highly ornamented with flecks of coloured stone and with narrow gold rims, was a jug, three little pots and a plate of square yellow cakes.

The boy started to pour. "This is pomegranate wine." Rameses leant forward and whispered conspiratorially. "It comes from Jericho, the very best!" "He, he, he," he giggled. "Drink, my friends," he ordered, raising a cup to his lips, then smacking his lips in appreciation. I took a cautious sip. Ugh, it was bitter, not like the stuff I've had before mixed with a bit of honey, all nice and sweet. He must have seen the involuntary expression of disgust on my face.

"Ah, take a cake. They are sweet." Said he with emphasis and gesticulated towards the cakes. I picked one up and took a suspicious bite. It was delicious, crisp and with a strong nutty taste.

"You taste the fenugreek." He did not seem to expect an answer. "Ah, but where were we?" he said, taking another sip of his disgusting wine. "Yes, Barak, your friend?"

Barak replied with nonchalance, "This is Ehud. He is Micah's new camel boy." Then he laughed and went on, "But you know about him, Rameses, you know everything. That's your job, you old spy!"

"Indeed, indeed." Sighed Rameses with mock diffidence. "People do tell me things, but it is good to put a face to a name." He looked back at me. So I was something, in spite of appearances. He continued, "Yes, you bested General Zemri. He speaks highly of you." He leant forward and put his hand on my knee. I recoiled slightly. "There is no higher praise," he murmured at me directly.

"But now, as we do in Egypt, first the news, then the business," said he, settling back on the huge gold fringed cushions. "Tell me, what news do you have?"

Barak told him shortly of the events of the day, of the cage of prisoners and the fighting in front of Jericho. Rameses nodded away. One suspected that he had already had a version of events from earlier visitors.

"There will be rich pickings in Jericho one day." He hesitated. "Your generals are confident that they can storm Jericho? I mean, apart from Joshua?"

We both laughed. Barak turned to me. "You know how the vultures follow us around? They know eventually they'll get a good feed. Rameses is the same. He wouldn't be here, amid all the discomforts of camp life," Barak gesticulated mockingly at the rich surroundings, "unless he was pretty certain that Jericho would soon be ours and a good percentage of the gold, silver and precious stones would pass through his fingers."

Rameses laughed off Barak's mockery. "And do you have anything for my fingers today?" he asked politely.

Barak opened the string on his bag and took out the heavy silver brooch with the glittery gems, handing it to Rameses.

"Lovely, lovely," said he rubbing his hands over the gemstones and the silver. "But now, a little test, a test of honesty."

He picked up a piece of slate and scraped it along the edge of the silver brooch. It left a whitish scar on the dark stone. "And now, let us see how it compares with pure silver." He looked at his left hand and took the three silver rings off his third finger. He selected one, and scraped it. The colour was slightly different, slightly greyer.

"So this is not pure silver. It must be…"

"Oh, come on, Rameses," broke in Barak. "That's enough conjuring tricks for the day. You know what purity of silver this is without all the rigmarole. Consider Ehud impressed, and get on with it!"

Rameses didn't seem at all perturbed at being called out. He simply shuffled the rings back on his finger and announced, "The silver is 90% pure. The stones? The orange is Carnelian, and the red, ruby." He held up the brooch. "See it smokes!" The light caught smoky wavy lines seemingly moving through the rich redness of the stone. "The green one is, of course, emerald, my favourite." He put the brooch down in front of him. "This was made for a Philistine noblewoman in Ashkelon. I know the jeweller."

I was longing for Rameses to ask Barak how he had got this valuable brooch, but that didn't seem to worry Rameses at all. I was beginning to cotton on; this was a no questions asked, none given business. He drew out a notebook, and consulted some figures.

"You are on 'Generals rates', of course," he

murmured reassuringly at Barak. "Which means Tops!" Barak said, looking over at me, then back at Rameses,

"And that'll do for my friend too when the time comes."

Barak turned to me. "Come in here from the tents, you don't have a chance. There will be a great show of expertise and care, then Rameses will pronounce your silver is polished iron and your lapis lazuli simple glass. He will then, with great grace, grant you the favour of taking it off your hands for a few farthings. And no pomegranate wine either. Or cakes that matter."

With that Barak picked up another piece of the cake while Rameses simply announced, "At General's rates, I value this brooch at three shekels of silver, which I will add to your account." He dug into his folds and brought out a small silver coin and held it up to me. "An Egyptian silver shekel, not one of your local shekels of tin," he said with a knowing smile.

"Your friend is a sensible man," he continued addressing me. "He brings me valuable objects which he has no use for. I convert them into silver which I hold in safekeeping for him for when there is peace. Then, he will be a rich man!" Rameses declared triumphantly.

I said nothing. He must have sensed my mistrust.

"Trust, yes, you must have trust in this world, and Barak knows he can trust me! And I can do the same for you."

He flicked his fingers and the boy appeared with

another tray. On it was a book, a pen and an ink stand. He opened the book and started a new page. Taking the pen and dipping it in the black ink he wrote my name, then looked at me, and put a stroke beside it.

"There! You see! I have started an account for you. And I have given you one silver shekel as an opening present!" he announced beaming. I looked back in amazement. What a showman! He has just got himself a new client, a mere chariot boy at Micah's. Big thing? But I could almost see him shrugging his shoulders as if to say, some risks pay off some don't, we'll see!

The serving boy came in and whispered in Rameses' ear. He turned to us. "This is a busy day and I'm afraid that I have more visitors. It has been a pleasure to see you again, Barak, and…" – this he said in long measured tones – "to meet your new friend. But now you must leave. By the back entrance. Please follow my servant."

Out in the hot white sun and in the tangle of tents behind Rameses' quarters Barak put his hands on his hips and burst out laughing.

"Well, there you are, Ehud, I am your new best friend and I have put you on the path to fortune! You've got yourself a month's pay by sitting still and keeping your mouth shut."

"And you trust him?" was all I could stammer back. Barak sniffed contemptuously, "Of course, we can," he said and fell silent. Then he continued in his silkiest voice, "Rameses used to have a competitor, another Egyptian. I never knew what his real name was but we called him Amen after Amenenap, another pharaoh name. He was doing very well. Everyone high-up used him, priests, generals, the lot. Like Rameses, they gave him things. He put them in a big box, and he gave them credit in shekels. But one day, he decided to make a bolt for it. His timing was good. We were moving camp so his disappearance wasn't noticed for several days. No one knew exactly where he had gone, whether he was heading for Egypt over the desert or making for the coast and catching a boat. So Joshua sent out half a dozen strong donkey patrols. The Reubs were ordered to check the route to the coast, probably the most dangerous since that was through enemy territory. Anyway, the Reubs struck it lucky and caught up with Amen after a couple of days. So it all ended happily!" Barak finished breezily.

"You mean…" I started.

"I mean," continued Barak, clearly welcoming my little prompt, "that they escorted Amen's little gang – or most of them anyway – and his big black box back to camp and old Rameses was appointed the new guardian."

"And Amen?" I asked.

"Oh, they buried him and his close henchmen. Buried them alive, of course, and cut off Amen's little finger with his gold rings and sold it to Rameses just like that, dried blood and everything. To make a point! So Rameses knows what's in store for him if he starts playing funny. And he is under 24-hour guard. Those big oafs at the front of his tent are not just for his protection."

We walked back to my old tent to find Seth being

his energetic self, bossing people around.

"He's your tent commander, is he? Seth? I know him of old. He's frightened of me! You see!" Barrack murmured to me.

Seth came bounding up. "You, Ehud, where have you been? I'm having an inspection in ten minutes. Cut about!" Then he turned his attention to Barak. "And who are you?" he asked rudely, then looked a bit sheep-faced. "Oh, it's you, Barak." He stopped, not sure what further to say.

"Yes, it's me again, Seth, I'm to join you. For a short time only, you'll be glad to hear." Barak announced casually, looking around the tent. "I'll have the empty bed space over there." This was over at the back of the tent where it was less dusty.

Seth just stood there. I had never seen anyone treat Seth like that. I explained that I had become Micah's new chariot boy and was now living in his quarters. Seth nodded without interest, watching Barak sauntering over to the corner and dropping his bag on the empty mat. "He's a bad one, that Barak," Seth muttered through clenched teeth. Those were pretty much my suspicions as well.

Chapter 11

Tubal was there when I got back.

"Go up to Joshua's stables and get a good donkey for Micah. He doesn't want a chariot. Too bumpy, he says. And just one donkey, you'll be walking this time, chariot boy." *Thanks, Tubal, I thought, you said that almost gleefully.*

Joshua's stables, as they were rather grandly referred to, were the huge open- air lines of tethered animals to the east of the camp, so their stink blew away from us in the normally prevailing westerly wind. And did they stink! And the noise too of all that neighing and braying! There were short lines of horses for the chariots, and long lines of donkeys for everything else. There must have been nearly five hundred, and Joshua was very proud of his stables. The horses, all captured from the Canaanites, were used for pulling chariots because they were fast and willing and, in those days, their backs were not strong enough to carry a man. And they were delicate. Thinking back being a horse was a pretty good life in those days, well-watered and well fed and cared for. Not like the poor old donkeys which got nothing but beatings and the worst of the forage. Yet they did all the hard work. Every day you could see convoys of pack donkeys bringing up supplies. Their busiest time was when the camp moved. Then there would be a long procession of donkeys bearing heavy loads escorted by mounted drivers and long strings of families; the women riding and chattering with children scampering behind, and a great parade of whores travelling in brightly coloured and curtained boxes suspended on poles strapped to four donkeys. Five to a rocking box, they always got a cheer from us as they passed. The girls would respond, coyly pushing aside the curtains and waving their handkerchiefs, gold bangles and whitened teeth glinting.

"And what may you be doing here, my lad?" called out a cheerful faced man, lazily flapping a fly whisk and sitting in a small grove of palm trees near the stables. I immediately recognised that singsong voice as something peculiar to the Tribe of Dan, our close cousins and therefore allies. *He would be helpful,* I thought.

"I've come from Micah," I said, entering under the grove and crouching down in front of him. It is always a good idea, I have found, to get down to the level of the person from whom you are wanting a favour. Lower if you can!

"He wants a donkey for tonight. It's got to be steady since he can only use one arm," I went on.

He was looking at my head.

"That's a nasty crack you've had. Something you got today in front of Jericho?" he said.

I mumbled something about the earthquake.

"Oh yes, that was something. Think what it was like up here with five hundred terrified animals! Some of them broke away and ran off into the hills. They only came back when they got hungry." He laughed shortly;

"But now, your business! What's your name, lad?"
I told him and he paused, then whistled.

"You are the lad who put a slug into the knackers of that loudmouth." He mused, continuing to flap his fly whisk. "And you are now with Micah." Another pause, then, "Well…." He rose to his feet and put out his hand. "Grace and peace be upon you. I'm Shem, assistant Head of Stables. Let's see what we can do for you while the boss is away."

We started to walk towards the lines.

"Why a donkey?" he asked. I simply told him that's what Micah asked for. "I'll give you a mule, a Philistine mule. You can't do better than that." We walked over to a small group of animals, a bit taller than the donkeys and with longer thinner ears. A small man appeared from amid the grazing animals and Shem addressed him in Amorite, ordering him to saddle a mule for a top commander.

"Yes," said he, and in a quiet aside, "give me a mule any time over a donkey. Surefooted, stronger, faster. And not so bloody obstinate! Like the best kind of women, if they existed!" He chortled.

"Mind, I want the animal back as soon as you finish with it," Shem called after me as I walked away with a fully saddled tall brown mule twenty minutes later. "There'll be hell to pay if he's not there for the morning roll call!"

Back at Micah's tent Tubal emerged, and looked over rather crossly, shading his eyes and squinting at the animal. Then he fetched Micah.

"What's this you've got here? I said a donkey, that

looks more like a horse." Micah was not pleased.

I was about to mumble something when I thought, *Hold on, how would Barak have handled this?* And out it came.

"This is a fine Philistine mule, sir," I spoke up with confidence, then paused. "Much better than a donkey. Strong, surefooted, and faster." I found myself glibly reeling off Shem's description, adding finally, "and less obstinate. He will be perfect for you, sir," I finished triumphantly. I could just see Barak's sardonic smile.

"Will he, will he?" Micah murmured limping around and scrutinising the animal, which simply stood there ignoring us both.

"Yes, I got him from Joshua's Head of Stables. He promised the best!"

I wasn't sure if I was overdoing it a bit so stopped there. The important thing was to get over to Micah that I was more than just handy with a sling. I might not be Barak but I was catching up fast! Micah nodded. That was approval! Thank you, Barak. I may not trust you further than I can spit back but you are a good teacher.

*****

"So you are off, Micah?" It was hardly a question, more a statement from Joshua. He was lying propped up on his elbow dictating to a small boy sitting cross-legged in front of him in the bustling command tent.

Micah, back again in his black leather breastplate

but his left arm in a sling, stood in the doorway. I hung back. My role as chariot boy so far had been to help Micah back painfully into his armour, strap a sword to his waist, and give him something to lean on for the walk to the command tent. But once there he brushed me off and was now standing alone in the entrance in front of Joshua, his wounded arm tucked into his belt for support.

"Mordecai and his staff will accompany you to treat the wounded," announced Joshua rather grandly.

A harsh voice interrupted, "What's left of them, that is!" There was sniggering from a group whence the nasal comment had arisen. The look on Joshua's face changed from concern to a glance of sheer fury. In the abrupt silence which followed, Joshua under control again, said slowly,

"We tend our wounded and we bury our dead!" Then he nodded back towards Micah. "And we want their armour and weapons," he added. *Ever the old practical Joshua*, I thought.

Micah raised his hand as a salute and turned away. I sidled up alongside and, putting his arm over my shoulder, he limped off.

*****

It must have been about an hour before darkness. Already the western sky was ablaze with red and orange and the hot white and blinding yellow of the afternoon landscape was now swathed in pink. It was cooler and there was a slight breeze from the south.

Micah was now mounted on the mule.

Jubal, the commander of the Benjamite troops, reported to Micah who gave the order to move. We set off up the broad flat watercourse once again towards Jericho. Leading was one tent group of 30 men, then Micah on his mule with Jubal and me beside him, followed by the other two tent groups and a score of carts pulled by donkeys to carry back the dead and wounded. Amongst this last group were medical orderlies. The slow screeching of the heavy wheels eerily filled the night air.

Mordecai on a donkey trotted up and slowed to a walk by Micah, with me walking alongside. He seemed to be rather agitated.

"What's the matter, Mordecai?" Micah asked.

"You've got one of Joshua's mules!" he exclaimed angrily.

Micah gave a sideways glance at Mordecai's donkey, smaller by a full hand than his mule. *Ugh,* I thought, *I'm caught between two senior officers fighting over toys.*

It's something which has never ceased to amaze me that guys involved in serious policy making and operational decisions can get side-tracked by toys. I reckon it's all to do with winning. Being one up, you know! The largest army, the shiniest sword, the best woman, it's all one and the same! Anyway, I just hoped I wouldn't be involved but I needn't have worried. I think Micah secretly craved a tussle with Mordecai.

"He's very quiet, very surefooted," Micah responded breezily, as if he had just been congratulated on something. "Fast too, I'm told. Not like that bumpy little thing you've got there! Yes," he said, rubbing the hand holding the reins along the mane of the mule. "A very comfortable ride for a wounded man like me. Very considerate of Joshua."

That will stop him, I thought, I'll bet Mordecai was preparing to raise hell in the stables the next day, but he would not want to challenge any decision made by Joshua. He wheeled round and trotted back to his ambulances at the rear. Micah smiled, face straight ahead.

An hour later we emerged out onto the plain in front of Jericho. From the city, there came the sounds of revelry. It was dark now with no moon. The great battlemented walls were black and sharply delineated against a deep blue sky set with twinkling stars.

We heard a soft challenge up ahead and the column halted. Micah kept his mule walking, with me and Jubal following. There we met the commander of the Benjamites who we had left behind to watch Jericho. Micah dismounted, leaning on my shoulder. Then our small group set off slowly in the direction of the main gates, picking our way across the fields which a month ago had been waving with wheat. They were now flat, stubbly, and sharp even for my hardened feet.

We stopped about three hundred yards from the main gates. Even at that distance they loomed huge and threatening. On the battlements, there were lanterns lit at intervals. We could just discern the occasional sentry in the square openings along the parapet. *Normal guard roster,* I thought, *unless they're lying in wait for us.* There were signs of music and laughter from within. Nearer to us, the only sound we could hear was the rasping of that terrible cage against the wall in the light wind. Inside the cage all was silent.

I shaded my eyes against the illumination from behind the battlements and focused on the dark area in front of the gates. Gradually I began to discern darker lumps and strange shapes against the rough soil.

"Ahh!" I gave an involuntary cry. Micah and Jubal looked sharply at me. "There's movement," I said. "They aren't all dead. They're moving around." And, really, I thought one moment it was my imagination but no, the dark lumps were moving, slowly, criss-crossing and pausing.

Micah and Jubal shaded their eyes. Mordecai arrived and dismounted.

"Our sharp-eyed country boy sees movement. You have a look," greeted Micah. Mordecai knelt down and pulled a small pouch from his garment. I watched him take out a small glass object, the size of a silver shekel, and put it to his eye. He was very silent, moving his head slowly from left to right.

"Vultures," he pronounced, passing the glass to Micah. "They are gorged. Too gorged to fly." He paused. "It won't be nice out there." He added almost conversationally, and suddenly the air seemed to grow very cold. Or perhaps it didn't but I shivered all the same.

Micah, the glass still to his eye, nodded in the darkness. "We'll have to drive them away first." He looked at Jubal. "I hope your men have got strong stomachs!"

Like all good plans it was pretty simple. First, the vultures had to be shooed away from the bodies. Mordecai assured Jubal that they wouldn't be any trouble. "Just go in, herd them, shoo them, poke them with the blunt end of your spears."

Jubal looked doubtful. He knew what those pointed beaks could do. Mordecai said softly, "They don't want a fight. They're stuffed with food. They'll just waddle off and wait for more pickings in the morning."

The first wave of soldiers went forward, in a line, slowly, tongues clicking, tapping the ground gently with the blunt end of their spears. I could see the dark shapes of the vultures retreating with a heaving of wings before this quietly advancing line.

"Go, Jubal!" ordered Micah when he saw the area was clear. Jubal waved his arm in the darkness, and his men, having discarded their spears, rushed forward. "Help them out, Ehud," he called to me, friendly-like. Hm, I was not sure this was for me but I didn't see any way out of it. So after a moment's hesitation I joined the dash forward.

I think we all realised pretty quickly that this was no rescue operation. Everyone was dead, or rather we hoped they were. My first reaction was to raise the cuff of my tunic to my nose. A foul stench hung over the area. Searching among the debris of bodies perforated with arrows, bits of armour and broken weapons, the ground was slippery with human faeces and the regurgitated food of the vultures.

The men were working in pairs, grabbing the

corpses and dragging them back. I remember the noise well. Not the cries of the wounded, of course, because they were all dead. Not the grunting and soft swearing as we handled the dead soldiers. But everywhere, retching. Some stood aside doubled over, retching and then vomiting, continuing to retch when there was no more vomit. Others continued the grim task pausing and retching as they did so.

Rushing about and not really looking where I was going, I stumbled and fell alongside a body, lying on its side. Easy to see how that soldier had died. Target practice from the battlements. There were two arrows sticking out of his exposed side. I stood up and pushed it with my foot. The next moment I was doubled up and the vomit was spewing out uncontrollably.

I suppose I'd seen what vultures can do to dead sheep. They want the innards and the easy way in is through the eyes, nose, mouth and anus. In, they go with their razor-sharp beaks and long necks and eat the body from the inside out. Never a pretty sight but this was the first time I'd seen a human victim.

I was still retching when I heard calls from up above. Those poor devils in the cage had woken from their misery and realised we were down below. You couldn't blame them if they thought it was a rescue operation. They started to cheer. Then I started to see movement behind the embrasures on the battlements above them.

An arrow thudded into the sand a few yards away. I instinctively looked up at the battlements and could see that many of the embrasures were filled by moving black figures. More arrows fell amongst us. Then there was a sharp series of twangs from the night and I watched a flurry of arrows speed from the dark plain up at the battlements. Some glanced off the stone sides but others found their mark, leaving the embrasure empty and filled again with the blue of the background sky. They were picking them off now, our crack archers. As soon as an embrasure darkened with the presence of an enemy archer it drew a deadly fire.

It was quick work in front of Jericho. Soon the last of us were turning our backs with relief on the scene of carnage and returning to the column. Ringing in our ears as we loped away with our burdens were the cries of anguish, disappointment and furious accusation from the poor prisoners in the cage.

"Armour this way." "Bodies 'ere."

Instructions rang out among the carts so we knew where to put our burdens. I flung the small bronze shield and the broken spear into the back of a cart already heaped with filthy broken weaponry and made my way back to Micah.

He looked at me strangely when I arrived. Then I looked down. My tunic was gory with blood and filthy with vomit. The moon was coming up and I felt sure that by the light he could see the shock in my eyes and the grey pallor of my face. I remember thinking to myself, in slow motion, that I was pleased. Yes, pleased! The state of me just! He could see I had not been shirking! And this was no time, not now, not ever, to admit to him that most of the time I'd been paralysed by vomiting, and only sense and an instinct for survival had got me retrieving a couple of pieces of armour off the battle ground for appearances' sake.

Mordecai loomed up on his donkey. He didn't dismount this time. I couldn't get it out of my head that he was still angry about Micah's mule and was going to start a row. But he had other considerations.

"I'm taking my men home," said he shortly. "There's nothing for them to do here." Micah nodded, and Mordecai brought his hand up to his forehead in casual salutation and, wheeling his donkey around, departed.

"We don't want any of this stuff coming back into the camp," said Micah to Jubal at his side.

"We've got baskets," Jubal replied tersely. "We can drop them off in the Moschen caves."

I knew these caves from terror patrols. They were a series of caves high up in the valley walls but easily accessible, Gilgal's burial ground for those who had died in the town, mainly the elderly, babies, and women in childbirth.

We could already see the lights of Gilgal when we halted on the plain just opposite the caves, black holes puncturing the rocky grey face of the wall. The awful creaking of the carts ceased and Jubal stepped forward and called for volunteers. I slipped away from Micah in case he had any bright ideas about my immediate future.

The lines of men were motionless, no takers. Everyone knew the grim task ahead. Someone else's turn.

"An extra day's pay," announced Jubal and men

shuffled forward until a tent commander could count a dozen. He led them away to the carts. Soon they were using their spears to scrape and push the corpses off the carts into big straw baskets, the ones normally used for donkey fodder. Again, the cold desert air became a foul sweet-smelling fug and all around men started to retch. I pulled my scarf up to my nose.

"They're not stripping them?" queried Micah suddenly. It was true. The earlier orders had been for all corpses to be stripped but this was not happening. We could make out, in the now bright moonlight, that the sagging disembowelled corpses being pushed into the baskets, still had strands of clothing and leather armour.

Jubal sighed through his tunic sleeve. "I think they've done enough for today." Then he added, "And it would take time."

Micah did not object. I think I heard him retch but it was controlled, and over quickly. It wasn't on for senior officers to show squeamish.

Everyone wanted to get this over as possible and be away from this place and its evil stench. The burial parties grabbed the big rope handles and, four to a basket, hauled them up onto the ledge and pushed them into the caves with the butt of their spears, deep into the mountainside. Then rocks, large enough to stop a fox or wild pig, were rolled and piled sealing the entrance.

Back at the camp I helped Micah slowly off the mule. I think his arm must been hurting again. He could hardly stand. A couple of servants came out and took him off me.

Shem was back on duty at the stables. I was dead on my feet. I had been running on adrenaline for most of the day and now I felt utterly drained, utterly exhausted by fatigue and, I suppose, shock. He saw the state I was in and simply came forward and took the leading rein from my hand.

"Mordecai was not pleased," I burbled. I think I was almost delirious. Shem looked momentarily puzzled.

A voice shouted, "What about the baskets?" I shook my head at Shem.

"Off you go, boy, get your head down," said he taking the reins from my hand, and patting the mule. "Leave everything to me."

I just remember thinking, *What would armies do without the Shems of this world!*

Chapter 12

I was looking for a couple of sheep – odd, I mainly did goats – which had run off from the flock. I was carrying a spear in one hand, something which I never had out in the wild, but I didn't think that odd either. Then I came on the sheep in a stream, and they were giggling at each other. Even that didn't puzzle me, but then I slowly emerged from these dreams and my deep sleep and I just lay there. Even with my eyes tight shut it was obviously bright outside; the dream about sheep stopped but not the tittering.

"Look at him," one voice said, a girl's obviously. "Dirty boy," said another, archly giggling.

Where was I? I wondered. Yes, of course, I dropped off the mule, came back to Micah's tent and crashed out on the palliase. So what is this?

I rolled over onto my back and opened my eyes. There standing at the foot of my palliase were two girls staring down and laughing at me. One was holding a laundry basket.

"You must be the new Barak?" said one, laughing. She was simply dressed in a long blackish garment, loosely held together at her cleavage but allowing a narrow strip of flesh visible to the belly button. Big eyes, full mouth and lovely brown hair framed by a white scarf which folded down and across her left shoulder. Mock concern, Hmmm? Definitely sexy!

"Very dirty indeed," said the other, feigning horror

and tugging at a long tress of jet-black curly hair in a Protect-me-from-this-Monster way. All done very sexily too.

I'm not sure what I would have done normally, but of course this wasn't normal. I suppose I would have rolled over onto the floor, got up, stood sheepishly in front of them, a beast in front of a couple of grinning hussies and uttered some inane welcome. All very embarrassing and, in my experience, not how you impressed girls. I mean, when they came up on the hill it was all very straightforward. You both knew the game and off you went into the bushes. Similarly, now in the military, when you went to the camp brothel, you chose one of the girls sitting outside the boxes, paid some old crone the money and in you went.

I will do a Barak, I thought. I simply folded my arms around the back of my head and rested them there. I think I even smiled back at the girls. I suddenly felt I was being cool.

"Laundry time," cooed Big Eyes.

"Yes," echoed Curly Hair, "Take off that nasty dirty tunic. Here," she said delving into her basket, "is a nice clean white tunic. Put this on. Orders of Abigail, the general's wife! This may be a camp but you can't walk around this house looking like a common soldier," she added and really hammed up a stern look.

"Go on," urged Big Eyes, "we won't peek." And they both, tittering away put their hands over their eyes and pretended to look down.

Okay, girls, I thought, *if that's how you want it.* I swung my legs onto the canvas floor and stood up.

183

Both girls recoiled with a little shriek as my movement released a powerful whiff of the stench of the night. I held my breath as I folded my tunic up and over my head and threw it down in front of them, and stood there naked.

They were making little simpering noises, laughing at me. Of course, they were peeking. I made a sudden movement forward which made them step back. I laughed.

"Caught you out there," I said, and then I was hit by their scent of cinnamon and cardamom and I felt my body responding, after the violence of the battlefield, to the sweetness and softness it betokened.

I breathed in deeply. *Not now, not now, something for later*, I thought, and I bent down and picked up the clean tunic.

"You can look now," I announced cheerfully, adjusting the pleats carefully, and they coyly emerged from behind their bashful fingers. " I am Ehud, by the way."

"Macar," trilled Big Eyes, with an inclination of her head and a mock curtsey. "And Zepzi!" mewed Curly Hair. "At your service."

They both giggled, then wiggled at me, gave me a 'Lucky Boy' grin, turned and skipped out of the room.

Oh ho, another perk for being a general's chariot boy, I thought.

*****

It is a funny old job being a chariot boy. Like many

184

things I suppose it is what you make of it. Okay, your official role is to make sure the boss does not fall out of the back of the chariot. You are a kind of human gate, but most of the time, well, you are just there with him at his side in the field and you talk about things. Then back in camp you are living in his home as well with family and friends and all that. So, you either became a kind of full-time servant or something a bit more. And you can guess I was working to be a bit more.

That bit more came early on when I discovered we all ate together. Back in the old days when we were wandering around the wilderness the women would prepare the food and men would then eat. But in Gilgal it was different, even for a chief like Micah. There was not much space so everyone ate together, masters and servants in the same area and at the same time.

"So, Ehud, on a typical night there will be two groups," Barak warned me in his Oh-so-patronising way. "Micah in the place of honour with a few guests," he had gone on, "other commanders or friends who just dropped in, and the other males of the household; then the other group will be the delicious Abigail, in her place of honour, surrounded by her handmaidens all squawking away." Delicious Abigail indeed! I was already getting an inkling that Micah had been itching to see the back of Barak. Ammunition for another day, I mused, as Barak proceeded with his instructions.

I entered the tent and sidled round to the wall opposite to where Micah was sitting. True enough, that night it was as Barak described, and over in a noisy corner there, with the other women servants, I think I caught a glimpse of Macar and Zepzi. I waited and, phew, Micah looked up at me and ordered with a sweep of the hand.

"Sit there, sit there," he ordered, pointing at a place lower than his guests but above his house servants. Exactly as Barak had said! So, I had got my place in the pecking order.

"My new chariot boy, Ehud. Handy with the sling. Knew his father," he announced casually then turned back to his guests.

Chaggy arrived shortly after. He was still limping a bit. I got up and helped him down onto the floor of the tent. He immediately started talking about the prisoners in the cage. "You know, Micah, we've really got to do something. We can't just let them die of thirst in that bloody cage." Dear Chaggy, his heart was always in the right place and it was nice he cared about a few unfortunate prisoners.

Micah shrugged, "Joshua is no Moses, what's more he knows it!" He looked over meaningfully at Chaggy. "So, we can't go expecting a miracle."

"Why not?" questioned Chaggy. "We got over the Jordan without getting drowned. That was pretty spectacular. And there have been other things…"

Chaggy believed everything, but Micah didn't like this kind of conversation. Anything involving HIM made him uncomfortable. He wasn't sure that HIM intervened to order. HIM got the blame or got the credit according to High Command, or so a lot of us thought. But you couldn't quite say that, even a tribal commander like Micah, or there would be mutterings about blasphemy. So, he turned to me.

"And what does my new chariot boy think?" A few around him laughed, Micah's little joke, ha, ha, but Micah continued to look in my direction, an eyebrow raised and half smiling. The laughing petered out.

It's always tricky when seniors ask your advice. It is normally when they are at a bit of a loss of words and want time to think. Of course, they are not really interested in what you have to say, or expect anything clever; actually, quite the reverse, that would be annoying! But then, they don't expect you to be completely dumb, especially not on your first day, the new chariot boy, and Barak's replacement at that.

"I remember you commenting, sir," I found myself saying slowly because I was actually wondering what I was going to say next, "when we were in front of Jericho last night…" I paused again. Silence, suddenly I found I had the audience, even the squawking from the women had stopped. What was I going to say, they were wondering, and so was I! Then a lightning flash! "Yes, sir," I found myself finishing hurriedly. "You commented that the walls were very lightly guarded."

"So, what do you say to that, Chaggy?" Micah turned away from me. Off the hook, but he'd got the ball rolling. *Clever me,* I thought, and tried not to let a smirk spread over my face. The chattering started again over in the female section; disappointed, of course, they'd been hoping for a bit more fun, the new boy making a fool of himself, and something fun to talk about.

Chaggy was frowning and pursed his lips.

"Well, then," said Micah, ignoring Chaggy, "we had better make a plan." And he called for a servant to bring over more wine, and the conversation turned to other topics.

When the food was finished, the room gradually cleared as people disappeared to their own quarters until only Micah and Chaggy were left. I rose to leave.

"Stay!" ordered Micah. So there it was, just the three of us.

Not surprisingly I quickly discovered I was not there simply for the consultation. I was there to run about and fetch wine and summon people, so I only picked up bits and pieces of the discussion which followed. Chaggy kicked off with a plan for a frontal assault with ladders and all that but then seemed to get a bit stuck on how to get the prisoners down. They moved on to discussing an inside job.

"Let's interview a couple of prisoners," Micah said. I was sent off to the enclosure where prisoners were held, and returned with two surly young Amorites under guard, still in torn and dirty grey tunics.

"What are your names?" asked Micah mildly, but they looked back at him blankly.

"Answer the General!" ordered the escort commander, giving the Amorite nearest him a vicious dig in the ribs which had him bent over and coughing. I remembered the commander now; he was a Simeonite called Terak, all fists and mouth, typical of his tribe.

"You, then!" he barked moving round to the other

Amorite, who started to babble away. I started to get that awful feeling of being drawn in again.

Look, you can't blame me. I had had my share of prominence and action for the time being, and I was quite prepared for a bit of rest and cushy time as a chariot boy. Frankly, I could see myself enjoying it; buzzing around the camp on errands instead of freezing to death on sentry at night or baking hot patrols by day; a nice big comfortable tent with good food rather than a dusty great free for all and whatever the cooks were doing with barley that morning. Then there were the perks, yet to be exploited!

Do you see my problem? Yes, you see, I could understand that Amorite chap. I had picked it up from Rim and his pals. None of them could speak Hebrew. They laughed at our strange language, so we got to learn their lingo.

So there was this poor Amorite guy babbling away. Micah and Chaggy looking puzzled and slightly angry, and me understanding, if not every word, the gist anyway.

Terak, thinking he should do something, barked into the poor man's ear. "Speak properly!" Of course, this had the opposite effect, he just dropped to his knees and continued to babble. Micah waved his hand for silence, and sat there frowning. It seemed to me a perfect time to scarper, so I rose and picked up the brass tray all ready to play the servant and nip into the kitchen. But then it came;

"Wait a minute, wait a minute, Ehud," said Micah. I stopped dumbly with the tray held rigidly in front of me.

"I think you understand these guys, don't you? I mean you had quite a little conversation with Zemri," he continued, nodding towards the prisoners. "What are they saying?"

I was stammering a bit about not listening when Micah cut me short;

"Well, start now. Tell them I have some questions for them to answer." In other words, don't muck me about, Ehud.

I took a deep breath. Time to deliver and go in hard. Putting down the tray, I looked towards the two prisoners, both surly and silent again.

"Look here, you shitheads," I sharply commanded them in my bastardised Amorite. That certainly woke them up; they just looked at me in amazement. Of course, they were not to know that I did not have a very big vocabulary, just the stuff I had picked up with the herdsmen, joshing stuff and all that. Shithead was a kind of friendly term of abuse, but said in a certain way it could be, well, pretty threatening.

I went on, so far so good. "The general here wants to ask you a few questions.

Get it?" They looked stonily back at me.

"And you will answer them," I continued menacingly. "And if you don't, well, you know those poor blokes you've shoved in that cage hanging over your walls?" Another pause, and I began to see fear in their eyes. "They'll think they are the lucky ones," I went on. "Oh yes! Lucky indeed when they see you two nailed out there to ten-foot posts by your knackers!

Yes, so your mothers can hear your screams during the daily shop!"

I paused again; yes, they had got the picture.

"So let's start again, shall we?" I announced breezily, crossing my arms. Did I smile? Perhaps I did. "The general would like to know your names," I stated evenly.

They looked briefly at each other. "Kudur," said one. "Hanun," said the other.

I turned towards Micah and slipped back into Hebrew. "Kudur and Hanun at your service, sir." I gestured towards the prisoners and sat down.

They were compliant now, the prisoners. Micah asked a number of questions, which I translated, and we got a pretty good picture about the internal routine of the city, the guard roster and suchlike. Particularly interesting was the routine at night and about the section of the wall which included the cage. This had a guard of twelve men and a commander with four men up on the wall at any time doing two hours on four hours off. The commander and the men resting were in a small guard room below the wall. So if a sentry saw something suspicious, he could shout down and up would come the commander, pretty quickly, to have a look. To raise the alarm, the commander could either send a runner back to the reserve company or, in an emergency, there were a series of hanging metal pipes along the battlements which the guards could strike with their spears to raise the city.

"So," said Micah turning to Chaggy, "four men on the wall, another nine down below in the guard room, and the reserve company about five minutes away. What d'you think?"

Chaggy nodded but without much enthusiasm. "But how do we rescue the prisoners?"

Micah turned to me with a number of questions about how the cage was slung. The prisoners simply confirmed the supporting ropes were fastened round two of the thick stone uprights which lined the battlements at regular intervals.

"We need Obed," said Micah shortly. Chaggy look surprised. "Will he come?" he said cautiously. Micah shrugged his shoulders and turned to me. "Get him," he said.

Obed again! I got to my feet and left quickly. I went back to the cooking area and a few boys sitting around. "Excuse me," I said politely, no point in rubbing in my newly acquired superior position. "Micah wants Obed. Where do I find him?"

Leading the way with a lamp, a young servant boy took me through the maze of buildings and tents belonging to the commanders and senior staff. Eventually we came to one, the same old black goat hair exterior within a low stone wall. A man was sitting cross legged by the flap and asked our business. He called in, then raised the flap and I entered.

Another dark interior lit by smoky lamps but over in the corner was Obed in a long red robe crouched over a table. He was sideways on and scrutinising something under a powerful source of light. He didn't look up. I gave him the usual routine, a Micah summons. "Micah presents his compliments et cetera et cetera."

Didn't work this time though. Obed just continued to look at a parchment through some kind of white pebble. Then he said with finality, "So Micah requests my presence. Well, Micah must wait" – he paused, continuing his scrutiny – "Inform him that I will attend on him…" – Oh, and the way he said "attend" dripped sarcasm – "….at ten o'clock tomorrow."

Thank you, I thought, *so what next, trip back to Micah and tell him, not in so many words, he wasn't Joshua and therefore Obed was not at his bloody beck and call?* I just stood there. I didn't really know what to do; but then I started to take in the extraordinary surroundings of the tent. It had the usual fine rug and coloured wall coverings but all around there were chests of drawers and, on top of them, strange instruments. One was a globe surrounded by metal bands. Obed ignored me. As the seconds passed, it was clearly time for a new tack.

"I'm Ehud. I'm Micah's new chariot boy," I announced with some trepidation, I reckoned he could well have forgotten all about me.

But Obed rapped down the white pebble on the table and stood up with open arms;

"Ehud, my dear fellow, of course, and I invited you to visit me, did I not, and here you are! Forgive my incivility but I get many calls. Welcome!" He waved his arm at some cushions on the floor. "Sit, and tell me what this is about."

Five minutes later he clapped his hands and a boy appeared, dressed Egyptian style, bare torso and long white skirt. Obed gave him some sharp orders. It sounded like Egyptian and the boy returned with a camel hair cloak. With the houseboy leading, I accompanied Obed up the hill.

"So," said Micah, "in summary, we believe we can get men into the city, onto the wall and overcome the sentries but there we are stuck. With twenty men inside the cage, it is too heavy to haul up. Cut the ropes and it would crash thirty feet," Micah hit the table sharply with the flat of his hand, "killing and maiming all those inside. And even," he continued, "if we had time to release the men from the cage, how many of them would be strong enough to climb down?" He sat back and all eyes turned on Obed. He took another sip of wine from the silver goblet.

"A fine wine." He smiled back at Micah, swirling it slowly and then sniffing. "From Joppa, I suspect. May I see the amphora?"

"Of course, of course," replied Micah rapidly. "I will ask my chief steward.

Ehud, call Tubal."

I rose to my feet. Blast, I wanted to sit in on this. As I left, I heard Obed start; "I have some questions for you. What…" he continued to speak but I was out of earshot.

And where was that wretched chief steward? He wasn't in his little den outside. I went into the kitchen; there was a row of amphoras against the wall; some maids were laughing over in the corner round a table.

"Which one have they been drinking from?" I asked. A maid laughed and shrugged her shoulders.

194

"I don't know, they are all the same to me. Take your pick!"

It was tempting but I knew it would not do; I simply could not risk it. Imagine the scene. Me: "Here's the amphora, sir." Pause. Obed takes the amphora from my hand. He looks, he sniffs. "No, it isn't," he says. "This wine comes from further south."

Everyone looks at me. I'm busted, and that's me back in the tents again, Seth's daily kit inspections and parched barley three times a day.

"Well, where is Tubal?" I asked but the girls were getting irritated now. Who did I think I was ordering them about? Just another chariot boy putting on the airs and graces of his master? Well, they were not having that, well, not here in their territory, the kitchen.

"I don't know. Ask one of the house boys," said one carelessly, and shrugged. For two pins, I would have gone over to the table and tipped it up, but I just gritted my teeth and went outside.

I eventually found a room full of houseboys sleeping or playing cards. One of them looked up. I asked him about Tubal. Same reaction, he wasn't too pleased either.

"I'm off duty now. Find someone else." He grumbled but I had had enough and shook him roughly.

"Get up and find me Tubal or you will be in big trouble."

He looked at me suspiciously. "I don't know where he is." I could tell he was lying and gave him a kick. The other boys looked on in amusement; this was fun, the new chariot boy losing his rag.

"I take orders from Micah," I hissed at him. "And you take his orders from me. Now!" I was pleased that fear now loomed in his eyes.

He rolled off his palliase. "Okay," he said grumpily, "but Tubs is not going to like this. He's down in the markolith."

So that is what this is all about, I smiled to myself; Tubal has slipped away for a bit of fun.

The markolith was where everything happened, a maze of tents and buildings where you could get everything. There, the prostitutes, sitting in front of the boxes where they did the business, waved and invited; there you could drink a skinful of date wine for a day's pay; there, you could pick up or sell something cheap, no questions asked; there you could gamble the night away. There, if you chose, you could do all these things at once; there, frankly you could do anything. And 'there' was always there, it followed the army wherever it went. But 'there' was always camped out of sight of Joshua and the priests, and always to windward. None of the smells or noises of the markolith to disturb those leading their people into the Promised Land. I'm not saying they were hypocritical; it's just they didn't want their noses rubbed in it. I don't blame them. No general really wants to know, let alone see, what soldiers get up to in their spare time. As long as they're up the next morning for the first parade, that is.

The houseboy knew exactly where to find Tubal. Not for him girls, boys or getting plastered. It seemed gambling was his thing and we found him in a big tent with about a dozen men sitting cross-legged on the floor with dice. They were wearing house uniforms and had the look of senior servants. A boy was moving from player to player pouring wine into silver goblets from a large grey amphora. In front of each player was a pool of silver coins. Tubal was obviously winning; he had a larger pile in front of him, and he was smiling as he shook the dice in the little clay bucket.

"Place your bets, place your bets," he announced teasingly, and the others reached for the coins in front of them. Tubal looked around approvingly, then he saw us and frowned. The houseboy sharply pointed at me.

"What are you doing here?" Tubal asked me angrily. "I'm sorry," I said. "Micah wants you."

There was a bit of sniggering around the players and someone went 'Woof, woof'. Tubal was furious and came over to us.

"Do you seriously mean to say that I can't leave the household for five minutes without something going wrong? That you can't bloody well sort out? Well, what is the problem then?"

"That wine you are serving up there. Obed now wants to see the amphora. I don't know which one it is, and the girls couldn't tell me," said I po-faced.

Tubal turned around towards the players. "Yes," he now drawled, looking into their faces. "Duty calls, gentlemen. And," he said moving back to the circle and bending down, "I'll just take my humble winnings." He scooped the silver coins by handfuls into his robe to the groans of the players. "And," he went on, now upright again and striding towards the corner, "I'll take this too."

So saying, he picked up a grey amphora over in the corner and held it mockingly in front of the group. There were groans of 'Oh, you can't do that, Tubal!' and 'You old skinflint!' but Tubal just smiled back. *That'll teach you for mocking me for being at the beck and call of my boss,* I could see him thinking.

He gave the amphora to the houseboy and then jingled the coins in his pocket at the players. "Never mind," he sneered. "Perhaps you'll get your revenge another day!" And casting one last mocking glance at the players, he swept out of the tent.

When we got up back to Micah's, Tubal took the amphora from the houseboy, and looked sharply at us both.

"And we" – he emphasised the 'we' – "will keep our bloody mouths shut, won't we," he whispered at us menacingly. Then, with a lightning artificial grin at us, more a toothy grimace, he turned and stiffly entered the tent, once again the indispensable and virtuous chief steward bearing his master's most precious wine. The houseboy departed and I stood there a moment smiling to myself. Well, I didn't care if old Tubs enjoyed a bit of illicit gambling and nicking his boss's best wine. I certainly wasn't going to sing it to the trees, but you never knew when these kinds of things could be put to use, a favour to be called in or something. I mean, going to someone and asking for help sometimes works but, in my experience, if the bloke is shit-scared of something you can say or do cooperation comes all the faster and surer.

Inside I sat over in the corner while the commanders talked. No invitation to come up close. I think I must have dropped off to sleep because the next thing I heard was Micah saying with loud finality, "Right, we'll take the plan to Joshua in the morning." And I woke up with a start.

Chapter 13

The next morning, I was summoned to Micah. His leg was playing up and, in spite of his protestations, Abigail, amid much cooing and patting, insisted that he have me to lean on during our visit to Joshua. Of course, I murmured something about all the work that Micah needed doing, cleaning his armour, getting things patched up but she pooh-poohed, "The houseboy's will do it, those lazy houseboys, they sit around all day doing nothing. It will be good for them."

Well, that suited me perfectly. I obediently moved around and grasped Micah firmly under the right armpit. She smiled encouragingly at her husband.

"You'll be safe with Ehud," said she demurely.

I felt I was rather in her good books. I had heard that when Micah told her – ears everywhere, of course – about my saving his life before Jericho, or whatever, he had simply added, "Lucky me, that Barak of yours would have left me for the vultures."

It was the first time I had heard any criticism of Barak. The senior servants just sniffed when his name was mentioned, as if they were frightened to give their opinion. Abigail apparently ignored Micah's remark saying simply, "No more ops for you, Micah, for the time being."

So I can frankly say I was in a very good mood as I supported a limping Micah over to Joshua's headquarters. It was one of those lovely early morning desert days, still cool from the night and a blue sky bright with the morning sun. No windblown dust, no scorching heat, no plague of flies; those would come later. Nice day apart I reflected upon my position of only a few days ago! Always an important thing that, a bit of compare and contrast, and what a difference, I congratulated myself! Good for Abigail putting her foot down and telling Micah no more military operations until he was recovered. As my job was to stick around Micah, it looked like I was in for an easy week or so.

So they have a plan, I thought cheerfully as the two of us progressed up the hill. Good for them, I hope it works. But you know, did I really care? I mean, I felt sorry for those poor devils in the cage but, well, tough, that's soldiering for you. Sometimes you're lucky and, well, sometimes you aren't. If I'd been one of those in the cage, I would have been as keen as the next man to be rescued, no matter what it cost. You couldn't blame them! But I wasn't up there slowly burning and starving to death, and I didn't really see the point of anyone going out and risking their life for them. Certainly not me anyway! I was not saying, "Let 'em rot," in so many words, but I was thinking that if there was a call for volunteers, I certainly wouldn't be one of them. And, anyway, I was looking forward to some rest and recreation in camp. I was just thinking of a romp with Macar or Zepzi – Who cares which was which! – when we entered into the presence of Joshua.

I helped Micah over to the rug where Joshua and the other commanders were seated and eased him down. He flicked his head which I interpreted as 'Push off to the back of the tent and wait there, boy'. Which I did.

Obed followed shortly dressed in a simple white tunic with a narrow gold coloured belt, and accompanied by the servant I remembered from yesterday in his cotton kilt. All very Egyptian. I knew this really upset Joshua's commanders because Obed just looked too cool, or rather they, the commanders, looked like barbarians in their coarsely spun garments with rough leather and brassy bits. Amazingly, Joshua who was 'We are the best, we are the chosen' and all that seemed to tolerate Obed's refined Egyptian ways.

His boy came and sat cross-legged beside me.

"I'm Anik," he said in heavily accented Hebrew. I noticed his torso and legs were hairless, another Egyptian custom.

"I'm Ehud," I replied, returning the compliment so to speak.

"I know," said he, looking ahead at the commanders; then, as if he had a job to do and now was no time for small talk, he put his finger to his lips, folded his arms and lowered his head. *He's concentrating, watching, and listening but doesn't want any of the commanders to notice,* I thought. Well, I like to think I'm a quick learner so I quickly adopted the Anik position myself.

I suppose I have got pretty good hearing from all those years as a herdsman, sight too for that matter. The catching of a far-off bleat was often the clue to finding a lost goat, a breaking twig the sound of danger approaching, even the faint sound of a drip onto a limestone surface that there was water nearby. And I was good at honing in on a sound amid other sounds. So when everyone was talking at once on the rug, or rather one person was talking and others interjecting, I was able to focus on the main speaker.

Micah's plan was pretty simple, or rather it sounded so. First, a few guys hitch a lift on a contraband convoy going into Jericho. Second, the guys get up onto the battlements over the cage and knock out the guards. Third, they release the cage on some kind of device which Obed was thinking up. Fourth, they jump over the wall and go home. Just like that, a few hours' work. Joshua just listened, impassive, nodding his head occasionally.

It was a bit strange this contraband convoy business. Jericho was under siege but of course it was not tight; sieges seldom are. One reason is manpower; Joshua could not really waste soldiers on a 24 hour watch on every gate or door in Jericho's walls. But there was another reason; Jericho was able to send messengers to other kings in Canaan and these we occasionally picked up to find out what was going on. Useful, but we still liked to put our own spies into the city. So it was a two-way traffic which suited both sides.

But their messengers and our spies could come and go without the need of convoys, so they were always a bit of an issue with some commanders saying the convoys should be stopped. This morning Micah explained, it was the only way of getting a group of armed men into Jericho.

"I have Intelligence that a convoy is arriving tonight. It will hide up in the foothills in front of one of the smaller gates at the back of Jericho, wait for nightfall and then slowly and quietly make its way into the city," he explained. "About half a dozen wagons."

There was a bit of mumbling but no strong objections. Micah's 'Intelligence' meant that the convoy was 'his prize' and if he chose to forego a valuable cargo in order to get his men into Jericho that was his business. The other commanders were also thinking that if this convoy got through it might encourage other convoys which they could pick up. Oh yes, everything would, of course, be handed over to the priests, but there was a general acceptance among the commanders that 'everything' was about 50%.

They went on to discuss the rest of the plan without much enthusiasm. Obed took a few questions, his replies followed by that great booming laugh. I looked over at Anik; he smiled occasionally. Anyway, no one came up with a killer punch, or a better plan for that matter, so that seemed that. Frankly it all sounded a bit of a 'Death or Glory' operation to me and I was glad to be out of it.

The discussion then started to take a nasty turn. It appeared I was not the only one not keen to take part;

"They're all Benjamites in the cage, from your tribe, Micah. This is not an army show," growled Amram. Micah had all along been putting the case for the other tribes to be involved – 'an army show'– as Amram called it. He knew Joshua liked that kind of thing and tried to play down what he called 'Tribal Differences'. But it simply didn't work most of the time because the differences, not to say hatreds, were just too strong.

It was funny. Yes, if you came upon a man dying in the desert you would give him some water; you would not check first which tribe he came from, but if there were two of them you might. And if you heard that a dozen of them were dying out there and they were, say, Simeonites, well, it was not only their problem but you would probably joke with your mates and say, "Serve those bloody Sims right!"

In this case, it was 'Serve those bloody Benjamites right!' That is more or less what Amram was saying and none of the other commanders were disputing the point.

"We've done enough," added Amram somewhat brutally, just to make the point about the bloody trap they had walked into the day before.

Joshua just sat there, his usual impassive self. To give him credit he did try to rise above the inter-tribal rivalry, 'Onwards Chosen People' and all that! Even on very rare occasions he would play the HIM card – the wrath of the Lord will descend on you if you don't work together etc – but this was not one of them.

"This will be a Benjamite operation," he said after a pause. "Of course, the army will help you out with any special skills you need," he offered all conciliatory. "You will want archers, of course."

So there was a bit of chat about how many archers, donkeys from the stables, medical support and things which Micah needed for the operation. It was agreed that Jubal would be in charge.

"We will make a sacrifice in the Temple this evening." Joshua breezily was finishing and you could, of course, hear everyone concurring. I mean they didn't say 'Hear, hear' but the enthusiasm was vocal. Supporting the sacrifice was cost- free as far as they were concerned; Joshua would provide the bull calf or whatever the priests thought was appropriate.

It was very important to keep the priests happy. Before any activity, particularly a dodgy military operation, they would insist on sacrifice. It was not worth standing out against them. If you did, they would moan about HIM being angry and the terrible signs they had seen. That would make everyone jittery and put such a hex on the operation that it was doomed to failure. So they would be proved right and there would be a lot of knowing nodding among the priests with every nod screeching, "We told you so!"

The best way of turning a hungry priest into a happy priest was a big fat bull calf for starters. The sacrifice of the animal could involve various different procedures and outcomes – some bits were burnt to a cinder on the altar – but you can bet the bulk of it went into providing a jolly good feed for the priests.

All I was thinking, whilst just half listening to all this, was bully for the priests.

Then Obed leant over to Micah who started up again with a jerk.

"Vital to the success of the plan is the infiltration group, the men we have to get into Jericho and onto the walls. There's a good chance they will be challenged, so we need Amorite speakers. We would like volunteers from the other tribes. They will be well rewarded."

This was a tricky one. The only good Amorite is a dead one, that was the official policy, so to know Amorite was to confess to consorting with the enemy. That could mean anything from meeting them, like I had, out in the hills or having a playmate back in the camp. Quite a few of the camp followers, especially the prostitutes, were Amorite, and jolly good at their job too. They just had to be a bit careful – no Amorite hairstyles or make up, and to wear rough Israelite clothes around the camp. Of course, once you had paid your shekels and were inside the box they were, I can tell you, all Amorite!

The commanders knew this went on but no one was going to admit any of their men were so tainted. They shook their heads piously; this was an easy request to refuse. For one moment, probably in his intense irritation, Micah forgot the rules of the game;

"Oh, come on, you've all got Amorite speakers," he said plaintively, and there was a terrific huffing and puffing of outraged denial.

It was, of course, Amram who spotted Micah's weakness in his usual blunt way; "Well, you've certainly got Amorite speakers among the Benjamites. Who was that soldier who bought the message from Zemri?"

I suppose I was still only half listening but Amram 's words had me awake in an instant. I felt a chill and out of the corner of my eye I saw Anik slowly turn in my direction. I remained with my head bowed; perhaps I'd misheard; perhaps they would move on to other things. But the chill remained. *What next*, I thought with dread in my heart?

At the end of that wretched conference, I helped Micah to his feet. The commanders were continuing to talk amongst themselves but, without looking up, I could feel Amram looking balefully at me.

That'll teach you, you cocky little bastard, he was thinking.

On the way out, Anik rose and stood there impassively as Micah and I limped past. As I glanced over, he gave me a huge wink; *someone at least is getting a bit of fun out of all this,* I thought ruefully.

I had the feeling that Micah was going to say something apologetic as, once again leaning on my shoulder, we left Joshua. I just waited, saying nothing. I was not into starting the cheery small talk, thank you! *Yes, I did feel hard done by, so let him sweat,* I thought grimly to myself. But Micah was having none of this;

"Stop sulking," he said sharply. "You are on for tonight. That's all there is to it." He shrugged his shoulders.

I had, of course, been thinking about my excuses if Micah had been at all conciliatory. I would have blethered on about still being concussed, showing the barely healed scar across my head and all that. Perhaps even play the 'son-of- old-friend' card, but I knew that wasn't going to do and I was lumbered.

I had, of course another fear; this operation

required Amorite which sounded like Amorite. Okay, I had a bit of Amorite, I could make myself understood, but this was going to be an inside job; and I knew my broken Amorite was not likely to convince an enemy, let alone a suspicious one.

"I'll need to brush up my Amorite," I said, after a pause. Micah nodded, grunting. "She'll charge," I added casually. Micah's face was impassive but he nodded again, and we continued in silence down the hill and along to his house.

Tubal was at the entrance to greet Micah, all smiles and solicitation. Micah turned his head towards me;

"We were going to give the volunteers from the other tribes a week's wages for tonight's work. I think it's fair that we do the same for our men. Tubal will give you the money." His face softened and he looked at me sideways, smiling. "For expenses!" Then he added quietly, "You'll get the same again after the operation."

Well, thanks a bundle, I thought, and mumbled some words of gratitude. But both of us were thinking that there was a good chance that his money was safe.

A servant took Micah off my shoulder. Tubal, left alone with me, pulled out a money pouch and counted out seven army shekels. These were nothing like the silver shekels that Rameses dealt with, just rough copper circles imprinted with Joshua's head which we used around the camp and were not much use outside. In theory, thirty of these copper coins would make up one silver shekel but not in the real world. I bet Rameses would just laugh or offer absurd terms.

Anyway, we soldiers got one shekel a day, seven in a week. They did have some official name but we just called them shekels.

Tubal pulled the drawstrings of the money pouch together, and put it back in the folds of his robe. He was puzzled; he hated not being in the know.

"The boss is generous today," he called after me, as I slipped away.

*****

"You want something, sonny?" came the throaty voice. I stopped in my tracks. Spotted! That was the voice of Ma Miriam, the camp madam.

My chosen Amorite teacher was Zaki, one of the camp prostitutes and, of course, a proper pure-bred Amorite. Back in the tribal lands we had our own prostitutes but they did not come out on campaign. I think it was something to do with Joshua remembering how hard Moses was on prostitutes; so having Amorite girls in the camp meant the tribal chiefs could splutter and swear and deny, "Not our girls, oh no!" And it suited us too, the clients. These Amorite girls were different; brought up in the softer life of a city, they washed and oiled their bodies, their hands were soft and, frankly, they seemed more fun than our back-at-home whores. We sometimes asked them about Amorite men and they would giggle and say how they liked what they called our 'vigour'.

I had been with Zaki a few times. Unlike some of the other girls who did not do conversation, she had could speak a bit of Hebrew. Anyway, I liked her, she was fun.

The camp brothel was right in the middle of the markolith and wherever the army went it was the same. Slap bang in the middle were the six boxes, in two lines of three. In there, the activity took place and behind were the tents where the girls lived when not working. In front, under a red awning fringed with gold at a small table sat Ma Miriam, quite small and, with a receding chin and prominent irregular teeth. She certainly had never been beautiful but you could hardly see her for the glitter of gold ornaments, and did she have authority!

I remembered the first time I went to the boxes. It was late on a Friday night and business was booming. Each box was divided into three sections with a short queue outside of randy soldiers. When I arrived at Ma's table, she had looked me up and down. "You're new here, aren't you?" she stated all very matter-of-fact in that husky voice of hers. Before I could stammer a reply, she gesticulated, gold bangles clanging on her wrist, over to one of the boxes.

"Go to the far queue. Her name is Zillah." She now looked me in the eye and added with a meaningful look. "She's my best girl, so treat her nice!" I was to discover that she said that to all the new boys.

She had looked at the copper shekel I placed in her ringed claw of a hand. "No silver, no ornaments, luv?" She asked sounding disappointed. Another of her tricks I was to discover! Effectively, she was the camp fence. No Rameses rigmarole with her though; she just would take the object from you, weigh it in her hand and announce her decision, like, "For this I'll give you half an hour today or two quickies within a week."

Of course, she was robbing you blind but then it was not that easy to get rid of the things we picked up. Joshua was very firm about this; any gold, silver or jewellery had to go to the priests. 'Looting for personal gain', which is what he called it, was punishable by death. Of course, we all did it, from the top down.

"You've got ten minutes," she shouted after me as I, the new boy, headed for the box.

She was very tough on timings and these were enforced by Ham, a huge lumbering figure of a man, totally bald, who never spoke. He was a eunuch, of course, and he had been picked up in Og. Joshua didn't feel threatened by Canaanites who could not breed so Miriam had been able to buy him cheap and keep him on.

"Number six." Miriam would call out. "Time's up!" And Ham would lumber over to a box and beat with his hand on the flap and out would shoot an embarrassed boy guilty of overstaying his time.

By now, I more or less knew the ropes with Ma Miriam and, of course, today I wasn't looking for sex. I knew things were always quiet in the morning, so I had been hoping I could just nip around to the tent at the back and grab Zillah – or rather Zaki which was her real name – for a quiet chat.

But that hoarse shout from underneath the gold fringed awning knocked that hope.

"Just come over to gives Zaki a message," said I lamely. I had suspected there might be a confrontation like this and I had worried about a good cover story to get past old Ma Miriam. Too right!

"You can start by coming right over here," she purred slowly. As I stood in front of her, she looked me up and down.

"You mean Zillah, I suppose," she said huffily. "I don't run Amorite girls." I could have kicked myself, a bad start with the old whore mistress. Of course, she was sensitive about having Amorite girls and insisted on each having a good old Hebrew name. Zilah, you could not get more ancient Hebrew than that but, once in the box, all that stuff was dropped and it was Zaki. Ma did not wait for me to answer.

"You want to see Zillah? You can see her in a box. Like any other visitor. Usual terms," she looked at me with hard black eyes. No discounts from her in the early afternoon even when business was quiet. She put out her hand.

Zaki was waiting for me in the cubicle, sitting with her knees up to her chin on the white cotton covering of the broad straw palliase. In truth, she was not a great looker, a little too much fat here and there, slightly funny teeth, but she took trouble – sexy make-up, smelling good, and fun and welcoming.

She stretched her smooth bronzed and slightly oiled legs across the length of the palliase and leant back.

"Bit early, Hoody," she cooed under the heavily darkened eyes and the short black shining hair. "And for half an hour? You want the works this time?" says she with eyes widening. I had asked Ma Miriam for half an hour and paid the going rate for three ten – minute sessions at one copper shekel each.

A ten-minute session was a quickie, that was all there was to it. Ma liked you out after eight minutes so the girl could get ready for the next punter. But 'The Works' was a full half hour, and you even got a good clean before hitting the palliase. How could I forget my first experience of 'The Works'! Oh yes, 'the Works' was really something, and very Amorite. Trick Number One: off came the dirty tunic and Zaki sprinkled me with some kind of powder, I think it was soda ash, and then, using a piece of glass, in long slow strokes, she scraped the dirt and sweat off. It was almost too much!

"No, no, not yet," she murmured, pouring scented oil from a glass bottle and rubbing it gently into my limbs and back. Trick Number Two!

"Good, good," she then murmured approvingly as she rolled me over onto my back for Trick Number Three, a final oiling. The pain, albeit exquisite, was intense and I kept my eyes clenched shut.

The hands lifted. "You can open your eyes now," she whispered. Her bra fell to the floor followed by the G string and she slid beside me onto the palliase and our oiled bodies entwined. "Gently does it," she admonished, and then I was in Paradise.

But today was not the time and place for Paradise. I winced; there she was the same old Zaki, soft green eyes, that shimmering skin, and a whiff of jasmine.

"Oh Zaki, I hate to tell you but I'm not here for that," I started. She opened her eyes wide in amazement. Sexy is not the word! *Don't do that, Zaki,* I thought, *please, please!*

I persevered. "This half hour is for lessons in Amorite. Old Ma wouldn't allow me to see you except on her terms, the old cow."

I was not sure if Zaki was beginning to cry; tears of disappointment – rather flattering to my ego of course – or tears of fear – being rejected and all that. I could not be sure but the last thing I wanted was a scene on my hands and to waste my expensive half hour consoling a sobbing girl. To boot I would probably get a black mark from Ma.

"Look, Zaki, there will be another time soon but please, please, go along with me." I shuffled in my tunic. "Look, here's a little extra." And I put the two copper shekels onto her crossed hands.

Good girl that she was she brightened up immediately.

"Well," she said, "a girl can do with a holiday from time to time." She lay back on the palliase leaning on her elbows. "Sit over there like a good boy and let's see what we can do."

Of course, I did not dare tell her what it was all about, going into Jericho that night and all that. Nice and trustworthy she might be but, in my experience, it is not fair to push a girl. Ma Miriam liked to keep herself in the know and rewarded the girls for useful titbits which she put to lucrative use. I doubt there were many secrets between the girls back in the tents.

I went on to explain that we had just captured some soldiers and Joshua wanted them interrogated that evening. Since knowing Amorite was a suspect talent no one had come forward and then someone had mentioned my name. So here I was to get up to speed. Try as I could it all sounded a bit hollow to me.

"Let's start then. In Amorite, begin." She smiled and wagged a finger. "Starting now!"

"What did you have for breakfast?" she asked in a school ma'am voice. I stumbled my way through some kind of response. Dammit, what was the word for barley? I made a guess and Zaki laughed. "That's linen, luv, unusual breakfast food!"

Then we really got into the swing of it. It was rather lovely being taught by her, really one long flirt with lots of 'Naughty!' here and 'Good boy!' there.

Of course, I had been racking my brains about the kind of phrases I might need for the situations we might face; a false word meant discovery.

"Let's do military for a bit," I asked after we had covered food, my family, the weather and similarly boring topics. So we played a game of soldiers; 'Who goes there?', 'Take me to your commander', 'Sorry, I have forgotten the password', 'I am just having a piss'. All those kinds of things which might come up, and we did it in earnest. I half wondered if she suspected, but she did not let on.

The flap of the box by my head suddenly shook with blows. It was Ham, our time was up. Zaki got up. I put my hands on her cheeks and drew her head to me. We kissed.

"I'll be back," I said softly.

"Look after yourself, Hoody," she almost whispered and looked down.

I could feel Old Ma Miriam's eyes boring into my back as I slowly turned down the hill towards the camp. She may not have said she cared about what went on in a box once you paid your money but, sure as hell, she wanted to know if it was something unusual. Poor Zaki, she was going to be in for some tough questioning, so I was glad I had given her the cover story of the prisoners. Ma would continue to suspect, of course; you do not become a successful Madam with a trusting nature.

Chapter 14

Down in the tents Seth was getting ready. He seemed in quite a good mood. I glanced over to Barak's mat but it was empty; no blanket or kit on it. So he was gone. *Not a man to hang around,* I thought, *and I bet Seth's pleased.*

There were five of us in all for this so-called 'water patrol', all part of keeping the operation very hush-hush. There was Seth in charge, me, Gam, Big Ab and a newish guy, Koresh.

I suppose 'water patrol' was a good enough cover. We were always looking for new sources of water, and this was normally done at night. I had always kept clear of water patrols. They were slow-moving and I much preferred the fast-in and even faster-out of the Terror patrols. Anyway, 'water patrol' is what Seth told us with a "And you! Keep your bloody mouth shut!" look at me.

Actually, I was glad that Seth was in charge. For all his bossiness in the tents, kit inspections, occasional bouts of obsequiousness and 'Yes, sir, no, sir' bullshit when any senior officer appeared, he was competent alright.

That evening he was taking preparations very seriously. He checked each one of us carefully. We all had more or less the same kit; a brown robe and scarf for night work, a dagger stuck in the belt, and a short throwing spear with a good iron point. We were each given a skin for water.

"And there's an extra bag for each of you. Sling it over your shoulder with the waterskin." He pointed at a pile of bags, each one about the size of a large head. *Awkward*, I thought.

"And if I catch any of you opening that bag before I say so, I'll have you!" Seth stretched out his arm and pointed his finger at each one of us in turn.

"Understand?" Not a question, of course!

"Now, jump up and down!" he ordered. "I don't want you sounding like a lot of rag and bone men clattering about in the night." There was a tinkling noise from the midriff of Koresh.

"What the hell's that? Let's see you!" Seth rounded on the soldier angrily, who sheepishly pulled out a purse containing some copper shekels. Seth took the purse, then leant over and put his mouth very close to poor Kor's ear.

"Oh, so it's a night out we are expecting, is it?" He hissed. "Need a bit of money for the beers and perhaps a girl?" We all laughed dutifully at Seth's humour. He shook the jingling purse and thrust it back rudely at the soldier. "Get rid of it, lad!"

That evening, behind the camp, we practised moving in a kind of arrowhead formation, with Seth at the front, pretending it was night-time, then obeying his hand signals to stop or lie down.

"You there, you'll wake up the whole of Jericho if you rattle like that tonight," he snarled at Gam who, getting down, allowed his spear point to hit a stone.

After we had practised crawling; not easy over

219

rough ground, only elbows and knees for propulsion, Seth finally paraded us in front of him.

"Show me your daggers," he ordered tersely, then proceeded along testing the edge of our weapons.

"Not bloody sharp enough," he rebuked Gam, feeling the edge. "Get down to the blacksmith now with that joke of a dagger."

Full marks to Seth; if you want a really sharp edge, you need a blacksmith with a grinding stone. But a mere Seth does not have access to the blacksmith without orders from on high. The other guys could sense something was on and there was a nervous titter. But Seth became angry and rounded on us. "And that goes for the rest of you. I want those daggers razor-sharp. Give them to Gam."

We quickly drew out our daggers and handed them over.

"Now, you, move!" Seth almost spat at Gam. Poor Gam was wide-eyed; we had never seen Seth so edgy. Gam slowly turned around and set off; Seth looked after him, shaking his head. He then appeared to recover his composure.

"Okay, lads, that's all for now. Back here at six," he announced and walked off.

"Bit of an overkill for a water patrol. The services of a blacksmith, the strange bag!" Abs voiced the thoughts of all of us; well, all of us, that is, except me because I knew what was in store.

Yes, I thought, *and nothing to it*! Kids' stuff! Jump on a convoy, get up on the walls, knock out the guards, release the cage, jump over the wall and go home. Just like that, and a week's pay for a few hours' work. A simple plan, yes, but that was about the only thing in its favour.

Four simple steps, I thought ruefully as I made my way back up the hill, but each one fraught with difficulties. If I had been a casual onlooker – if only! – I would have rated the chances of success at Nil minus and, more importantly, the likelihood of my evading capture or coming back alive at even worse odds. *Blast*, I thought, *this is nothing more than a suicide mission to save Micah's face*. This time tomorrow those guys in the cage will be dead or carrying on dying and I – Well, it did not really bear thinking about it – would either be dead with a quick stab wound, dying out there somewhere with the spear in my guts, or trussed up in some Amorite hellhole awaiting interrogation and a man with red-hot pincers.

It must have shown on my face as I arrived at the entrance of Micah's compound.

"You're looking a bit glum today, Ehud," was Tubal's jolly greeting. I sometimes wondered what he did all day; he seemed always ready to pounce out on any visitor.

"Well," he went on, "Let me cheer you up! You have got a secret visitor." He put his finger to his lips. *Thanks,* I thought, *that's all I need.*

"No guessing." He pursed his lips archly. "It will be a lovely surprise!"

I was in no mood for a guessing game, but I suppose I should have guessed. I pushed past Tubal and through the empty corridors to my room, and stopped abruptly. There, lying on my palliase, head resting on folded arms, eyes closed was Barak. Yes, and I do believe he was asleep.

My first reaction was blind fury. Kick the bloody bastard! Boot him off the palliase. My palliase! No longer his bloody palliase! No longer his bloody room! And he's not going on some bloody stupid operation. He's not risking his bloody life out there tonight!

Kick, kick, and kick him again! It was tough, but I didn't. I just smiled down at him, and smugly congratulated myself on my self-control. And, truth be told, I was learning to be cool, and learning that from him.

I think he was actually a bit disappointed, me taking all this in my stride, treating him like an unimportant interloper. I was wary though. Barak was not here for small talk.

"Ah," he murmured, opening his eyes wide and yawning. He sat up. "You've been a while. Nice of Tubal to let me in." Turning the knife, yes, just what I expected. Don't rise, keep smiling! Of course, they are in cahoots, what did I expect?

I heard myself saying, "Good to see you again, Barak."

Non-committal, semi-welcoming, just the right tone, so I thought. Barak pursed his lips. "Preps went okay with old Seth, did they?"

If there was anything further to convince me that Operation Water Patrol was doomed to failure, this was it. If bloody Barak knew, then who else?

Barak was reading my thoughts, "Barak knows

everything!" He crowed with a laugh, adding, "But I am here to help."

He took up a seated cross-legged position on the palliase; generously, I thought sarcastically, leaving enough room for me as well.

Sitting opposite, Barak now took a packet about the size of a small perfume bottle out of his tunic and gave it to me. It was light and wrapped in stitched plain canvas.

"When you get into Jericho, I want you to place this in the wall. For a friend." He smiled at me and went on to explain minutely where it should be put. Then he made me repeat back the instructions. *What next*? I wondered.

"My friend inside will signal its safe arrival tomorrow night with a light from the walls," he added confidentially, "and then you will receive a reward."

He leant forward and tapped me on my knee.

"Yes, enough for a whole night in the box with the lovely Zaki, eh!" He smiled at me knowingly. *Yeah, great stuff,* I thought. *She's in on this too, is she?* Still, the money was all adding up...and perhaps I would come back so I simply nodded agreement back at him. What did I care what was in the package? Why ask him anyway? Barak was not going to let me in on his little secrets.

Barak drummed the fingers of his left hand on his knee. "Now tell me." He cocked his head on one side and laid a questioning finger on his shaven chin. "Just how are you proposing to hitch a lift on the convoy?" He smiled that false smile of his and opened his eyes very wide.

Come on, Ehud. I knew he was mocking me. *Be a big boy now! Tell Teacher!*

Don't be shy!

Of course, feeling like a complete fool, I had to explain to him that Seth had told us nothing about the operation, just told us we were off on another water patrol. Barak nodded. "He's probably being briefed now." He made a grimace, then laughed. "Lucky old Seth, no imagination. Otherwise, he would probably be shitting himself right now."

So far as imagination went, he was dead right. Seth could certainly think on his feet. When things came at him, he reacted fast and well, and that got him out of trouble. But that was about all. He did not look ahead or think of ways to avoid the trouble in the first place. Barak had put his finger on it; doubt had lurked in the back of my mind how we were going to hitch a lift on this blasted convoy.

"So," said Barak slowly, "let's look ahead, shall we? In a few hours' time you will find the convoy, half a dozen wagons drawn by oxen in the hills outside Jericho. They are waiting for nightfall; the drivers get down and, with the escorting troops, hunker down in a nearby cave. It's safe in there so they light a fire and start to cook. You see all this from a safe distance. Now is your chance!"

Get on with it, I was thinking, and Barak smiled in acknowledgement. "Well, it's easy, isn't it? You just jump on the biggest and most comfortable wagon, probably one with sacks of barley and sit there, six armed men, and wait for the guys to finish their meal and give you a lift into Jericho. Yes?"

Ha, ha, I thought and Barak continued. "Or do you spread yourself out and find little hiding places on the wagons? Five men, five good chances of detection." He sighed. "Or," he continued, with a short bark of a laugh, "will good old Ehud in his best Amorite ask the chaps for a lift?" Barak finished mockingly.

I put on my best face and managed a kind of I'm-enjoying-the-joke-too titter. But frankly I felt like Seth; I didn't know the answer, I just hoped something would crop up. But inside I suspected that what Barak had yet to say was our only chance, and I nodded back at him.

Barak put his hands together, fingers uppermost, and pressed them to his chin.

"There are four steps to this," he continued, no whimsy now, just bald step- by-step instructions.

"Step One; the second last wagon has barrels of oil on board, big barrels, a head shorter than you. Four men can manhandle a barrel. You will offload two of the barrels. Step Two; you will carefully carry – Carry, not roll, mind! – those barrels fifty yards back from the convoy and place them underneath an acacia tree. There is one you can't miss. You will cover them with an awning you will find there. Step Three; you all get back on the wagon and huddle into the middle, swivel some barrels round so the load looks intact from the outside. An hour later you rumble into Jericho. How does that sound?"

I have to confess it did not sound bad. "Okay so

far," I mused, "but you mentioned four steps, Barak."

"I did indeed, how could I have forgotten?" he looked at me with that insincere smile of his.

"The fourth step," he went on smoothly, "is payback time. When you have done your business in Jericho and returned safely, you get a month's pay, credited with Rameses."

Well, that did surprise me, and it must have shown because Barak clapped his hands. He then put up his hand to stop me saying anything.

"Now, what's been missing in the camp, Gilgal, Shittim, Abila or wherever, in the last few months?" he asked. "Why are all the women so surly and so many stink of stale nuts?"

Well, I didn't know that and I can't say I had really noticed. No one smelled good in the camp except those using perfume. Give me the honest stench of sweat and dirt any day rather than that sweet cloying muck some of the women called perfume.

"Because they all like to oil their precious bodies," smoothly continued Barak, "and the only olive oil currently available is that rubbishy stuff, like thick yellow soup, which in normal times you take when you are bunged up or use for fuel in outdoor lamps." He laughed scornfully. Barak was getting into his stride. He enjoyed playing the sophisticated expert to my unlearned savage.

"Think of it. All those bodies, now sun-dried and wind-roughened by the rigours of camp life or stinking with stale oil. Untouchable! Men passing on the other side of the street, husbands complaining of headaches!

Ha!" snorted Barak with relish. "I can tell you, this stuff from the barrels will be down in the marketplace this time tomorrow and gone in the evening. There will be no shortage of servants queueing to pay top prices for their mistresses. Of course," he went on, enjoying my attention, "our best client will be Old Ma. She needs to give extra sheen to her best whores now and again."

You had to give it to him! But I wasn't going to go telling him what a clever chap he was. I clicked my tongue in a business-like way.

"You say one month's pay. That's too little. Make it three months," I heard myself saying.

Barak made a face and shrugged his shoulders. I wondered what odds he placed on me coming back and claiming my share, but he couldn't say that.

"Split the difference then. Call it two," he said carelessly, "and that's final." He put out his hand. We shook.

I was now doing some thinking for myself. "You'll be moving the barrels first thing, will you?" I asked, pretending to look concerned.

"At dawn," Barak replied casually. "I don't want some damn fool patrol stumbling on them."

I nodded. Perhaps I might be able to pull a fast one on the great Barak himself?

*****

I suppose I was not looking my most enthusiastic when I joined the others outside the tent at six promptly. Big Abs started to laugh, the others following; "Well, guess who's chipper today?" said Seth, joining in the merriment. "Get fell in, Ehud, lad."

There was some joshing about going from pampered chariot boy to stinking camel dung and learning to piss again like a dog. All very funny, meant in good spirit, but not so funny for me. Well, I knew what was in store.

By the light of the reddening sun, Seth checked our water skins and gave each one of us a ration of bread.

"That's your last food for at least twelve hours, till we get back to camp. So, no scoffing until I say so."

"A bit long for a water patrol, Seth," said Abs in his innocent but lugubrious way.

"Yeah," said Seth uninterested, and indicated the mysterious bags for each one of us to pick up. "No looking, mind, until I say so." Abs was silent now.

Two soldiers emerged from the tent with a man who looked like a shopkeeper. He was middle-aged, short, fat and waddled. He looked incredibly surly and was gabbling away in Amorite, protesting. I noticed he had a rope round his waist which was attached to the wrist of one of the escorting soldiers. *A friendly Amorite, and coming with us. Seth's taking precautions!* I thought mirthlessly. The soldier jerked the rope; the man grunted in surprised and the gabbling stopped.

"Let's go," said Seth, not deigning to give us an explanation for the Amorite, and led us off in single file down into a maze of narrow watercourses. It was twilight, darkening, so we kept fairly close together, a yard or so apart, with Seth leading accompanied by the Amorite and the two soldiers. Seth would stop and look carefully ahead. There was not much likelihood of Amorites picketing the heights but we did not want to chance on one of our patrols, doing the same as us and keeping to the watercourses. But if we did, we wanted to be the ones doing the spotting first. Seth was good at this.

Seth put up his hand, and we again halted.

"Okay, lads, gather around," he said. "And you," pointing at the Amorite and the escort, "stay over there." We drew off the watercourse into the rocks and crouched down in the sand around him. Seth looked across his shoulder to see that the Amorite was out of earshot. *Good,* I thought, *Seth's taking no chances.*

"Well, lads, as some of you have guessed this isn't a normal water patrol," he started.

Seth then explained that he was under orders not to reveal the true nature of the operation until we were well out of the camp. What he was really saying is that no one trusted us to keep our mouths shut! Of course, he was right; but if Barak knew who else? Everyone listened impassively as Seth explained the phases of the plan from hitching a lift to escaping from Jericho.

"Now you can open your bags," he said. We all emptied them out. Inside was a grey tunic, a simple bronze helmet of the type worn by the Amorites, a coil of rope with a hook on the end and some rough leather mittens.

"You'll be changing into those later," said Seth, "but try on the helmets now.

229

Make sure you have got a fit."

"And this rope here. That's how you get back over the wall. Fasten the hook, thrown over the rope and down you come. Forget to put on the mittens and you won't be using your hands for a month." He paused, then snapped, "Any questions?"

Seth did not like questions, mainly because he did not know the answers until the situation arose. But Koresh nervously put up his hand.

"Yes," said Seth frowning back.

"But how do we know who is an Amorite and who isn't?" Koresh complained. It sounded a perfectly reasonable question to me. I could just see us killing each other in the dark but Seth sneered back.

"We are smaller than the Amorites, we have got our own belts and weapons, we know each other. What more do you want?"

There was silence. No one quite liked to contradict Seth but then I found myself saying, "Micah asked me to give you a password."

This was, of course, complete nonsense but the odds of me being caught out were small and it might make the difference between living and a slow death tonight. I mean, if it worked, Seth was hardly likely to challenge Micah; and if it did not, well, that would be that!

Seth looked at me rather irritably.

"I was told to keep quiet until the briefing," I explained and Seth nodded. *Of course, if it was from Micah, that was all right, not from little smart arse me second-guessing him,* I bet he was thinking.

"It's two Amorite names," I went on, then hesitated. All right, I did have a bit of Amorite language but at that moment my mind went blank and all I could think of was Zaki holding my hand during our teaching session in the box and calling me Adoni Zedek, which in Amorite means Lord of Righteousness.

"The challenge is Adoni and the response is Zedek," I heard myself saying. "So if you actually challenge an Amorite, he will just think you've got his name wrong."

There was a pause but Seth picked it up and was all business. For the next minute or so, we practised challenging and responding to each other, and 'Lord' followed by 'Righteousness' in broken Amorite went around in a little circle. *Fine,* I thought, *someday, if I survive this lunatic operation, I will dine out on the tale of a famous patrol with passwords chosen by an Amorite whore with buttercup cheeks.*

We set off again, now into a dark blue night with stabs of orange on the horizon and a half moon above us.

Chapter 15

We must have been going a good hour when Seth clicked his fingers, the signal to halt. In front, there was a low-lying broken ridge and Seth and the Amorite with the escort trailing behind with the rope crawled up to the summit and looked over. I could hear them talking, very low. Seth was asking the Amorite some questions and getting irritable. Then the soldier gave the rope to Seth and slipped back.

"Where is Ehud?" he asked in a loud whisper. In the darkness, I waved my hand.

"Get up there. Seth needs some help."

Up on the ridge we were looking down into a narrow valley. Seth was agitated. "You translate for me, Ehud. Where's the bloody convoy? How does he know we're in the right place?" I turned to the Amorite. "What's your name?" He glowered back at me, gleaming hostile eyes in the dark; clearly a pressed man, I judged, and none too pleased with it either. Well, now was not the time to be asking what the deal was, how much he was getting for co-operation and all that. He gave a sharp short cry as I put the point of my dagger into the flesh of his shoulder and held it there.

"And now you will answer my questions," I murmured slowly in his ear.

This was a line I had practised with Zaki so I was pretty confident, but I gave the dagger a little push so that he did not think I was going soft. I could feel

Seth's breath on my shoulder as he watched my questioning technique.

I thought I would go for a bit of the back story, partly out of curiosity, but mainly to get my ear tuned in and make sure he could understand me. He now told me his name; it was Oth something something. So many of these Amorite names are like someone gargling, the sound coming from the back of the throat. "So I'll just call you Oth. Okay?" said I, slightly increasing the pressure of the dagger.

Now, if not the best of friends at least with an understanding of each other, he became quite cooperative. It seemed he was an ox driver and a regular on convoys to and from Jericho from all over Canaan. Somehow, he got sacked and then got picked up by one of our patrols. They were going to kill him when he had the bright idea of spilling the beans about the next convoy.

"What's your reward?" I asked.

He shook his head in the darkness. I turned to Seth and spoke briefly with him, asked him when the moon came up or something like that. Seth, of course, had the answer. Who cared! I turned to Oth.

"The boss says, if you cheat us," I said, probing slightly with the dagger, "we'll cut your throat just like that and leave you for the vultures. But play us straight and you will get ten shekels."

That, I thought, *with any luck is a good enough carrot to keep him going with any luck.*

"Slow down," said I sharply when he started to babble again. I asked him a few questions; like where was this convoy? He motioned towards the moon and explained that probably they would be using the moonlight to bring the convoy near to Jericho. Then they would lie up until the moon went down before making the run to the city.

"So, the convoy should be here in the next two hours or so?" I confirmed, then passed the information to Seth who just grunted.

"And this is the right place, where they stop?" I asked Oth.

By the waning moon, the rugged desert landscape was still brightly pallid and marked with the dark patches of trees and the shadows of outcrops. It all looked the same, no distinguishing marks and none of those signs – small walls, shelters – which indicate the activity of man. *No, it was just another bloody watercourse in a land of numerous watercourses,* I thought grimly. Then I kicked myself. Get your brain into gear, Ehud!

"So where's the cave?" I demanded.

Oth was not in the least surprised. He simply pointed his finger to the dark broken wall rising on the other side of the watercourse. I followed his finger to a black jagged hole about thirty foot up, hardly different from the other surrounding shadows, but darker, more intense. I looked hard and could just discern a track, slightly lighter in colour than the surrounding rocks, leading up to the hole. *Barak's cave,* I thought. W*ell, that fits.*

Then the landscape fell into place more or less. In front of us, the watercourse widened and there was a flattened area which had been cleared of stones, obviously a parking area for convoys. I now needed Barak's tree. I looked back up the watercourse. There was lots of light scrub and then, a bit further back than I expected and bigger than the surrounding stuff, a dark flat dome, the familiar shape of a mature acacia tree. I smiled to myself. So far so good, another fit.

I informed Seth, who nodded impassively. "Keep your dagger stuck into him," he said curtly.

I looked at my new friend and he looked back at me with calf-like beseeching eyes. *No, you aren't planning anything funny,* I thought. *You've no master plan up your sleeve.* Seth must have been thinking the same but Seth liked to be sure. Seth spelt it out.

"Any funny business from him, you know what to do, Ehud, and we'll scarper." In Hebrew, of course, but stabbing his finger at the poor man. No need for translation or explanation, Seth had made his point. I think I heard Oth whimper.

Back off the ridge we changed into our Amorite grey tunics.

"Leave the helmet in the bag," ordered Seth, "and you'd better keep your brown capes. It could be a long cold wait." As if to prove his words a sharp wind rose from the East and we all shivered.

"You come up with me, Ehud," ordered Seth, and turned to the rest of the patrol. "The rest of you stay down here. Get down among the rocks. And keep alert!"

235

I scrambled after Seth up to the ridge line, joining Oth and his escort. I wrapped the brown woollen scarf tightly around me, right up to my ears. Everything was still in the bright moonlight, and silent, apart from the sudden and occasional swooping and twittering of bats above us.

Peace really hits you at the end of a long day when darkness falls and the cold air of the sunless desert drapes you like a clammy shroud. 'Keep warm, keep warm', the brain orders; but you can't do anything about that, so the brain says 'Deaden the pain, deaden the pain'; which means go to sleep. 'Keep awake, keep awake', the soldier and survivor in me urges, so that is what I want to do. I focus on the moonlit ghostly landscape of sharp rock, scrub and shadow. Something out there seems to move; I shake my head and look again, and it moves again. I look at another object a bit further off; it moves too. It must be an illusion. I test my theory and yes, every time I look at something it moves or grows into a fantastic shape; or rather it does not. That is what the imagination does at night when the brain is tired. I dig my fingernails into my arm under my scarf; I need pain to keep awake.

"Oof," I let out an involuntary sigh as Seth's elbow rammed me in the ribs, and I raised my head.

"Ssch," Seth hushed in my ear. I blinked and looked at the unchanged landscape.

"Can you hear anything?" asked Seth intently.

All I could hear was a light snoring noise, probably Oth, on the other side. I shook my head, I wondered if Seth was imagining things. Then there was a puff of wind and I caught it momentarily, a crunching rasping noise from up the watercourse.

"Yes," I whispered to Seth. "I can hear something too."

Seth spoke sharply to the escort beside him and the soft snoring noise stopped in a low groan. Another elbow had been at work.

"Get down and warn the others and then come back up here," Seth ordered me.

I did not find much readiness as I shook the crouched and huddled soldiers.

"Get ready, get ready, they're coming. Keep quiet," I urged.

Back on the ridge, Seth had slid back with the others, eyes just above the line of the ridge, fearful of an alert escort in the convoy spotting our heads against the dark sky.

I listened and the noise came closer. Then suddenly they were in sight. First, I saw a couple of scouts out in front picking their way, spears in hand, through the scrub; followed by the first wagon hauled by oxen, the dark muffled figure of the driver looming above his bench.

One, two...I counted six wagons, all heavily loaded, pass about fifty yards in front of me. The rasping of the heavy wheels on the rocks was joined by the clinking of the harness, the panting of the oxen, and the soft voices of the drivers. For a moment, I was gleeful thinking they were not stopping. *Abort plan, done our bit, return to camp!* But suddenly the noise of movement ceased as the convoy drew up on the far side and stopped. The drivers jumped down from their seats and I could see them stamping their feet and waving their arms.

Now, Barak, I thought, *everything now depends on your forecast.*

The men hung around the convoy for a few minutes, checking their loads. Then, in a kind of black group, they took the track up the rocky side opposite. I counted about a dozen. They disappeared into the black hole Oth had identified as the cave, and soon there was the flickering of a fire and the sound of cooking and voices. Not the kind of activity of those expecting trouble; that is, unless we were walking into a carefully laid ambush.

I could almost hear Seth's brain clunking away as we peered over at the convoy, now quiet except for the shuffling of the beasts and occasional grunting. I'd better go down and have a look now, I reckoned Seth was thinking, find some places to hide. Clunk! But what if there's a sentry there? I can't see anyone but they might have left someone behind. We might stumble on him and that would be that. Clunk again! He would raise the alarm and they would come rushing down. We would then scarper, and that would be that. Failure of operation!

Poor old Seth! I, of course, had my own agenda thanks to Barak. For that I needed Seth right where he was and out of the way.

"Seth, let me go forward with a couple of guys," I heard myself saying. "I'll check the convoy for sentries because I can speak Amorite."

Seth was not going to let on but I detected his relief. He nodded.

"Okay, Ehud," he agreed. "We'll watch the cave and give you a warning signal if anyone returns to the convoy." He paused. "The warning will be the hoot of an owl." *So be it, Seth,* I thought. *The hoot of an owl it is.* Although that's a pretty suspicious sound out here. I haven't heard the hoot of an owl for ages.

l slipped back off the ridge and grabbed Abs and Gam. Armed with our short stabbing spears we set off parallel to the watercourse and then crossed into it beyond the acacia tree and out of sight of the convoy. Keeping to the far side we slowly made our way forward. There, round a curve, we soon could see the last wagon of the convoy and further off up the side of the rocky wall the flickering of the fire from the cave.

Keeping in the shadow of the rocky wall we softly made our way towards the wagons, stopping every few paces to listen and look. We came level with the last wagon and crouched down looking around wheels and animal legs, searching. No sign of any sentry. I stood up and inspected the first wagon. I could not tell what the load was, it was tightly enclosed by a tarpaulin. Looking down the line in the waning moonlight they were all like that.

I have always found that, however well things are planned, however brave and bold the execution, success or failure all comes down to luck. Yes, sheer bloody luck! A single moment, a single act will determine the outcome. In our case, right now, it was the call of nature, and our good luck.

As we moved forward, suddenly, out of the darkness from beside a wagon a figure stood up. Another pace and I could have touched him with the point of my spear. I heard the hoot of an owl from up on the right. *Good old Seth,* I thought, *you are on it anyway.* The Amorite seemed to pay no attention; he just stood there and spat on the ground; if he had only turned his head slightly, he would have seen the three of us frozen like statues. Then he shuffled forward a dozen paces to one side and stopped, his back to us.

Those who make their money out of selling warfare to kids always put an emphasis on the trial of strength, superior skill, the triumph of our chaps, and all that, with a bit of chivalry thrown in. That's what girls like to hear too; their brave boys triumphing over a worthy adversary. And sometimes it is like that, a good clean fight, hurrah, hurrah! But not always and certainly not this night. Call it what you like, killing a man having a piss does not really qualify!

I looked back at Abs, and nodded towards the man and the sound of his urine splattering the rock at his feet. *Lucky me, we have you with us,* I thought. Abs was the tent butcher. On those rare meat days, he would go off to the quartermaster's compound, choose a goat, cut its throat, and then bring it back to the tent for skinning, butchering and cooking. So he was the obvious choice for a bit of slick bloodletting. Abs nodded back and handed me his spear; then pulled a dagger soundlessly from the scabbard in his waistband. I remember thinking, that thing will be sharp, razor-sharp, thanks to Seth's fussiness.

For a big man, Abs could move remarkably swiftly and silently, and was behind the man in an instant. All we saw was his left hand move round and jerk the man's head back, simultaneously there was a flash of the dagger in his right hand. Then there was a soft gurgling noise. It seemed to go on forever, then stopped and Abs let the body drop gently to the ground. He wiped the dagger on the man's clothes, stood up straight, and turned back to us.

"A lot easier than a billy goat," growled Abs softly. Gam and I almost collapsed in silent laughter, bent double and covering our mouths with our hands. It was a sign of how wired up we were.

"We'll hide the body later," said I recovering, and we crept forward cautiously wary of another sentry. When we reached the end of the convoy, we crouched down and looked up. The cave was less than 50 yards away, flickering with flame; they must all be inside getting warm and having something to eat.

All the wagons looked the same, stores heaped high above the wooden sides and covered with tarpaulin.

The second last wagon, that's what Barak had said. Finding it I started to try and undo the knot of the rope passing round the edge of the tarpaulin and looped over wooden cleats along the side of the wagon. Abs came up behind me; simply grabbed the rope and yanked it down releasing the tarpaulin. We lifted a corner of the heavy canvas and, yes, there they were, tall wide barrels.

I think that Abs and Gam just assumed I was in the

know and had some kind of authority. True, to a certain extent, but this was private business and none of theirs. Absolutely no point in explanations, unless they became difficult.

I briefed them on what we needed to do, especially the importance of hiding the barrels. No discussion!

We dropped the tailboard and Abs put his huge arms around one of the barrels and slid it with a swivelling motion over the edge of the platform with Gam and me on either side to catch the weight as it slid clear. Slowly, slowly Abs pulled the barrel, it's bottom scraping along the platform.

"Got it," I said as I gripped the rim of the barrel, my cheek hard against the rough wooden staves slightly moist with sweet smelling olive oil.

"Me too," I heard Gam say. Abs pulled the barrel the last few inches off the platform. We knew the barrel was going to be heavy but clear of the platform it just seemed to drop until Abs got a hand underneath. He grunted with the exertion.

"There, got it now," he said, and together we lifted back the barrel until we all three were upright. Okay, with Abs the barrel was manageable and we started a crablike walk back away from the convoy towards Barak's acacia tree. We ducked under the bristly dark canopy.

"Gently, gently," I said as we put the barrel down with a collective grunt and hurried back to get the next barrel. It was much easier; this time Abs had his hand under the barrel when it came off the platform.

"That it?" said Abs, after we had lowered the

242

second barrel into its hiding place and covered it with some spare awning lying on the floor of the wagon. Then I heard myself say, "Just one more one."

Well, it had just struck me, the deal had been for two barrels, but why not a third barrel for Ehud? Okay, I had not really thought it through; how to get the barrel back, how to tap into the lucrative olive oil black market; but those were details for later. No time for explanations to the boys and, yes, of course I would cut them in, I said to myself without much conviction.

Good for Abs and Gam. Soon there was a third barrel hidden under another tree further up the watercourse and covered with branches.

I was getting worried about the timings. The moon had almost gone down. "I'll go and get Seth," I whispered. "You take that body and hide it a good way from the convoy. And cover up the blood."

I went back up the watercourse until I was out of sight of the flames of the cave and raced across and up to Seth. He already had the rest of the men ready on the ridge. Oth was tightly secured between the escort and gagged. There was no good reason for Oth to start blabbing but Seth wasn't taking any chances. He was good at that.

"You've taken your time," was all he said as I flopped down beside him. It was much darker now. Soon they would be coming down and setting off.

"Okay, there's room for us all on the second last wagon but we need one of these guys." I motioned towards the two soldiers with Oth, 'to secure the tarpaulin over us'.

Abs and Gam were waiting by the wagon when we got there.

"Hop on then, lads," said Seth now back in charge and in his element. Abs swivelled some barrels round to the back and flipped over the tarpaulin before settling down with us in the middle. We heard the escort soldier slip the rope over the cleats. He gave a couple of taps on the side of the wagon, then he was off.

Underneath the tarpaulin the five of us sat cross-legged leaning against the barrels. It was pitch black and the air quickly became stale and sickly sweet with our breath and the seeping olive oil. We were dead silent. All we could hear was the shuffling and the stamping of the oxen and, further off, the occasional clash of a cooking pan amid the low buzz of activity from the cave.

Shortly after we heard the clatter of stone as the Amorites came down the track, talking quietly among themselves. The wagon tipped slightly as three men clambered one after another onto the driver's broad seat.

The leader started to pass down from the head of the convoy, stopping at each wagon.

"All set, ready to go?" I could make out the simple question in Amorite. Our driver followed the others in giving an affirmative grunt. We heard the commander brush by the wooden side and call up to the last wagon.

"We're missing Dag," called the driver. "He was sentry." I went tense.

"Blast him." The commander got angry. Clearly Dag was no favourite of his and he was now in a hurry. "Where the hell can he have got to?"

He paused, then brusquely ordered two soldiers to get down and check around and about the convoy.

"Quickly," he said, "I will check the wagons."

I could hear the carefully quiet breathing of the men around me and gripped my spear. I wondered what Seth would do if the tarpaulin was swept back. Would we lie doggo and hope the commander could not see us amid the barrels? Or would Seth order us up and away, no more fighting than necessary, and we would race back into the darkness of the desert, and a long walk back to Gilgal to report our failure?

The commander moved quickly. As he came to each wagon he rapped on the wooden side and said tersely, "Dag, are you there?" waited and passed on.

Having finished his checks, he returned to the last wagon and waited for the soldiers to return.

"No sign. Nothing, sir. Had a good look around," one reported. *Abs and Gam, good on you*, I thought.

"Hm," re-joined the commander. "Well, he has probably deserted, the fool.

Well, we can't waste any more time. Get up and we'll get started."

There was no more talking, just the soft cracking of whips, and one by one, the six wagons started their journey once again down the watercourse towards Jericho.

Chapter 16

I can tell you it is no fun sitting on the floor of a wagon; bumping and crunching along, limbs crushed together, faces almost touching, breathing each other's breath and the sickly smell of olives, and in the pitch dark.

Around me I felt our euphoria collapse. Yes, we had found the convoy. Yes, we had smuggled a lift – had to kill someone, of course. And Yes, we were heading towards Jericho. *But*, I thought grimly to myself, *these were just the preliminaries, the opening stages of one hell of a challenge.* What we were going to do once we got through the gates of Jericho I had absolutely no idea.

I bet Seth had no clue either. I wondered what he was thinking, or rather I didn't because I knew. Seth was thinking, I am pretty sure, 'I have no idea what I am going to do but I have always worked it out at the time, and this time will be no different'. In fact, I bet he was quite relaxed. *Lucky him*, I thought.

Then I had this additional task, this package of Barak's to drop off. I felt deep into the pocket of my tunic and grasped the package in its oiled packaging.

With darkness and the rhythmic motion of the wagon, I soon was aware that sleep was our biggest and most pressing enemy. Because with sleep comes the snore! Over across from me I could hear someone breaking into that steady heavy breathing of a man who has fallen asleep. It grew louder; then there was a low grunt and silence; Seth's elbow had been busy. In the darkness, we heard him hiss.

"Keep awake!" then added. "Nudge your neighbour if you are in any doubt." Then there was the danger of the accidental noise, enough to give the game away. I could just visualise the sequence; a cough in the darkness, a furious growl from Seth, a call from the driver on our wagon and the convoy stops, the tarpaulin is undone and swept back, and there we are cross-legged, cramped and stiff, surrounded by very angry men with spears and in a hurry.

So we ground on in the dark.

At last, the wagons stopped and we heard a low call from ahead and above. Must be from the walls, I guessed. In the dark we all stirred, flexing our stiff knees and shoulders. I gripped the haft of my spear. There was a wooden thumping noise and then the squeak of heavy gates and we heard the sound of men tramping and surrounding the convoy.

"You want to check our loads?" we heard the commander say, and I froze.

So did the others, I bet. No real need for translation. *So this was it,* I thought. "Nah, get moving. A patrol is out there."

I heard the response with relief. The man banged twice on the side of the wagon, which started forward again. Slowly we felt the wagon move from the mush and scrape of the sandy rock-strewn track to a grinding squeal as the wheels slithered and gripped on the paved and inclined causeway leading up to the gates. We knew we had passed into the city when light started to penetrate our dark awning, and once again we could faintly see each other. I glanced around; most of us had our chins down, only Seth was looking straight ahead, his head darting, all alert. He looked like an eagle thinking, choosing his next attack.

We lumbered on along a street. There was a lot of noise, music and shouting, and the smells of meat and baking bread joined us under our canopy. Had not someone said that it was party night and all the better for our operation? *Well,* I thought glumly, *I hope so, but roll on silence with the city in a drunken slumber.*

The wagon halted and I heard another gate open and some shouting. We rolled forward, away from the noise and the light, and stopped.

"Okay, lads, well done, gather round," we heard the convoy leader shout. I heard him brief the drivers to unharness the oxen and follow him to the barracks. "And then you can get out on the town, lads, but back here an hour after dawn to move and unload the wagons."

Seth leant forward, his forehead almost touching mine.

"What's he say?" he hissed. I explained and he thought I saw a smile pass over his face and he leant back again.

We heard the unbuckling of the oxen; our driver swearing at the stiff leather straps securing the yoke. The long wooden shaft fell to the ground with a clunk and we heard the driver leading off the oxen. Gradually, the sounds diminished until there was the creak and slam of a heavy wooden gate shutting and the sound of a bar falling into place.

The cacophony of the city suddenly lessened. Around us there was silence. Looking at Seth he raised his finger to his lips and put his hand to his ear. We nodded silently.

We waited in the dark for any sound of a guard, or someone being left behind with the wagons. It must have been after about ten minutes that Seth, with a slight scraping noise, drew out his dagger and cut into the canvas above us. He poked his head out and looked all around, swivelling on his knees. Then he stood up to get a better view. He seemed satisfied.

"Stay here," he ordered the rest of us as he clambered carefully over the barrels and jumped down. A short while later there came his urgent whisper, "Okay, lads, down you get. It's all clear but keep it quiet."

One by one we stiffly got up and jumped off the wagon. What we saw was not encouraging. The wagons were parked in a courtyard completely surrounded by high white buildings except for the heavy gates by which we had entered. Doors were set at intervals around the courtyard with shuttered windows marking out the three storeys of the buildings looming over us.

The five of us crouched down by our wagon while Seth went round checking the gate and doors. He returned. "They are all locked," he told us without emotion.

Well, that was cheering, I thought. *Here we are, stuck in this bloody courtyard.*

First we tried the big gates. It was a simple design; two flaps meeting in the middle. Looking through the central crack we could see there was a heavy beam of timber keeping the gates fast. Seth put the point of his spear underneath the beam and tried to raise it. It would not budge, probably some kind of locking mechanism on the other side. *That was no bad thing,* I thought ruefully. A heavy beam falling off a gate seemed just the kind of thing to raise the suspicions of a passer-by, and we could tell by the noise that the street outside was busy.

We followed Seth round to the first door in the wall. It looked solid and ancient, with a brass keyhole.

"Well, they all look pretty stout but this one looks a bit lighter than the others," Seth growled and nodded at Abs. The big man put his shoulder against the flat wooden surface and heaved. It barely budged. Then he bounced against the door several times hoping to shatter the lock on the inside. The heavy thudding filled the courtyard. I looked up; the shutters remained closed and there was no sign of a light. Abs stepped back and shook his head; he was already sweating in the cold night air.

"There is some give." He turned to Seth. "Not much, but a ram should do it." *And wake up the neighbourhood,* I thought, but there did not seem any other option. The shuttered windows were too high to reach and there were no footholds on the wall.

We chose the largest wagon and the five of us lifted up the pole and, with a couple of heaves, broke it away from the heavy wooden mounting with a crack. We carried it round and lined the pole up with the keyhole of the door, three of us on each side with our hands underneath.

Keeping stationary we swung the heavy pole back and high and then let it fall forward. Crash. Our arms shivered as the pole hit the wooden surface just above the lock, and the door shook. Seth leant forward and inspected the door. It looked as solid as ever.

"Not a mark, lads," he stated simply. "Put some muscle into it next time."

We must have all had the same feeling of being watched because suddenly we were all looking back and around the courtyard. There was movement; over against the opposite wall and highlighted by its white background was a dark figure. By the flickering light of the flame-lit sky, I could see it was a woman. Behind her we could see an open door and, within, a faint light.

Without a word from Seth our reaction was automatic. We were already dropping our battering ram and grabbing our spears when she started to advance slowly towards us with a finger raised against her lips. We just stood there while Seth came round and stepped in front of us. She stopped a pace away. She was middle-size, a scarf covered her head and the lower part of her face.

"Do not fear." The voice was throaty but soft, speaking Hebrew but with an Ammonite twang. "I am Rahab and I will be your guide and protector."

Rahab! We just stood there. Surely not! Was this ordinary looking woman really the legendary Rahab, the Ammonite prostitute, bar girl, or innkeeper if you prefer, who had sheltered Joshua's spies and helped them escape from Jericho? But we didn't doubt long; this was a woman accustomed to command.

"Tidy up your mess, try and cover up your traces," she urged in a low clear voice. "The watchman will be doing the rounds soon."

We set to, dragging the pole back and propping it back onto the broken mount of the wagon, and flipping back the canvas awning over the barrels. Okay, the scene would not bear a careful scrutiny but you don't expect that from a bored, tired, and probably drunk watchman late at night. Anyway, it was just another risk forced upon us, I glumly calculated. Like the rest of us, I was simply thanking our lucky stars at the miraculous appearance of Rahab, particularly with the news that a watchman would be around shortly.

We followed her through the dark doorway. Inside there was a small oil lamp which she picked up and led the way up some stairs, eventually pushing up a trap door. We clambered after her onto the roof and, following her example crouched down. It was really noisy; there was obviously some big festivity going on, the booming of drums and the crashing of symbols, and the whole city was lit up by the flames of bonfires. Rahab finished consulting with Seth.

"Okay, lads, we are going to follow Rahab," he told us. "Keep down and quiet."

We started to crawl after him on our hands and knees keeping below the level of the low wall surrounding the roof.

"And reverse your spears, I don't want a bloody

accident!" Seth snarled back as an afterthought. He was right, of course, it wouldn't have taken much, one man to pause, another to continue forward and then the man in front gets a spear up his arse, just the kind of additional complication we could do without.

Over the roofs we went; crawling along gutters, swinging over parapets, occasionally dipping down through a trap door and following Rahab along corridors before emerging again onto strange roofs. We were certainly nearing the external walls of the city. We could see the high white towers, flickering yellow and orange with the flames from the city, and standing out sharp against the clear desert sky of deep dark blue. We stopped by a large trap door and Rahab spoke to Seth.

"We're going in here, lads," he whispered. "Got to lift this one off, it'll be heavy."

We gathered around the four sides. "One, two, three," he counted, and we heaved away. The trap door broke away from its bitumen surround and we slid it aside onto the roof. Rahab with her small lamp stepped down through the opening onto the stairway below.

We followed her down into a long room. She put the candle in an alcove in the wall and motioned us to sit down on the bare wooden floor. There were sacks stacked against the wall and some broken chairs and bits of bed. It was clearly a lumber room. There was music and revelry from below. Rahab spoke in normal tones.

"Now listen to me," she addressed Seth, and went on to explain forcefully that we could hide here until the great bell rang and the sentries changed over.

"Then you can go out," she continued huskily, "and do your business."

She stood up. "You've got a bit of time," she said. "I will bring you up some bread and water. You, boy." She motioned towards me. "Come with me. You can leave your spear."

It was funny; while she was speaking to Seth, she was looking around carefully at all of us, and then seemed to fix her gaze on me. I almost thought she winked.

I looked at Seth who shrugged his shoulders in acquiescence. She opened the door onto a candlelit stairway and I followed her down a flight of stairs, the noise getting louder as we descended. She knocked on the door on the next landing. There was silence, so she pushed open the door into a small bedroom, just like one of old Ma Miriam's cubicles. It was lit with oil lamps. She sat down on the crumpled bed and held out an open hand.

"Give it to me," she ordered, which was the last thing I expected, not that I was expecting anything in particular. I was nonplussed. She stood up abruptly and put her hand up on my shaven head and ran her finger along the rough scabby edges of the cut.

"Yes, you're Ehud, all right." She was talking to herself, and sounded relieved. "Hand it over, the package from Barak."

Of course, I had completely forgotten, I still had that bloody package to drop off! I instinctively went to my pocket and felt its shape. She folded her arms and looked up at me. She was smiling.

"Now, Ehud, you are just wondering who is this aging madam demanding Barak's package?" she purred. "How do you know this is not a trap?"

What eyes she had, big and round and looking straight into mine!

"You think that," she continued, "once I get the package from you." "Phoo!" She waved her hand. "I give a signal and soldiers will fall upon you and your gang, and that will be the horrible end to Operation Water Patrol."

She paused, clearly enjoying herself.

"Well," she said after a pause, "I will give you some kind of proof. I will tell you exactly where you were meant to leave the package."

I listened as she recited Barak's instructions about where to leave the package in the wall.

"Happy?" she concluded once again putting out a hand. There did not seem much for it; I drew the package from under my tunic and handed it over to her. *Well, that's one less thing to worry about,* I thought. It had struck me anyway it was going to be difficult to get away from Seth and the others on a package dropping mission.

"And now I have a little job for you," said she, drawing a small parcel from underneath her dress. "Give this to old Ma Miriam" – she chuckled – "and she will reward you." Another chuckle, we both knew what that meant! I took her parcel. *It too was light, no gold or silver in there,* I thought.

Rahab seemed in no hurry and once again she sat

down on the bed and looked back at me.

"I've heard about you," she went on throatily. "You are quite a lad." She nodded her head up and down. "We heard how you saw off Zemri, not once but twice with that sling of yours. He told me himself! And that great oaf Zophar will still be rubbing his groin for some time to come. How we laughed!" She paused, and then continued with a low laugh. "Not that it will make much difference! All talk that man, according to my girls!" She laughed, a low gurgling noise.

"We know everything here. Nothing is secret long from my girls, I can tell you. And it gets a bit boring in Jericho at times, so it's good to have some tales of what you boys get up to."

Then she rose.

"We'll be getting busy again quite soon. I must go. Wait here, and I'll bring you up some bread."

I waited in the room and a short time later up she came with a bag and a jug encased in straw.

"Here you are," she said and turned to go.

Then I did something that really surprised me. As she began to move, I found myself taking her gently by the shoulders; then I leant forward and kissed her full on the lips. We looked at each other wide-eyed in mutual astonishment. Then she smiled, took my wrists gently and dropped them from her shoulders.

"I'm a mother too," she said softly, tears in her eyes. "I won't betray you boys." She finished and passed out of the room.

"You took your bloody time," rasped Seth, the point of his spear glinting at me momentarily as I pushed open the door and put down the bag of warm flatbread and the jar of water in the centre of the group. I sat down and we all grabbed some bread and passed round the water.

"We are missing someone," I said.

"On the roof. Keeping an eye out," Seth answered shortly.

"D'you not trust her?" I murmured. Seth gave a sardonic laugh. "Trust her or not, I believe in precautions."

Many a time I have fried on a hillside in the midday sun, frozen in the night of the open desert, or endured any one of the physical miseries which go with a campaign. Quite apart from heat and cold, there is damp, hunger, thirst, pain and so on; the list is endless. But I can tell you with absolute authority, whatever you are suffering at a particular time, that is your Number One Hate. When you are cold, you would give anything to be warm. If dead hungry, you reckon you could cope with thirst. And so on. Sitting round the campfire we sometimes talked of the challenges in the field and how we dealt with them. Everyone has their little tricks to make the agony easier; grit your teeth against the cold, swear against the heat, suck a pebble for thirst. But we all agreed that the worst battle is against the agony of waiting; that time when you are still, motionless and doing nothing. Those long slow ticking moments before the shout of the leader, the wave of the arm, and suddenly you are in battle.

Yes, you try fantasy, or put your mind into neutral by an effort of will; any way to deal with the waiting, anything to stave off the dark thoughts. And, I reflected, it is worse in the darkness; somehow, fear and apprehension are more bearable by the light of day.

Looking over at Seth I almost doubted my 'waiting' theory, in his case anyway. There he was, candle flame flickering on his face, as impassive as a stone statue, and looking straight ahead. And motionless! Unlike the rest of us who, just like him sitting around uncomfortably on the dusty floor, were giving way to bouts of shifting and fidgeting, or, head down, trying to sleep without him noticing.

Business was building up downstairs. We could hear raucous joshing outside and rapping on the door or the ringing of a bell. Then Rahab's voice would ring out, "Welcome, boys, come on in," and then, always, "Remember this is a respectable house. No rough housing!" She would admonish to friendly laughter. I bet there was a big man down there to emphasise the point.

We continued to make out Rahab amid low conversation and some giggles and shrieks. Then there was the rapid patter of feet coming up the stairs and doors closing on the numerous rooms; the business of a brothel on a busy night; and not more than a few yards away from us and discovery. Every time we heard footsteps coming up the stairway, I sensed we all held our breath; well, perhaps not Seth. Would they stop, or would they stump up the extra storey and crash in on us?

So it was with relief when Seth leant across to me.

"Ehud, your turn for stag on the roof."

I got to my feet, heaved my way up through the trapdoor opening and, spear in hand, crawled on all fours over to where Gam was sitting, his back against a chimney.

Gam shook his head in response to my 'Anything?' and crawled away.

I sat back against the dark stone of the chimney. It was a good place; I could see anyone coming up on the roof before they saw me, and anyone looking up from the street or over from the battlements would just see the chimney as my dull grey uniform melted into the dark sooty stone.

I looked over to the battlements and the tall twin towers over the main gate of the city. To the left, I could just make out the thick ropes wrapped and knotted around two of the thick symmetrical buttresses which formed the battlements. Up there on the narrow walkway the sentries were patrolling casually, occasionally leaning out over an embrasure and looking out into the desert; or spitting more like on the poor devils in the cage below; bored, like all sentries, and doing anything for a bit of fun. Except I was not just a bored spectator, I reminded myself. At some stage, tonight and sometime soon, we would have to be up there to do our job and...? It was no consolation to consider I had not the blindest idea, how we were going to do it.

Time passed. Down below on the street there were still people coming to Rahab's door but not the same raucous crowd of a bit earlier. The noise from the centre – shouting, music and crackling of a giant fire – seemed to be diminishing. *Well,* I thought, *if Jericho is at last going to bed it will not be long now.*

A patrol came swinging up the street. "Left, Right, Left, Right," called the commander, and brought them to a sharp halt below me, then a 'Right Turn'. All this in Amorite, of course, and something I had not thought of asking Zaki about. Ugh, an omission I reflected; then for a moment I could not help giggling at the thought of old Ma Miriam hearing Zaki drilling me in the cubicle, left, right, left, right and so on.

Then more commands from below and also easy to interpret.

"At ease!" rasped out the voice. Then, minutes later, "Attenshun!" and with a 'Quick march' the patrol was off again. Drilling a squad is the same everywhere; same words of command and, of course, same insults from a mock- furious commander but at least I did not have to worry about those.

I was saying these words of command over to myself. Actually, in my imagination, I was drilling Zaki, her boobs wobbling from side to side as she marched when Clang, Clang, Clang went the great bell in the left-hand tower. That was the signal, I recollected, for the night watch to take over. *Bye Zaki,* I thought switching off my fantasy. Now we are on! You can't go into battle with a woman in your head! And, yes, once again I felt those butterflies in my stomach.

Seth called.

In our dusty upstairs room, we quietly got ready.

There was not much to do really; take the Amorite helmet out of the bag, put it on fastening the hard leather buckle, grab a last swig of water and a scrap of bread, and we were ready. In the half-light, Seth carried out his final checks.

"Spear," he called and we each raised our spear; "Dagger," and we each drew our dagger and showed him the shining blade; "Helmet," and we each shook our heads.

"Tighten that strap there," rasped Seth to Koresh whose helmet had slipped onto his nose.

"Now," he continued, "we wait for Rahab. From now on, we are an Amorite patrol on duty."

He then went on to remind us of what we had to do. He did not half keep it simple. Get up on the wall, get rid of the sentries, check that our boys on the other side of the wall are there and ready, then with a 'One, Two, Three, CUT' from Seth, Gam would cut the ropes. Crash, bang! Down and away would go the cage. Then sling our ropes over the wall, down we go and hotfoot it back to Gilgal. *Oh yes,* I thought, *Seth, tell us about the heroes' reception!*

"And don't forget the bloody mittens, or you will burn your hands to pieces on the rope," Seth finished.

Typical Seth! Broad-brush plan and no evidence of any thought of the challenges we faced or what might go wrong, except getting a few blisters on our hands. I even smiled to myself; if sore hands were the worst we got out of this evening's fun, we could count ourselves lucky.

We heard soft steps outside and a triple knock on

the door. Rahab entered and pointed to the opening in the roof. We followed her up the stairs and into the open air.

Once again, we followed her gliding figure over the roofs and back a bit from our recent hiding place opposite the main gates. Eventually we found ourselves overlooking a courtyard. There was a narrow set of external steps zigzagging down to the ground, four storeys below.

"Go down here," she said in a low voice. "The gate of the courtyard is open. Then you are in the main street." She looked at Seth. This was the moment of parting, I guessed.

"Thank you, ma'am," said Seth tonelessly and started to lead the way down the steps. I brought up the rear and looked back. There she was still standing there. I thought I could see her eyes glistening under the shadow of her hood. She raised her hand to her mouth and blew a good luck kiss after us.

Chapter 17

Down in the courtyard we formed up in a single file facing Seth with me on the left.

"'Ere, Ehud," Seth demanded, "what's the Amorite for left, right, left, right?"

That's it, I thought, *Seth, one thing at a time! And aren't you lucky to have Ehud here with his wits about him?* Not that you will display any gratitude.

I took him quickly through the simple orders. "Got that, you lot?" he said, and slowly surveyed our line from left to right.

"Attenshun – Right Turn – Quick March." Seth's dodgy Amorite words of command echoed in the quiet courtyard; and through the gateway, left arm swinging, right arm grasping a spear, we marched out into the street.

The earlier crowds had thinned out but the coffee shops and inns were still busy with drinkers and old men playing backgammon. Seth marched straight ahead, not deviating to left or right. No one looked up from their pleasures. Those on the street never gave a passing look, or simply sidestepped out of the way; proof that there are few things more invisible than a file of soldiers marching through a city under siege. Or rather we were simply commonplace; an unfortunate presence to be avoided where possible. No citizen wants to see his streets suddenly filled by young men recruited hastily from the countryside and put into uniform. The prudent lock up their daughters and double the bars on the shutters; that done they just try and ignore the randy, pilfering rabble from the countryside marching up and down their streets and hope for a return to normal life as soon as possible.

So we swung along untroubled to Seth's occasional 'left, right, left' until we were in sight of the twin towers branching up on either side of the main gate of Jericho.

"Squad, halt, left turn." We halted in the square and turned to face Seth.

I bet it was the kind of warrior who never went further than a desk who pronounced that war is 90% boredom and 10% excitement because but it has always struck me as nonsense. All right, perhaps correct on the 10% 'excitement' bit, if that is what you want to call 'Terror and Desperation', but boredom simply does not describe the other 90%. More like hard grind and misery all along the way. Take tonight! We had marched for hours, waited freezing in the desert night air, bumped along in a cart under a stinking awning, and hidden upstairs in a brothel. Not forgetting the silent killing of an unsuspecting sentry having a pee. And you call that boredom, give me real boredom any time!

But all that was to be as nothing for what was in store, I thought grimly. *Now we are into 'Excitement' time!* 'Excitement' resulting in success or failure, glory or ignominy, life or death. Okay, and the possibility of capture as well. How nice, and all to be determined in the next half-hour!

"At ease!" ordered Seth, and we grounded the butts of our spears. The great bonfire in the centre was dying. Looking up, the walls now towered darkly over us. On the battlement walkway, we could just make out the shimmering helmets of the sentries doing their beat or leaning over an embrasure to look out over the desert. Descending from the walkway a wooden stairway zigzagged down the wall to a small, whitewashed guardroom. This section of the wall, so we had been told, was guarded by nine men and a commander; three men as sentries up on the wall at any time and the others in the guardroom resting but dressed and ready for action.

I wondered what Seth was planning. The only way up that wall was those zigzag steps with the guardroom at the bottom. So one option was to take out the guardroom; which would mean crashing in, five against six but with surprise in our favour. A bit of butchery and then hell for leather up the steps onto the walkway and do the business. But the guys on the wall would see and hear the commotion in the guardroom, raise the alarm, and be ready for us at the top. *Not so good,* I thought. The only other option I could think of was, at a sharp word of command from Seth, we belt over the square, roar past the guardroom and clamber up the steps and onto the walkway before anyone really knew what was happening.

Sitting outside the guardroom was a great bear of a man, the watchman, with his timekeeping lamp. When the oil reached a certain level, it would be midnight, which he would announce in a loud voice in the square before setting off for his rounds bawling his message. His announcement of midnight would be the signal for Jubal and the reception committee on the outside, and for us to take the wall.

"Won't be long now, lads," murmured Seth turning his head slightly so we could all hear him. The watchman had risen and was pulling his boots on. Seth walked out in front and turned to face us.

"Now, lads," he continued quietly, "let's just go through things once more." This was a different Seth; gone was the sarcastic and nit-picking bluster and bawling of the camp. Now he was quiet, almost conversational, he could have been describing a trip to the barbers. Finishing with, "And I'll be the last one off the wall." He paused, then smiled. "Remember to use those mittens!" Were we about to snigger? We did not have time.

"Right," he continued. "And in case you're thinking how we get past the guardroom, up the steps and onto the walkway it is simple. We march!"

Was there a collective intake of breath? Possibly, but he got us there. *Good old Seth,* I thought, *that good old military trick.* Look shifty, act hesitant and people will immediately notice. Move fast, orderly, head straight ahead and people will think you are official; well, for those vital few moments before you have to break your cover and all hell breaks loose.

"And you, Ehud," continued Seth in his low monotone, "stay in the rear. If anyone questions us, give him your best Amorite."

That certainly got my mind working. What would

I say if we were challenged by a sentry on the wall? Or the guardroom commander? He would hear us marching past and up the steps. Surely, he would be out in no time and demanding to know what was going on?

Big Abs caught Seth's eye and nodded over towards the guardroom. The watchman was now standing and stamping his feet while strapping on his sword belt. Seth looked at him quickly, then took his place on the right of us standing waiting in our single file.

"Midnight, midnight," bawled the watchman, first to his left up to the men on the walls and then right into the city in general before setting off on his patrol. "Right turn. Quick march." Seth gave the Amorite words of command, not shouting, just a firm late-night-not-to-wake-good-citizens kind of voice and we trooped off behind him, parade-ground style, across the square, necks braced back, looking straight ahead, in time and with our free left arms swinging back and forth.

"Left, right, left, right," we continued mechanically past the guardroom and started to mount the steps. They were a bit more rickety than I expected and shook as we ascended. To keep balance, we slowed up from a fast trot to a more deliberate pace.

I was kind of aware that the two sentries nearest on the wall were looking down at us. They were probably no more than a bit puzzled at this break in the routine, and curious to see what was going to happen next.

Seth had just reached the first platform when I

heard the door of the guard room below open and an angry voice shout up, "Ere! Where do you think you lot are going?"

"Keep going, lads!" I heard Seth hiss back as he kept climbing, turning from the first platform onto the next quaking stairway. One more platform, another stairway, and we would be up on the walkway but the Amorite commander was already onto us.

I suppose I had rehearsed in my mind for this kind of thing happening. Option One, play the 'Denial' card; ignore the shout below and keep on going. No, any half-reasonable guard commander would have his men out and clambering up the stairway after us while he beat the alarm on the long hanging pole outside the guardroom door. A great prospect for us, caught between the guards charging up the stairway and a gathering reception committee on the battlements.

So it was Option Two, 'Bluster'. All we needed was a few precious seconds; time to get us all onto the walkway, and it was up to me to win that respite. I put my head over my shoulder and shouted down to the angry guard commander in my best Amorite;

"General Zemri's orders. He will be here shortly."

I almost felt sorry for the man. On the angry frowning face, I could see him agonising; here I am, the poor fellow was thinking, Saturday night guard duty and all pretty quiet when suddenly these men turn up and, dammit, without so much as a 'With-your-leave-or-by-your-leave' sweep past my guardroom and up onto the wall shouting something about orders from the general. Well, I could show them! Easiest thing in the world, play it by the book, sound the alarm and have the guard after them. Killed or captured in a jiffy that lot! Job done, good on me and the lads! But then, horror of horrors, General Zemri turns up, some mess-up in communication or something, and finds I have chopped up six members of his personal bodyguard.

You really cannot blame the commander, and I bet Seth – denying it vehemently of course – would have done the same in the circumstances. I saw 'Puzzle' leave his face and replaced by a kind of gleeful determination; he had made a decision; he would show the General a spick-and-span guard when he arrived!

"Turn out the guard!" He roared at the guardroom and stepped inside, like he had done a hundred times before, to chivvy and bluster bored, sleepy men to get on parade outside the guardroom and impress a senior officer.

With those precious extra seconds, we gained the walkway. Seth and his three men raced off to the right while Abs and I stood at the top of the stairway and looked along the parapet to the left, and the bored gaze of the other guards stationed at wide intervals along the wall.

There was a long agonised scream followed by the thump of the body hitting the ground. That was the sentry opposite the cage; amid his confusion and terror he had half got out a challenge when Seth had simply flicked him off the walkway with his short spear.

The scream had hardly finished when the rapid clanging of the alarm pole below rang out and was picked up along the walls. From every side, we could hear the beating of poles, and shouts as soldiers were called to arms all over the city.

Whoosh, whoosh, whoosh. Flaming arrows passed not far above my head in a wave and fell onto the thatched roofs of the city. I looked through the embrasure. Suddenly, there was another volley of flame rising from the darkness of the desert. I instinctively ducked as a second fiery wave, spitting burning tar, passed over my head.

Phew, I thought with relief, *at least our guys are bloody well out there and, thank you very much, setting the city on fire is a handy diversion.* But Abs and I had more immediate concerns. Threat Number One was the previously puzzled sentry to the left of us along the parapet, now galvanised into some kind of action. A middle-aged man, probably a shopkeeper by day, with a weekly guard duty on the walls which was a steady night-time job where all he had to do was put on a grey tunic and helmet and muffle up well against the cold. Then stump along the wall, spear over the shoulder, occasionally looking out over the battlements into the desert. Never anything to report, but now this!

He was advancing on us, slowly, hesitantly and holding out his big long spear, shouting for help from his mate, similarly armed, fifty paces behind, or anyone who was nearby. I reckoned we could deal with him.

Much more serious was Threat Number Two below us, as the first soldiers of the guard mounted the stairway urged on by a furious guard commander with a reputation to salvage.

The stairway shook under the weight and clamber of the armed men. We would be no match for their long spears once they neared the top.

There was only one thing for it. I pulled out my dagger and started sawing away at the ropes securing the stairs to the walkway. It was a temporary stairway put up, no doubt, when we first turned up outside Jericho, an additional way of getting men onto the walls quickly. It was really three wooden ladders, each section secured to a wooden platform with poles sunk into the great walls.

"Help me," I called to Abs and together we sawed away at the ropes. It took just a few seconds with sharp knives in the hands of desperate men for the bonds to part and fall away.

"Push," I called and we both heaved against the ladder. *Thank goodness for Ab's giant strength,* I thought desperately, as the top of the stairway swung out from the wall. For a moment, it swung just a few inches away, then snapped back against the wall. The whole stairway shook and we saw briefly the men below lurch then steady themselves on the shaking treads; then the headlong ascent resumed. Desperately pushing once again against the stairway I found myself looking into the eyes of the leading soldier, now on the second platform.

"Where was bloody Abs?" I cursed. Looking behind me I saw him wrenching the long alarm pole with its chain out of the wall. Then seated with his back propped against the castellated wall, he thrust against the stairway with the long pole. Using all his great strength, with every squeal of the ropes and crack of wood the space between the stairs and the walkway increased.

I flung my spear. That sentry on the wall was almost on us. As I followed the point of my spear into his black beard there was a horrible gurgling sound. Behind me more cracking sounds and shouts from below.

I looked back just in time to see Abs now lying down, arms fully extended, with the tip of the pole against the top of the stairway. This was now bent and twisting several feet away from the wall. But even fully stretched Abs was unable to do more than prod the stairway as it bounced back against the pole. Fascinated I watched this battle, prod, bounce, prod, bounce; and the soldiers were climbing again.

Then another prod from Abs and suddenly a long cracking sound; more shouts – or shrieks rather – and the whole stairway tipped over in a giant arc, and in slow motion with its screaming and shouting human load, crashed abruptly onto the street and the burning roofs below.

In the strange lull which followed, I suddenly became aware of other sounds. Still the tap, tap, tapping of the metal poles all over the city, still the rough orders of soldiers being turned out; but now there was the crackling of the flames as the thatched roofs took light and the shouts of the firefighters as they formed human chains with buckets of water. But penetrating this cacophony there was another sound; it was a kind of scraping noise, like rough iron bars rubbing against a stone wall. Suddenly I realised the noise was from the other side of the wall and was human. I looked over the battlements and traced the sound along to the cage now illuminated by the flickering light from the flames of the city. Looking down, I could make out a whirling of naked limbs, faces with bright eyes pressed to the trellis ceiling of the cage, and mouths, opening and shutting, emitting this croaking rasping sound; all these poor devils could produce after their long imprisonment of thirst, hunger and the burning sun.

"Ropes out," I heard Seth shout and two escape ropes snaked over the battlements into the darkness. Seth and Gam secured them to metal hooks sticking out of the wall.

"Ready yet?" Seth shouted down over the wall. I could see giant beams being wrestled up out of the darkness and propped under the cage. There was an answering cry from below. "Wait, wait!"

"Better be quick!" shouted Seth. He and Gam stood ready, daggers in hand poised over the heavy ropes knotted around the two crenellations and secured to the cage below.

"Ehud," Seth's urgent voice shouted out. "Take my place." It was almost a scream; Koresh was in trouble.

Koresh had been designated the task of taking on any sentries who came along the parapet from the right while Seth and Gam could get on with the job of releasing the cage. It should have been another case of confronting another slow-moving very reluctant part-time soldier but Kor's adversary was different. I was

273

just in time to see Koresh backing away from a slowly advancing grim- faced Amorite with a long spear, then buckle up as the point emerged bloody and dripping from his back. Seth was already running to meet this new threat.

"They are ready, they are ready," shouted Gam as I dashed past him to Seth's place and reached for my dagger. I could hear the croaking noises from below growing louder.

I did not bother to look over the wall but simply looked back at Gam.

"One, two, three, cut!" he yelled and started to hack away at the three thick strands of the massive rope. "And shout when you've cut two strands!"

I blessed that blacksmith. He had done a good job on my dagger. I knew it was a good bit of metal but I had never been able to get an edge on it like he had. Anyway, most times all I wanted was a reasonable cutter of bread or a bit of canvas not something with the razor-sharp edge he had given it.

The blade almost hissed as it cut through one heavy strand of the rope and then another. As they sprang apart the remaining strand quivered; the threads starting to burst apart with the new strain.

"Ready!" I shouted, dagger touching the rope.

"Cut," I heard from my left and start to saw. Suddenly the remaining strand I was trying to cut tightened, and there was a grinding cracking sound above the excited croak of the prisoners. Gam had cut his rope and the left-hand side of the cage was now slipping down Obed's platform. I sawed away in desperation.

My strand snapped suddenly striking back and knocking the dagger out of my hand and high into the air. I looked over and saw my side of the cage now slipping down the platform. Over to my right there was a short scream as Seth dealt with his man.

"Off you go, lads," I heard him shout.

I was about to un-sling my bag from my back when I looked down and saw Seth's mittens beside his leather bag where he had thrown it down on the parapet. *No time for the bloody mittens,* I thought, *I'll leave those to Seth.*

I grabbed his leather bag and scrambled through the embrasure. I lifted up the escape rope dangling into the darkness and wrapped the leather bag around the coarse thick fibres. Grabbing it with my right hand I launched myself into the darkness and the noise and the shouting.

I swung in hard against the wall and managed to get my other hand onto the bag around the rope.

"Get going, get going," Seth was shouting from above.

I eased my grip and abruptly started to slip at speed. I could smell the burning leather and feel the heat through my hands as I desperately tried to slow my descent. Suddenly my legs crumpled up to my chest as I hit the ground below, winding me. Then something crashed into me from above and I was out.

*****

I came to upside-down and bumping along in the darkness. Over someone's back and with my head down, all I could see was my porter's heels rising and falling as he raced to get away from the noise and light of the city. Arrows still whistled over my head, now going both ways.

A trail of dark spots fell in the sand behind me. My blood, I realised, when I put my hand up to my skull finding it warm and slippery. The bang on the head had opened up my old wound and I was gushing. I kept my hand clamped to my scalp; the blood continued to ooze through my fingers but the trail on the ground got less.

"There you are, lad," a jocular voice rang out as I found myself pitched onto the sand. It was Seth. He had been my porter. Then squatting on the sand beside me he lifted my hand away from my head. His grasp was rough and calloused, I realised he was still wearing leather mittens.

He swore gently. "We'll get that looked at in due course." He drew off a mitten and gave it to me.

"Take this," he said. "Keep it on your head for the time being."

I looked down at the mitten. The palm was scorched black and blistered, clearly a faster descent off the wall than mine. I guessed he must have crashed into me at the bottom. Well, I was not going to wait for an apology.

"Thanks, Seth," I said. Turning over the mitten I clamped the rough unscorched back to my wound.

"Wait here while I gather the others." Seth rose and set off into the darkness shouting.

I swivelled round and looked back towards the city. The black battlements were silhouetted against the flames and, above them, a huge pall of grey smoke was rising into the deep blue sky. I could make out the movement of running men on the battlements as the embrasures filled and emptied repeatedly, but the great gates remained closed. With a jerk, I realised the cage was gone. But where? I shaded my eyes against the flames. I half expected to see the cage intact or, more likely, smashed at the base but no, it wasn't there; but I could still see, propped up against the wall, the dark lines of the beams.

I looked up to see Abs towering above me.

"So you got out okay," I said. "What about the others?" He crouched down then sniggered.

"Sorry, Ehud," he said, putting his hand over his mouth. "But you do look funny with that mitten thing on your head. Glad you are okay though." Another shadow loomed and Abs looked up. It was Gam.

"Yeah, I think we're all here, apart from poor Kor. He got a spear in the guts." Abs paused. "You remembered to use the mittens?" he asked, nodding at my head and then showing the undamaged palms of his hands. "Me too!"

I explained that I had used Seth's leather bag and Abs smiled.

"Up you get," Seth's voice came out of the darkness and he was there above us. I struggled to get up but my legs just crumpled. Abs and Gam on either side heaved me up. Seth looked at us narrowly.

I am not sure what we were expecting from Seth.

Perhaps a bit of congratulation, some kind of acknowledgement of a job well done, and against pretty stiff odds. But no, that wasn't Seth's style and we knew it. So, no surprises, he simply looked us up down and along.

"Everyone okay?" he asked tonelessly, adding, "I know about Ehud."

Gam piped up, rubbing his thigh, expecting some sympathy. "Hurt my leg when I hit the ground."

"More fool you," pronounced Seth. "But looks like you can still walk."

So poor old Gam had had a hard landing as well, I thought. So I wasn't the only one. Lucky old Seth! Without me for a soft landing he might be hobbling himself!

"Hands okay?" demanded Seth without much interest, just following procedure. "Everyone use the mittens, okay?" He did not wait for a reply.

"Follow me," he growled and turned on his heel and set off alongside two lines of heavy planks which stood out white and skeletal against the greyness of the desert.

It was a trick from our days in Egypt building the pyramids. My grandfather– Well, Dad's father if you prefer– used to tell us about hauling these huge stones across the desert. They would take and strip four straight trees and lay them in parallel lines a yard apart. The worst job was heaving the stone onto these rails. Then the towing would begin, often requiring two hundred men tugging away, whipped on by overseers. As the stone reached the end of one set of wooden rails the next set was laid down and so on, often for hundreds of miles. It was slow work, so Grandfather said! But the same principle had been adapted for the cage, which was much lighter, of course, so the towing was speedy but they therefore needed more rails – planks in this case – to keep up.

Half a mile back from Jericho we came on the main force and, of course, the cage. There the orderlies, some with scarves over their mouths against the awful stench, were at their grim work sorting the former prisoners into three categories. Already there was a line of the dead, not stretched out full length with their hands folded and crossed on the chest, or something decent like that, but stiff and contorted in the cramped position they had died in. Others could barely move and were carried out and laid flat. There they were inspected by the medics to see who was likely to survive. The third category, those who were able to stumble out of the cage on their own, were ordered to sit down and were given lukewarm gruel and some water.

A line of six wagons drawn by donkeys drew up and Seth was called over to help load.

"We've got one here who needs a lift," he said to the lead driver.

"Put him on the last wagon. This one's for stiffs," the driver growled down from his box, motioning with his whip towards the back of the convoy.

The last was a much larger wagon pulled by four donkeys. The driver was dropping the tail board as we arrived, me more or less being dragged along, and he

279

looked at us suspiciously.

"He can't walk. Got permission for a ride," announced Abs.

"Put him up then, over in the far corner. We are going to be crowded enough as it is," said the driver grumpily.

I was pushed up onto the wagon. I managed to wave at Gam and Abs and then crawled over into the far corner where I tried to prop myself up. I still had the satchel with the rope and gloves. It dug into my back so I slipped it off and held it over my knees. *Bloody useless thing now,* I thought, *but I had better hold onto it.* Seth would want every bit of kit returned or accounted for, which means I had better not lose his wretched mitten, still clutched to my head. I gingerly put a finger up to feel my scalp, rough now with dried blood. I gently tried to move the mitten but it appeared glued to the wound. *Leave it there,* I thought, *until I can get proper treatment.*

I must have dropped off. I jerked awake with a fright as the tail board crashed down, and I saw the wagon driver heave himself up, cursing. He ignored me sitting upright in the corner and made over to a pile of blankets. He grabbed a couple, wrapped them around himself and climbed back onto his box.

I shivered. I was cold through and through and I knew, just knew, that I had to get warm. Or I would die. *After all you've been through, Ehud,* I told myself, *you would be a fool to let yourself die of shock.*

The sky was a piercing dark blue, and light from the stars illuminated the desert like a full moon. How long had I been there? Why weren't we moving? Getting a lift on a wagon did not now seem such a smart idea. Probably Seth and the gang are already back in Gilgal and hitting an amphora of warm wine. I looked over at the pile of blankets. Wait if I must, I snarled to myself, but freeze no longer. I stood up and stamped my feet and flapped my arms. The driver looked round, half mumbling to himself half to me, "Way past the time we agreed, and I've got an early job tomorrow." He was still grumbling away as I cautiously made my way over to the blankets. "Bloody medics, never touch anything to do with bloody medics!" he moaned on.

"Yes, help yourself, they're not my bloody blankets," he asserted with some jubilation. "Come up on the box if you like."

I wrapped myself up in the blankets with one carefully over my wounded head and clambered up beside him. I dropped off again, then more crashing woke me. At last, they were loading the wagons in front, dropping the tailboards and sliding on the loaded stretchers.

The wagon in front was for those prisoners who could still walk. They were helped over and lifted up onto the wagon. A man on top was distributing blankets. An awful mewling noise reached us. It came from the poor wretches in front as they sat down. It was the sound of men crying.

"They're mad, out of their senses!" murmured the driver, looking across at them a bit in awe. "Anyway, we should be off soon," he muttered. The tailboard crashed down behind us, and the medics clambered aboard. There was some cursing and an angry head appeared between the driver and me.

"Where are the bloody blankets? We're missing half of them," said he. *Leave the talking to the driver,* I thought.

"I don't know," the driver shook his head sullenly. "Some guys came and picked them up a while ago. Said they were for the cage blokes." Very matter- of-fact, a bit irritable, hard to be challenged on his lie, and he knew it.

Angry Head snorted, and turned his wrath on me.

"And who the hell are you?" he hissed. "Those are our blankets. I recognise them."

The driver came to my help.

"He's wounded, can't you see? Arrived with those blankets. They're not yours."

I slipped the blanket off to show my head. I must have looked a ghastly enough sight in the starlight, my face covered in blood and then that ridiculous leather gauntlet still stuck to my scalp.

Angry Head looked briefly at me, then gave up, but I wasn't going to get any sympathy from him.

"You can get treated when you get back," said he dismissively. "And you lot!" he shouted back. "Stop complaining. Sit down and we will use the blankets like a tent."

I put the blanket back over my head and my arm through the wooden railing. I had had enough excitement and bumps for one night and falling off the box was not going to be one of them.

There was a cracking of whips and braying of donkeys and we slowly started moving forward.

Chapter 18

"You're awake at last." Spices Junior sniffed. "They wouldn't let me in while you were asleep."

You could hear the resentment in his voice. I was sitting up and sipping the tea which Zepzi was holding out for me.

"I have been waiting," he continued unnecessarily.

He stood there, his portly little figure in the medic's uniform of brown tunic and yellow scarf with an assistant behind him holding a black bag. He oozed contempt; I might be Micah's chariot boy, I might be one of the hero rescuers but, as far as he was concerned, I was still a dirty little Benjamite and treating me was way beneath his dignity.

I stared back at him. I realised that I must have looked pretty fearful. I was not sorry! *Enjoy the frontline,* I thought with malice. *It'll make a change from the high priest's haemorrhoids!*

The wagons had moved very slowly and it was early morning but still dark when we creaked into Gilgal camp, the tents and buildings speckled with dew. The tailboard dropped and the orderlies tumbled out swearing at the cold and fighting over the blankets.

"Get down now, lad," rasped the driver from the depths of his blanket layers, only his face showing.

"'Ere, and you can leave those blankets behind!" he shouted after I had stiffly made my way down from the box and was walking away.

Give him those blankets? No bloody way! I thought to myself. I did not look round but continued up the hill. I think he shouted after me something like 'ungrateful little bleeder' but what did I care?

Outside Micah's tent there was the night guard sitting at a table with a small oil lamp. He challenged me as I approached. I must have just looked like a bundle of blankets to him.

"You stop right there," he called out, not too loud, he did not want to wake up the household.

"It's me, Ehud." I opened the flaps around my head and showed him my face.

He recoiled briefly, then laughed.

"So it is, so it is." He smiled to himself. "We weren't expecting you, y'know?"

What the hell! I thought.

"No one gave a dog's chance for you lot getting back. Been quite a clamber back here to replace you." Chortling, he shook his head. "But Tubs had his nephew lined up."

I remembered that skinny little black-haired boy who was always sitting about scowling in the kitchen.

"He's there now," the watchman continued.

I just saw red and stormed past him and down the corridors to my chamber.

It was dark inside but I could see a figure stretched out on my palliase.

"Get out, you little shit," I cried kicking him furiously, I did not care where. He gave a cry and rolled off the palliase and started to crawl away. I landed one last kick on his back. That was the last of him as he scurried on his hands and knees out through the flap.

I was not going to bother about washing at this stage, I flopped down on the straw and arranged the stolen blankets because I was beginning to feel cold again. A sickly smell of jasmine enveloped me. That boy's been at the scent pots, I remember thinking, he will never make a chariot boy. Then I must have passed out.

The next I knew it was bright daylight and I heard a soft female voice saying; "Are you awake, Ehud?" I opened my eyes and there was Zepzi kneeling beside me, all sweet and soft, with slender cool hands holding out a cup of herbal tea. I sat up and, lo and behold, from under the flap entered Spices Junior and his servant. You could have left me alone a bit longer with Zepzi, I cursed silently. "You might have washed," Spices started again with disgust in his voice. "And you, be off!" He curtly ordered poor Zepzi who scrambled to her feet and left. I turned my head and followed her out of the tent.

"And what's that ridiculous thing on your head?" he demanded, angry that I was distracted from his great presence by the curvy bottom of a servant girl. I put my hand up to my head, I had forgotten about Seth's leather mitten, now completely stiff with blood.

Frankly, when it comes to doctoring or patient care, give me the female gender any time. The blokes may have a string of qualifications, learned words by the ream, and all the herbs in the world but what really heals is female care; the kind words and the soft touch. While Zepzi was there with her warm tea, I had almost forgotten about the crack on my head, but now Spices was here, and that wound must be made important and deserving of the privilege of his presence.

The next few minutes were some of the most agonising I have ever endured. I don't think Spices was deliberately causing pain but, frankly, did he care? Yes, he did get the orderly to swab a bit of water around my blood-caked scalp and where the mitten was clearly stuck fast; but rather than wait for the blood to soften or wash away, he was out with his little knife scraping away and tugging on the mitten at the same time.

"Keep quiet and be still," he ordered. I ground my teeth and gripped my arms around my back.

"There!" he said flinging Seth's mitten on the ground. "Clean that wound now, I want a good look."

He motioned to his orderly who came forward with a bowl of water and a rough towel and started to clean my face and scalp. Nothing gentle about him either; he could have been cleaning the arse of the donkey at the end of a long day.

"You have broken your stitches," Spices announced, accusation in his voice. *Thank you*, I thought. *I – Yes, I have broken my stitches, have I? A self-inflicted wound, is it? A bit of outstanding carelessness, eh? Something for which further punishment is due possibly?*

Oh, yes, I bet Spices was thinking all these things, just not saying them out loud. Wounded men disturbed the smooth tenor of his life, and it was their fault! I kept my mouth shut, then let out a cry and jerked my head away as Spices pulled at the newly torn flesh.

"He's a wriggler. Put on some myrrh," Spices called over a shoulder. "And pass me the needle and thread."

I shut my eyes tightly and prayed; Yahweh, Baal, whoever you are I don't care, do something for me, just no more pain, please! The orderly came forward and poured the liquid over my wound. It stung at first with an oily fragrance and then the raw pain of the wound receded. Relief! All I could feel as Spices worked the needle to and fro was a light tapping over the wound. I breathed out noisily.

I felt the draft of the flap being raised and, even with my eyes shut, saw a shadow rise up in front of me.

"Well, I say," I heard a familiar voice announce. "If it isn't little Spices practising his butchery on my good friend."

It can't be, I thought. I opened my eyes and there, of course, standing in the entrance, was Barak, his eyes twinkling and that cool mocking smile. I smiled to myself, a contest between Barak and Spices would be entertaining. I had never heard anyone call him 'Spices' to his face.

To give Spices his due, he was up to this impertinence.

"What are you doing here, Barak?" said he casually, acting bored, not even bothering to look round. He continued to ply his needle.

Barak simply laughed.

"Visiting my heroic friend, of course," said he, crouching down and pretending to take an interest in the operation. "Mmm," he mused, "That's quite a responsibility you've got there, Spices." He paused, Spices lips tightened, and anger shone on his face.

"I mean, old Josh..." Barak continued. *Wow, I thought, rather gleefully, no one refers to Joshua like that, well, only in the tent or around the campfire. Barak must be very sure of himself!*

"Old Josh," he continued easily, "wants the boy alive. Kill him off with your dirty needlework and I wouldn't like to be in your sandals. Back with the pack animals again before you can say..." he paused, searching – I think he was going to say something blasphemous, but thought better of it – "Saddle soap!" he declared triumphantly. *You cruel bastard, I thought, but lay it on, good for you!* Spices continued to work the needle. "I heard you were back in the tents," he said with disdain in his voice. Barak neither moved nor spoke, just remained crouching and smiling at me.

"And you will go while I am treating a patient," continued Spices. "Be off, or I will call Micah's chief steward."

Barak seemed in no way discomfited by this or in any hurry to go. He just crouched there. *What next? I* wondered. Then he leant forward and patted me on the knee. Once again that cool smile, with just a touch of menace.

"I'll be back, Ehud, my old friend," said he and left the chamber, the heavy flap falling noisily behind him. I reckon he felt that he'd had his fun with Spices and whatever business he had with me could wait.

Spices did not say anything as he continued with

his needle. Then, in that superior voice of his, "Barak is a friend of yours?" he questioned me. I explained how I had supplanted him as Micah's chariot boy.

"But he's been pretty good to me," I added, and immediately felt foolish. "A bad friend to have," announced Spices primly after a long pause. "He'll get you into trouble." I remained silent. I wondered how Barak had crossed Spices.

Spices finished his work. "I have cleaned out the old stitches and put in new ones. I recommend light duties for a week. Then report to the San and we will take out the stitches." He rose while the orderly came forward and cleared away the bowl and the other bits and pieces. Spices was frowning, he appeared to be thinking, wondering how to phrase something.

"Report to the San immediately if the wound opens up or starts to ooze. Keep your head covered when outside," he continued. I smiled to myself. Barak's threat about Joshua was clearly rankling in his mind.

"And if you hear anything suspicious about Barak report it to me immediately! Immediately! It's very important!" With that parting shot, or surely there was a threat too, Spices bustled out of my chamber followed by his orderly.

I slept. No one disturbed me until sundown when Zepzi bought me some food and a little date wine, which Micah had ordered for me.

"He says you must rest, and he'll see you tomorrow. Well done, he says!" Her dark eyes glowed at me. I almost purred; there is nothing like a bit of praise and admiration from a sexy little piece.

Of course, hero worship does not last long.

"I want it back clean," Seth said shortly after a sniff of disgust, handing me back his leather mitten still encrusted with blood. I took it back murmuring an apology.

"And I have put in a report to Micah on the operation. He wants to speak to you to. So don't show off," he added.

"I think there'll be some kind of victory parade," he announced with his customary disdain. I suppose that was as near as he could get to 'Well done'.

I duly saw Micah. That was a bit more encouraging.

"You did well, all of you." He lazily congratulated, taking a sip of wine. "Better than that, it's a triumph! A great day for the tribe of Benjamin!" He nodded. "But I need a bit of colour for the boss. Seth's a good commander. He did well, very well, but he's no storyteller."

Yes, I could just imagine Seth telling the story to Joshua and his generals. It would go something like this:

Seth speaks: "We found the convoy; we entered Jericho; we mounted the battlements; we cut the cage ropes."

And that's all Seth would have said, although he might have added, "And now we are here."

Then he would already be saluting like mad and wanting to get away. Mentally I shook my head; Reliable, good in action but junior commander was his absolute ceiling.

Micah wanted more. He even gave me a cup of wine and enquired after my head. Then he sat back and I gave it to him. Well, not everything! Nothing about the barrels of oil of course, and oh, he loved it. I did not spare the detail, the bolshie spy, the guard having a pee, the stinking wagon, Rahab…

"Yes," I heard Micah say. "Go on." He was puzzled because I had suddenly stopped speaking. I collected myself quickly and rattled through the rest of the story. But I was now in a panic, a panic to get away. I could hardly wait to leave while Micah drawled out his thanks, and murmured about seeing Tubs for my payment.

Rahab! Of course, I had not mentioned anything to Micah about the package Rahab had given me, or for that matter anything about the package Barak had given me; *but where the hell was her package?* I thought furiously. I really started to worry. *Had I lost it? Had it been stolen?* I thought back. No, I clearly remember feeling it in my bag on the wagon. Yes, the bag was still there beside my paillasse when Spices visited. Yes, it was there when Zepzi dropped in. I thought I could almost visualise it this morning when I got up. But I had not looked inside. Was the package still there? I rushed back to my chamber.

Tubal, standing outside the entrance to Micah's quarters had just started his smile of welcome, preparatory to some mocking banter, as I, mumbling an excuse, swept past him along to my room. I hurriedly pushed past the flap and, well, you might have guessed it, there was a Barak in his favourite visiting position, stretched out on my paillasse with his eyes closed and hands clasped behind his close-cropped fair hair. He wasn't playing doggo this time though, but opened his eyes and looked at me with that ever-mocking smile.

"At last, Ehud, on your own at last! We have business to discuss." He paused, cocking his head to one side, and continued slowly, "By all accounts, you performed well, very well. Of course, our serious friend, Seth, will get the public credit but," he added tapping his nose with a long forefinger, "those in the know…" He smiled and jabbed his finger at me.

I was starting to mumble some kind of thanks when he sharply interrupted me. "Where is it?" he demanded sitting up and looking hard at me. Oh yes, the smile was still there but I detected anger.

"Yes, you gave Rahab my package after some checking. That was fine. You will get paid."

He gave the briefest of small smiles and then opened his eyes very wide. "And she gave you a package for old Ma Miriam. Where is it?"

I kept my temper but, yes, I really resented Barak's superior attitude towards me. Of course, what really pissed me off was that he was clearly ahead of the game – whatever it was – compared with me. Or was he? I wondered. Sometimes, but perhaps not always? I warmed to the little voice inside me saying, "Time to stop playing his puppet, Ehud boy, time to give it a go."

"It got lost," I found myself saying hollowly. "I lost everything after I jumped over the wall. Seth just picked me up and ran." It sounded a bit lame. "These things happen," I continued mulishly and shrugged my shoulders. In other words, Barak, not everything goes right in a fight, not that you would know! And things sometimes get lost.

Barak just smiled back.

"It's storytelling time!" he chirped merrily, and leant forward.

"Once upon a time there was a lad, not a bad lad, actually quite a good lad, and very much out for the main chance." He looked at me meaningfully, big smile, of course.

"The lad gets in a bit deep, gets given a package by the enemy, told to give it to a secret enemy in his camp. Oh yes, there's a bit of a reward." Barak smiled encouragingly, then continued in that sweet voice of his.

"But someone gets to hear of it." He flicked his fingers in the air, like a summons, and waved towards the doorway. "Soldiers arrive and search the room. Here!" Barak gestured with both hands looking around, "and the package is found!" Barak clapped his hands and looked at me closely. "What do you think will happen then to our lad?"

Well, I knew and he knew. A simple matter; arrest and put before a military judge; and you do not go before a military judge with much chance of being found innocent. Guilt is the usual verdict, popular too for the judge normally picked from one of the tribes which hate all Benjamites. Sentence passed and out I would be taken to the local execution site half a mile from the camp. There, almost always the first thing ever set up with a new camp, would be a stout post set in the floor of a narrow watercourse. I would be tied up to the post and along would come a few thugs, the professional executioners from the tribe of Simeon, and start chucking stones. And their laughing and joking, by all reports, would be the last sounds I would hear apart from the flapping of the wings of the vultures arriving and their cackling at the prospect of a good feast.

As this ignominious procedure flashed through my mind, I suddenly caught sight of the leather bag, it was just beside the top of the paillasse less than a couple of feet from Barak's head. He turned around, following my eyes.

"Ah," he said looking back at me and lightly clapping his hands. "If bad lad becomes good lad, we may have a happy ending after all."

To say I felt foolish would be an understatement. I just stood there, inwardly glowering, but I knew, just knew, with a silly guilty smile on my face. Barak leaned over and took the leather bag. Looking up at me he shook the bag and gave me a 'I-do-believe-there's-something-in-here look' as if he was playing some silly child's game, and all with that irritating smile of his. He untied the noose and emptied out the bag on the paillasse. There tumbled out the rope with steel hooks, one leather mitt, then another, and finally Rahab's package.

"Ah," said Barak lifting the package and looking at it carefully, turning it over in his fingers. He then held it out in front of me. It was the first time I had seen it by daylight. It was just a thick tube wrapped in canvas and sewn shut. Along the seam was a hard green wax finish which was slightly cracked at one end.

"And your instructions were to give it to old Ma," he mused. "Well, we had better not waste any time."

He rose, and slipped the tube into the side of his tunic.

"And now I will tell you what happens next." Barak almost sighed, raising his hand at me as I appeared to be about to step forward. Then his mood changed, and he rubbed his hands together, chuckling.

"It's time I congratulated our hero. It's time I bought you a drink," he said now oozing geniality. "I will see you at Eli's house at six, and afterwards" – he patted the side of his tunic – "you can give this to old Ma."

It sounds silly but I still said it. "What are you going to do with it?"

Barak just smiled. "Suffice to say when you receive back the package, the sewing will look original, the wax seals intact, the damage at one end still entirely credible." Barak shook his head. "Old Ma will have no suspicion that the message has been read. You can then claim your reward; which she will give you, albeit grumbling."

"So, at Eli's then, at six," he finished brusquely, turning around to leave. He paused. "Oh," he said, "there is another thing we have to discuss." With a final flash of that disingenuous smile of his, he swished the flap and ducked out through the entrance.

I did not like that last shot one little bit. I suppose

if my conscience had been squeaky clean, I would have just shrugged my shoulders and reckoned that this was just his way of finishing the deal, sorting out the loose ends – like paying me! – over a drink, all very civilised. But, of course, my conscience was not clear, well, not entirely. Yes, I had done everything he asked; I had rolled off those two barrels from the wagon and put them under his damn tree, I had delivered the package to Rahab, so there was a 'Yes, yes, yes', I had fulfilled his instructions. But to the letter? Looming in my mind was a big 'No!', and that barrel we had sneaked off into the bushes.

Chapter 19

It was dark when I arrived at Eli's, another tented building in the markolith off a busy street. Outside a flame blazed from an urn of oil on a silver tripod illuminating the two huge Nubian guards, their naked torsos wrapped in giraffe skin against the cold night air. They stood there with their swords drawn, hands resting on the ornate bronze pommels of long, curved shiny blades with points resting lightly in the sand at their feet. The naked blades were a warning of their readiness to deal with anything from a few drunken tent boys making a big mistake to an assassination attempt; because this was where the top guys; the commanders, the men of good family and the rich came to drink and plot, and be safe from interruption. I knew, because my dad had been a member.

Their heads turned slowly towards me as I stood in front of the entrance. I could see them eyeing my bald scalp with the black line of stitches wondering what this young skinhead was up to. I stepped forward and quickly one of the giants moved to block my passage, close enough for me to catch the reek of giraffe hide.

I looked the surly bastard straight in the eye. Stonily, he returned my stare. I could tell he was itching to slap me down.

"I have an appointment with Barak," I announced shortly.

For one fleeting moment, I wondered whether

Barak had, in his cruel whimsical way, simply set me up for a kicking. Where better, where more humiliating than in front of Eli's? Ha, ha, Micah's cheeky chariot boy sprawling in the dust and, of course, the story would be around the camp in no time. Thankfully, that was just my guilty conscience pricking away because the giant, after a brief pause, stepped aside and I entered the tent.

Inside on the left as always, according to my dad, sat Eli. According to convention, the front-of-house man was always called Eli, as were all the other servants. It made things easier, my dad used to say, and laughed that the chaps at the door always had a mournful expression.

"Good evening, Eli," I announced to the gloomy-looking man city sitting at the desk. He had a sheaf of papers in front of him which he was checking with a quill. He looked up dumbly, clearly a bit surprised at being addressed so familiarly by a complete stranger. I told him I was here to meet Barak.

"And your name, sir?" he started to consult the list in front of him. I almost laughed. Me, Sir! Was it ironic? I wondered. More likely he was simply playing safe, but I smiled inwardly all the same; so I was 'Sir' now, well, there's a first time for everything! I told him and he frowned, clearly searching his memory.

"Yes," he said, more to himself than to me. "You are the son of Nathan, are you not, sir?" I almost saw him smile. I think he was rather pleased to demonstrate the legendary recall of the good club servant rather than admit to a bit of prior briefing.

"Yes, sir," he continued, "Barak is waiting for you." He flicked his fingers and a servant came over.

Behind the front desk was the main room of the club with dark rich rugs on the floor and lined with woven panels showing life in Egypt. It was open in the middle and around the sides were booths each with cushions and a small table and candle. I followed the servant over to a small booth in the far corner. I thought I recognised Amram with a large group on the right.

"Welcome." Barak rose, gesturing me to sit on the other ornately embroidered cushion in the booth. "You got past the gorillas all right!" He laughed. "Now, let us have some wine. Eli," he called out, and a servant shimmered towards us.

"The Commanderia," he ordered, and turned back to me. "It's from Cyprus, Ehud. Only the best to celebrate your triumph!"

Well, that was fine by me. Shortly after one servant was kneeling in front of me with a bowl and I was washing my hands in water scented with balsam, while another servant was pouring a dark red liquid into silver goblets from a tall narrow-necked jug.

"Leave it with us. Thank you," bid Barak to the servant and raised his goblet to me. I followed suit and we both sipped. I suppose my face must have shown appreciation because Barak just laughed.

"Not your usual vinegary stuff, is it?"

I had to agree. This was sweet and light with a flavour of figs and honey. It had a kick too; I would need to watch Barak.

But it was Barak who was watching me, or rather

my left hand holding the glass. He leaned forward, took the glass and turned my hand over into the candlelight exposing the purple ink of the entwined snakes on my wrist.

"Ha," he laughed. "A tattoo! I say, that is a bit risky of you; the Moses ban still exists, you know."

I wanted to snatch my hand away but his grip was firm.

"Well?" he asked again and laughed shortly. "Don't worry I'm not going to tell. Anyway, I can see it is old."

All I could stammer out was that I did not know its origin; how it was done when I was too young to remember, before I was with Nathan and his family. Barak just sat there scrutinising the tattoo.

"Ever seen a similar tattoo?" he asked. I shook my head and he placed my wrist slowly back on the table. For a moment, he was silent.

"Now," he started again with relish. "Let's have the whole story from beginning to end!"

So I blethered away; Barak sitting there nodding and sipping, occasionally saying things like 'So I heard' and 'Oh, it was like that, was it?' which was rather irritating, as if he had been an eyewitness to the whole thing and was just checking to see if I was lying.

"So here I am once again with another great big crack across my head!" I finished jocularly, and Barak was quiet for a moment.

"You did well, Ehud, or should I call you Babyface?" He laughed, and I froze. That was Zemri's name for me! Okay, I laughed along with him but that shook me.

"Yes," Barak went on, "You are quite a well-known figure now among the Amorites. That trick of telling the guard commander that Zemri was coming probably saved the day. Indeed, there is a price on your head! You should be flattered!" He paused while I smiled away in the flickering candlelight. Barak's face suddenly contracted, he looked puzzled.

"There's just one thing." His brow wrinkling. "The extra barrel. I don't think you mentioned it. You know, we very nearly didn't find it!" he chuckled knowingly.

So this was it, what the 'other thing to discuss' was all about. I shrugged my shoulders, playing cool I hoped, and muttered something about needing more space on the wagon and another hiding place for the extra barrel. I thought I was pretty convincing but I was grateful for the darkness of the booth as I knew my skin was glowing.

"It's very lucky we did find it," continued Barak, shaking his head, "or there would have been hell to pay! The deal was for two barrels, not three." He gestured with his hands, signifying helplessness. "We can't get the barrel back to the merchant so we'll just have to give him the full retail price. And, of course, the extra oil is going to depress the price we get for the other two barrels."

He was laying it on, and enjoying it. He knew that in the shadows I was squirming with embarrassment.

"So we all make a little less money in the circumstances," said he shaking his head, then looking at me with false commiseration. "Which goes for your share as well, I am afraid." He leaned forward. "You do understand, don't you?" he finished all syrupy kindness. "Of course, that share will be credited to your account with Rameses. He likes you, by the way!" he continued to smile at me. *Bastard!* I thought. Yes, I understand all right. Don't play with me, Ehud old son. I can recognise another boy on the make a mile off. Try your tricks, by all means, but not on me, not on Barak. Not on your best friend!

I think I muttered something about doing the best I could in the circumstances, needing the extra space on the wagon, and a few other excuses. I even did a bit of apologising but it all sounded a bit weak. He just sat there nodding, then reached into his tunic and put something on the table between us. I darkly made out Rahab's package.

"There you are," said Barak, as I took it. "Old Ma won't suspect a thing."

No explanation, of course, and he forestalled any possible question by raising a finger. Then it was time. Barak seemed to nod to someone over my shoulder, and rose.

"Now, my dear friend" – he bent forward as I scrambled to my feet – "you must go. You have an important package to deliver. Hurry!"

As the servant showed me out, I half glanced round and already Barak was welcoming his next guest.

*****

"You took your time, sonny," rasped Old Ma,

fixing me with her small black bead-sharp eyes.

There was a small queue of five soldiers waiting for the boxes when I arrived. Old Ma was in in her familiar station with an awning protecting her from the cold night air and a brazier of olive husks flaring beside her. I decided to wait my turn and joined the queue rather than stump up to the front waving the secret package in the air.

She always saw chaps one at a time; assessing which girl to offer, how much and for how long, but once there in front of her she was quick enough. In response to her angry accusation, I pointed to the scar on my head and explained that the medical treatment had put me to sleep. She continued to regard me, suspicion in her eyes.

"Not here, you fool," she hissed at me as I put my hand into my tunic. She called out and Ham lumbered over from behind the tented area. She addressed him sharply; I could not make out the language, but he turned away and went into one of the boxes, emerging a few seconds later.

She looked back at me.

"Go into that box and put the package on the table. There is no one in there now. Wait until Ham bangs on the door, then come out." She paused, and I wondered what was going to come next.

"No one knows about this package, do they? You have not been blabbing, have you?" she questioned me intently. I shook my head and she almost smiled. "Keep it like that, sonny," she almost whispered, then, "Come back in a week and you will get your reward."

She looked past me at the queue. "Next," she called out.

I went into the box. It was empty. I put the package on the table beside the small flickering lantern and sat down on the palliasse. The room had the usual stench of oil, sweat, and the cheap perfume which old Ma insisted the girls use and which they had to buy from her. I waited. I supposed that Ma wanted to give the impression I had slipped in for a quickie. Anyway, a short while later Ham banged on the door and I emerged into the cold darkness and, a bit shamefaced like any other client, slunk away.

*****

Everyone loves a hero, so the saying goes; but to be the hero everyone loves you really have to work at it. Operation Water Patrol, the rescue of the prisoners in the cage, had frankly been an unexpected success. It had, of course, only got dumped on Micah because none of the other tribes wanted to get involved in a dismal failure. There was a bit of hearty backslapping from the commanders of the tribes, like us descended from Rachel, but the others merely shrugged their shoulders and did their best to belittle the success. Amram was, of course, right up there;

"I mean how many men were rescued?" he complained. "About a dozen? And these were soldiers..." – Here Amram looked contemptuously towards Micah as if to imply that Benjamites were on the whole a rotten lot – "...who had been caught asleep on sentry duty or wandering around miles from the camp. Probably trying to desert! Well done, Micah!" he continued sarcastically. "All you did was risk many of your best for a few of your worst!"

I have never seen Micah so angry. I really thought he was going to thump Amram but Joshua hastily intervened.

"Send for the commander," he ordered loudly. "The gallant commander who led the patrol. Let him tell us, the senior commanders, what bravery can do in the name of HIM."

Good old Joshua! You could tell what side he was on and I rather think he felt this was a good opportunity to make Amram and some of the others squirm a bit. Anyway, in a long campaign, every general needs to declare a victory now and again to keep morale up.

"Seth will be a disaster," muttered Micah gloomily as we left the council. "I can just hear him. *I-went-I-did - and Is-there-anything-else-sir-or-I'll-be-off?* That's all they'll get from Seth." He clicked his tongue. "Joshua will not be pleased; I will be a laughing stock and we won't get proper credit for this whole damn thing!" He was thinking of himself, of course. I waited. I guessed what was coming.

"You'll have to do it, Ehud," Micah continued more happily. "You know how to tell a good story."

I think I mumbled something about only being there to help, which got a slightly sharp look from Micah. He was beginning to recognise my lapses into false humility.

"Yes, Seth can have a private audience with

Joshua, if that's what he wants.

Then I will present you to give the story to the commanders."

I accompanied Micah to Seth's private audience with Joshua and, I tell you, it was painful to watch. There was Seth in the limelight, hating every moment, and showing it. It's not that he, Seth, the cool confident commander in the field, was a gibbering wreck in front of Joshua but he became all rigid, almost terrified; he could have been a prisoner facing his first interrogation with a red-hot brand. Yes, he actually shook! But Joshua, bless him, refused to notice and Seth's reward was promotion from tent commander to commander. That was, of course, in name only; he still had the same old tent, the same old soldiers and the same old job but everyone was happy. Oh, and he got a few sheep as well.

The next day it was my turn and I got a full house. There was Joshua surrounded by his senior commanders as usual and quite a few others. Obed was there, at Joshua's right-hand side and I noticed Barak at the back standing beside a hawk-faced older man.

For the occasion, I had been well and truly tarted up with a nice new tunic and my head carefully shaved to show the long wound with the jagged stitches. There were a few adjustments to the story; like Micah and I both agreed that the crack on the head needed to come during the battle on the walls and not from Seth falling on top of me.

"Keep the funny bits for jawing around the campfire and your grandchildren, Ehud!" Micah warned. "And don't get too cocky," he added. "You won't do yourself any good. They're not fools and they'll see through you with relish, especially Amram and the likes of him; they haven't forgotten the Zemri business." He paused. I think he was wondering if a presentation by me might be a big mistake. "At least, you've got Joshua on your side," he grumbled, "for the time being anyway."

So, while I gave them the Boys Own, Brave Lads, and Clean Fight version, I was careful not to take all the credit and, when they looked particularly interested, gave them an extra bit of juice which they seemed to like. I laid off the Moses stuff, no bits like 'The Lord strengthened my arm' or 'I prayed and behold' which I had rehearsed, thinking mainly about impressing Joshua. By and large, I gave them a pretty accurate account of what happened although if Seth had been there, he would have been frowning and mumbling about inaccuracies. But he wasn't, of course: he was back in the tent happily organising a lice inspection or some such.

There was one hiccup in my presentation where I nearly came unstuck. I had got to the bit where we were clumping up the stairway and I had conned the Amorite commander. Well, this was my big moment and frankly, without my quick thinking not one of us would have got off that stairway alive and those men would still be rotting in the cage. So you can't really blame me if I paused at this stage to let it all sink in;

let Joshua and the generals imagine us marching up the stairway dressed like Amorites and them down there in a panic getting on parade for a non-existent senior visitor. Yes, all thanks to me! I must have smiled, even smirked, but they all just looked coldly back at me, and I froze. In a rush, I realised, with mounting panic, they did not like it! If the ruse had come from Seth it would have been all right, but from me? Well, that smug look on my face was just what they were waiting for. In the silence which followed, I could see Micah inhaling and looking cautiously about when, thank goodness, Obed, at Joshua's side, loudly announced;

"Well done, Ehud. Well done, indeed!" followed by a long loud guffaw of a laugh and kept nodding round at the other po-faced commanders until they reluctantly joined in.

But I was still frozen. *When do I start again?* I was thinking. Joshua came to my rescue.

"Continue," he said, raising his hand to quell the laughter of those feeling obliged to follow Obed's example, and smiling at me approvingly. I continued to the end of my narrative and then stood there. *Don't smile at them,* I urged myself. Play it straight, play it Seth – like, then just stand there impassive, the good soldier awaiting orders.

Got it right this time, I thought, as I heard Joshua announcing simply that I had done well.

Just as I was wondering what to do a priest came forward, almost pushing me out of the way, and stood stock still in front of Joshua. There had been quite a throng that day. I suppose I had hardly noticed various groups of priests in the gathering. I mean they just looked like any other old men in ankle-length white linen with flowing white beards, and they normally kept to the hill with the Ark of Covenant with their sacrifices and services. On the occasional day when the wind was blowing from the north, you got the delicious smells of roasting flesh and could hear their gloomy singing. You had to be from the tribe of Levi to become a priest and, of course, there was considerable competition among the older men of the tribe because it was a pretty cushy life.

Their job was to keep us sweet with Yahweh with services and sacrifices. Effectively, their message was that, if we displeased Yahweh, they could help us buy our way out of trouble; and the same thing if we wanted something. Did we believe all this? It didn't really matter, Moses had declared it, and Moses was always right.

Anyway, the priest standing in front of the council was very angry indeed. He did not half give it to Joshua and the commanders. Recent events, according to him, and in particular the mess in front of the walls of Jericho, had occurred because they had displeased Yahweh.

"And now," he went on, his voice rising, "when the Lord smiles on you and gives you victory, and you rescue the prisoners, you fail to praise HIM!" He paused here for effect, looking around to make sure that Joshua and the commanders were looking appropriately solemn, if not contrite. "Not only do you fail to praise HIM but" – another pause, then a thunderous finish – "you fail to thank HIM!"

Everyone knew what that meant. He wanted lots of animals for sacrifice and there would be much joy and feasting up on Temple Hill.

Of course, the commanders were unanimous, except poor Micah; that the tribe of Benjamin should provide animals in Thanksgiving, but the old priest was having none of that. He wanted animals from all the tribes. Jericho, he said, was the gateway to the Promised Land, Jericho was proving a hard nut to crack, and no success could come without the help of HIM. Of course, he dressed it all up with grand language and gestures but the gist of the message was 'This is going to cost you a lot!'

It was a racket, of course, but Moses had said you had to have priests and, of course, they had to be fed, but Joshua, sitting there rather bemused by the row going on around him, could not say that.

"Put me down for five goats," boomed out Obed, coming to the rescue. That silenced them. They all looked at Obed, they knew he was Egyptian, Yahweh was not his God. Did they not worship cats or something in Egypt?

But the priest did not object. He just stood there, even allowed a deferential nod towards Obed, so it was okay by him. Of course, the others joined in. Obed's handsome offering as a private individual required the tribal leaders in their turn to be generous. When Amram volunteered twenty goats, there was general laughter as his meanness was notorious.

"I knew this was going to be expensive," grumbled Micah as we walked away from the council. "Any success, any failure is an excuse for the priests to fill their bellies."

Tubal was at the door to greet us. He frowned when Micah addressed him, "It's sacrifice time again, Tubal," he said. "You had better get up there" – Micah nodded towards the hill with the Ark of Covenant – "and negotiate. It's under tough new management, a chap called Phineas, so I'm told."

Tubal's eyes simply widened. "Phineas," he murmured. "Not THE Phineas, surely?" But his boss was not listening and continued, "Take Ehud with you, he looks slim so the priests won't all think we're feeding well."

Of course, this was a jibe at Tubal who, fat cheeked and plump, looked very well fed indeed. Micah stumped past him into the tent leaving us together.

Tubal looked back at me. "You look tired," he addressed me kindly. "This can wait. Go and sleep."

I remember slipping past him and actually touching the skin walls for support as I made my way to my chamber. My last memory was flopping down on the straw bed with an enormous deep breath of relief and downright exhaustion.

*****

I do not know how long I slept but eventually I saw myself in a dream lying on top of that roof in Jericho overlooking the battlements with Abs at my side. He

312

started to beat a tattoo with his spear on the parapet. This annoyed me. I woke up to see that hangdog nephew of Tubs in the doorway tapping with a stick on the table.

"Tubal wants you," he gloomily announced.

"All right, all right. Tell him I'll be with him soon," I said sitting up abruptly and wincing in the bright sunlight.

Bloody rude, cheeky brat, I thought, as he turned abruptly and left. *You are lucky to have your uncle looking after you! You would not stand a chance in the tents!* And that rather cheered me; the very idea of Seth putting that boy to rights.

Chapter 20

I found Tubal in the large anteroom looking down on a backgammon board. As I entered, he clapped his hands.

I tell you one of the things I have learnt is that, if you think that top servants enjoy being servile, think again. Given the opportunity, put them in 'Master's' sandals, and they will be as imperious, demanding, and *when-I-say-now-I-mean- now* as the best. Clearly the girl in the kitchen knew this as Tubs had barely finished clapping his hands and leaning forward to grasp the dice holder when she was there standing over us, all fluster and wiping her hands.

"You must be hungry," Tubs addressed me, and ordered the girl to bring tea and cake.

"Do you play backgammon?" he stared at the ornate board. Well, of course, I knew the game; I remembered seeing my father playing it with his friends but they were a bit coy about it because they were gambling and that was forbidden. Moses, or someone like him, had condemned it saying, "Whoever gambles it is as if he puts his hand in the pork and pig's blood." You cannot really put it stronger than that. In other words, a stoning offence; but we all did it. It whiled away the time. Out in the remote pastures with our flocks and, in the absence of a jazzy cedarwood backgammon board with counters of ivory bleached white or reddened with dried beetle juice, we played a game which did not really have a name but we called 'Shits' because it was played with balls of dried camel dung.

I nodded, explaining that I knew the game from my father but had not played it except as a child.

"Then you don't know the key to winning at backgammon. The first rule, say?" Tubs asked, raising his eyebrows.

I searched my mind and babbled away hopefully. Yes, you had to put both dice in the pot, I started. Yes, you had to keep your pieces moving clockwise: or was it anticlockwise? Anyway, hardly the stuff for victory! Was it about knowing the odds, perhaps? Tubs nodded encouragingly, amused at my efforts. "And then, of course," I spoke up, "there is luck, that plays a big part…and then there's…" and here I paused, *what the hell could this damn thing be?* Then with relief, I thought, I volunteered rather triumphantly, "experience!"

"Good, good," said Tubs. "All good. But it is not what I was looking for. The best way of winning is to cheat! So the first rule is to watch your opponent."

He threw the dice onto the board and looked up. "You throw a lousy five and a four." He gesticulated towards the dice. "You play a sweet five and a three. Your opponent does not notice and it is now his turn."

He gathered the dice together in the pot and handed it to me.

"By that simple move, that simple act of cheating, the game may have been transformed, from defeat into victory."

I picked up a piece of cake. It was one of those sweet semolina things with honey. I had not realised how hungry I was; all I knew was that my stomach was calling more urgently than the desire to win at backgammon.

Tubs noticed, and smiled. "Eat, boy, eat," he encouraged as I wolfed the cakes down. He clapped his hands again and more cake arrived. I put my hands up in mock surrender, I had had enough for the time being.

"Yes, the first rule of backgammon is 'Watch your opponent'. Of course," he hesitated, then continued smoothly, "he may not be deliberately cheating, it may be a simple mistake…" – he paused here – "but you should be aware of the, ah, error."

I nodded, not sure where this was going.

He tapped on the table – "You then have to decide what to do about it. If he is your friend, you can denounce and laugh and the matter is resolved. But if he is not your friend it is different," said he raising his eyebrows. "Then you have to decide. Make a scene, and he will never play with you again; but that may not be what you want. Or do you overlook the deceit? What is the gain in that, you may ask? I tell you." Tubal leant forward and tapped me on my knee. "You know him better! You know he cheats and you know how. So, perhaps you lose the game, but you win the war!"

Tubal snapped the backgammon board shut with a rattle of counters and dice and sat back. "What do you know of priests and sacrifice?" he asked with a certain disdain in his voice.

Well, the truth is I didn't know much, or rather this

was the first time I had come across the world of priests and trumpets and flowing vestments. Of course, I knew about sacrifice at home and I could remember accompanying Dad on a number of occasions. He was rather grumpy about the whole thing but there was always Ma egging him on. So off we would go to our flocks of goats with Ma shouting after us something about only taking the best.

I will never forget the first time and being a bit surprised when Dad chose a really weak goat and rather triumphantly put it under his arm. We then set off out of sight of the camp and tethered the poor animal. Nearby we built a rough stone altar and piled some brushwood on it.

"It's our best goat, remember to tell that to your mother!" Dad growled at me, putting a clay cup down in front of him and drawing his knife. "Bring it over it now."

I untethered the goat and brought it over. My father knelt over the animal. He swept back its head with one hand and smoothly sliced through the hairy throat with the other. The poor goat gurgled and my father caught the welling blood in the cup.

"So far, so good." He looked into my eyes and I think he winked. "Remember the detail for your mother!" I nodded back.

He stood up and, dipping his hands into the cup, sprinkled some of the blood over the brushwood and reciting, "Blah blah blah," he babbled away. It sounded strange. He then wiped his hands on a towel.

"What was that you were saying?" I asked him

puzzled.

"That was an incantation," he said shortly, lifting the dead animal up onto the pyre. "Now, get the fire going."

I scraped the back of my dagger with a small piece of flint and the flying sparks quickly lit the dry brushwood. I leapt back as it flared suddenly.

My father went forward with his hands together.

"Blah blah blah," he went on again and for a while in a singsong voice. I just sat and watched bringing my shawl up to my nose at the stench of burning flesh and hair.

There was a slight breeze from the north so my father motioned me over out of the wind and the smell of the sacrifice and we sat down.

We waited until the fire died down and then approached the altar. The goat's head continued to loll down but the body was black and charred and continuing to smoulder.

"A burnt offering," my father announced grimly. "No bloody use for anything. A complete waste of good goat flesh, hide, hoof and horn." He sniffed.

"So, is Yahweh happy now?" I asked tremulously and my father paused.

"Perhaps he is, perhaps he isn't," he said, then stopped. "Perhaps he was watching, perhaps he wasn't," he continued, then another pause. "Perhaps, frankly, he doesn't care," and he looked at me forcefully. "But the important thing is that it pleases your mother."

So that was sacrifice for me at home, something we

had to do to keep Mum happy, and Dad had to go through the motions.

"You were quick," Ma remarked suspiciously when we returned and were washing off the blood.

"You know, Dad," I said drying my hands. I could feel her eyes, doubting, trained on my back. Dad just laughed.

Of course, I only gave Tubal the gist of my experience of sacrifice, and he smiled when I finished.

"Those were the days back in the wilderness but here and now sacrifice is a business." He nodded his head towards the Sacrifice Hill. "All those priests, pomp and ceremony. They come expensive, and we have to pay for it."

I kind of knew that every month each tribe had to provide the priests with a number of goats and sheep according to the size of their flocks. Moses had, of course, ordained it so there it was. No one really opposed Joshua when he insisted on its continuance.

"But now," said Tubal, "every now and again the priests decide on a push, a one-off demand of animals, to boost their coffers."

"And this is one of them," I stated flatly.

"Yep," replied Tubal. "Any disaster or victory will do, and the rescue of the chaps in the cage happens to be a victory. And, as Micah said, the priesthood is under new management. Phineas is a common enough name but if their new agent is the Phineas I am thinking of, he is a very slippery devil indeed. Phineas won't cheat unless he has to, his game is to bend the whole system in his favour." He opened the backgammon board and carefully turned the two dice six upwards. "So for him it's double sixes all the way!"

He sighed and gently closed the backgammon board again. "Anyway, we'll go up and sniff the air." He laughed, suddenly more cheerful. "Did I tell you the second rule of backgammon?" I shook my head.

"The second rule is when you know you are playing someone better than yourself then you can only win by luck. So take more risk. Perhaps Micah thinks you will be my lucky charm."

He rose and turned to me and smiled. "Let's see, shall we?"

*****

We walked slowly out into the bright sunshine. Sacrifice Hill was easily visible against the clear blue of the late morning sky. There were figures in white clustered around the summit and a thin plume of smoke rose like a white marble pillar into the still air.

"And it's all go, already," Tubal said briefly as we threaded our way through the maze of buildings and throng of off-duty soldiers and bustling servants.

It was busy at the big Temple complex, a conglomeration of black-haired tents and white buildings. We just stood and watched for a bit. The new regime, which Micah had referred to, had not changed the external organisation. There were the usual queues of people; mainly women, bringing animals or carrying sacks of grain or food, tribute for the priests; and seated opposite them across tables were the usual clerks and Temple servants in white tunics fringed with green. Their job was to manage the queues, check and receive the goods offered for sacrifice and note down the names and quantities. Over on the left were the red desks of the moneychangers, hard-faced men with their scales, scrolls and bowls of money. They too now were in uniform – different from Temple servants – in white tunics fringed in red.

Normally it would be all bustle and business-like but today it was all screech and anger; tables occasionally erupting into a short angry shouting matches.

"That animal is not pure enough for sacrifice," one clerk was saying scathingly, pointing contemptuously at the miserable-looking dove in a cage belonging to a furious-faced woman, adding, "You may have got away with that kind of thing in the past but not now."

At another table, a man was exploding. "How much?" he demanded. "How much were you saying?"

Outraged and insulted, he was leaning over, fists clenched on the table, at the clerk on the other side who simply scratched his nose and responded: "That's the going rate, mate," said he with a sarcastic emphasis on 'mate'. "And we want to be paid in Temple money." He nodded towards the red tables. "You can get it over there." The man said something, turned back and barged past us mumbling furiously.

Looking around there were also angry scenes at the red tables.

"It's always been a bit of a racket," murmured Tubal. "If you want to buy any Temple goods, like an

321

animal for sacrifice, you have to pay in Temple shekels and you can only get those at the red tables at a rotten rate of exchange." As he spoke a woman slapped down a small heavy leather bag on a table and berated the money changer opposite. "Shame on you for cheating an old woman," she screeched while he simply opened the bag and started to count the silver coins.

"Seems like the rate of exchange just got a bit worse," announced Tubal starkly. "Well, let's see what the score is for ourselves."

We went over to a queue and waited our turn. The conversations were usually quite short; those waiting in the queue now knowing to expect the worst and being resigned to it. Just occasionally there was an outburst and everyone looked at each other sympathetically.

A man in front of us with a lamb left and headed off towards the red tables grumbling. We sat down. The clerk continued to write, head down.

"Yes," he drawled shortly. Tubal waited until the clerk looked up rather angrily, then rather changed his tone when he became aware that he was dealing with a chamberlain.

"Yes, sir, what can I do for you today?" he now asked amiably enough.

Tubal explained who he was and asked to know what the Temple quota for the tribe of Benjamin was for the Cage Thanksgiving. The clerk picked up a scroll and ran his finger down the list. "Samuel…Manasseh…Dan…" he read out the names as he came to them on the list. "Ah, here we are,

Benjamin. Yes, you are down for fifty goats. Everything is by percentage," the clerk explained, "Samuel has much bigger flocks, about double yours, so they are down for one hundred. Can't get fairer than that, eh?"

"That's still double the normal amount for a Thanksgiving," protested Tubal frowning. The clerk shrugged his shoulders; there had been similar conversations earlier and there was no point in arguing. Move on quickly!

"Do you want to pay now? Today's price? Fifty Temple goats at ten shekels a piece, that's five hundred Temple shekels." The clerk was getting his confidence back; he was back on safe territory. This chamberlain fellow could bluster all he liked but these were official figures. He looked up to see if Tubal was carrying a bag of money, and then at me. I could see him wondering, *what's this brat with a great scar on his head doing here, but who cares anyway!*

"Thank you," replied Tubal a touch coldly. "We always bring our own goats and that is what we will be doing this time. As you know, if you check," and here he beckoned towards the clerk's papers – "they have always been approved as Temple Standard in the past."

I could tell it was not going to end there. What had Tubal said earlier? The game's rigged and it's double sixes for them all the way. The clerk looked positively pleased; yes, another good throw was coming up.

"Well, that may be but the past is the past and out here on campaign standards have been allowed to slip. So," he continued with evident satisfaction, "by all means bring along your goats but they will be subjected to our tests and purification procedures before they can be accepted."

Tubal just looked back at him while the clerk scrutinised a clay tablet with some figures.

"Goats, let's see. There's the purity test first. We only take perfect specimens so none of your one-eyed, one-legged animals that have been in a fight. That's two shekels for the test. Then we need the animals in for three days to get rid of any impurities. That's three days feed and care at one shekel a day, another three shekels. So, bring your own," he finished triumphantly, "and there will be a five shekel charge per animal."

At last, Tubal was getting angry. "So, if I bring along a goat that would fetch ten of your shekels on the open market you will charge me another five to make it acceptable for sacrifice?"

"That's about it," the clerk smirked back. "So it's much easier to buy the Temple goats in the first place, isn't it?" He pointed to the red desks. "The gentlemen over there will oblige you with Temple shekels."

And stand by for another rolling over when you get there, you fat pompous chamberlain with your airs and graces, I could see the clerk was thinking, *and take away that little tough of yours who keeps giving me the eye.* He was, of course, quite right about me, I was itching to get my hands round that scrawny throat of his.

I felt quite sorry for poor old Tubs as we walked over to the red tables. Of course, he could be a bit pompous at times, *I am my Master's voice et cetera*, but he was not a bad chamberlain and not always having servants whipped for minor offences. But there in the crowds before the Temple, he just stood out like a sore thumb in his smart house uniform and chain of office. *Give me special treatment*, it cried out, inviting every minor Temple official to have a go at the poor fellow. We sat down at the next vacant red table marked Abdul in chalk. On it glistened small piles of gold coins, silver shekels, bowls containing precious stones and bits of jewellery alongside bronze scales and small round shiny weights. I noticed too a stone, like I had seen Ramesses use. In a tray alongside, there were the Temple shekels, short oblong blue clay tablets with the Ark symbol embedded on one side and the denomination on the other.

We sat down and the money changer looked up and across at Tubal with hard black eyes and waited.

"I am the chamberlain of General Micah," Tubal announced without any answering flicker of respect on the face of the money changer. "I believe I need Temple shekels for the purchase of sacrificial animals, about five hundred. I have silver shekels."

The reply was quick, matter-of-fact. "The rate is two silver shekels for one Temple shekel, so that would be a thousand shekels." Tubal was immediately frowning. "But what about payment in tent shekels?" He pointed angrily at a pile of dirty white tent shekels on the desk in the corner.

The money changer almost sneered. "Tent shekels." He sniffed and shook his head. "Sure, we take Tent shekels." He consulted the papyrus in front of him with black ink figures. "Current rate is twenty tent shekels to the Temple shekel."

Tubal exploded. "Only a few weeks ago it was one silver shekel or ten tent shekels to the Temple shekel. You have doubled the rate of exchange. This is simple robbery!"

The clerk looked back coolly. "I wouldn't make accusations like that around here," he said flatly. Tubal looked across at me. I was not sure whether he was looking at me for sympathy or actually thinking I could help; but suddenly his words came back to me about the second rule of backgammon, take more risks when the odds are stacked against you.

"We can get a much better deal from Ramesses." I found myself lying without effort. "He does the old rate. Probably even better for a larger amount." Before Tubal could react, there was an explosion from the other side of the table. "You can only purchase Temple shekels here," the moneychanger almost shouted across. "Everything else is black market. And impure! Ramesses is a crook!"

But Tubal had seen the chink. He leant forward and picked up a Temple shekel with the denomination ten imprinted on its blue clay surface and laughed; "My good friend," he announced almost patronisingly, "they over there." He gesticulated towards the other clerks. "They don't care where your precious shekels come from."

He held up the blue tablet. "Black market or red table, it's all the same to them."

Before the angry clerk could say anything a voice, cheery but sardonic, cut across from the entrance to the Temple.

"Hello, hello, what have we here? And who is talking about black-market?" Tubal looked up and raised his hand in slow acknowledgement.

"Well, I say," said he slowly, "if it isn't old Phineas himself!"

You would not have noticed Phineas in a crowd. He looked like just another comfortable official in white robes, sallow faced, clean-shaven and, if not corpulent, certainly not a man short of regular meals. But he didn't have that serious look, that frown denoting heavy responsibilities, that 'get-out-of-my-way-I'm-important' look which many officials wear as they go about their mundane duties.

Phineas put his hand on the moneychanger's shoulder. "It's all right, Abdul," said he consolingly to the angry man, and then brightly at Tubal.

"Well, what a pleasure to see an old friend," he observed playfully.

"Well, well, well," Tubal bantered back, "when I heard that 'A Phineas' had taken over as Temple Chief Executive, I just wondered if it was you. Then there were rumours of a shake-up which raised my suspicions. Coming here and my experience today has simply confirmed my worst fears." He shook his head in mock sorrow.

Phineas laughed but I could tell he didn't really relish Tubal teasing him in front of the moneychangers.

"Indeed, you are right and I will show you round. But come, first some refreshments. Follow me…and your friend of course," says he, looking at me carefully. "That's a nasty cut you've got on your conk," he added with apparent kindness, but I could see him wondering where I fitted in.

"He's the one who's been using the black market. Using Ramesses!" blurted Abdul keen to impress his new master, but we were already following Phineas into a white-walled courtyard bustling with the shouting of the Temple servants, the snorting of beasts, and especially the chink of the heavy bags of money.

Phineas took us into another walled room; it was light and cool and protected from the sun above by a thin canvas awning suspended on pillars. All around were cubicles furnished with ornate cushions, each with a low polished dark wooden table. Most of these were occupied but Phineas beckoned us over to an empty cubicle on a low dais over in the corner. He motioned to us to sit down on the heavy cushions.

"This is my favourite place in the Temple," Phineas confided to us. "This is where the action is! From here, I can see and hear everything!"

A man appeared, in a uniform of green and gold with soft yellow leather slippers, and stood silently over us.

"Not too early for you?" asked Phineas, and Tubal shrugged.

"Some Egyptian white okay with you then?" Phineas gave the order to the servant and then looked back at me, plainly curious.

328

Tubal took the hint. "Ehud is Micah's new chariot boy. He was a member of the patrol which cut the cage," said he all very matter-of-fact.

Phileas's eyes widened in polite astonishment. The servant set down three silver goblets and poured the clear slightly yellow wine from a bronze jug.

Phineas raised his goblet. "We may not be Pharaohs, Tubby, but at least we can drink their best wine! To a return of the good old days, eh?" He looked over at Tubal and sipped his wine. We both followed suit.

There is a very good reason why we – 'We of the Chosen People' – drink beer rather than wine and it is quite simply this; we were clearly not 'chosen' to make wine. Most of the stuff we make ourselves is disgusting and why people go to all the trouble of adding expensive ingredients like honey and raisins is beyond me. It is still disgusting. Of course, if you just want to get drunk then it's okay, you frankly can't taste anything after the first couple of goblets. But this stuff of Phineas's was different, it was light and sweet and actually cool. Phineas noted my surprise and smiled. "The ice was delivered last week from a north- facing gully on Mount Hermon."

I could see Tubal was enjoying it too.

"Only the best!" He leant forward and patted Phineas on the knee. "Always the best with Phineas, eh?" He congratulated our host.

"And you've fallen on your feet, Tubby, old boy. A chamberlain, no less, to a general!" Phineas fingered the heavy silver medallion hanging round Tubal's neck. "A better billet than being a priest, eh?" said he letting the medallion go and blowing on his fingers, then laughing as he saw me sit back sharply in surprise.

Tubal frowned. "Yes, yes, I was an apprentice priest once, Ehud, but I don't go on about it now," said he a trifle petulantly. I could tell he was not that pleased about his past being brought up but it was now Phineas's turn to have some fun. "Tubal, Priest of Baal," he announced with mock pomposity. "Has a ring to it, Ehud, doesn't it?"

This was getting nasty. I mean, you do not mention Baal at the best of times let alone in the Temple, and you certainly didn't go around calling people a 'Priest of Baal'. It was an insult beyond insults! Of course, we swore in the tents and called each other rude names, the usual bits of the reproduction organs of both sexes occurring with most frequency. We were even used to Seth bawling us out with 'You prick of a pig', and that was pretty fierce, but Baal...! We were Yahweh men, one and all, and Baal was the big competition, the God of the Amorites and all that lot in Canaan.

"You were one too, Phineas," returned Tubal evenly, then turned to me obviously feeling some kind of explanation was necessary. "Years ago, it wasn't so straightforward. There was nothing to choose between Baal and Yahweh but Moses opted for Yahweh. At about the same time, I resigned from Baal because I couldn't take the human sacrifice, throwing babies into blazing furnaces and all that. I don't think that upset you, Phineas, did it?"

"You big softy," Phineas chortled, then started

wagging his finger. "No, but what I did discover was that there was no money in human sacrifice; whereas here…" His voice trailed off as he waved his arm towards the centre of the room. "I've made quite a few changes," went on Phineas. "Put the whole place on a business footing. Got rid of some of the old priests who objected to staggering up Sacrifice Hill four times a day or refused to do miracles. Put the priests into a proper uniform. Cost an absolute fortune! But the worst of it was the waste when I got here. And Joshua's really chuffed. He's given me Carte Blanche. Now, stay a bit, enjoy your wine and watch with me." He paused and waved towards the cubicles. "Where humble priest meets rich punter."

Chapter 21

Most of the cubicles were occupied by priests in Phineas's new uniform looking anything but humble in conversation with someone who, from their rich clothing or the number of gold bangles, clearly fitted Phineas's description of rich punters.

Phineas nodded and we followed his glance towards a particular cubicle. There, a priest, fairly young and with well-oiled black hair was smilingly listening to a richly dressed heavily wrinkled woman with a gold chain around her neck. She was complaining.

Phineas turned back to us. "That's old Orpah with her bowels. She comes here every week, and she likes her priests young! It's always the same sacrifice, a white kid and lots of incense."

Tubal irreverently scoffed. "Can't be very pleasing to Yahweh if she has to come back week after week."

"Not at all, not at all," responded Phineas seemingly unconcerned at the accusation. "Her bowels always improve immediately and are okay until she slaps a servant or does something which displeases Yahweh. And then, the bowels start playing up again! So, it's back again for another sacrifice." He paused. "Okay, it's up to the priest to keep this a regular thing, find out what's displeased Yahweh this time. Then he'll probably throw in a bit about the sacrifice contributing to her immortal life and a place in

Paradise."

As he spoke another priest came over towards the cubicle next to us. It certainly was a gorgeous uniform; first a white ankle-length robe with a wide embroidered hem, then a kind of blue short-sleeved knee-length shirt with golden tassels, and then a shorter heavily embroidered jacket with a gold and red belt. Yes, it oozed expense and I think I caught him winking at Phineas before he sat down. A Temple servant brought over an angry-looking elderly man, obviously another version of a rich punter.

"Another regular," confided Phineas. "Got a new young wife who wants a son. Giving him hell, she is, and, of course, it just makes him nervous, angry and useless!" Phineas chuckled. "Of course, he's got a bit of a record, a bit of a sharp dealer so that's why Yahweh has it in for him."

The chap also sounded pretty sceptical to me, and was angry too.

"I wouldn't be coming here on my own account. It's just my wife thinks it might work. But it hasn't. How many bloody kids have I sacrificed! And all those extras, incense, sung prayers and that man playing that horn thing. Cost me a fortune it has, with nothing to show for it."

Phineas made a mock, shock, horror face and held up his finger for our silence. We listened.

The priest was talking. "Prayer and sacrifice, my son, and nothing else. Think, think, how else you may have displeased Yahweh," he said earnestly, then paused and almost man-to-man continued, "I mean

333

have you not been taking those pills as well?" There was a pause and then an exclamation of impatience from the priest. "Well, what do you expect? You sacrifice to Yahweh, and you take those pills. That is highly displeasing." We heard some more mumbling from the angry man. I wondered if the sceptic in him knew what was coming.

"We must start again," the priest resumed again with confidence. "No more kid goats…let me think…ah, just arrived is a batch of pure white goats; bred high in the mountains specially for the Temple and priestly sacrifice for noble causes. We call them 'The Chosen People' goats. They are very pleasing to Yahweh."

He went on a bit, did that priest, but the end result was Old Angry agreed to a course of sacrifice of those white billies and, as a special privilege as the priest put it tapping his nose, he was taken out to choose one from the batch.

Phineas shook his head. He looked pleased. "Nice bit of work there," he mused, then turned to us. "We are trying to move people away from the 'One- year-old kid without blemish' choice into bigger older animals. It's not just that it's a crying waste of a young goat but there is precious little meat on them, and these young priests are big eaters!"

Now I am not a prig; business is business and, as a young herdsman I have done my fair share of pilfering, almost always, I hasten to add, from those tribes which don't like us like the Sims. And I know that things, a fiddle here, something shady there, go on in every organisation, but what Phineas was bragging about was different, and must have shown on my face.

"There, there," said Phineas leaning over and patting me on the knee and looking at Tubal. "I've shocked the young boy!" Then he laughed. "But I'll tell you what, everyone is a lot happier with my new regime including the priests; they are busy, they are well fed and we are putting good money aside for when we take over in Canaan."

He pointed west towards our promised land.

"And the punters are happy too. Sacrifice succeeds! Sacrifice works! Most of it is in the mind whether it's Orpah's bowels or Old Angry's impotence."

Seeing the doubt on my face he continued.

"Yes, even for Old Angry and that new wife of his. She desperately wants an heir for when he dies. Not for her the fate of a childless widow being pecked to death by the older wives! I tell you she will be pregnant within the month amid great rejoicing, and a further sacrifice of thanksgiving with Old Angry paying up like a lamb." And he rubbed his hands together.

"But come on, you've now seen the 'Front-of-House'. Now finish your wine and I'll show you the rest."

We stood up and followed Phineas out into a large open courtyard filled with the noise of animals. There were goats, sheep, rabbits, and even some birds in cages.

We stopped by one enclosure filled with young goats looking rather miserable.

Phineas opened his hands. "You see before you the impure ones, goats brought here by clients for sacrifice. Here they will be checked for blemishes and then fed Temple food for three days to become acceptable to Yahweh." Phineas bowed his head.

"Yes," huffed back Tubal. "We heard all about that. It means an inspection fee of two shekels to kick off and then sparse rations at one shekel a day each. After three days of shitting out your rubbish, the poor animal is declared pure and ready for sacrifice. And all paid for out of Temple shekels at an exorbitant rate." Tubal paused – I think Phineas was actually humming to himself. "So a much better idea to buy a Temple animal at a premium price in the first place. Of course! I think I have it right, Phineas?" finished Tubal with mock innocence.

"Something like that," agreed Phineas pleasantly enough. "But an astute man like you will not be surprised to find that it gets better."

We moved on to another enclosure, goats again. I know a bit about goats and they looked much the same as the last lot except their coats had been glossed up a bit and glistened with oil.

Phineas raised his arms.

"Behold, goats without blemish, born in the Temple and raised by our own shepherds," declared he rousingly. I think he was aware that he now had a bigger audience; some of the Temple servants were certainly watching him. I caught one or two of them smiling, not jeering him, just appreciating their boss and a class act.

"Yes, ready for sacrifice, pleasing to Yahweh, and excellent rates of customer satisfaction!"

There was a short snort from Tubal and he mumbled something.

"Oh, you want guarantees?" asked Phineas. "Well, nothing is guaranteed for man. But as we all know, Yahweh likes a white goat so, for the more devout customer we have guess what?"

"White goats," Tubal answered dutifully, "and at one hell of a price no doubt."

"Indeed, indeed," agreed Phineas, "and, surprise, surprise, here they are."

We came upon a smaller enclosure with a dozen larger white goats being groomed by two men, combing and cleaning. A Temple servant approached Phineas and whispered in his ear.

"Yes, white goats. Most are pleasing to Yahweh and the bigger the better. I have just heard that an important member of the tribe of Dan has selected Big Billy." Phineas waved towards a much larger white goat which returned his stare, 'for his sacrifice this week'.

A priest approached the enclosure as we stood there. With him was a finely dressed middle-aged man with a stick, leaning on the shoulder of a young servant. Phineas put his hand up so we could listen. Out came the priestly patter. "I think you said your budget was a hundred shekels," the priest was saying, "and for that you can get a very acceptable sacrifice. We have just had some very fine goats come in today, fresh from the pastures in the high hills behind Ebrei where the best and biggest goats breed. Moses sacrificed an Ebrei goat before the confrontation with Cora, and we know what happened there." The priest allowed himself a little snigger, and then stopped clearly wondering whether that was appropriate in the presence of an important potential buyer.

Phineas looked at Tubal and winked. "Works every time," he said. "Every time! We call it Cora's gambit."

Oh, ho, I thought, *that's a good one!*

I mean, I think you can gauge that most of us thought this sacrifice thing was a bit of a racket, certainly in the hands of the dodgy Phineas. By most of us, I mean the guys my age. Sitting around in the tents when the subject came up the general view was that Yahweh did not pay the blindest bit of attention to the antics of these priests or care whether the offerings were young meat, old meat or even camel in disguise; let alone get involved with Orpah's bowels and Angry's impotence.

Of course, it was the job of the priests to pretend otherwise; to convince punters that miracles did happen, or it just needed one more sacrifice. And then, even if the 'wish' was not granted, the priests could play the immortality card, that sacrifice was important for a life after death skipping around in some heavenly garden called 'Paradise'. That certainly pulled the older generation and they did not like being teased about that. I suppose the older you get the more you think about these things and then sacrifice becomes a sensible insurance policy. But in the tents, over an amphora of strong beer, we only laughed at such things; we were immortal!

But sometimes the mood deepened and we recollected some very funny goings-on indeed. I mean Moses. Miserable old Rule-maker that he was, he certainly did things. And that's where Cora comes in. Of course, we had been brought up on the parting of the Red Sea and the water from the rock and all those things which happened in the distant past, but the terrible fate of Cora was only a few years back. He was a cousin of Moses and a bit jealous of him. Well, Moses could be maddening! So, when Moses appointed his brother, Aaron, a complete shyster if ever there was one, as high priest, Cora challenged him. Moses suggested a sacrifice competition to settle things.

So the next day you have Cora with his censor, praying and doing his sacrifice over there with Aaron doing his thing over here. Now some say there was a huge bang, others a ball of fire. But anyway Cora and those around him, his immediate family, simply disappeared. Just like that! All that remained was smoke and the smell of burnt flesh. Yahweh had decided! Did Moses say 'Next'? I wondered, but there had been no challenges ever since.

Of course, I wasn't there; I was probably about two at the time and I don't know anyone who was there. But one of the guys said he talked to someone who was there, which is I think as good as it can get. So, we did reckon that Joshua, as Moses' heir, could call on Yahweh to intervene; but here and now, hearing the priest invoke Cora's fate in order to meet his weekly sales target seemed a bit cheeky. Not to Phineas, of course. The sales pitch continued, "And most pleasing will be this magnificent goat here." The priest pointed and an attendant grasped Big Billy by the horns and paraded him in in front of the small group. We listened as the priest pushed the price up to two hundred and fifty shekels which the old boy agreed, and they turned back into the meeting hall.

Phineas looked after them. "And, you nice old man, you'll get a nice goblet of wine to see that seal the deal. Not, of course, the Egyptian stuff you've been drinking," he added to us.

"Hold on," said Tubal. "I thought that the Danite had just bought Big Billy.

Your priest has just sold him again to this guy!"

Phineas led us away chuckling. "Those white goats are just what we call 'Display models'. They are very hard to get, you know, so we can't waste them. Yes, each of those white goats get sold two or three times a day and Big Billy a bit more. It's just business. No one knows, so no one cares! That's the mantra here! Come on, let's get some fresh air. There's more to see!"

Phineas led us out of the emple complex and along the watercourse a short way until we came to more tents and several rough stone-built enclosures, one containing a dozen or so forlorn looking goats.

"This is where the animals are killed prior to sacrifice. We've arrived just in time," announced Phineas with satisfaction, but Tubal was not impressed.

"They look a pretty mangy lot to me, and pretty

elderly some of them. Talk about perfect specimens! Look," he said, pointing at a dark brown-haired goat which was clearly hobbling. "He looks a bit poorly, and," he continued, "over there in the corner, that one's missing an ear." He was right, of course. They were all rubbish.

Of course, I knew the game. Looking after a herd up in the hills was always a difficult business. Okay, you lost a goat or two to wolves but the main challenge was to keep the animals in tiptop shape for their eventual destination, the market. There you got the best prices for the young and the beautiful, but these dropped like a stone for the old and the ugly. You always had a good number of goats in a herd which were sickly or injured, or even good to breed from but past it now and old and tough. Disposing of these was a bit of a problem. It wasn't just the peanuts you got for them in the market, but they created an oversupply of meat and depressed the price for your better specimens. I shook my head in admiration; some smooth cookie of a herdsman had clearly done a deal with Phineas and was offloading his rubbish for sacrifice.

Tubal looked as if he was about to protest further but Phineas forestalled him. "Tut-tut," he murmured. "No whinging please. Yahweh abhors waste!" he pontificated. "And it's again a case of 'Nobody knows so nobody cares' and that is how we intend to keep it! But come now," he continued to Tubal in a more conciliatory tone. "You remember those human sacrifices we did to Baal?"

Tubal nodded but said nothing, clearly not liking these references to his past. "How we were meant to take the first born and throw them into the furnace?" goaded Phineas. "You remember what we got? It was sickly children, babies without arms or legs, wasn't it? Well, it's the same here!" Tubal was silent and

I tactfully looked down.

Just then a wagon drawn by two oxen rolled up and reversed into an empty enclosure. The driver dropped the tailboard to reveal a full load of goats. *That's funny,* I thought to myself, *whoever heard of goats being carried to market on a wagon?* I remembered some goats might take a bit more prodding than others but we would surely get them to the market in the end.

The goats were just lying there. The driver climbed up on the wagon and picked one up by the horns and threw it down into the sand. It just lay there and, seconds later, another goat thudded down and lay still. All the goats on the wagon were dead; probably with scrapie or one of the other horrible things which can sweep through a herd under sloppy management.

Phineas knew he had to say something. "That lot will be incinerated today," he said shortly. "Can't have better veterinary practice than that," he finished smugly.

"Yeah, yeah, more burnt offerings pleasing to Yahweh!" Tubal drawled, then shook his head. He was now angry. "Don't you think one fine day Yahweh might pay attention to all this and come down and thump you?" Phineas did not answer. Back in the first enclosure a strongly built young man was grappling with a goat. He grasped a horn twisting the head on one side, then pushed open the gate and hauled the animal out. The other goats started to bleat. "I'm afraid they know what's coming," sighed Phineas.

The young fellow dragged the goat a short way from the enclosure to where thuggish-looking men in bloodstained rags were standing. One had a large knife and the other a basin. As we approached, the flies got worse and Phineas flapped his hand in irritation.

"Let's not go any nearer. The flies are awful here. But just so that you can see, Tubby, whatever else you may say or think about my operation, the killing is kosher."

I must say it was quick work. The man with the knife gave the goat's throat a couple of gentle strokes with the edge and then cut swiftly. The blood gushed out into the basin as the goat's struggles grew feebler. The strong young man was already walking back to the enclosure for the next victim.

"Well, I think we've seen enough of that," declared Phineas. "Over there" – he pointed to another waist-high enclosure inside which we could see men chopping away with cleavers – "is the butchery area but you don't want to go in there, Tubby, the flies are even worse and you might get your nice white tunic spattered with blood. And the stench!"

And the rest, I thought, *but you reckon we'd seen enough for the moment!*

It was pretty clear to me that any animal arriving here, dead or alive, got the same treatment. They were flayed and chopped up; any good bits put on one side for the hungry priests and the rest, the guts and all the horrid bits, went up as a burnt offering on Sacrifice Hill. Oh yes, and the priests were entitled to the skin of the animal, another good little earner.

You could tell there was no waste around here. There was no caw cawing of vultures!

"Fit for a walk up Sacrifice Hill, Tubby?" Phineas asked. "Bet you have never been up there, you irreligious man," he scoffed and looked up, shading his eyes. Sacrifice Hill was not far away and there was an easy path straight up to the summit a few hundred feet above us. There was a single sacrifice taking place. Smoke was rising and we could see the glinting of a censor in the hands of an elderly priest.

"Oh yes," said Phineas, "that's old Enoch. He is one of the old school." "You mean he's not a salesman and doesn't have weekly targets." Tubal laughed back now and off his high horse.

Phineas went strangely quiet. "Well, he's one of the few we had to keep on. He sacrifices every day; gets a proper kid goat without blemish, blood for sprinkling, proper incense and all that. He goes first thing in the morning before the others. That gets him out of the way." He paused. "Moses used him. Joshua swears by him. If Yahweh listens to anyone, it's him."

Old Enoch, preceded by a small boy carrying the censor and accompanied by two Temple servants, slowly made his way down the hill. He was very bent and his long white beard hung down in front of him nearly touching the ground. He looked towards us briefly, mumbled something, and moved on down the hill. "That was a blessing, I am almost sure," said Phineas when he was out of earshot. "Although he loathes me, I still get one of his bloody blessings whenever he sees me." He laughed. "Which probably means he's a vindictive old bastard beneath it all!"

Phineas paused and watched old Enoch teeter down the hill.

"I bet you're hoping he'll fall over and break his pious neck," drawled Tubal sensing discomfiture in our host.

But Phineas paid no attention. He was watching carefully the activity around the Temple at the bottom of the hill.

"Ah, here they come," he announced, as if presenting the opening of the main act after a slight hiccup in the preparations. "And we seem to be starting with a biggie," he added with satisfaction as the rams' horns started to blast out their mournful call.

It was certainly quite a procession making its way up the mountain. First there were the musicians, as they called them, which was a bit of a joke since all they did was make an ugly noise puffing into an extra-large ram's horn. I suppose it harked back to our nomad days when we used to send messages across the valleys to each other. It was amazing how far this deep sound travelled. Anyway, Moses or someone like him, no one quite knows, decided that the ram's horn should provide the sound effects for the Temple and hence declared it a musical instrument. All you needed were strong lungs to get the horn to work, and these guys, as they passed us, looked built for strength.

Then came a couple of boys carrying armfuls of faggots, then another couple with a huge, covered brass bowl on a kind of stretcher.

"The meat's in there," said Phineas out of the corner of his mouth. "Big Billie rides again," replied Tubal caustically.

Then came two guys holding censors followed by two fit young priests in very splendid robes and white shaped hats. And after them came the sponsor – a short fat man wheezing with the exertion of the climb – accompanied by his family and a few servants.

"I try to make a bit of a day out of it," said Phineas. "It helps keep sacrifice popular and everyone gets a good feed back in the Temple area." He paused and turned towards Tubal. "Another innovation. Another extra!" Tubal bowed in mock deference at this disclosure of another fast one.

The summit of Sacrifice Hill had been levelled to provide a space for eight altars of rough stone with one big one in the middle. About ten yards from the summit the fat man and his family halted and the ghastly ram's horn sounds stopped. They stood and watched as the priests and the boys continued the ascent. There was a bit of bowing and scraping at the top and then the main priest went forward with a little pot and sprinkled blood on the altar in best sacrificial fashion.

"Something genuine at last," whispered Tubal.

"Not a bit of it," re-joined Phineas. "Real blood attracts the flies. Water with a bit of henna in it makes for a cleaner event for all. Keeps the complaints down especially from the womenfolk whom we now encourage to come along too."

The boy put the faggots on the altar and the heavy brass bowl was emptied over the wood. In the still air, there was a sudden draught of wind from the west. "Ahh," rasped Tubal, putting his scarf to his face at the foul smell. "That's old meat if ever there was."

"Hmm," responded Phineas unperturbed by the stench of the rotting meat, adding, "won't be long now."

As he spoke there was a roar of flames as the dry sticks caught fire. The two priests stepped back and started to sing, if you could call it that, a kind of groaning noise. Out of the two censors billowed dense white smoke towards the burning sacrifice.

"Bit wasteful on the old incense, aren't you?" commented Tubal.

"An important extra," agreed Phineas. "Can't have a proper sacrifice without incense and that means frankincense. Fifty shekels a pound, you are paying nowadays, if you can get it at all," he added.

"So, this stuff is another phony," shrugged Tubal.

"Well," agreed Phineas slowly, "just understand we don't waste good frankincense at the top of a hill. No, that man who does the blood also has found a wonderful way of producing lots of smelly white smoke from simple ingredients. No complaints so far!"

He stopped, shading his eyes and looking down towards the Temple;

"Ah," he said with satisfaction, "here come the B Teamers." And he rubbed his hands together. "I like a full house on Sacrifice Hill. Yes, this is a good start to

347

the week."

Snaking up the hill was a procession, lots of sacrifice groups but on a smaller scale than the first group. Each was still headed by a priest with boys in uniform carrying the sacrifice and the firewood, followed by the family members. When they arrived on Sacrifice Hill, they were allocated to an altar by an imposing man with a giant black stick. Then the same old ritual for each sacrifice; sprinkling of the altar with fake blood, dumping of the rubbish meat on the firewood, lighting of the fire with a hidden flame, a bit of singsong prayer from the priest and a few puffs of white smoke smelling of acacia and back down to the Temple. Soon there were six plumes of smoke rising into the clear blue windless sky from the sacrifices and the air was filled with the chanting of the priests and the murmurings of the attendants. You had to admire it.

As if he was reading my thoughts Phineas cut in. "Joshua will be looking up at this moment. He will see all this and will say to those around him, 'Behold the faith of your people, Oh Lord'." In the embarrassed silence which ensued Phineas turned to Tubal.

"So, what do you think of it all?" But he did not wait for a response adding quietly, "And this is just the beginning. When we get to Jerusalem, there's a ton of work ahead of us and I will need a deputy, someone I can trust." Here Phineas tapped Tubal on the arm, smiling. "And we know each other from the old days, don't we?"

So this was what all this was about; why he was

letting Tubal in on the secrets of his racket. Phineas put up his hand as Tubal started to protest.

"Don't give me all that stuff about the honourable position of being chamberlain to Micah. You know you are just a glorified flunkey, and there are a couple of other problems, aren't there?"

You bastard, I thought, *I wonder what you've got on him.* Poor Tubal looked anything but comfortable. My immediate thought was that he simply did not like these things being discussed in front of me, but Phineas showed no sign of excluding me from the conversation. So I just stayed put and pretended to be studying the flattish plain to the west while, of course, hanging on every word. I may have moved away a tiny bit but I have got sharp ears.

"There are rumours her ladyship is not satisfied with you." At this, Tubal just grunted something. "That she wants a younger man as chamberlain, someone who, how shall I put it, can relieve Micah of some of the burdens of office…" Phineas paused and then added with a little giggle, 'or of his marital duties'.

He shook his head. "You should never have let Micah get rid of that Barak chap. He was keeping her ladyship happy, and you in a job."

So that was it. Thank you, Phineas! Frankly it had always slightly puzzled me why Micah had let him Barak go so promptly. Now all was explained, Barak was knocking off his wife. It just shows that if you hang around long enough with mouth shut and ears open all will be revealed.

I had to laugh. So much for the great Ehud, the boy

who saved his life and the hero of that rescue expedition; which is, of course, how I was beginning to see myself. I might be that and all to Micah but, first and foremost, I, with my sunburnt scar and woebegone face, was the handy excuse to get rid of the chap who was cuckolding him in his own house.

"And there's the other thing, of course," went on Phineas smoothly. Did Tubal know what was coming? I suspect he did; he just stood there grimly and Phineas was silent, letting him sweat a bit. I broke my intense scrutiny of the hot rocky valleys with the vegetation beyond to look back sharply to see what was happening, straight, of course, into Phineas's unswerving eyes. Back I was like a shot to my precious landscape studies.

"You are on a losing streak, my friend," he continued quietly, "and for all your fancy theories backgammon was never your game. How much do you owe? Hundreds of shekels, so they say, and I hear that old moneylender, Jethro, is beginning to get tetchy."

"You know what will happen next? Jethro will start talking and Micah, once he hears of your little hobby, will give you the sack. So there you will be, unemployed, up to your ears in debt and – oh yes! – with the dreaded reputation of a gambler. Especially backgammon! What did Moses say? 'Whoever plays backgammon puts his hand in the pork and pig's blood'. Oh dear!"

Phineas allowed this all to sink in before continuing. "I tell you what; if you join me, I'll settle your debts. Back to zero! You will be debt-free, and you'll start here on a salary double what you are getting with Micah. You can bring that lad along with you too." Phineas nodded over at me. "It will be a big operation in Jerusalem. Behind all the priests and the sacrifice stuff, there will be a lot going on. I'll need young guys with initiative."

Well, that was a bit of a surprise. So I was getting a look in on another act. Getting out of the tents and becoming chariot boy seemed such a giant step that I had not thought about 'What next'? And, frankly, I had had other preoccupations, had I not? But perhaps this was it? And the next step was working up at the Temple, at what only Phineas knew!

Chapter 22

I was enjoying these warming thoughts while still resolutely staring into the distance; sightless, of course, because I was not actually looking, just focusing on the conversation going on behind me. I suddenly became aware that my subconscious was registering some kind of activity down there on the plain, and when it kicked in, I froze. Emerging from a wide valley and flooding onto the plain were chariots, hundreds of them, and heading towards Gilgal and the camp below.

"Look, look," I cried pointing and turning towards Phineas and Tubal. They stopped talking and came forward abruptly.

"It's the raid," declared Phineas sharply. "It's come at last. Nothing you can do up here." As he spoke, from below, long blasts on trumpets sounded the alarm. If I had been thinking that a surprise raid by the Amorites with hundreds of chariots was going to upset today's sacrifice routine that did not last long. Up on the hill the priests continued their rituals and were replaced by others from below. "We're fine up here. Business as usual! The tribe will surround us. The easy meat is down there." As Phineas was speaking we could see below us on all sides soldiers from the tribe of Levi taking up their positions.

"I guess it'll be a hit-and-run," Phineas continued. "Looks like your old friends, the Gads and the Sims, are going to catch it. Probably the market area as well. Bet it will be all over in half an hour."

I just loved his detachment. It could have been a delivery of old camel meat rather than a massacre in broad daylight before his very eyes. I was learning too though; swiftly acknowledging I could live with any amount of trouble for those smug bastards, the Gads and Sims, and all the good weapons they had courtesy of being the favourite tribes of old Amram. But I wondered about the marketplace and my life savings, such as they were, with Rameses. And then poor little Zaki, would she be all right? Looking over, Tubal seemed unmoved. I wondered if he was praying that Jethro with his little black book would be one of the victims down there.

I must say it made a change not being in the thick of things. For once, I could watch the fray below without having to worry about my own skin. For a brief moment, I wanted to get down there and stuck in. That that quickly passed and I was soon thanking my lucky stars to be up on the hill under the protection of the tribe of Levi, and whatever competent arrangements Phineas had made for the preservation of his set-up.

And he was right, of course. It was a hit-and-run operation. The alarm trumpets continued to blast above the rising clatter and crash from below as the Amorite chariots swept through the camp and market area. But it did not seem long before they were trailing back onto the plain and back up the valley leaving behind the crackle of flame, black oily smoke and the steady sound of wailing.

*****

353

"I wonder who Joshua is going to blame this on," said Micah who was standing looking down on the carnage below, as Tubal and I arrived back at the house.

"Yes, yes," he reassured somewhat tetchily Tubal's hasty enquiries, the kind of things a chamberlain should ask and worry about even when the crisis is over. "We were fine up here but, of course, the women took fright. They shut themselves up in the kitchen and have been screaming blue murder. That…" Micah nodded indoors to a whimpering noise more like a few dogs in pain, "is nothing to what it was."

"I'll go in and see them," said Tubal warily, recognising a nasty duty. "I've got some of those Egyptian salts. Ehud, get some water and wait for me here."

Tubal disappeared and returned with a small polished dark wooden box. He lifted the lid and sniffed and turned his head away.

"Still got a kick, this stuff. Go on, Ehud, sniff away."

I came forward and Tubal once again opened the small box and turned it around in his hand. In it were large white crystals. They looked like salt to me and innocuous enough. I leant forward and, with my nose almost touching the crystals, started on a long deep sniff. Next moment I was bolt upright with the top of my head blown off, my nostrils on fire and Micah and Tubal both laughing at me.

"That'll sort them out," assented Micah grimly. "Go to, Tubal!"

Actually, it was a bit of an anti-climax after that. As we walked towards the kitchen the whimpering turned to wailing again and there were cries for help and calls on Yahweh to preserve them and all that, but this stopped immediately when Tubal simply announced, "Madam, it's all right. You are quite safe. You can all come out now."

In the silence which followed, the door opened a crack and one of the maids peered out. "Yes, Madam, it's the chamberlain," she said in a small voice before being yanked back from the opening and replaced by a rather cross looking Abigail who took one look and then opened the door. Inside, the women were all sitting around looking glum. Some were fanning themselves, then the whimpering started again.

"I apologise for the dreadful experience you have had, Madam," said Tubal formally. "I have these Egyptian salts here." He opened the box and proffered it. "But take care," he added in a low voice.

She brushed him aside. "I don't need those damn things but give all this lot a dose," said she through clenched teeth. "One moment, they are screaming their heads off about the prospect of being raped and killed. The next moment, they're whimpering in disappointment!"

Most of the women bucked up marvellously after the first had been almost flattened by a sniff from Tubal's box. Soon, shamefacedly they made their way out of the kitchen urged on by sharp words from their mistress.

Tubal looked after them smiling slightly and

flipped the lid closed. "Yes, the best Egyptian smelling salts," he said quietly to himself. Then waiting until Abigail was out of earshot, murmured to me, "Made from burnt dung of a camel!"

*****

"I'll get down there and see if I can help," I said to Micah with that little- boy-brave look on my face I use when I am dressing up something I want to do; which was a mistake as I immediately remembered that Micah pretty much knew me now. He just looked back with a slight smile and nodded. What did he care what business I had down there? Also, in the back of his mind I bet he was thinking that I normally came back with a useful titbit of information.

So down I went to the devastation below; tents freely burning, people rushing around with water, and the screams of the wounded being helped by clumsy soldiers. Worst of all was the horrible frizzy smell of goatskin and burning leather, worse even than Phineas's slaughter area.

I had to give the Amorites credit for a great hit-and-run job. Lurid accounts were to be had from a number of chaps standing around playing the brave survivor and professional witness, and loving the attention to bits. Even making allowance for some exaggeration it seemed that this part of the camp had been hit by over two hundred chariots; each drawn by two horses and carrying five men; the driver flanked by a couple of archers loosing off arrows left and right, and a couple more men ready to step down to do what other damage they could.

The first casualties were those fools who rushed out of the tent at the sound of the alarm and got an arrow tipped with camel shit in the gut for their pains. Keep down in those circumstances is my motto and nine times out of ten you will get away with it; or rather I have so far. But the raiders also had a secret weapon; oily burning stuff which they threw onto the goatskin tents and into the buildings. That is what created the real devastation. Water only made the fire worse. Some of the soldiers, the really unlucky ones, had received horrible burns, their screaming growing worse as the fire just seemed to burn deeper into the flesh. Nothing – not oil, water, or even sand in their desperation – could douse the fire. They, poor devils, just lay there writhing and screaming in their agony. Elsewhere men fussed about; cutting the burning goatskin flaps and throwing them into the sandy street while others, puzzled and fearful at the strange nature of this new fire, warily collected smouldering bedding and wooden furniture to add to the growing piles.

"Baal's Fire!" I heard someone scream. Suddenly all around the cry went up until many were tearing at their garments and shouting to the sky and Baal for help. Fat lot of good it did them of course; the fire just continued to burn, fizzle out for a few seconds at each dousing of water, then start again. Hot, oily, smelly with an evil black smoke!

Now it is all very well to claim to be cool after the event but I won't lie to you, I was scared. Fire was always Baal's thing; what with throwing living children into great flaming furnaces and allowing his priests to walk across burning coals barefoot and unscathed. Here, before my very eyes, was Baal's magic and Yahweh was just letting it happen! Joshua was always banging on about Yahweh being our protector and Baal being a false god but here it looked distinctly as if Baal had the upper hand.

All around the cries erupted but, amid the 'Help us, Yahweh, help us!', you could hear others calling on Baal.

It seemed to me that the screaming for help was roughly divided into two; half sucking up to Baal and the other half calling on Yahweh. Curiously, you can normally rely on the women to make all the fuss while the men stand around and look slightly embarrassed. But no, this time the women were fussing away and whimpering quietly and it was the men who were making all the noise. Very undignified it all was! I suppose it is all to do with temperament and how one reacts when frightened with no idea what to do; some scream and shout and go to pieces, others, like me, just freeze and go silent. Beneath we are the same, in a state of high panic.

I don't know what worked quicker on Joshua, the cries of help to Baal or having a bit of his camp on fire, but he was there pretty quickly on the spot with his entourage all jabbering at him. Not surprisingly the faction calling for a top priest from Sacrifice Hill won the day and shortly after, there arrived a very out of breath and almost flustered Phineas. In his wake was one of the oily young priests. I can tell you it was a pleasure to watch how his face changed when Amram, standing by the side of an ever-impassive Joshua, gave him his orders to the effect that he was to put out the fire and be quick about it! Poor Oil, or rather Horror-stricken by the look on his face, gave a quick panicky look at Phineas, but got no support there except a nod as much as to say, "Get on with it, boy!"

I will give him credit; the oily priest put on a good show, just as if he was up on Sacrifice Hill earning good money for the Temple. By standing in front of the flaming goatskin and waving his arms a bit and calling on Yahweh in a loud voice, he got everyone to shut up. He then he settled back into a priestly routine of kneeling, standing, singing and shouting. Indeed, his best moment, after a bit of quiet chanting, was to raise his arms and look to the heavens, and shout 'Yahweh' several times and then everyone else would join in the yelling. Of course, the fire continued to flicker and hiss.

I felt a tap on my shoulder. It was Phineas. "You know where Obed lives, don't you?" There was urgency in his voice and he did not wait for me to reply. "Go to him, quickly, and tell him exactly about this fire, what it smells of and its reaction to water and sand. Everything!"

The cool unruffled figure of Anik was standing at the entrance of Obed's quarters and, as I gasped to a halt in front of him, the trace of a smile briefly distorted his impassive face.

"So, it's you and you've come for some magic!" he

asked carelessly, and raised his hand as I started to jabber away about the fire, Phineas and his priest. I stopped and Anik raised the flap for me to enter. Obed was leaning over a table and pouring blue powder into some white mixture which he was stirring.

He paused and shook his head smiling without looking up.

"Back in my country, Egypt, the fire which never goes out is called Pharaoh's flame. It was invented over 500 years ago and its secrets held by the priesthood." He laughed shortly and continued, "So the Amorites have got hold of it and today it is Baal's fire! Well, with this pot" – and here Obed gestured towards the blue powder – "the priests of Yahweh will conquer the fire of Baal."

Anik, standing by my side, put his hands together and looked piously at the ceiling. Obed smiled briefly at Anik's posture and then frowned formally at this impertinence. I guessed they were both enjoying this and would have a good laugh after I had gone.

Picking up a brush with a short bronze handle he said, "Take this to Phineas. All the priest has to do is dip the brush in the powder and shake it onto the fire." From outside, the roar of the crowd had started again and the cries for Baal could clearly be heard. Obed picked up a green cloth and threw it over the pot and brush.

"Here, take it, go quickly," he said.

I sidled up to Phineas with the pot. The priest had gone through his antics and was now kneeling in front of the fire with his head on the ground and his arms stretched out before him. Playing for time obviously and I felt quite sorry for the poor fellow. Joshua's hangers-on were standing around, looking rather uncomfortable, occasionally snatching a glance at the boss. He simply stood there observing the scene with his arms folded.

I have always admired nonchalance, that cool unflappability when faced with a dire situation. I can't do it. In a crisis, I become an all-action scratching and biting man and emerge – well, I have in the past – if not triumphant certainly surviving but with blood and bruises to show for it. The cool types just stand there. Of course, there are those who try it on and they simply get flattened and forgotten. But the others, like Joshua, just come out on top without a scar to show for it, and not even out of breath. I mean, you got the feeling with Joshua that he knew it was going to be all right. But how did he know? I could bet anything that he did not know what was going on behind the scenes with Obed and his magic powder.

So Joshua just stood there. The fire blazed away in front of an exhausted kneeling priest. Behind him his entourage was beginning to whisper, and there were more cries from the crowd for Baal to save them. But there was not a flicker of concern on Joshua's face as he watched Phineas come forward with Obed's pot and place it ceremoniously between the priest and the fire. The priest then went through a quick bit of bowing and bending and chanting, and the whisperers and bawling stopped as this new act began. Then the priest knelt, took the cloth off the pot and, incanting as he did so, dipped the brush in the blue powder and flung it onto the flaming goatskin. A grasp of astonishment went up as the flames flickered briefly with sparks of green and went out.

Good old Phineas, he was the first to start the 'Yahweh, Yahweh', chant which was quickly picked up and spread to the crowd. Did Joshua smile or look around triumphantly? No, he just looked on! You could tell he knew something would save the day, there was no sign of pleasure or even surprise. Cool guys just don't show it, they never do. It's baffling and makes the rest of us feel like lesser beings, which we probably are, but we don't like having our noses rubbed in it.

Things quietened down after that. Anik turned up with another pot of the magic blue stuff. Another priest arrived and the two priests set off with one pot each putting out fires. Of course, with Phineas watching, they were careful to do a bit of chanting and waving of arms before they did the sprinkling.

After Joshua departed, bossy junior commanders started rounding up those standing around to help in the clear-up operation. This sharply reminded me that I had other things to do. I turned away and started to walk swiftly to my first stop, Rameses. Yes, I was worried. Apart from scaring the shit out of the camp what was the purpose of that Amorite raid? Perhaps they were after Rameses and his treasure? Certainly, the best way to upset the top brass would be to go after their secret savings accounts. *But bang would go my precious shekels too,* I thought grimly.

"You too," a laughing voice called out behind me.

Oho, I thought, *I might have guessed.* I turned round to find Barak loping up beside me. "Going to check on Rameses, are you? So am I. He should be okay, but you can never be quite certain." He paused and we both looked back at the busy scene below.

"This was just a killing-and-destruction exercise. They weren't after loot. Your piggybank is safe!" he laughed. I could not work out whether he was making a statement or putting up a theory.

Of course, he was right. It looked like it was business as usual at Rameses' shop except outside there was no sign of the two big black Nubians, ornamental in a thuggish way but fit for nothing except to look impressive and curl their lips at unwanted visitors. Instead, guarding the doorway, were half a dozen soldiers, well-armed with spears and some with bows, Simeonites, I reckoned, tough lads from the tents who knew how to fight and showed signs of having done so. They were now just lolling around the entrance.

The commander seemed to know Barak and they conversed briefly. Someone had gone off to find the Nubians and coax them back.

"We will hang on here until they return," the commander said. "You will let Rameses know?" he added meaningfully and Barak nodded.

"Come on," Barak said turning to me and in we went.

"There was some noise and shouting but nothing more," smiled Rameses lisping slightly, taking a puff out of his hookah and offering it to Barak.

"Those men, those guards you provided, Barak, they did a good job. A couple of chariots came rattling past but they saw them off sharply." He took another puff. "Those men must be rewarded. What do you think? A week's worth of tent shekels for each man, would that do?"

He opened the small brass bound wooden box in front of him and took out six small pouches.

"Quite right." Barak laughed, gathering them up. "No point wasting good silver on simple soldiers."

"Where you are off to now?" Barak asked after as we once more stood outside in the street and he had finished paying off the soldiers. I shrugged my shoulders. I am not normally emotional but I could only think of Zaki.

"I'm off to see how the girls are," said I offhandedly.

"They're on my list too. I'll keep you company," was his jolly response, and we set off together in silence.

As soon as we came in sight of Old Ma's empire it was obvious things were not right. All three sex boxes had been overturned and one was still smoking; a few men were squirting the smouldering wood from skins filled with water. Several miserable-looking scraggly-haired girls were standing around. Some were in pyjamas, some in their working kit, and giggling or crying. I could not work out which, probably both. There was no sign of Zaki.

In Ma's old place, a sour-faced woman sat. I recognised her as one of the older prostitutes and definitely a Hebrew with that big, hooked nose of hers. She simply stared at us as we approached.

"We're closed. You can see that," she said shortly looking daggers. "Go away."

But Barak was having none of it; he tersely explained that we – I smiled to myself – were from the Head of Intelligence and required a report of what had happened.

"In your own words, in your own time." Barak encouraged her briskly. "But let's keep to the facts, please," he added coldly as Sourface broke into a furious rant about Old Ma and her betrayal.

Well, you have to give Old Ma full marks. Last night had been business as usual; the shop had closed at the regular Monday night time of midnight. Nothing to suspect but when Sourface woke up in the morning, "Miriam and her Amorite sluts," she spat out, "had gone, disappeared!"

"Of course," she continued, "the takings were gone as well. So, she's gone with our wages for the last fortnight, the old cow!" And then she went on a bit.

"What about Zaki?" I interrupted. Sourface shot me a dirty look. "Zillah, you mean. She went with the other Amorite bitches."

Well, that's no surprise, I thought. *Zaki was not going to hang around while the other Amorite girls scarpered.* Of course, I was relieved. I was fond of Zaki and would not want her to come to any harm but, dammit, she did owe me an all-nighter.

And then Barak and I both started to laugh.

Yes, it was a bit cruel but it was a bit funny all the

same. You see Old Ma Miriam had a good business model; for her shop window, her poster girls if you like, she had imported these bright pretty sexy young Amorites like Zaki, and she was careful how she used them. I had been very lucky to get Zaki. But the main business, the real money spinner, were the gangs of boys later on in the evening. Along they would come, roaring like water buffaloes after hitting the rubbishy plonk bought by the skin for a few tent shekels. Of course, by that time, whether they got their mother's cousin or a goat, it was all the same to them; so Miriam had an easy job supplying them with her mingas, and Ham beating 'Time's up' on the door of the box every ten minutes. Poor old Sourface, it was going to be hard to get the business going again.

"Where d'you think she's gone?" asked Barak with a certain innocence. "Obviously, bloody Jericho," she snorted. "Where else? Into the bloody desert?" She paused. "Yes," she continued, and here she gave a gurgling noise which could almost pass as a laugh, and there was even a grim smile. "She and that old tramp, Rahab, will be back in business this very evening, I bet."

The mention of Rahab had me looking sharply at Barak but he looked as impassive as ever. He then became quite kind to old Sourface asking her name and promising her some soldiers to set the boxes back up and do any repairs.

"I'll come back, Adah, and see how you're getting on," he said to her, but now with an ominous note in his tone. From an intelligence point of view, the pillow talk gleaned from the boxes was an important source of information. Oh yes, Barak's message was loud and clear; I'm not having the stream of information drying up. You've got Miriam's old job; you do Miriam's real job! I looked between the two and I could see that Adah, her face hardening, had got the point. Things might be tough but now she was the Madam, and she was going to keep it that way.

Chapter 23

"I'm looking for Ehud," a lisping voice which I thought I recognised sounded from outside the tent. I had time off and was visiting Abs. From the mat where I was sitting, I turned around and squinted into the sunlight. It was Anik, Obed's servant, looking very out of place in his pleated white Egyptian kilt and funny green and white striped headpiece, and utterly impervious to the looks he was getting from my tent mates.

Before any ribbing started or even the odd sandal was thrown, I hastily stood up and went outside. Anik slowly turned his head towards me, not his body of course, that would have been too much trouble. But he did smile.

"You owe Obed a visit. Can you come with me now?" I shrugged my shoulders.

As I entered, Obed, dressed in a short heavily embroidered white tunic but bare headed with his fine yellow hair, was bent over a curious machine into which he was controlling a supply of water.

"My clock," he said. "So I do not have to look outside to estimate the time of day. It is very accurate. The day is divided into twenty-four periods. See, the arrow is pointing at the tenth period and is slowly moving towards the eleventh. When the sun is at its highest, it will be pointing at twelve." He waved his arm. "All it requires is Anik here to fill it up with water twice a day, and may Yahweh strike him down if he fails." Obed sniggered slightly.

"Yes, we have unfinished business." He sat down and gestured me to join him. "You will remember your scene with Amram when he accused you of blasphemy and the whole camp shook and the tent fell down?"

"Yeeess," I said slowly. I mean so many things had happened since then I really did not want to revisit all that. Old Amram was a vengeful type, and if he thought that one fine day it was time to make an example of someone, he could well remember the blasphemous goatherd with the sling and the Big Shake.

I cannot even remember discussing it much in the tents; it was just another of those things which was a bit inexplicable. But then, that was HIM all over; things just happened. People would scratch their heads a bit and then someone would announce 'the explanation', and that would be that. I did hear that 'the explanation' in high places about the good old shake HE had given the camp was not about 'Little Me' but more a message from HIM to the bosses to stop fooling around with gladiatorial combat in the late afternoon and to get on with the serious business of taking Jericho. So I kind of got left out of the picture, which suited me fine. There was a bit of teasing at first but Seth quickly put a stop to that. He was superstitious, was old Seth.

"You still think it was a miracle?" Obed asked smiling at me with his soft brown eyes. "And you would be right but we have miracles all around us." He waved his arm towards the outside. "The sun rising in the morning is a miracle, and setting in the evening another. Trees growing, water flowing, goats bleating; these are all miracles but we see them every day, so we call them normal."

I was not sure where this was all going but keeping my mouth shut and looking interested certainly did not seem the wrong thing to do.

"Your miracle, that shaking, it happens every twenty days around here. I call it an earthquake. And in exactly ten days' time about mid-afternoon, it will happen again. Most people will be going about their normal business, or not. Perhaps at the moment when the world shakes, someone will be doing something bad; then everyone will say that the earthquake was Yahweh speaking."

"You are sceptical." He smiled at me and gave a deep guffaw. Then he turned to Anik. "Shall we show him, Anik?" he continued in his booming voice. "The chariots are outside?"

I just gaped. I suppose it should not really have come as a surprise that Obed could flick his fingers and summon up six of Joshua's precious war chariots just like that. Obed laughed.

"I do not like the night. That is for your terror patrols. So we visit the Promised Land by day."

I nodded. One of the chariots was empty except for the charioteer, his multi- coloured headband showing him to be a Benjamite. This I noted with relief since the escort were all from the tribe of Gad with their black and white headbands, and they loathed our Benji guts. Yes, it was a strong escort, I mused. Five chariots with two archers each, more than enough to see off your standard Amorite patrol. For someone who had spent the last six months of his life lying up in caves by day and going taut with fear as these patrols went clattering past, this was reassuring.

"You know there is a price on my head, a thousand silver shekels. It is flattering," Obed added. *Stick close to Obed and I'll be ok*ay, I thought.

We walked over to the empty chariot. It was painted red with elaborate scroll work. We mounted while the charioteer held the horses steady.

The pace was fairly leisurely and our first stop was in a valley just to the west of the camp. We got down. Along the valley ran a seam about a foot wide. I looked over at Obed to find him smiling at me. Then he pointed, saying, "Observe the rocks on either side of this seam."

I frowned. I did not really know what he was getting at, but then I noticed there was a difference. Where we were standing the rocks on the left of the seam were all reddish and chunky and, on the right, they were much smaller and lying there in the sand.

Obed pointed at the rubbly rocks which had a reddish tinge to them and I followed him along the seam until he stopped and pointed. There, on the right similar red rocks.

"You see, Ehud, that the earth has moved along this seam; only a dozen yards or so but it was enough to shake the camp and bring the tent down."

He went on a bit about dry land being composed of massive platforms which bumped into each other creating, among other things, mountain ranges which did not sound very likely. Anyway, according to him we were standing at the place where two of these platforms were rubbing alongside each other.

"So here's ten days ago. Now, let us go north and travel back in time."

He called to the escort. A rather surly looking commander dismounted and came up to Obed. He was clearly not pleased.

"We've been out here an hour, sir. I'm sure we've been spotted. It's time to go back." I cannot say that I blamed him. *Lose Obed and that's me at the stoning post,* he was thinking. But Obed was dismissive.

"Let us proceed quickly then, commander," he said decisively, pointing north. "Up that valley and at your best speed." He could have been a pharaoh calling on a slave to bring some figs or something. The commander mumbled something and turned on his heel.

I have never liked chariots. Yes, they look glamorous and intimidating; there you are with two snorting horses in front of you standing on a platform looking down on everyone. Yes, they are great for a parade and at walking pace along paved streets, but out in the country and at anything faster than a walk, chariots are hell. You have to hang on for dear life. At best, you are shaken to bits; even worse, you risk dislocating an arm. And, of course, you cannot fight because you do not have a loose hand. So there you are, a sitting, albeit a moving – or rather shaking – target.

The other thing, more important than the ability to

fight, is you lose your senses. Out on patrol, spotting, hearing, even smelling the enemy before he does makes the difference between death and glory, or rather surviving to the next day. On a chariot, you are too busy watching for the next big bump to spot an enemy hiding in the hills; all you can hear is the grinding of the wheels on the rocks below, and all you can smell is the stink of the horses.

As we rattled dustily up the valley at a fast trot, I could guess the commander was grimly thinking, "I'll show that milky faced bastard!"

Half an hour later we halted. Obed unwrapped his white linen stole from around his face and carefully dismounted. He did not appear discomfited by the journey, or at least was determined not to show it. He beckoned me over to another seam running along the valley floor. Once again, the rocks had been displaced by several yards.

"That miracle took place thirty days ago," Obed guffawed. "Anything within a few miles of here would have had a terrible shaking." He gestured with his arm. "Look at those ruined towers. I bet they were brought down then."

It was those towers which did it for me. I squinted up the mountainside. It had been a proper fort; not just made of rubble and loose rocks but of stone roughly dressed and built with mortar. In other words, it would have needed an almighty crack to bring that lot down.

"Well," Obed said looking at me quizzically. "Satisfied?" But he could see I was not.

"What are you thinking?" he asked because I was

just standing there, and then I laughed and laughed and laughed. I could see all the other guys looking at me and getting impatient. I knew what they were thinking, this was no place to hang about.

I grabbed the charioteer's spear from the wicker basket and drew a line in the sand.

"That's the Jordan, right?" I said looking up at Obed. Then I drew another line parallel to the Jordan. "And that's the line where these platforms are rubbing. That's the seam."

I drew a cross on the seam. "Here we are. Right! And Miracle Number One, thirty days ago. The next day some passing herdsman sees that an abandoned fort has fallen down. He just shrugs his shoulders." Obed chuckled.

I drew another cross on my line in the sand.

"That's the seam near our camp. Ten days ago, we had Miracle Number Two and I get a crack on the head." Obed was now looking at me, genuinely curious.

I scrawled in the sand again. Another cross, the same distance again from the last cross.

"So," I said, "according to your theory Miracle Number Three will take place about here in ten days' time." I stabbed the sand. "Slap bang opposite Jericho…" and here I pointed dramatically towards the ruined fort. I think I was going to say something like 'And down will come the walls'. Yes, I was enjoying myself, savouring this moment, and thinking Clever me. I even think I saw Obed smile and beginning to clap when all hell broke loose.

Arrows were falling thickly among us finding targets in men, horses or the sand. An arrow bounced with a hard click on a nearby rock and the terrified neighing of frightened and wounded horses started. From the ruins of the fort on the hill, I could make out a dozen archers.

There are only two real options when you are caught in an ambush; fight it out or scarper. The escort commander clearly decided on Option One and his soldiers were quickly sheltering behind the chariots and the horses and firing back at the archers in the fort.

You bloody fool, I thought. *It's Option Two for me.* Obed was still standing there in the first shock of surprise, his mouth slightly open when I cannoned into him grabbing his arm and steering him towards our big red chariot. I shouted at the charioteer to mount up and seconds later he was whipping the horses into a gallop.

Okay, I may have been rude about chariots and their general usefulness, but in the hands of a good charioteer they are worth their weight in gold as getaway vehicles. And he was good, that charioteer; he cottoned on immediately; we were to get out and fast, no hanging about for the others.

I pushed Obed down on the floor and crouched behind him holding the grips on either side, closing the back of the chariot. At that speed, the big wheels hardly touched the ground and there was even less clatter and shaking as the chariot became almost airborne.

Up the valley we raced, the charioteer watching carefully ahead and weaving skilfully to avoid the many big rocks. Just one of those could take the wheel off the chariot and leave us sprawled in the sand and sitting ducks for any enemy following behind. I looked back and saw with relief that we were now out of bowshot; arrows were falling in our wake. Back opposite the fort I could see our escort were having a hard time of it. Several men were down and some Amorites were starting to descend from the fort.

"We can't just leave them," said Obed almost magisterially above the noise, turning his head towards me with his hands clenched on the side of the chariot.

"Can't we!" I snorted back and looked at the charioteer. Good fellow, as if in answer and to show that he did not share Obed's qualms, he cracked the whip the harder on the horses' backs and the chariot spurted forward.

At that speed, it did not take long for us to reach the first sentinels of Gilgal. We slowed to a walk and Obed stood up again. He then insisted that we stop, and he just stood there with his arms folded looking back up the valley, while I sat down on a nearby rock looking bored. Eventually, after about five minutes he turned to me.

"You are a callous bastard, Ehud," he said and I just shrugged my shoulders. "Only thing to do, sir," agreed the charioteer. "No sense in sticking around when the arrows start flying."

*****

Of course, there was a bit of a fuss when we got back. Night fell and still no sign of the escort. Then,

376

when the next day dawned, there they were, all fifteen of them, stuck on poles on a high hill in full view of the camp with the vultures flapping around. They were picked men too, from Joshua's own bodyguard, and then there was the loss of the five chariots as well. The rumour going around was that Joshua was pretty angry and that possibly he had not known about Obed's little expedition.

I had been off duty anyway so back in my quarters in Micah's household I was able to be fairly noncommittal about where I had been. I took the precaution of a good wash before returning and frankly was only too glad to lie down because that last gallop had well and truly shaken me to bits. But I guessed it still had not ended as far as I was concerned. I was not entirely surprised therefore, or even sure what to expect, when I heard the door flap and Arik loomed over me as I lay quietly on my bed the following afternoon. He just said 'Obed' and I got up and followed him.

Obed seemed entirely recovered from the experience and was in his same old form, the cheerful boffin at work in his laboratory surrounded by metal contraptions and glass jars. He wiped his hands on a towel and bade me sit down. "You were saying?" he opened his clear blue eyes wide at me. I looked back blankly.

"Well," I said slowly, "I thought the best option was to get out fast when they attacked us. Otherwise, we'd have been up there." I nodded towards the hillside with the corpses of the escort. *Are you going to say 'Thank you'? Better still, give me some money,* I was thinking, *or rather hoping.*

"No, no," guffawed Obed, "and yes, yes thank you for your quick thinking and saving my life, but do you remember what you were saying when the arrows started falling?"

I suddenly remembered and was about to open my mouth when he interrupted me.

"Yes, my clever Ehud, you were pointing out that in nine days' time there will be another miracle, but this time it will take place opposite Jericho. The ground will shake and the walls of the city will come down. Just like that fort on the hill. And Joshua and the army need to be there when it happens."

"It's a bit of a long chance, isn't it?" I managed to stutter.

Obed shrugged his shoulders. "I have done the measurements and estimate the fault line will lie less than half a mile from Jericho. That's near enough. And now" – holding two silver goblets and proffering one to me – "we will drink to your brainwave."

I am sure the wine was good stuff but my mind was in such turmoil I did not taste a thing. Obed saw my discomfiture and laughed.

"Don't worry. If it doesn't work, I'll take the blame and Joshua will just have to find some Yahweh-based explanation for the troops. He's good at that."

*****

I know when to keep my trap shut so I certainly

was not going to brag about all this to Micah. But try as I might, I could not get rid of the nagging 'What ifs?' I could just see us marching out and sitting there in the sun all expectant. What if there was no earthquake? Or what if the ground did shake and a bit of dust fell off those mighty towers? Then there would be us creeping back to Gilgal with our tails between our legs and Amorite jeers ringing in our ears? It did not really bear thinking about.

But, hell, I consoled myself, it's not my problem, and perhaps it is just not going to happen. Indeed, I had almost persuaded myself that Obed had either been joking or failed to persuade Joshua when the camp was put into uproar. All over commanders were briefing other commanders and the men in the tents were being put on alert. I guessed Seth was down there breezily announcing his usual, 'Start panicking. Details later' to the usual routine groans.

Micah appeared confused by it all so I easily got his permission to nip down for Seth's briefing. I think he just wanted me out of the way and not asking awkward questions.

Seth's 'Details' made no mention of earthquakes. It was all about HIM and how HE had appeared to Joshua and promised victory. It was going to be another Red Sea Moment, just do what HE says and it will be all right on the day. Seth made it sound all very straightforward, like the arrival of rations or another lice inspection.

I furtively looked around. There was no disbelief on the faces. No 'What are you talking about, Seth?'

No 'How are we going to get victory, Seth?' No 'Frankly, you are talking through that nice bronze helmet of yours, Seth!' Nope, nothing, just a lot of nodding.

But there was some scratching of heads when it emerged that the 'More Details' involved the whole army decamping to Jericho; then marching round with the priests blowing on trumpets and the walls would fall down. Just like that, so Joshua had been assured by Yahweh!

But, just to make sure, yes, Seth finished gleefully, there was to be plenty of sacrificing.

*****

"Hello, hello." I was merrily greeted. It was Phineas doing a round of the reception desks up at the Temple. The white kid goat by my side, Micah's a grudging contribution, bleated and tugged on the rope.

"That's a nice one you've got there. Very acceptable!" he added in his mock reverential voice, out of earshot of course, of his staff and the other sincere arrivals with their offerings for sacrifice.

"Yes, we'll keep him for the big day." I just looked back at him and Phineas had the grace to smile. Oh yes, there was going to be a lot of old meat going up in flames on the big day, and this kid of Micah's was going to be sold twenty times over.

"So you are not coming out yourself?" I asked, and Phineas shook his head. "No, that is a job for fit young priests. I'll be back here busy sacrificing," he chuckled. "If there is no miracle, I don't want anyone pointing the finger of blame at the Temple," he added reflectively.

"Give my regards to old Tubal," he said turning away. "Remind him that the job offer is still on. And that goes for you too."

*****

You can bet that every man jack in the army, once he had dismissed the nagging thought of how they were actually going to get into Jericho, could think of one thing and one thing only and that was loot. All that gold, all that silver, all those jewels just there for the taking. Oh, and perhaps another thing, all those sweet-smelling Amorite girls!

There was a bit of argy-bargy about which tribes would invest Jericho and get first dibs. Joshua came down on the side of Leah and co's descendants, that is those tribes, led by the Simeonites, which hated us. So theirs were the smiling faces going around the camp. And our lot, those tribes descended from Rachel, were allocated the task of hanging round the perimeter just to make sure no one escaped, so missing out on the real fun.

This had our guys going around looking a bit glum but that soon changed and it was our turn to laugh. Yes, looting was on but, Ha! everything had to be handed in to the Temple. Yahweh's orders! And as for girls, no such luck. Once again it was massacre time! Yes, Yahweh's strictest orders were everyone was for the chop. Well, that certainly took the thrill out of being the first into Jericho, and those grinning triumphant faces turned a dark shade of sour.

Actually, I was quite relieved. I had had my fill of massacre. Okay, they were mainly stabbings in the night in a dark tent, but not always without an occasional glimpse of a terrified child's face, or an agonised scream from a young mother; the stuff of things that stick in dreams for a long time.

Chapter 24

Well, you all know the story; how the army marched round Jericho once a day for seven days with trumpets blasting and on the seventh day and after the seventh circuit the walls fell down. Just like that, and all according to the master plan, good old Joshua! But in my experience the official version is always tweaked a bit; what's left out is what might be called 'The Colour', in other words the things which went wrong and therefore unsuitable for 'The Record'. So I will tell you as it was and, yes, I was there and the walls did fall down; but even now I am not sure what actually happened.

"I think we will pitch about here," said Micah, gesturing vaguely while standing beneath a nice shady tree and squinting at the glistening white walls of the city.

We were to take up position opposite the south gate of Jericho and our tribal cousins, also descended from Rachel, had the West and North gates while the bulk of the army comprising Leah's lot were opposite the main gate.

"Bit too near, sir," stated Seth baldly. "Still in bowshot."

"Really, Seth?" queried Micah with a slight frown. Seth turned away from him, with his back now to the city.

"You see that acacia tree there," he said pointing to

a tree about two hundred yards away. "No one closer than that, sir."

Then he turned back to Micah with that 'Whether you want my opinion or not you are getting it and you would be a damn fool not to take it' look on his face. Seth at his usual irritating self, competent but completely unpromotable! I often wondered if other senior tent commanders ever tapped him on the shoulder to say, "Seth, stop being so obviously right the whole time and rubbing our noses in it."

I could see that Micah was about to complain but he was interrupted by Seth.

Right again, of course.

"And here they come," he announced flatly folding his arms.

We followed his gaze as the shafts from the battlements rose up black against the blue sky, higher and higher they went until they turned and were lost as they came straight for us and soon were hitting the rocks and sand around and about, mostly in front but a few behind. No one was hit except a donkey which started to bray.

"Well, that was close," Micah said after a pause but Seth had already grabbed him by the arm.

"Get the other side, Ehud," he called and together we marched or rather ran with Micah to the Acacia tree. Another volley of arrows thudded behind us.

"Phew," said Micah sitting down and mopping his brow. "I agree with you, Seth. No troops further forward than here."

Actually, our little HQ was not that uncomfortable.

We simply spread goat skins over the Acacia tree and propped them up with poles so it was just like a big tent and fairly cool inside. The other soldiers, poor devils, did as best they could with the other sparse trees to create some kind of cover so they were not just sitting in the sun; because that seemed to be our job, just to sit there and keep a watch on the south gate.

It was all a bit boring at first, which is what most things are when they go according to plan, and this was no exception. The following day I had just finished the very adequate breakfast which Tubal had sent out for Micah's household – figs and some sesame cakes, if you must know – when we heard the first roaring of the rams' horns. Not exactly early risers those priests! Over on the right we could see a glittering phalanx starting its procession.

We had a grandstand view, of course, and along they came. In the lead was pretty much the whole tribe of Reuben, about a thousand men, with the Ark of Covenant and half a dozen priests blowing the rams' horns. We watched them weaving towards us, very carefully keeping their distance from the walls – and those deadly shafts.

All captured kit was theoretically handed in to the priests, or rather Phineas, so the Levites, the Temple Guards, got first grabs at any armour and weaponry. I think the logic was that their main job was to guard the Temple and look impressive; so standing there barefoot, in a loincloth with a sharp stick was out for them. But anything left over went next to the Tribe of Reuben, and today, I admit, they did look smart as they passed in front of us. Each soldier had a fine brass helmet with a feather dyed red – the Reuben colour – glossy black leather armour and a shield studded with bronze or iron. Of course, there was some pretty smart weaponry; spears, swords and the like.

Then came the priests, the Levites, with their horns in their long white robes and, behind them, the bearers with the Ark of Covenant. As they passed us, they gave us a roar on their rams' horns. In normal times, we would have done what we always do and blown raspberries back at them, but here they had the Ark of the Covenant so there was respectful if grudging silence from our ranks. After them, came the rest of the army, tribe by tribe and all descended from Jacob's whores, finishing with a few bedraggled soldiers from the tribe of Asher.

And then that was them, and they were past us and continuing round the city, dust in their wake. We just continued to sit there baking in the sun, well, they were, the poor blighters out there on the plain, but I was okay sitting in Micah's nice big cool tent pretending to be useful.

Nothing happened, that day anyway. I knew, of course, what we were meant to expect, a bloody great earthquake and, too right, I kept my mouth shut.

"I wonder what it will be this time," opined Micah sitting in his comfortable wood and ivory chair, expressing a widespread view as to what method Yahweh would use to destroy Jericho. Slithery old Barak had joined us. He started to count off his fingers.

"One, there's Fire. That's the usual. Then there's

Two, Thunderbolts. That would bring those towers down. Three, Flooding but that seems unlikely. Four, Plague, but that's not quick. Five, a heavenly host. Mmm," he mused, "that would be interesting. Then there's Six, the Earth opening and swallowing them up."

He paused, and I just wondered whether he knew the secret.

"What's your money on, Uncle?" he addressed Micah with that ultra- respectful tone which he used to tease.

Micah mumbled something to the effect that all were possible, but Barak had not finished with him.

"I mean," he continued, "you've seen them all, or your father did, Uncle."

Micah continued to mumble; this time something about his father not being very specific on these things. I think Barak realised that he had done enough uncle-teasing and turned to other quarry, Me, in a word!

"So what about you, Ehud?" he said turning his Cheshire cat face to me. I boiled. Barak really knew how to get to me, and of course I rose.

"Real money? Good odds?" I asked.

I was pleased to see Barak rather taken back. Micah got up and left. I know what he was thinking. Gambling is strictly forbidden and betting on what Yahweh will do next can only be blasphemous. But then boys will be boys.

"What odds do you give me on the sky raining down thunderbolts?" I asked. "Oh," said Barak carelessly, "that would be spectacular. I'll give you 10 to 1."

"And what about the earth shaking and all that?"
"Less fun. I'll do 8 to 1 on that."

"Done," I said quickly. "Ten shekels on the earthquake at 8 to 1." I leant towards him. "Silver shekels!"

That stopped him. What on earth was I doing taking on such a ridiculous bet, he was puzzling. As for me I was kicking myself. After all, this Obed thing was no more than a hunch.

"I'll pick up your stake at the end of the seventh day," he said. "Or you can just give me a chit to Rameses," he continued over his shoulder as he left.

"Not so cocky now," commented Big Abner who had joined me at the front of the tent as the first files plodded past already sweating in their big heavy armour.

Thanks, I thought. *That's what I get for confiding in you, mate!*

*****

It was the seventh day and nothing had happened. Jericho still stood there; white, glistening, towering and defiant. Anyone venturing within bowshot got a sharp reminder from those high walls.

Along they came again. I almost felt sorry for the poor sods as they clanked past in front of us. All that fine kit they had was taking its toll; great for taking a stand in or a short charge but not the kit you want for trogging round a city perimeter under a hot sun with archers taking pot shots at you. This might be the last and seventh day but Joshua had declared that they had to march round the city seven times. Seven times!

"Well," continued Abner, "looks like we'll be going back to Gilgal this evening. That'll be good."

Looking back on it I realise that was the moment it started to happen. I was silently cursing my rash bet with Barak when the tent shook slightly and Abner and I found ourselves looking at each other in surprise. It was another hot windless day, but of course there were always sudden gusts and we thought no more of it.

Then it was the animals.

"Looks like they've got bored too," commented Abner as the local vultures, our companions for the past seven days and occupying a shady outcrop between us and the castle walls, suddenly flapped their wings and caw caw cawed off to the west and out of sight.

Micah's dog got restless and started to whine. For the last week, it had just lain there on the floor of the tent.

It must have been around the sixth circuit of the army, well into the afternoon, that I almost fell over. I was fetching some water from the well a couple of hundred yards back and the ground was rough, so I thought I had just stumbled. There were strange lights too. At first, I thought it was things moving about and glinting in the sun; then perhaps it was my eyes acting funny. But others saw them too; there were definitely shafts of lights suddenly spurting from the ground.

"Mmm," buzzed old Micah, and commented that he seemed to remember his father had said something about funny lights. "I think I will go and lie down."

As he spoke Barak appeared at my side out of nowhere. *Bastard,* I thought, *come to collect my chit for Rameses.* Did I even have ten silver shekels with Rameses after Barak had done me over the oil?

But he was looking at me oddly. "You are a curious creature, Ehud," he said casually. *What on earth did he mean?* I wondered and shrugged my shoulders in response. "I've heard your life story. How you became a Benjamite. Turning up with your mother out of the blue all those years ago."

I was silent, none of his bloody business! *And so what anyway?* I thought to myself. *That happened a lot in those days!* All the tribes were a pretty mixed bag; it just was not something you talked about.

"Can I see your wrist again, please?" he asked with unusual politeness. "There," I said curtly, proffering my arms with palms down.

"Now, Ehud, you can do better than that. Please turn them over."

He stared for a moment at the tattoo on the inside of my left wrist, the snakes entwined in blue. Then he gave a short laugh. "Indeed, my information is correct," he finished.

Then it happened. Even now I cannot quite remember the sequence but I think it started with the dog's whine turning to a howl. Then the ground wobbled so hard I fell down flat on my face – we both did – and I simply could not get up it was shaking so

390

much. All around men were, like us, on all fours and trying and failing to stand up. I heard a crash which was the tent collapsing. Then, lying shaking on the ground, I looked around and then towards Jericho….at first, I thought it was a wavy effect of heat haze.

"Look, look," I heard someone cry. "The towers!"

Yes, the whole right-hand section of the wall and the two high towers over the main gate appeared to be bouncing up and down like toy bricks. That did not last long though; suddenly they stopped moving and just dropped with a long grinding thudding noise while simultaneously up rose a huge white cloud of dust.

The ground had stopped shaking so I stood up. A great cheering broke out. "They're going in," announced Barak now standing beside me again. We could see the attacking force on the right surging forward disappearing into the dust as they entered Jericho. The screaming and shouting began.

I think I was numb with surprise and shock. I heard myself saying, "That's ten silver shekels at 8 to 1, Barak. I'll take a chit of course." It sounded silly and hollow but I could not help it.

But Barak was not interested. Perhaps he did not care, perhaps he had no intention of honouring the bet, perhaps he knew I was going to die shortly.

"Well," he said, "that was genuine enough. Whatever it was!"

Yes, clever old Barak was beginning to wonder; and for once he did not have the answers. And I knew ruefully that I would not get any credit, nor would Obed for that matter – not in public anyway – and instead this would be declared a Yahweh event, a miracle that HE had performed for his 'Chosen People'. And three cheers for Joshua.

"Won't be long now, I guess," said Barak.

I did not have to wait long to see what he was talking about. He had hardly finished speaking when the great double wooden doors in the southern façade opposite us swung open and out flowed a glittering black mass of horses, chariots, and fully armoured men. The flow seemed endless. Out they poured, then spread out and formed a huge black square. Then the commander trotted out into the front. I had seen that bronze helmet with the red coxcomb before. *It must be Zemri,* I thought. And then they charged.

I know I have been pretty scornful about chariots before, called them parade toys or battlefield taxis, but get them in a mass to charge over good ground and they are terrifying and unstoppable.

I did not run away, no one did. Everyone all about grabbed their weapons and waited, helpless and hopeless. I managed to loose off a couple of stones from my sling into the throng galloping towards us. I just aimed for the centre; I could not avoid hitting something but they just came on. I got a fleeting glimpse of that red coxcomb and a horse hit me. I spun around and fell to the ground. A blow on the head and I was out.

I do not know how long I was unconscious, probably a few minutes. When I came to, it was carnage all around me. Micah lay there with the top of his head cut off, and Amorite chariots were touring the battleground in a leisurely way killing off the wounded.

"Keep down, keep still," muttered Barak in my ear, his fair hair caked with blood. A chariot ground up and came to a halt, the horses gasping for breath. Twang, followed by a thud and groan, more tidying up.

Barak was suddenly sitting up. "It's me, Barak," he called out. I looked up and there was the red coxcomb and the heavy bearded face of Zemri looking down from his chariot. Behind him an archer was fitting another arrow to his bow, and turning it to point at me.

"Don't kill him, Zemri!" Barrack shouted urgently, grasping my left arm roughly and turning my wrist towards the commander. "He's your son."

Zemri dismounted and looked down at the entwined snake tattoo, and slowly he raised his own left arm. I saw in exactly the same place on his wrist the same tattoo.

He paused, then spoke.

"What do they call you?" he asked. "Ehud," I replied.

"I knew you as Zemri, named after me. Will you come with me now?" he added softly.

I looked back into those deep brown eyes. My eyes. I know I yearned to say 'Yes, Father' and jump up on his chariot; but I knew that after all those months of terror raids and killings I could never be Zemri and an Amorite.

"I can't," I said slowly. I think he understood, was not surprised. He just nodded, turned, mounted his chariot and left.

And sitting in the middle of the battlefield, dead and wounded all around me, I just wept.

October 2021

Milton Keynes UK
Ingram Content Group UK Ltd.
UKHW010734070823
426447UK00001B/5